ABILITY INC.
David & Goliath

P.G. MacDonald

D1051400

Ability Inc.: David and Goliath

Copyright © 2015 by Patty and Garry MacDonald

Published in the United States of America

ISBN: 978-0-9966182-0-5

Book design by Patty MacDonald

Dedications

Ability Inc. is dedicated to all the disabled young people in America and around the world. Stay focused on your abilities and all you can achieve.

We would also like to dedicate this novel to all the animals who have been abused, tortured, forced to fight to survive, or abandoned. We would like to thank the tireless efforts of all the people who open their hearts and homes to the millions of rescued animals yearly.

Special thanks to Jonathan, DeAnna, Jessica and Jacob P. for being the first to join David and his friends and helped make their adventures even better.

A portion of all book sales will be donated to spinal cord research and animal rescues.

Prologue

Twirling his lucky silver dollar between dirt-crusted fingers, Hank watched the pit bull puppy play cat and mouse with a young girl in her front yard. The yard was fenced but the gate unlocked. He stood quietly by the deserted bus-stop bench and waited, careful not to appear too interested in the girl or her dog. Three buses had passed, their irate drivers cursing at him after having stopped and he merely waved them on. *Screw them,* he thought, *it's still a free country and there's no rule that says everyone standing at a bus stop has to get on the stinkin' bus.*

Hank flipped the silver dollar high into the air, caught it as it fell, and slapped it on the back of his hand. "Heads, I take him. Tails, I walk away," he muttered before lifting his hand. And there she was—sweet Lady Liberty.

He pulled the grungy baseball cap low over his grizzled face, keeping his face shadowed in case the girl saw at him. Heavy-lidded eyes followed the movement of the sturdy pup. Impatiently, Hank watched the puppy churning circles around the girl before collapsing on the grass. Whenever the little brat got close, the pup eluded capture by agilely leaping forward between her legs or dodging her outstretched arms. *This young pit's a clever one*, he thought, nodding in approval. *A useful trait in the ring.*

When the girl's giggles turned into grumbles of annoyance, Hank saw his chance and pulled a dog biscuit out of his pocket. Slamming the wooden screen door open in a fit of pique, the girl stomped into the house. "Fine, Spot! Don't come! Stay out here all by yourself then!"

Hank rushed across the street. "Too easy," he snickered, stepping up to the gate. Now tired, the pup lay flat on his belly, legs splayed out in all directions, nose snuffling slowly in the dirt and grass. Checking up and down the street, Hank crouched down. He quietly lifted the latch and opened the gate. Whistling long and low, he held out the biscuit.

Hearing an unfamiliar noise, Spot got to his feet and waddled over to investigate. Black nose held high, the pup wiggled with excitement as he picked up an interesting scent. Fearlessly, he rushed at Hank, eagerly nudging the man's hand.

Grabbing the pup by the back of the neck, Hank stuffed him under his jacket and quickly crossed the street at a jog while Spot continued to happily gnaw on the tasty biscuit. Convinced they were far enough away from Spot's home, Hank slowed his pace to a brisk walk. Pulling the wriggling puppy from under his jacket, he held up his newest acquisition for a closer inspection. With his mouth wide open and panting slightly, the pup wiggled forward to lick enthusiastically at the man's face. Hank frowned before cradling the puppy under his arm like a football.

"You're a cute, friendly thing, aren't cha?" he muttered, before smacking the pup under the chin. Whining softly, the confused puppy responded by licking Hank's fingers. "You're in for a lot of changes. And the first thing that's gonna change is that stupid name of yours. Spot?" Hank sneered. "Your old family didn't show much originality, did they? Your new life calls for a new name. You're gonna be a fighter. And a fighter needs a strong name. Say hello to your new life, Goliath."

***

"I wish I had a dog," David sighed. He gazed out the car window at the man walking quickly across the street with a puppy's head peeking from under his arm. David stared wistfully and smiled at the sight of the cute wrinkled face, white with a large liver spot over its eye, and crooked black-spotted ears.

"If I had that puppy," he said, "I'd call him Max...or Patches...or maybe even Spot."

"David, you know we don't have the time for a puppy right now. Not with your mother in the middle of her bar exams and twins on the way."

Sighing, the boy twisted in his seat to continue gazing enviously at the man and the puppy. "Yeah, Dad, I know, but I'd rather have a dog than a baby brother or two."

The man was now crossing the street toward the park and bouncing the puppy in his hands. David wondered briefly what the man could be saying to the dog. He grumbled quietly but loudly enough for his father to hear, "He's probably telling Patches that he's the luckiest guy in the whole world 'cos he's got such an awesome dog."

His father slowly pulled out into the intersection and chuckled at the obvious attempt to make him feel guilty. Letting out another loud and obvious sigh, David turned around to look at his father.

For a moment, time seemed to stand still. But as it always does, time eventually moved on, taking David through a surreal set of events that not only altered his dream of becoming a fireman but changed his entire way of life.

He froze in stunned horror as his father strained to control the car; his strong hands on the steering wheel spinning it madly to the left; the shiny silver grille of the Mack truck bearing down on them from the right, looming closer and closer. Horns seemed to blare in stereo from every direction. Angry screeching tires tried to stop tons of metal as the

Mack truck's back section spun sideways, and the two vehicles collided. The metal of the compact car crumpled from the weight of the behemoth as it continued through the intersection, dragging them with it. Their windshield buckled and shattered. Tiny lights and slivers of rainbows rained down, covering his father and the front of the car. Then the front airbags exploded. David was driven forward against his seatbelt and felt a brief weightlessness as his legs lifted from the seat.

"Dad!" he screamed.

The truck crushed their car and the door pushed against his body. He threw his arms up to protect his face and squeezed his eyes shut. His head whipped sideways and cracked savagely against the side window. And then he drifted down into a black abyss from which he would awaken into a new and different world. Unlike Alice in Wonderland, David's new world included things like oxycodone, neurologists, physical and occupational therapy, adaptive equipment, wheelchairs, and handheld urinals.

1

Punked

D avid sat quietly by his locker, feigning interest in the *Popular Science* magazine in his lap. Every few seconds he glanced up at the bathroom door and smiled despite trying not to. He had outdone himself this time. Last week's payback for Brian and his jock buddies had been itching powder in their jock straps the day before a big game. They had spent more time scratching than passing during practice that night.

Of course brainless Brian hadn't figured out who did it but no doubt had his suspicions. David and Brian's rivalry went back to the first grade when a roly poly Brian decided to sit his big butt on David's dinosaur diorama. Brian should know by now that when David got even, he went all out.

Two weeks ago on the way to school, Brian rode by on his mountain bike and threw a cherry slush on David in passing. David spent the entire school day with bright red stained clothes. Kids thought David had spilled his drink. Even after having to endure hours of "smooth move, Ex-Lax" and teasing about butter fingers, there was no way he was going to rat Brian out—he preferred to get even.

His best friend had badgered him enough that he did finally tell her what happened, and Aimee offered to go beat the crap out of Brian. While definitely tempting, David liked to fight his own battles and had something much more devious in mind. And now he waited patiently for that plan to come to fruition.

"Ouch! That's gonna leave a mark," David muttered, hearing the muffled pinging of a metal bucket bouncing across a tile floor followed by a howl of outrage. A string of loud curses came from behind the closed door of the bathroom before it slammed open.

Too bad the bucket didn't plop on his head. That would have been classic. David stifled a chuckle.

"Look at what they're doing with recycled food waste these days . . ." David greeted the other boy as Brian burst from the boy's bathroom, head and shoulders covered in the remains of the high school cafeteria's mystery lunch. "So, you leaving that trail behind you in case you can't find the bathroom again, Hansel?"

"Did you do this, gimp?" Brian growled. He self-consciously peered up and down the empty hallway before storming over to David. He slammed a beefy paw into the nearest locker above David's head, causing some decomposing particles to fall off his beefy arm.

If it wasn't for the recycled food covering the upper part of his body, Brian might have looked more intimidating standing over David. *Who knew Brian would turn out to be such an environmentalist?* David thought. *I mean, really! Wearing compost is about as green as you can get.*

"Hey, don't look at me. I'm waiting for Aimee, you know, chilling and sitting here reading a magazine. Minding my own business. Wrong time, wrong place, buddy. But I must say that getup will be a hit with the cheerleaders!" David snickered and brushed off the remains of someone's lunch from his pant leg. He hoped Brian would take a step back before the brute sloughed off more reeking mystery meat.

"Was that an insult?" Brian sneered. "You think this is funny, Wheels?" Brian tried too hard to be witty and as usual came off as lame-o. Wheels was seriously unoriginal but definitely an improvement from gimp. At least Brian was able to put two lines of speech together, which wasn't bad for a throwback to the Neanderthal man. Beady eyes glared down at David from behind a curtain of thick brown bangs and strings of slime-covered spaghetti.

"Adding insult to injury. What a concept," David muttered, realizing his cleverly orchestrated plan had worked too well.

Brian actually looked ticked off. Crossing his compost-bearing arms in front of his chest, Brian towered ominously over David. From where David sat, Brian looked enormous and meaner than his not-so-distant cousin, the mountain gorilla. Yeah, Brian was definitely two-hundred pounds of angry Silverback at the moment.

"I asked you a question, nerd!" Brian practically snarled. He put his foot on David's low-profile ROHO cushion and leaned in close.

Dead animal, some fruits and veggies, ewww sausage with a pinch of garlic, David thought. That smell wasn't the garbage Brian wore; it was his horrid breath that wafted toward David, choking off his reply. Gagging, David managed to wheeze out with much less force than he intended, "No one touches the chair! Back off, dude!" He sounded slightly strangled and squeaky.

"Whatever, gimp," Brian snarled and pushed David's chair with his foot. The wheelchair rocked back and sent David tumbling forward, almost knocking him to the floor. Before David lifted completely out of his chair, he grabbed the wheel rims and stopped the chair's backward motion. The front wheels banged heavily against the ground, causing David to slam back into his chair with a sharp click of his teeth, catching his bottom lip. With an angry growl, he propelled the wheelchair forward toward Brian.

"Yo, David, what's up?" Aimee asked brightly. She pushed past Brian and interjected herself between the two boys. Aimee's service dog, a tricolored Basenji, barooed a welcome before sitting against the lockers.

David braked hard and fumed, wiping his sleeve against his bloodied lower lip. Facing Brian, Aimee quirked an eyebrow, face smug, taunting him to do anything while she stood there. Sometimes being the captain of the volleyball team had its perks; besides giving her a huge ego and an attitude the size of the Goodyear blimp, it also came with a reputation of having a deadly spike. After holding his sullen gaze for a moment, she smirked at Brian before turning her head back to David.

David grinned sheepishly up at Aimee and shrugged. He began to quickly sign. "Brian's modeling the new, eco-friendly school uniform, which apparently includes that fancy banana peel logo and some kinda ABC food stain on the shirt." David spoke more for Brian's benefit.

Reaching down, David scratched the Basenji, Hoku, under her little service jacket where she got itchy. She yodeled up at him, and he had to smile as he read the jacket. *Can't you see I'm working here?! Hands OFF!* Typical Aimee attitude.

"That gimp...that loser..." Brian stammered, his arms flapping like a drunken seagull. His face flushed a dark, splotchy red, which definitely didn't make him look more attractive.

David suspected an explosion or take-off was imminent. He wondered briefly what Brian's reaction would be if he started counting down out loud. He nodded at Brian to let Aimee know that the boy was about to speak.

Aimee whirled around to face Brian, her straight black hair slapping him across the face. She put one hand on a hip and thrust her other hand out, index finger pointing, almost up Brian's nose—at least that's how it looked from David's seated position.

"You need to take a shower and cool off, Brian. I'd head for the boy's locker if I were you because even my dog wouldn't want to roll around in your stench—and that's saying a lot!" Aimee waved her finger from side to side as she gave the boy attitude, her voice accented but understandable. "And Brian? Don't even think about getting into it with David. 'Cos you'll have to go through me first, dude, and personally, I don't think you're up to it. Trust me. You wouldn't like me when I'm... ferocious!"

8

At the cue word, Hoku went from adorable little Basenji to snarling Tasmanian devil with hackles raised. David couldn't help but laugh. When angry, Basenjis actually did sound like a cross between the Looney Tunes' version and the undulating growling cries of the real-life marsupial Tasmanian devil. It was too bad Aimee couldn't hear all the great noises her pup made.

Hoku bared her canines to full advantage and snapped at the air in front of Brian, who quickly backed up a few steps. Aimee tried to suppress a grin as she slapped her leg to get her dog's attention. The Basenji immediately stopped acting demonic and placidly sat back on her rump, her curled tail waving from side to side. She narrowed her eyes and smiled, letting out a little yip.

Aimee focused her attention back on Brian.

"You know he's not innocent, Aimee!" Brian blustered. "He's gonna pay for this!"

"Did you just seriously threaten David? David is in a wheelchair, you moron! Did he suddenly sprout wings along with a whole herd of pigs? There's no way he could have put that bucket over the doorway." *Unless I helped him that is*, she thought. "Gawd! What is with you? You do have a brain, don't you, Scarecrow?"

At five-foot-nine inches and drop-dead gorgeous with a sharp-edged tongue known to make guys bleed, Aimee could stare down any boy her age without much effort. She could actually stare down any guy twice her age. Brian was no exception; he deflated like a helium balloon at high altitude. Sputtering and muttering, he threw his arms up in the air, grunted out several inappropriate words, and stalked off.

Once Brian was out of sight, Aimee turned back to David and raised her hand for a high five. David's hand shot up and out as Aimee's hand fell down and forward, slapping him squarely on the forehead. Some day she might actually give him a high five without almost knocking him out.

"Geez, my head's not a volleyball! You gotta go easy on the merchandise," David grumbled, rubbing his forehead. "I am handicapped, you know."

"Yeah, whatever. And I'm deaf and dumb." Aimee rolled her eyes.

"Well, definitely not dumb, and at least you're able to stand up to that bully while all I can do is sit and plot my revenge from this chair."

"Cry me a river, build a bridge, and get over it already!" Aimee smiled and the hallway seemed to disappear for a minute.

While David was a little smitten with Aimee, the hallway disappearing was more from the conk on his forehead, which had scrambled his brains and blurred his vision for a few seconds. *Note to self,* David thought, *never ever get on Aimee's bad side.*

"He'll be back, but whatever. I can't believe you spiked my head, Aimee!"

"Would you like some cheese with that whine?" Aimee made a snorting noise and waved her hand at him as if blowing off his girlie complaints. "I take it pig-face got more crap from the crapper than he anticipated?" Aimee laughed uproariously at her own joke.

"You should have seen his face," David said, signing as he laughed. "He came pushing out of the bathroom door and—splat!—the bucket of cafeteria dumpster grossness splashed all over his head and shoulders." David laughed so hard his sides ached. "That look was totally priceless! Too bad we didn't have any cameras set up."

"Like that wouldn't give the prankster away! Ashton Kutcher you are not, my friend. Anyway, you better get to class. I gotta bail. We're cutting out early for agility practice tonight, and Manny's dad doesn't like when we're late."

With a flip of her hair and a prancing Basenji at her heels, Aimee walked away from David before he could reply. He knew Aimee was an expert lip reader, but she didn't have eyes in the back of her head.

Therefore, it was pointless to attempt a witty reply as it would fall on deaf ears...literally.

2

Fight Club

I t felt good to roll in the grass after a bath. He never understood why that annoyed the big people so much. Lying on his back, his body wiggling back and forth to get that itch between his shoulder blades, he eyed the laughing girl. He let out a happy whimper of excitement, docked tail churning a small hole in the dirt. Waiting until the last second before her hand touched his belly, he scrambled to his feet and raced away.

Sprinting past the wooden deck, he caught the enticing aroma of cooking meat. He stopped dead in his tracks and lifted his black nose, inhaling deeply. As he started to follow the tantalizing scent, the girl scooped him up in her arms. She laughed and pulled him close, tickling his belly. She made some noises at him while she carried him closer to what he hoped would soon be his dinner. He whined expectantly as she held out a tasty treat. Licking his chops, he opened his mouth...

And bit down onto the cold steel bars of his cage. Yelping in surprise and disappointment, Goliath opened his eyes and was greeted by the sight of his cruel master taunting him with a piece of barbeque-lathered pork.

"Stupid dog," Hank said. He kicked the cage and popped the piece of meat into his own mouth. Grabbing a broken curtain rod in one hand, he thrust it through the cage into the dog's ribs, scraping the dog's side. "I hope you were dreaming of killin' that mutt in the fight tonight, Goliath!"

Hank prodded Goliath several more times until the dog finally rose to his feet. At one end of the curtain rod, Hank had wrapped a raccoon skin. Poking the skin through the bars of the cage, he jabbed it roughly into Goliath's face. Goliath hunkered and looked away, his ears laid back low.

"Goliath, kill!" Hank commanded, with another stab at the dog's jaw.

This time Goliath obediently attacked the end of the rod and savagely ripped a strip of skin from the pole.

"Now that's what you call a fighting dog, Carlos," Hank sneered and turned to face the other man in the room.

Carlos gaped at the savagery of Goliath's attack. "Man, that is one loco brute. You been workin' him? 'Cos I've never seen him do that before. He's shredding that skin to bits!" Carlos exclaimed, pointing at Goliath who lay at the back of the crate, tearing lengths of skin into smaller pieces.

Hank shrugged and threw the curtain rod across the kitchen. It bounced off a wall and fell onto a heap of other animal skins. "Yeah, I've been workin' on him. Haven't fed him much in a couple days, so he's hungry but not too weak to put up a good fight. Plus he's in the right weight range for that other dog that I'd like to see him whip. You know, that joker from Palmetto, his dog Brutus. I wanna take him down a few notches. This time when I say kill, he'll do it."

"Well, I don't know what happened last time," Carlos said, sounding skeptical. "I was sure he was gonna finish off that other dog, but all he did was hold it down 'til you pried him off." Carlos grabbed another helping of barbequed ribs from the table and started gnawing on the bone. "What's it matter if he doesn't kill as long as he keeps winning his fights? He wins—we win. Nowhere in the contract does it say killing required." Stripping all the meat from the bone, Carlos reached for another rib.

"People wanna see blood. They pay to see gore. More people, more bets. More bets, more payout for us. Got it? When I tell him to kill, he better kill or else!" Hank snarled, slapping the piece of meat away from Carlos. "Besides, it was his eighth straight win without a kill. If he kills tonight, he'll be one of the most valuable fighting dogs in this area. That means no more street fighting for us. We'll be moving up to the pros, Carlos. The pros! Now quit eatin' and let's get goin' before you have to waddle your way down to the warehouse."

Hank grabbed a muzzle, pinch collar, martingale, and leash from the hooks by the refrigerator. Carlos hastily washed his hands before grabbing the dog's first-aid kit. Opening the crate door, Hank lured Goliath out of the crate with a small piece of pork. Hank then half-carried, half-dragged the dog by his collar out to the old Ford van and threw him into the crate in the back. Shaking his head, Goliath drew in a deep breath and sneezed several times. Hank shut the cargo doors, leaving Goliath in the dark. He heard a chain slide outside the door and the loud click of the padlock that held the broken doors closed.

"When are you gonna fix this broken door?" Carlos complained. "It don't look right, driving down the road with a padlock on the back."

"It works fine. Stop your whining and get in before we're late for the fight!" Hank hissed.

Several minutes later two doors opened and closed as Hank and Carlos got into the vehicle. The engine rumbled several times before turning over, and soon the van moved out of the driveway and onto the street.

Goliath huddled in the back of the crate while the van sped toward the abandoned warehouse. Gas fumes wafted through the corroded floor of the van, making him nauseous. He knew what was coming. The only time he left the house was to fight or train. He also knew he would eat tonight. His hunger was like a living thing, gnawing at him from the inside out, aching almost as much as the beatings. Sometimes his stomach shouted at him as loudly as his master did. It was like this every time before a fight. Hank would make him go days without much food followed by an evening car ride and then fighting. The fighting was all a blur to Goliath. Then afterwards Hank (or more often Carlos) would feed him. But sometimes Hank would beat him before he fed him. But at least it was followed by food.

The van hit a bump. Goliath's cage bounced and knocked him off his feet. Metal objects rolled and pinged loudly against the bars of his prison. Whining soulfully, he lay where he fell and waited.

Soon the van stopped, and Goliath heard the front doors open and shut. Within seconds, the cargo door slid open. Rough hands strapped a muzzle around his face and hooked a pinch collar around his neck. Immediately, Goliath felt the sharpened needle-like prongs digging into his throat.

Giving the leash a vicious jerk, Hank pulled Goliath forward, growling, "Heel!"

Goliath resisted briefly, standing his ground, but another hard tug and painful pinching of the skin folds on his throat had him obediently crawling from the crate. Hank hauled him roughly from the back of the van onto the gravel-covered ground. Another sharp tug found Goliath walking reluctantly beside his cruel master from the parking lot toward the dark warehouse.

Hank jerked the leash upward, keeping the dog's head held high as if Goliath was parading around the Best of Show ring at the

Westminster Kennel Club dog show. Sneezing to clear the gas fumes from his sensitive nostrils, Goliath tried to identify his surroundings by smell.

A hundred different scents assailed him as he followed Hank and Carlos toward the noisy building. Somewhere close by was the stink of a recent death. The dead dog's blood, urine, and feces mixed with the reek of smoke, beer, and food. One smell overpowered the rest, meat being grilled. As the aroma grew stronger, Goliath began to drool. Thick tendrils of saliva dripped from his muzzle as his empty stomach growled and gurgled, demanding food.

Carlos was at the door of the warehouse when Hank and Goliath approached. In one hand was a charbroiled drumstick, and with his other hand, he opened the door as Hank and Goliath approached. Both men seemed oblivious to Goliath's hunger. There were food smells everywhere, tormenting the dog as he passed through the doorway.

The room he entered was large enough to comfortably fit fifty people. As the doors slammed shut behind him, Goliath's keen senses reeled. He could smell cooked meats, potato chips, and pizza. Once again the smell of fighting, fresh blood, and death hung heavily in the air. In addition, pungent odor of cigar smoke mixed with the acrid tang of spilled alcohol assaulted him.

With sensitive ears rang from the clamor of the cheering spectators and the barking, snarling dogs, Goliath shivered in anticipation and fear. He passed several sweating men and growling dogs as he moved through the warehouse toward the center ring. His hunger was momentarily forgotten when he reached the fighting pen.

The square fighting pen was a twenty-by-twenty foot enclosure that had been hastily erected using old plywood boards. A bloodied carpet covered the hardwood floor. Encircling the three-foot-high pen were eager gamblers raucously waiting for the next dog fight. At the other end of the pen, Goliath's adversary jumped against his constraints. Brutus, a caramel-colored pit bull with a black muzzle, was also undefeated. They had saved these two undefeated young fighters for the last fight of the night. Unlike Goliath, Brutus had fatally wounded or killed his opponents.

The ring steward signaled the two owners to bring their dogs to the scales hanging from the rafters to be weighed before the fight. After getting weighed, Goliath was grabbed by the collar. Hank took off the muzzle and pinch collar before tossing Goliath over the plywood boards. Hank then climbed into the ring.

"It's time to earn your keep, mutt," Hank said, giving Goliath a kick to move him toward Brutus.

Both handlers circled their dogs around the pen, letting them come within inches of each other without touching. Goliath laid his ears back, growling menacingly to warn the other dog to back off. Snarling, Brutus lunged forward, momentarily pulling his handler off balance. The crowd began to chant, "Fight! Fight! Fight!" as Goliath and Brutus closed in on each other.

Sensing the crowd's eagerness, Hank and Brutus' handler nodded at each other and released their dogs behind their respective scratch lines before jumping out of the ring. Brutus immediately charged at Goliath who braced himself for the rush. Goliath waited until Brutus was almost on top of him before dropping down with his belly to the ground. As Brutus' jaws closed on empty air, Goliath lunged forward and up, grabbing Brutus by the throat and rolling him onto his back.

Goliath held his opponent to the ground with jaws that could easily rip through the muscles of Brutus' neck and crush his windpipe. Brutus whipped around in a frenzied rage, snapping at empty air, his claws digging into Goliath's skin but ineffectively finding leverage to break himself free. Finally, Brutus stopped struggling, and the crowd grew quiet. The fight, which could have lasted half an hour, seemed to be over in less than a minute.

With his mouth still around Brutus' neck, Goliath looked toward Hank and wagged his stumpy tail. Someone in the crowd snickered loudly and a beer can hit Goliath's side. Face twisting in fury, Hank leaned forward over the side of the pen and growled, "Kill, Goliath! Kill!"

The ring steward looked at Brutus' owner and lifted his stun baton inquiringly. With a nod from the owner, he would dislodge Goliath from Brutus with a quick stun blast, separate the dogs, and let them rest a moment before starting the fight back up.

Cursing loudly, Brutus' owner kicked the side of the ring. He made an obscene gesture in Hank's direction and turned to leave Brutus to his fate. After this humiliating defeat who would want to fight a dog that had been taken out so easily?

Goliath continued to wag his tail but did not obey Hank's command. Enraged, Hank stalked over to Goliath and screamed, "Kill, Goliath! I said kill!"

By this time, the crowd had started to boo, and people were throwing more beer cans at Hank and Goliath. Someone shouted, "Kill, Goliath, kill!" The angry crowd picked up the chant.

Brutus' owner turned back toward the two dogs still locked together in the center of the ring. Hearing the crowd getting more worked up, he hoped Brutus might have gotten free. Mockingly, he shouted at Hank, "Some killer you got there! Maybe you should change his name from Goliath to Pee Wee!"

Hank stalked over to the ring steward and grabbed the stun baton. Rushing over to Goliath, he reached out and zapped the unsuspecting dog, all the while screaming, "Kill! I said kill him!"

Momentarily stunned and confused by Hank's attack, Goliath released his grip on Brutus with a loud yelp. Taking advantage of Goliath's confusion and momentary pain, Brutus scrambled quickly to his feet and snapped at the Goliath, missing Hank's swinging foot by inches. Even though pit bulls were bred to be aggressive toward animals and not men, Hank wasn't taking any chances and scrambled back out of the pen.

The fight continued with a vengeance, and the crowd was riled up. Even Brutus' owner shouldered his way through the masses to return to the edge of the pit. Having learned from his mistake, Brutus attacked more carefully this time. Keeping his head low, Brutus charged forward, savagely tearing into Goliath's exposed right shoulder. Goliath turned to meet the attack but was too late to avoid being bitten. He snapped back, biting Brutus' ear in retaliation. On hind legs, they ripped into each other with fangs and claws.

After ten minutes of fighting, both dogs were covered in blood and beginning to tire. Goliath limped from a deep wound on his right shoulder and bled from numerous punctures around his face, shoulders, and legs. Deep gouges crisscrossed his chest and neck. Bleeding profusely from a score of wounds, Brutus had not fared much better. Aside from the many punctures and ripped flesh, he had lost the use of his left eye, and his left ear had been partially ripped off.

Sensing the fight would soon be over, the crowd began chanting again, "Kill, Goliath, kill!" The ring steward had requested the dogs be given a break several times, but with no one listening, he gave up and watched the fight with the rest of the bloodthirsty spectators. He didn't care who got killed, the white one or the brown one; this was the best entertainment he had witnessed in several months. Either one of these dogs could make it to the professional level—that was if one of them survived.

3

Busted

S lamming on the brakes of the company's Ford F150, Greta Shultz from the Animal Rescue Co. skidded to a stop behind a parked police cruiser. It was her passion for dogs that had dragged her away from a *Buffy the Vampire Slayer* Netflix marathon and into the shadier areas of downtown St. Petersburg. After rolling her head from side to side to release some tension from her neck and shoulders, she extracted her six-foot-four-inch frame from the vehicle. She took a deep breath to keep the gagging feeling of adrenaline from rushing up past her throat. Greta was excited but scared as she surveyed the premises.

An anonymous caller had given the police a tip there would be a dog fight in a supposedly abandoned warehouse at this location tonight. Mobilizing the troops had taken less than two hours. Whenever animals were involved, staff from the Animal Rescue Co. were called in to assist. When it came to dog fights, Greta was the one on call to supervise and handle the more aggressive situations.

Greta Shultz was blonde with blue eyes and built like a German Panzer tank. That is to say, she was not a small woman and was of German descent, and to her a pit bull might as well have been a Pug. She had a strong love for German Chocolate Cake (tons of it) and animals (tons of them). She ate the chocolates but not the animals, being a vegetarian. At this moment, she could have used some chocolates to help her compose herself. Unfortunately, this was the calm before the storm, and there was a big storm brewing that was about to crash through a dog fight.

Checking the back of the pickup, she counted the crates again. She hoped she had enough to contain all the dogs they rescued tonight. She always fretted about numbers, because with raids she never knew what to expect. She could make educated guesses but nothing could be guaranteed. And, of course, she could always call for backup. Hopefully, this time there would be more alive than dead. She wanted to save them all, but realistically knew if she could save even one, it would be a good night. After assuring herself everything was ready, she marched over to the police cruiser. Her stomach did a little jitterbug when she spotted who was on duty tonight. Excited, she leaned into the open window and slapped Officer Slimka on the shoulder.

Officer Mike Slimka spewed coffee across the dashboard and onto the windshield in a passable imitation of an erupting volcano. He coughed up a piece of cream-filled doughnut as Greta helpfully slapped him between the shoulder blades. He was sure his spine would pop out through his chest at any moment. Holding up a hand for her to stop, he managed to draw a shallow breath and squeak out a few words between coughs.

"Geez, Greta," he choked out, still gasping and wheezing. "You almost made me wet myself!"

"Hallo, mein schätzchen," Greta purred near Officer Slimka's ear, her plump body filling his entire window.

Not understanding a word of German, Officer Slimka wasn't sure if Greta was flirting or insulting him. He hoped for the latter. Being muscularly built at five-foot-ten inches tall with chocolate-brown eyes and sandy-brown hair cut in a military style, Mike Slimka still maintained a boyish look some women found attractive. He hoped Greta was not one of those women. He was in denial and refused to acknowledge that this blond Amazon had a huge Amazonian-sized crush on him.

Officer Slimka's partner, Edgar Connelly, was a thirty-year veteran of the Tampa Bay police force and the complete opposite of his young partner. He grinned at Greta and winked. "Er ist ledig," he said in passable German.

"Gut zu wissen," she winked back, beaming a smile at Officer Slimka before walking back to her vehicle.

Officer Slimka made a face. He had a suspicion they had been discussing him, and with his partner being such a comedian, who knew what had been said to Greta. He agitatedly mopped up the coffee from the dash as Officer Connelly chuckled.

"Well, let's get this party started," Officer Connelly said, glancing in the rearview mirror and noting the rest of the team arriving in their unmarked vehicles.

Climbing out of his squad car, the short and rotund Officer Connelly quickly established control over the operation. Within minutes he had organized the assembled officers and Animal Rescue Co. agents into working units, and had outlined their basic plan of attack. He and his fellow officers would enter the building first and arrest the dog handlers and gamblers. Once the area was secured, Greta and her group would then round up the dogs.

At Officer Connelly's signal, the heavily-armed officers carefully advanced toward the warehouse. Each officer wore a Kevlar vest with a two-way radio strapped to his or her shoulder. Some carried Mossberg 590 sawed-off shotguns while others used their standard issue Glock 22, .40 S&W pistols.

The warehouse was a two-story, steel-framed building with several doors and windows that could be used to enter and exit the building. Busted windows, broken doors, and graffiti-painted walls indicated the building had not been an operational warehouse for many years.

As Officer Slimka crept closer to the warehouse, he stepped around broken beer bottles and other debris littering the ground. The closer they got, the louder the racket became. At first the many voices were an indistinguishable hullabaloo, but as he approached the broken doorway, Officer Slimka realized the noise was actually the crowd chanting, "Kill, Goliath, Kill!"

Man, these people are sick! What are we—some throwbacks to bloodthirsty Romans? Officer Slimka thought, shaking his head in disgust. Stopping outside the doorway, he looked quickly to his right and left, signaling his fellow officers to enter the building on his command. Taking a deep breath, he lifted his right foot and kicked the half-broken door down. He could hear his partner on the bullhorn.

"This is a police raid—everyone on the floor. Now!"

Pandemonium erupted throughout the warehouse as officers entered the building while gamblers and dog handlers tried to exit. For several tense minutes, it appeared the situation might get out of hand. Shots were fired from both sides, but more people were looking for an escape route rather than trying to stand their ground.

Unbroken windows shattered from bullets and other projectiles as people scrambled over each other and their dogs, trying to escape the building. A few made it, but many were tagged and cuffed. Some handlers grabbed their dogs and tried to run, while others released their fighters to add to the chaos in the building and hopefully buy them some time to flee the premises. Several of the pit bulls started attacking each other while a few ran around confused or merely cowered in the crowd.

Swinging his Mossberg like a club, Officer Slimka fought his way through the crowd, pushing people to the ground and fending off disoriented canines. Luckily, there seemed more flight than fight tonight. As he pulled out a pair of handcuffs from his belt to cuff yet another lowlife, he heard a window shatter behind him and quickly clicked the handcuffs closed. Turning toward the sound, he witnessed a mullet-haired man on the other side of the room with a shirt-covered fist break the remainder of the glass at the bottom of the window.

"Freeze!" Officer Slimka ordered.

The mullet-haired man shouted something and gestured wildly at a short Hispanic guy who dragged a bleeding black-spotted pit bull toward the window. Dropping the dog, the shorter man hoisted himself out the window. The other man lifted up the limp dog and shoved it outside to his accomplice before climbing through the opening himself.

Shouting into his two-way radio, Officer Slimka warned his partner two men had escaped through the south wall window with a wounded dog and were headed his way.

4

Run, Run Away

Hank gunned the accelerator, sending dirt and gravel flying. Weaving across the lawn and through the ditch, the white van lurched onto two wheels, almost flipping over before righting itself and landing hard on the asphalt. Goliath bounced against the side of the van as it careened down the service lane and away from the warehouse. Officer Connelly gave chase in his cruiser, sirens blaring.

"Hey, man, we need to ditch the dog! We can come back for Goliath later!" a terrified Carlos shrieked, his hands and knees bleeding from the broken glass of the warehouse window. Trembling, he fumbled with the police band radio. "Do something! The pig is right on our tail. Hank! What are we gonna do? They can't find us with him!"

"Shut up! Shut up and let me think," Hank screamed. He had lost the biggest payday of his life, and he was in no mood to listen to Carlos' blubbering. Glancing in the rearview mirror, he spotted Goliath trembling in the back and focused on the dog as the source of his frustration and anger. "This is all your fault, you worthless mutt!"

Hank turned the steering wheel hard to the left, almost tipping the van on its side as he rounded a corner and stepped down on the accelerator. Luckily at two in the morning, there weren't many people out driving. Checking his mirror, Hank could barely see the police car following them. It was almost a block behind but coming fast. Running a red light, Hank turned sharply to the left, sideswiping a van parked on the side of the road. Metal grinding on metal, the two vans briefly touched and moved apart like two punks dancing in a mosh pit. Carlos yelped. Hank would have slapped him but couldn't afford to take his hands off the steering wheel.

Then out of nowhere two kids sauntered into the middle of the road directly in front of the van. The girl walked with a long white stick testing the ground in front of her. Cursing, Hank swerved left, then right, causing the van to fishtail around the pair. He missed the tall boy completely but knocked the stick from the girl's hand.

Tires squealing, the police cruiser skidded to a stop to make sure the teens were uninjured, giving Hank a few precious seconds. Making several quick turns, he was able to put some distance between the two vehicles. After several more turns, the sirens faded into the distance.

Warehouses soon gave way to ranch-style homes as the van roared into a residential area. Rounding a corner, Hank let up on the accelerator and turned up the police band radio to hear if there was any mention of the chase underway. He heard the description of their van and the street where they lost their pursuer. They might get out of this mess if he kept his wits about him. *Momma didn't raise no fool!* he thought. Slowing down, he turned into a side street and looked for a place to ditch the van.

"Hank, we're headed into the city. Shouldn't we run for the interstate?" Carlos asked. Not bothering to answer, Hank hit the brakes hard and turned sharply into a service lane used for collecting trash behind some office buildings. Practically standing on the brakes, Hank brought the van to a grinding stop beside a large dumpster.

"End of the ride, you worthless piece of crap!" he snarled. Carlos shrank back from Hank and covered his face with his arm to fend off the attack.

"Not you! The other worthless piece of crap," Hank hissed at Carlos. "Idiot!"

Kicking his door open, Hank practically flew from the front of the van to the back and ripped the cargo door open. Grabbing Goliath roughly by the skin on his back and collar, Hank snarled in the dog's face. "When we come back for you, you're going to be working overtime to make up for all the money you cost me tonight!"

If he wasn't in such a hurry, Hank would have vented his anger on the dog with feet and fists. Instead he gave a mighty heave, lifting the wounded dog out of the back of the van. Without another word, he swung Goliath up and over the lip of the dumpster and let go. With a startled yelp, Goliath plunged into the depths of the garbage container and landed in an open cardboard box. Scared, exhausted, hungry, and hurting from a dozen wounds, he lay down inside the box and closed his eyes. The last sounds he heard were Hank cursing at Carlos as they abandoned the van and ran down the service lane on foot. Too tired and sore to even lick his wounds, Goliath whimpered and closed his eyes.

5

Luck O' the Irish

Manny reacted instinctively, reaching up to grab Siobhan's shoulders. He pulled her back in the nick of time as a white van sped by, hitting Siobhan's cane and sending it flying through the air.

"Are you okay?" he asked.

"What the heck was that?" Siobhan yelled, her Irish temper flaring, her freckled face flushed as red as her hair. Shrugging out of Manny's grasp, she shook her fist in the direction she heard the van speeding away. "Idiot, learn how to drive!"

Seconds later a police cruiser screeched to a stop beside them. Manny took Siobhan's elbow and pulled her back a little, taking a step in front of her. A concerned-looking officer rolled down the passenger window and leaned toward them, asking, "You kids okay? Anyone hurt?"

"He t-t-totally missed us. Everyone's fine, sir," Manny stammered nervously, dropping Siobhan's elbow. He groaned inwardly, imagining the fight that was sure to erupt at his household when he called from the slammer. After all, they were out after curfew. Since his family emigrated from Mexico, no one had been in trouble with the law, and Manny didn't want to be the first. Thankfully, the distracted officer merely nodded his head and sped off in the direction the van had driven.

Heaving a sigh of relief, Manny walked to where Siobhan's white stick lay in pieces on the road. He picked up the pieces and handed them back to her. "Sorry, Siobhan. Your walking stick got mangled."

"Son of a biscuit! This has been such a bad night. First, the stakeout was a bust, and then we nearly get turned into pavement pizza by some drunken lunatic. And to top it off, my favorite walking stick gets whacked!" Siobhan sighed and dropped the pieces of her stick into her backpack. "I told you I was having a bad karma week. My constellations are all out of alignment."

"Well, look on the bright side. We didn't get whacked by the van, and the cop was in too much of a hurry to ask why we were out so late," Manny offered with a smile, which was totally lost on Siobhan who was legally blind. "Besides it's nothing a little super glue won't fix."

"You're such a dweeb!" Siobhan said with a giggle, accurately punching him on the arm.

"Ouch! Not so hard," Manny laughed. "I bet I get a bruise there tomorrow."

"Yeah? Well, it serves you right for some transgression I'm sure you'll soon commit!" Siobhan smiled and punched him again. "Take me home. It's late and I'm beat. Besides we need to skedaddle before the fuzz comes back and busts us this time for being out past curfew." She offered Manny her arm, and the two headed toward Manny's moped parked down the street.

6

School Daze

Rain, rain, and a 100% chance of more rain. Some weather forecast, David thought, pulling the poncho out of his backpack. *Florida may be the sunshine state, but when it rains, it pours, and obviously, it has to pour on me right before I get to school.* He gazed skyward at the angry cumulonimbus clouds and imagined that somewhere in the heavens Thor struck his mighty hammer against a shard of hot steel, causing a loud rumbling crack of thunder. Flashes of lightning lit up the dark clouds as sparks from his forge dropped to the earth.

Oh Mighty Thor, can't you wait another fifteen minutes to start your work day? Give a guy a break! Without further ado, the clouds purged their overfull bellies and dumped buckets of rainwater on top of his high school. Of course, the rain couldn't wait until he was actually in the building.

David quickly pulled his poncho over his dark brown hair and shoulders. Down the sidewalk he sped with the wind whistling through his hood and the water beating against his head and back. Rounding the corner of the school, he ducked his head and gave a strong push that sent him rolling up the ramp that led to the school's back door. Only teachers and kids with wheels were allowed to enter through this door. He felt so very privileged... not.

With a deep sigh, David pushed the oversized silver button and waited for the door to open wide enough for him to fit through. Once inside, he removed his poncho and shook the rain off it as best he could before shoving it into his backpack.

Dull, grey-painted walls lined a long hallway to its ominous end—the school's main office. Each morning he was forced to wheel up and knock on the locked door while the office secretary sat somewhere inside—no doubt enjoying his misery since it seemed to take her forever to get off her overdressed, gaudy-from-the-jungle, could-a-woman-seriously-have-that-much-leopard-print butt and open the door.

Today, as usual, she greeted him with a false, bright, red-lipped smile and an insincere comment about how she was worried about him being out in this weather. If she had been so worried, she would have been waiting at the back door for him with a plush towel. David almost asked about that nasty smudge of lipstick on her front tooth but instead gave her his best village-idiot smile before accidentally rolling over her blindingly pink, high-heeled shoes on his way through the door.

"Ouch!" she yelped, jumping back slightly.

"Sorry," David muttered.

Hmmm, was that petty or what? David wondered briefly to himself as some rain dripped from his bangs. *Maybe.* But she had been the one who kept him waiting until 8:30 every morning and making him late for class. If he could enter through the front door like every other student in this school, he would be on time, but as of yet he wasn't as skilled going up stairs as he was going down them. David did not get mad. He did, however, always get even. As the saying went, "vengeance was a dish best served cold." And vengeance liked to run over gaudy-covered toes.

***

Tick, tock, tick, tock. The second hand laboriously tried to make its way around the face of an oversized clock. *Who made clocks that big anyway?* David stared up at the clock and sighed. Five minutes to go. He glanced at the test on his desk while using the pencil eraser to scratch between his eyebrows. His dark brown eyes skimmed over the test papers for the third time.

With a cough to get the students' attention, Ms. Lenz rose ominously from her desk, spread her feet shoulder-width apart, and placed her hands on her hips. "Time's up! Please put down your pencils and pass your tests to the front of the class," she ordered in a passable imitation of a military drill sergeant.

All writing stopped. All thirty grunts looked to the front of the class and saluted—actually some yawned, some stretched, and some insubordinate even passed wind to the snickers of many. *Dad's always saying better in than out. Guess he never sat behind someone who let one out*, David thought, holding his breath.

David reluctantly turned in his chair and collected the papers from the ape-thing named Brian who sat behind him. Snatching the pile of papers from Brian's hands, he whipped back around and almost tossed the papers into Ms. Lenz's eager hands. She smiled down at him with a pitying look on her face that seemed to say, "I am so sorry you're a cripple" or maybe she was simply thinking, "Would you like fries with that?" As Ms. Lenz moved to the next row of desks, David's thoughts were interrupted by a small jab between his shoulder blades.

"I'll get you for your little prank, dork," Brian hissed close to David's ear. "You're dead meat!"

David's stomach troll started doing little somersaults. It wasn't that he was afraid of Brian. Sure, most people would be, but David knew from past experience, Brian was usually more bark than bite. But David didn't handle confrontation well. Bullies, girls, teachers—all made him nervous. And then, of course, when he was nervous, his mouth seemed to get him into even more trouble. Plus he was sure Brian wouldn't let the garbage-over-the-bathroom-door thing go without some form of idiotic retribution, especially since Aimee was there for Brian's humiliation, which would be unforgivable. So, it was a good thing Brian was more brawn than brain, and David could normally hold his own against Brian's brain—or lack thereof.

"You're gonna be sorry, gimp. I swear you're gonna get it," Brian threatened. David waved his hand back at Brian like he was waving a pesky mosquito from his ear.

Ms. Lenz turned to face David's row. With an exasperated smile on her face, she looked at Brian expectantly. "Brian, was there something you wanted to share with the class?"

"No, ma'am," Brian grumbled. David heard the desk groan as Brian moved away from David's head and back into his seat.

Brrring! Brrring! The ear-splitting school bell rang. *Ah, the signal of the end of yet another day in the life of the brave adventurer, David the Bold. Or maybe it should be David the Brave or David the Lionhearted.* David knew Brian was definitely going to be up to something today, and he would need to be ready. Heaving a deep sigh, David waited patiently as the classroom erupted with the sounds of textbooks slamming shut followed by thirty bodies rising almost simultaneously from their seats. The mob fled past him, emptying out of the classroom on their way to freedom.

David leisurely scooped his books into his backpack, as the stampede momentarily bottle-necked at the doorway. Ms. Lenz stared at him as the last of his classmates did everything but run from the room. David gave her a thin smile while he waited for the onrush of students to trickle off before he made his way to leave the class.

"See you on Monday, David," Ms. Lenz said, patting him on the shoulder when he rolled by her, missing her feet by mere inches. Just a warning pass. She hadn't crossed the line yet.

"Not if I see you first," David whispered under his breath as he smiled and waved goodbye. He wasn't in the mood to respond to her. He didn't care for the special attention she gave him. Oh, she didn't mean to watch him a little more carefully than the other students. In fact, she probably wasn't even aware that she did it. But the fact of the matter was she did, and it annoyed him more than running over dog crap in the middle of the sidewalk. Some of his teachers were cool. Ms. Lenz wasn't one of them. Anyway, David knew she meant well. Usually adults around him meant well, but they were oblivious of how stifling they could be.

David took his time and let the crazed mob rush out of the school before he made his way to his locker. It was easier not having to deal with the congestion of eager bodies slamming and dropping things in and pulling things out of their lockers at the end of the school day. He had been given a locker on the bottom row, even though he was a decent five feet ten inches tall. Well, okay, maybe four feet six inches when sitting. Granted he was always technically sitting but that's beside the point. Luckily, the owner of the top locker had cleared out and was probably already getting on the bus.

David's locker was extremely clean and organized with stickers and pictures on the inside of the door in straight rows and columns instead of haphazardly stuck on and around each other in every direction possible like most of the walkies' lockers. David called people who were temporarily not physically challenged "walkies" because they walked instead of wheeled. Not that David was prejudiced against walkies. After all, it wasn't their fault they were not physically challenged yet. David figured he was fifty to sixty years ahead of most of the people he knew in the physically challenged department. Not that David would ever consider himself too physically challenged. He understood he had some limitations but had dogged determination to learn, adapt, and be able to do pretty much what anyone standing was able to do, and he was probably better at basketball than a lot of guys standing on two legs.

Snapping his earphones on, David pulled on his fingerless leather gloves and wheeled to the school's front entrance. He lived fairly close to school, so he didn't have to rush to meet a bus or have a parent wait for him in the car lane. The first week he had wheeled to school by himself, Mom had secretly followed him and attempted some pretty high-level, covert, James-Bond moves along the way.

Unfortunately, he spotted her minutes after leaving the house and did his best to ignore her lack of faith in him, although he did burst out laughing when she tripped while trying to duck behind a tree. Dad, on the other hand, had waved from the kitchen window and went back inside to finish the morning paper before heading off to work at the hospital outpatient therapy clinic.

7

Dumpster Diving

David hummed happily out of tune to the fast-paced Fall Out Boy song thrumming loudly in his ears as he bounced down the front steps and across the street. He may not be able to go up the front steps that well, but he could damn skippy go down them. He waved cheerfully at the school's crossing guard as he careened across the street and pulled a wheelie to get over the curb.

He turned down the deserted service lane a few blocks from his house. It was rough going as the service lane had potholes and uneven gravel from one end to the other. He was assaulted by the unpleasant aromas coming from the dumpsters that lined the service lane, but it was a small price to pay for his freedom after school.

Phew! That one beside the white van must have a dead body in it, David thought, picking up the pace. His meandering thoughts were abruptly cut short by a smack to the back of his head. His earphones slid in front of his face, and he grabbed at them while whirling his Quickie Eclipse space age-designed wheelchair around to see what had hit him. With his hand, he felt something slimy sticking to the back of his head and neck.

Looking at the goo in his hand, which strongly resembled decomposing garbage sludge, and at the source of the goo, David did his best Vin Diesel I'm-gonna-kick-your-butt look. Standing about twenty feet away was none other than his arch nemesis Brian. It appeared Brian felt he needed backup and had brought along a couple of his demented cronies. Apparently, Brian was more steamed up about the garbage dumping than David expected.

"Look. I know you're ugly and your mother dresses you funny, but is that a good reason to act like a schizophrenic homicidal egomaniac?" David cocked his head to the side and flashed his best you're-a-total-moron smile at Brian. "Oops, did I use big words you didn't understand?"

Brian's acne-marred face screwed up in anger. David wondered briefly if it was possible for Brian's eyes to become even beadier. They were small and pig-like to begin with, and the red blustering cheeks didn't do much for Brian's complexion. The zits were fiery-looking enough without the added flush of rage. Someone seriously could use the benefit of Proactiv.

"You are so dead, dork!"

"Dude, seriously. What is your major malfunction?" David tried diplomacy.

"I know it was you! You dumped the garbage on me! It's payback time, gimp!" Brian sneered. David thought he more closely resembled someone trying to hold back a wave of gut-wrenching diarrhea. *Constipation has a new name and its name was Brian.*

The three bullies stood shoulder to shoulder, their backpacks now resting on the ground at their feet. Brian was slightly overweight and wore his shirts one size too small so that one couldn't help but notice his girth—his bowlful of jelly that shook when he laughed. Or ran. Or walked. Or pretty much whenever he did anything but sit and pick his nose. It was that girth and not his charming personality that landed him a position on the Junior Varsity football team.

Bulldozer Brian is what a lot of kids called him. Not that it mattered to Brian. In his mind he attained his popularity because he was on the football team. However, had he truly been popular, there would have been a crowd with him instead of two other boys. Well, if he'd truly been popular and widely liked at school, he wouldn't be cornering some disabled kid in an alley, no matter what smelly pranks that kid had come up with.

Leroy and Gerald, the two boys with Brian, were also on the football team. They were both bigger than David. If he was a horse in a race, David wouldn't bet on his chances of winning at the moment. Or even finishing the race for that matter!

Leroy swung his baseball cap so that the bill faced behind him and took a step toward David. When Leroy smiled, the world became a brighter place. Actually, Leroy's smile was a good look at a PPO dental plan gone wrong. Leroy grabbed David's backpack and, showing more of those rotten bicuspids, upended it and dumped all of David's things onto the ground. He then threw the backpack at David, which David caught with a pained grunt.

Be calm, Grasshopper, wait for the right time, David thought and tried to stare down Leroy. Or more accurately, stared up at Leroy. "So, does that make you feel like a man?" David asked, gesturing to his books in the dirt and miscellaneous papers floating around.

Leroy cackled. "I'm more of a man than you'll ever be, gimp."

"Ah, wounded to the quick," David grabbed his chest in imitation of a heart attack.

David's dad had always told him to turn the other cheek and walk away when facing a bully. Well, David only turned the other cheek to prevent getting sores on his butt, and he obviously couldn't walk away. So, here was the dilemma. Should he stand and fight, or wheel away? A Clash tune popped into his head. *Should I stay? Or should I go now? Reality check!* Instead he opted for a third approach. He would use his superior intellect and talk his way out of trouble—or at least make the attempt.

"Seriously, guys. Let's talk about this. Do you really want the school paper to write about this? Imagine, if you will, the headlines reading Three football jerks—I mean, jocks!—corner poor, defenseless, disabled kid in back alley! I mean, c'mon! What would the cheerleaders say?"

"What did he mean by that?" Leroy asked Brian. "When did that happen? I didn't see that."

Gerald looked perplexed. "What would the cheerleaders say?"

"You think Coach would make us run extra laps for this?"

"Never mind! Wheels is blabbing, so let's make him blubber instead. Payback time!" Brian grinned. "Talk all you want. This time you're going to walk the talk instead of talking the walk!"

Leroy and Gerald looked more confused than normal. "What?" they asked simultaneously.

"Touche. As always, Brian, your oratory genius again leaves me speechless with wonder—as in I wonder if there is anything up there." David tapped his head as he spoke.

Brian's friends both laughed until Brian glared at them before lunging forward and pushing David hard in the chest. David's attempt to block the attack only earned him two bruised forearms. Grabbing the front bar on David's chair, Brian gave a mighty heave, lifting the front and throwing David off-balance.

Guess you can only talk your way out of something if the other party is willing to listen, David thought. *Lesson learned.* He gripped his wheels tightly and tried to push them forward to ram the wheelchair into Brian in a futile attempt to get free.

"Give me a hand," Brian grunted. Each of his cronies grabbed a wheel and lifted. Together, they carried David toward the dumpster. Getting roughly jostled, David was too busy hanging on to effectively fight back. He felt like the unwilling sacrificial offering to the primitive dumpster god of football imbeciles.

Had he been in a mood to reflect upon recent events, David would have seen this as an ironic twist of fate as it appeared the dead-body smell had been a foreshadowing of things to come.

"Come on, guys! This isn't funny anymore. Put me down!" David demanded.

"What's wrong, smart boy? Nothing smart to say?" Gerald asked.

"Wow, Gerald. Finally he speaks! You write your own material or does Brian help you?" David replied before good sense could stop him. Gerald growled in response. *Yep. Brian definitely did have to help him write his own material.*

Reaching the dumpster, Brian looked David directly in the eye and smiled. "Up, up, and away! S'matter? Cat got your tongue?" For once David was, in fact, speechless. Did Brian giggle? "Let's see you talk your way out of this one, gimp."

Together the three boys gave a mighty heave, lifting David, chair and all, up toward the lip of the dumpster. Forgetting he had his seatbelt on, David struggled frantically as he tried to jump from his chair onto the three goons. He wasn't going to go down without a fight. As the chair reached the apex and started to tilt back, David thought he heard a low, menacing growl coming from somewhere below.

Too late, he finally got the seatbelt undone, and David felt himself slipping forward off his chair. The wheelchair balanced on the edge of the dumpster where it teetered but did not fall in. For a moment David thought he was going to luck out and manage to swing his weight back toward the ground instead of into the dumpster.

"Since you like playing with garbage so much, you should feel right at home, Wheels." Then Brian, always the helpful one, gave one last heave and over the edge David and chair went to join the other dead body already inside the dumpster.

8

Pittie Party

Computer geeks would one day rule the world! Aimee knew this for a certainty, just as she knew that she would be a computer master. Computers were how she had gotten her part-time job at the Animal Rescue Co. during the volleyball season hiatus. Although she was still in high school, she was already doing college-level computer courses. She had a way with computers like some people had a way with, say, horses. Yes, that was her—the computer whisperer. But that sounded too geeky, and she was seriously way too kewlies to be a dweeb.

She wasn't your stereotypical computer nerd unless tall, athletic, Hawaiian beauties were considered nerds. She was often told how pretty her brown eyes or long black hair made her. She didn't believe a word of it. She believed that anyone could see she was too heavy in the hips and her nose was way too small to be in proportion with the rest of her face. As she liked to tell everybody, she had a Mr. Potato Head nose. Not everyone saw that though. One boy had even suggested she looked like an exotic dancer. She had knocked him down and made him take it back. But that was when she was only thirteen. Now that she was older, she liked the compliments, depending on who was giving them, of course. Orlando Bloom could give her a compliment any time!

Aimee looked up from her computer screen when she felt the breeze from the door being opened as Greta entered the Animal Rescue Co. main office. At the same time, Hoku's paw batted Aimee's leg to get her attention. Greta's eyes were bloodshot and her hair more disheveled than normal, which was actually saying a lot. Her clothes were crumpled like she had slept in them, and they were covered in blotches and streaks of dried blood. It was obvious Greta was a person with a serious curling iron phobia on a normal day, but being up all night made her look like a Sasquatch's sister, twigs in hair included.

"Rough night? You look like something the cat dragged in," Aimee said, smirking. "Or should that be some*one* dragged in? Hmmm? Possibly one of Tampa Bay's finest? Officer Slim Jim? Officer Simpleton? What was his name again?"

Everyone knew about Greta's crush; she did a horrible job at keeping it a secret.

"Slimka, you silly girl." Greta laughed good-naturedly at the none-too-subtle teasing. "As a matter of fact, I did see him last night but got dragged home by a bunch of pitties instead. We received an anonymous tip and successfully raided a dog fighting ring last night. I didn't get much sleep." Greta yawned as she spoke, covering her mouth with her hand.

"What was that?" Aimee asked, watching Greta's mouth carefully.

"Ah. Sorry, pumpkin." Greta moved her hands and repeated what she had said. Since she wasn't good at signing, she needed that subtle reminder to slow her words and speak more clearly for Aimee's benefit.

"Were you able to save any of the dogs?" Aimee missed most of what Greta said but got the gist of it. She swiftly rose to her feet and moved toward the door to the kennels. She signed at Hoku to sit and stay. Hoku plopped back down on the dog bed next to the computer desk and resumed her search for the elusive squeaker in her stuffed teddy bear.

"We have twenty dogs total. Four are in surgery now, and four were either killed or died on their way here. We don't know how many escaped," Greta explained.

"Poor things. Can I see the ones you rescued?" Out of habit, Aimee's hands moved swiftly as she spoke.

"Sure, pumpkin, but I warn you some of it won't be pretty," Greta replied.

Greta led Aimee into the back kennels where new animals were kept until they could be examined and were being treated by a veterinarian. Depending on the animals' temperament and condition, they were either moved to a holding area for rehabilitation or adoption, or humanely euthanized. Aimee stopped following Greta when she reached the first kennel occupied by one of the pit bulls and read the name tag on the door—Smiley.

Smiley was obviously a young dog as evidenced by his happy demeanor and lack of scars. The exuberant brindle puppy squirmed in delight at seeing Greta and Aimee. He seemed totally unaware of the seriousness of the situation he was in as he bounced in high spirits, unable to stop squirming, his front end unable to catch up to his back end. Aimee watched him bark in welcome and, kneeling down, wiggled her fingers through the mesh for him to lick.

"You're such a good boy, Smiley. Such a sweetie! Oh, yes, you are! Who's a cute little boy?" Aimee cooed. "I love me some bay-beh puppies! Yes, I do! You can never get enough puppy kisses." Aimee was definitely a puppy junkie. She was in need of attending Pup-aholics Anonymous to get over her addiction. Her name tag even read *Hi! My name is Aimee and I'm a pup-aholic.*

Greta placed a hand on Aimee's shoulder. She tugged her away from the kennel and stopped the nauseating gush of baby-talk, a major symptom of pup-aholism. Aimee looked up and quirked her eyebrow questioningly. "Sie vorsichtig! Some were abused and might bite you," Greta admonished.

Aimee rolled her eyes. "I wasn't born yesterday, you know! And do you seriously think this little guy's capable of anything but licking someone to death?"

"Too true," Greta laughed, "but you can't hear them growl."

"Well, yeah, but I can see them growl long before they actually make the noise," Aimee retorted before moving down the line of kennels and greeting each new resident in turn. Her anger rose with each innocent victim she met. A few were friendly like Smiley and not that badly hurt, if at all, while others hunkered in the back of their kennels, licking their numerous injuries.

It hurt Aimee's heart to see them like this—to know they had been cruelly abused by monsters instead of having the love of a family that they deserved. She ached to see them hurt and scared and suspicious, but it was also devastating to see them acting still so very loving towards people after all they had been through. They were so forgiving and didn't deserve to be hurt or abused.

One small black male had a foreleg cast and was too traumatized to even look at Aimee when she tried to say hi. He pressed himself into the far corner of the cage, his head down, body shaking. Others with more grievous injuries had either already been put to sleep or were still in surgery.

When Aimee approached the last kennel, she crooned to the reddish-brown pit bull. He had a missing left ear, stitches from recent eye surgery to remove his left eye, extensive scarring over his face, and numerous staples over his chest and legs. He lay on a pile of blankets but had perked up at her approach. His head weaved, his one eye slightly dulled from the pain medications.

"Oh, you poor baby. How could they allow this to happen?" Aimee glanced at the name tag, which simply read No. 9, which meant he recently got out of surgery and hadn't been named by a staff member yet or had any identifiers on him. "You're okay, baby boy. The bad men won't hurt you anymore."

No. 9 responded to Aimee's sweet voice and licked at her fingers through the gate. As she knelt down to give the injured pit bull more affection, the puppy in the next kennel poked his paw through the gate to get some attention from her as well. No. 9 suddenly lunged at the paneling toward the other dog. He slammed into the wire cage, his shoulder level to Aimee's face.

Holy guacamole! Where did that come from? Aimee thought, falling back against Greta who had been trailing the girl. The puppy yelped in alarm before scrambling to the far end of his kennel. Greta quickly went into the scared pup's kennel and moved him down the hall. Snarling viciously, the caramel-colored pit bull continued to attack the cage for several seconds until the puppy was no longer in view.

During this time, Aimee had attempted to talk No. 9 down by trying to project calm energy, but the berserk pit bull didn't notice her until the puppy was gone. Not until the other dog was actually out of sight, did No. 9 sit with his back against the paneling, his hackles raised, his head resting against Aimee's fingers.

Still in shock, Aimee sat and stared at the poor beast while she continued to stroke the top of his scar-marked head. Even after his ferocious attempt to attack the dog in the kennel next to him, all Aimee wanted to do was give him a hug. *It's not your fault that you had scum of the earth for owners.* She looked into his remaining sad brown eye. *It's not your fault you had been forced into this life. You shouldn't have to suffer because of them. It's not fair!*

Greta walked back to Aimee. Greta's heart lurched to see the beauty taming the beast. But this wasn't a fairy tale, and unfortunately, this story wasn't going to have a happy ending. Greta tapped Aimee's shoulder to get her attention. Aimee looked up at her with a questioning expression on her face.

"He probably won't be one of the lucky ones, pumpkin." Greta reached down and helped Aimee to her feet.

The pit bull gently licked Aimee's fingers as she stood. Aimee bit her bottom lip hard to keep from crying at the bereft look on his face as he watched her walk away. It was always hard for her to see the dogs in cages. She was even known to spill a tear or two when the Animal Rescue Co. commercials came on TV. She went through boxes of tissues watching any episodes involving abused fighting dogs. Of course, no one would ever tease her about that unless they wanted a smack upside the head.

"But why!" Aimee asked. "I hate this!"

"If he doesn't calm down and pass the temperament testing, he will be humanely put to sleep. It's the only way for some of them." Greta heaved a deep sigh and led Aimee back down the long corridor toward the front office.

"Why would anyone do this to an animal, Greta?" Aimee's face flushed, and her eyes were starting to mist. She blinked her eyes rapidly or she wouldn't be able to clearly see what Greta had to say, but things like this made her so angry! *You protect those smaller than you. Not abuse them!*

"The jerks who own them call it sport. They fight for money. It's not hard to train them to attack other animals because they want to please you so much. They're fiercely loyal to their owners. Their ancestors were used to taunt bulls in the ring. And now this..." Greta smiled sadly and patted Aimee's back in commiseration. "These monsters don't care about what their dogs want—a warm bed, a good belly rub, a loving home, a person to call their own."

"I hate them. Every single one of them!" Aimee growled. "They should all be rounded up and put in a ring to fight it out against each other."

"I agree, pumpkin. Wholeheartedly. But let's look on the bright side of things, okay? Some bad people are in jail now. We did save these dogs from a life of pain and abuse. And after all of this is said and done, I'm hoping that most of them will be adoptable." Greta stopped by Smiley's cage. "Like this little guy."

Smiley resumed his happy bouncing now that he was away from No. 9. "He is loveable and friendly with people, as are most of the other dogs. So far it seems he has an excellent temperament. We need to test him for animal aggression and food aggression, but I think he should be okay for adoption. Hopefully, the case against the dog fighters won't be drawn out for too long, and he'll be able to go to a home soon."

Kneeling in front of the puppy, Aimee asked, "How could anyone do this? How could anyone maliciously hurt these dogs and make them attack each other and consider that fun? Sickos! How could they exploit abuse like that? With a total disregard of their feelings and their injuries! How could they make them suffer like that and not care? Ugh! Wait until I can vote. I'm going to badger my Congressman! My Representative! My Senator! All of them! They need to put an end to this. Don't make me go up to Tallahassee!"

Aimee wiggled her fingers through the kennel door to get a calming dose of exuberant puppy love. Greta patted Aimee's back in sympathy before walking down the hall to the vet's office. Aimee hadn't seen Greta's reply, "Because they're not human."

With her anger spent, Aimee sighed and got up to go to the office to hug her dog. Hoku always knew how to make her feel better. *I wish there was something I could do to help.*

Her cell phone began to vibrate. Taking it out of her pocket, she flipped open the cover and saw that she had received a text message. Text messaging definitely made her life a lot easier to communicate with her friends. As she read the end of the message, her mouth dropped open. She didn't know if she should laugh or worry.

Aimee quickly looked up to see if Greta was watching her. Fortunately, Greta had gone back into the holding area, probably in response to a call. Aimee returned to her desk, scooped Hoku up in her lap, and quickly began typing out a reply to the strange message she had received.

9

Barking Dead

David's head pounded like all seven dwarves were mining for diamonds in his brain. He didn't remember passing out, but fortunately, the sun was still up, so he knew he hadn't been out for long. Gingerly touching the bulge on the side of his head, he grimaced from the pain while surveying his surroundings. The interior of the bin was not as large as it looked from the outside. In fact, with all the garbage inside, it was cramped—not to mention, extremely nasty and foul smelling from years of built-up decomposing waste. A torn garbage bag oozed rotten food. A cardboard box, which at one time claimed to have held a 42-inch TV, was currently seeping unidentified liquids.

Fortunately, David hadn't landed on the broken coffee table missing two legs that also occupied the bottom of the dumpster. Somehow when he fell, he had managed to twist around so his wheelchair was now on top of him. An armrest poked into his rib cage and one tire rested against his head. The wheelchair falling on him must have been what had caused him to hit his head against the side of the metal bin.

He was aware of his own labored breathing and wondered briefly if he had punctured a lung. He remembered reading about soldiers being shot in the chest and dying from fluid filling their lungs. Moving his wheelchair slightly so the armrest no longer stabbed him in his ribs, he felt the pain ease off slightly. *Ah, that's a good sign.*

Quoting *Monty Python's Holy Grail*, he tried to let Brian and his goons know he hadn't been beaten. "It's only a flesh wound!" he shouted. "Come back and fight me, you cowards!"

No one answered him with a strangled roar of rage or hurled insults. The only response was the caw of a startled crow as it flew from the top of the dumpster. Apparently, his assailants had fled the scene. *Oh, well, unlike the dark knight, I seriously doubt I'll fight them off with my teeth.* David laughed out loud.

A low, rumbling growl came from somewhere to his left. It appeared to be coming from the seeping box. *Zombies!* The dead body in the garbage had come back as a zombie, and David was sure that he was going to be its first victim. Obviously watching *The Walking Dead* didn't help calm his hyperactive imagination. *I need a stake or garlic! Wait a minute. Stakes and garlic are for vampires and silver bullets for werewolves.*

If I remember correctly, which I usually do, zombies have to be hacked to pieces or shot in the head. Hmmmm, shot in the head. Sooooo, if zombies are reanimated flesh, how would a bullet to the head re-kill it? Not that it mattered because David didn't have a gun and was currently trapped under his wheelchair. *This is freaking craptastic! Where's Daryl and his crossbow when you need him!*

The growling grew louder as the occupant of the box shifted slightly. David quickly reviewed his situation and tried to develop an action plan like his parents had taught him to do in a time of crisis. Unfortunately, they had not anticipated him and his wheelchair being dumped in the garbage by a trio of Neanderthal jocks. The growling became more of a muted gurgling sound followed by a whimper.

"Whatever you are, come out of there. You're not scaring anyone," David said loudly, trying unsuccessfully to steady the quaver in his voice.

He pushed the wheelchair up and away to the side. Then he maneuvered his body into a sitting position before grabbing his backpack and looking inside it for something to use as a weapon. He still had his cell phone, a water bottle, and a severely squashed peanut butter sandwich. Good thing Leroy wasn't bright enough to unzip all of the compartments in his bag and had only dumped out his paperwork and books from the main pouch.

Without warning, the box tipped over, shifting the wheelchair with a screech of tortured metal, and out spilled the zombie. David screamed high, long, and loud like a little girl who had a running mouse stuck in her pants. Fortunately, it wasn't reanimated flesh, but to David's mind, it was much, much worse. It was one of those vicious pit bull dogs everyone was talking about these days.

Pit bulls were all over the headlines for dog fighting and attacking people and killing little babies in their sleep! And this one's face was covered in blood! David only hoped it went for his leg first because he had less feeling down there then, say, in his arms or face. He tried to shift his upper body away from the dog's face, but the wheelchair was now angled from the top of the TV box down on David's head.

David eyed the dog warily; it glared at him, its blood-stained muzzle crinkled to show its sharp canines. Neither moved and neither seemed to breathe for a long time. Since it was snarling, David got a good look at its huge, saliva gleaming, sharp teeth, which, unfortunately, all seemed to be there.

Finally, David broke the stalemate. "Soooo, what brings you to this neck of the woods?" No response. *Well, it was worth a try. Man! I wish I knew how to handle dogs better.*

David had been volunteering at the same shelter with Aimee for the past year, but he did more office work than handling the animals. He hoped his parents would eventually let him adopt a dog if he showed them he could be responsible enough. Now he wished he had been allowed to work with the dogs because he had no idea what to do. Fumbling in his backpack, he felt his cell phone.

Does a cell phone seem like a good weapon against eighty pounds of hungry pit bull. Hungry pit bull? Ah ha! David pulled out the peanut butter sandwich and unwrapped it. He broke off a small piece of bread and threw the chunk at the dog. After the bread bounced off its nose, it grabbed the offering and swallowed without chewing.

David threw a few more pieces, and as the dog loudly chomped away at the gooey mess, he felt brave enough to offer a piece on his outstretched hand. Sniffing, the canine moved an inch closer. How it could smell anything in the stench of their container was beyond David's imagination. Trying to cement their relationship, he slowly fed it the rest of his sandwich.

With the sandwich gone, the pit bull laid his massive head next to David's knee and drifted off to sleep. It was difficult to get a good look at the dog as David was still firmly wedged under his wheelchair. It was hard to tell exactly what color it was since it was covered with blood and random pieces of garbage. He reached out a tentative hand to gently stroke the muscular animal's neck. A low rumbling growl warned him he had not yet earned that right, so he withdrew his hand and went searching in his backpack again.

Pulling out his cell phone, David flipped open the cover and saw that it was 5:30 p.m. He should have been home almost an hour ago. He grimaced, knowing his dad would be coming to look for him soon. There was no way he wanted his dad to find him like this or especially his mother. She'd freak and he'd be confined to the house for eternity. A plan slowly began forming in the depths of his mind and finally pushed its way to the surface.

Dialing his dad's cell number, he waited patiently as the phone rang. His father was an occupational therapist who didn't believe being in a wheelchair gave David an excuse to hide away from the world. He always encouraged David to make new friends and try new things. David played that trump card now.

"Hey, Dad. Um, sorry, but I was hanging with these guys from school and kinda lost track of time. Can I stay for a while longer?" In a way he didn't lie. After all, wasn't it his own mother, the lawyer, who always said, "There is a difference between lying and not telling the whole truth." Well, he wasn't technically lying. He merely left out a few parts— like the part where he was stuck in a garbage bin with a savage, possibly rabid pit bull.

"That's fine, David. I'm glad you're socializing. You should bring them around sometime, but for now, be home by eight or your mother will have a litter of kittens."

"Sounds like a plan. Bye!" David smiled. His dad had given him over two hours to complete the rest of his plan. Operation Save Killer Mutt was under way. He could have asked his dad for help. Maybe he should have, but that would mean explaining why he was in the dumpster and also would mean the dog being taken to the shelter by his parents. And then who knows what would happen to this dog. He had other plans for this pup.

David quickly typed out a text message and sent it to Aimee. **Need ur help 2 save dog. Come right away + I've fallen and I can't get up :0p.**

He only hoped she wasn't out sailing with his nemesis for her affection, Skyler Stoerm. Fortunately, it was only a matter of seconds before David's phone began playing Survivor's *Eye of the Tiger*. Hopefully, it was Aimee returning his text. Score!

He looked at the message. **Where r u? I'll be there ASAP.**

David quickly typed his location into the phone and pressed the send button. The shelter was a few miles away, so it would be a while before Aimee would get here. Putting his phone down beside him, David surveyed his surroundings again. This time he wasn't afraid of fictitious zombies caused by his wayward imagination. He was in planning mode. First though, he had to get out from under his wheelchair.

Lifting with both arms, he was able to maneuver the chair to its side on top of the box but wasn't able to push it back over the lip of the dumpster. Feeling much better about his situation now that he was able to check out his body, David was pleasantly surprised to discover he was mostly uninjured. No more than a few scratches and sore ribs.

Of course, on the other hand, he could have broken his legs and might not have felt it. Could that and handicap parking count as the advantages of having paraplegia? Not likely! Besides he didn't have a driver's license yet. David felt the length of his legs and didn't feel any bones sticking out. He worried briefly that he could have damaged some muscles or joints in his legs but was distracted by the whimpered groan emitted by the dog.

David eyed the pit bull sleeping beside him, twitching and whining as if in a nightmare. The poor guy was pretty beat up. Its entire chest and face were covered in dried gore, and a gaping wound on his shoulder still oozed blood. It appeared to be starving and dehydrated, although heavily muscled, with its skin hanging loosely over its rib cage like it had been meant to fit a larger dog.

"It's okay, boy. You're gonna be all right. I'll figure something out," David spoke soothingly in an attempt to wake his snoozing companion without getting his own head ripped off in the process.

Risking another growl, David gently unbuckled the dog's steel pinch collar and slipped it from around its neck. There was a tag with a name on it. After cleaning off the dried blood, David was able to read the name—Goliath. There wasn't any other information, such as a phone number or address. Only the dog's name. Not like he'd ever think about returning Goliath to an owner who would leave his dog in this condition.

The irony of the situation hit David like a ton of bricks falling on top of him. David and Goliath! Only in the Bible, David slew Goliath. Well, not this time! In this version, David would tame the ferocious Goliath and turn him into a friend. He only wished one of those dog guru people from TV was here to guide him through the process. At least he had Aimee with her knowledge and connections.

David rummaged through his bag until he found his half-empty water bottle. Pouring a small amount of water into his hand, he held it under Goliath's nose. Slowly, Goliath's tongue came out and licked David's hand. Encouraged by the fact he still had all his fingers, David poured more water into his palm, letting it trickle onto the dog's tongue.

Without moving his body or even opening his eyes, Goliath lapped up what was left of the water. He let out a deep sigh when he was done and his whole body shuddered. David couldn't imagine the pain the poor guy was in, but hopefully soon he'd be able to remedy that.

"It's gonna be okay. I promise."

There was the slight problem of what to do with a pit bull he didn't want his parents to find out about right away. Thinking was one of David's strong points, and think he did. *Garage? Nah. Too easy for Mom to find 'cos she parks the Prius in there. Darcy's princess castle? Now that had potential!* David wondered how they would sneak the dog through the backyard and into the plastic playhouse.

He could probably pull it off with Aimee's assistance. It wouldn't be that far-fetched of a scenario, but he'd have to figure out a way to keep the door shut and the dog inside, which wouldn't be anything a few bungee cords couldn't take care of.

With that problem solved, he looked over his wheelchair for damage. There was nothing but a few scratches that he could see. At about that time, an angel appeared over the lip of the garbage bin. Maybe not a real angel, but she was close enough that David wasn't about to complain. It was a definite *Wayne's World Dream Weaver* moment.

"David...David, you in there?" Aimee's sweet face peered over the edge of David's prison before reeling back in disgust. "Oh, wow! I think I just vomited a litte. This is rancid! Next time you ask me out, you'd better shower first. I don't care for eau de gar bahge."

David shrugged. Since he knew it would be easier for her to see his hands than his lips, he signed *Sorry* as his face went through several shades of red before stopping at bright scarlet. Aimee smirked at his obvious distress.

Are you alone? David signed.

"Well, duh! Do you see anyone else?" Aimee replied.

Score! No Skyler, oh yeah, oh yeah! David thought and would have done a little dance of joy if not for two reasons. One, he was in a dumpster, and two, he couldn't stand up to dance.

Kinda hard to see anything from down here, he signed.

David knew the moment Aimee spotted the dog because her face melted. He didn't know if it was because Aimee was deaf or if it was just her personality, but she was the easiest person to read. She never hid her emotions, and he could always tell how she felt by her facial expressions.

Pointing to Goliath who eyed Aimee curiously, David signed, *His name is Goliath.*

"You're kidding, right? Goliath? That's the best you could come up with?"

David rolled his eyes and signed, *That was the name on his collar.*

"David and Goliath?" Aimee quirked an eyebrow. "Lame."

Aimee jumped into the dumpster before David could reply. Guys in distress covered in garbage slop may not have tugged at Aimee's heart strings, but dogs in need had Aimee at their beck and call. She stroked the top of Goliath's head as she blinked back tears. Unlike a lot of her friends, she didn't cry at movies, sappy love stories, and sad plights of the human psyche, but hurt a dog, kill a wolf, commit any type of animal atrocity, and she would cry a river that would put the Rio Grande to shame.

Goliath groaned in response to her gentle touch and moved his head slightly to gently lick her hand. David frowned. *You ingrate!* he thought. *She gets licks and I get growls? What's up with that!*

David touched Aimee on the shoulder and signed for her to help him get his wheelchair out first then she could pass out the injured dog. Together they were able to lift the wheelchair up and let it drop down beside the can. Aimee wrapped her tanned arms around David's waist and helped him into a semi-standing position against the inside edge of the garbage can.

David was keenly aware of Aimee. She stood only inches away from him. Her hair smelled slightly of coconut even with the decaying aroma permeating the air around them, and her skin felt warm and silky. Self-consciously, he looked up and, for a moment, got lost in her chocolate-brown eyes. Even that crumpled pink plastic thing that managed to get stuck on her head looked cute, like a Hawaiian flower accenting her dark hair.

Aimee raised an eyebrow and looked questioningly at David. "Earth to David?"

"What?" David replied intelligently.

"Up and over." Aimee smiled and gestured with her eyes, looking outside the can.

"Oh, yeah." David's ears were definitely on fire, although Aimee didn't seem to notice. He couldn't seem to get a good grip on the garbage lip. Being around Aimee made his legs feel weak. Granted normally his legs were weak, but Aimee turned him into super spineless jellyfish boy.

"Umm...David?"

"Yeah?"

"Today...dog rescue...remember?" Aimee smirked.

With a heave and Aimee's hands on his butt shoving him up, David managed to slide up over the edge. He got a good grip on the lip of the bin as Aimee pushed his legs over the edge. He felt the weight of his body swing over the dumpster and held to the side like he was doing a chin-up. *Thank God for upper body strength!* David thought, positioning himself directly over his wheelchair then dropping ineptly down into it. A few seconds later his backpack landed on his head and Aimee's face peered over the top.

"Ready for the dog?" Aimee asked. "I don't know how I'm gonna do this. Hey! Wait...go get your poncho over there."

"Sec." David attached his bag to the back of the wheelchair and strapped himself in. He rolled over to where his school papers lay scattered on the ground and retrieved his rain poncho. Returning to the garbage can, he tossed it up to Aimee.

Aimee stroked Goliath's head, which remained between his paws as he gazed at her or sometimes at a noise David made from outside the bin. The only things moving were his eyes and eyebrows. "Hey, big guy," she said softly, smiling in reassurance. "Be a good boy, okay? I'm not going to hurt you. We'll get you out of here in a jiffy. Don't struggle too much, okay?"

Aimee didn't hesitate, didn't think about those huge sharp canines, didn't think about the possibility of the dog attacking her, didn't think about getting injured herself, while she carefully wrapped Goliath in the poncho. She frowned at the sight of his numerous wounds but continued to talk soothingly as she lifted him up and over the edge of the can. David had a heart-stopping moment when he wondered suddenly if Goliath would go ballistic and rip Aimee apart when she had the dog balanced precariously on the edge of the dumpster. Goliath groaned and whimpered at the movement but cooperated with his rescue effort. Using the poncho as a harness, she slowly lowered Goliath onto David's lap.

With the grace of a gymnast, Aimee vaulted over the edge of the container and landed lightly beside David's wheelchair. Heaving from exertion, she leaned against the white van parked beside the dumpster. Aimee gnawed on her bottom lip as she got a good look at Goliath. He didn't look good at all. She was worried. His wounds were bad, and she was sure the garbage bin wasn't exactly a germ-free environment. The last thing that dog needed was a serious infection on top of everything else he'd been through.

What moron would throw away a perfectly good animal? Aimee shook her head and pulled out her phone. "We have to get him to the shelter right away. I'll text Greta."

David grabbed her arm and shook his head, signing an emphatic *NO!* With the dog on his lap in such close proximity to his face, David was afraid to raise his voice. Aimee may have a way with animals, but he wasn't so sure about his own skill—or lack thereof.

"Why not?" Aimee asked. Aimee was on the verge of losing her temper. "I didn't come out here to rescue a dog, only to lose it."

David sat there, looking at Aimee for a long time before he could answer her. *Why not? It was a simple enough question. It was probably the right thing to do.* He looked down at the wounded dog wrapped up in his poncho.

No, he signed again. *I need to help him.*

"Then let's go to the shelter and have the vet look at those wounds," Aimee said, her tone deepened in exasperation, her accent thickened by her agitation.

"No!" David felt a little foolish at the moment. Would Aimee ruin his plan by turning Goliath over to the shelter? He had to think fast.

Sighing deeply, Aimee walked over to David's papers and books on the ground and began picking things up. David wheeled over to her and waited. After a few minutes she had everything sorted and put back into the backpack. She then walked over to her mountain bike, picked it up, and climbed into the saddle.

"Okay, now what?" she inquired.

"My house. I thought maybe I could keep Goliath in my sister's outdoor castle for a while. You know, use it as a doghouse until I break the news to my folks." There it was...his wonderful plan. Only now that he said it out loud, it didn't sound so good.

"Um, ok..." Aimee raised one eyebrow again. A habit that was beginning to get on David's nerves. What she left unsaid spoke volumes to him.

"You think this is a dumb idea, don't you?"

"Well, yeah...kinda." Aimee sneered. "Where's your brain? First of all, this guy needs a vet—like yesterday. He has some serious-looking wounds, and he's malnourished. Secondly, he's most likely part of the pit bull fighting ring that Greta and her hunka hunka burning love, Officer Slim Jim, broke up last night—which means this dog could be dangerous. If he's a fighter, he could be a killer, and I don't think you can handle that."

Aimee had a flashback to the dog at the shelter that had tried to attack the puppy on the other side of his kennel. She looked at the pit bull on David's lap and he looked at her with soulful eyes. The dog had licked her hand before she picked him up. He didn't show any signs of aggression even when she did pick him up. And he was badly injured and most likely frightened; those two factors could easily have led to her getting hurt...had she been thinking at the time. She frowned as her own words to David didn't make any sense to her.

"If he's dangerous, he would have ripped your face off...or even mine before you even got here. But maybe you're right, maybe he's more dog than I can handle." David felt powerless in the face of Aimee's logic. It had all sounded so good when he was sitting inside the garbage container planning.

Aimee remembered what Greta had said about the aggressive pittie back at the shelter, about the possibility of him being euthanized. Aimee stared into Goliath's sweet, mournful eyes. *I wanted to do something to help, and here's my perfect opportunity.*

"You know, for once maybe I'm not right!" Aimee had a wild look in her eyes. "Let's take him to old Doc Foyster! Let's do this!"

10

Fixer Upper

avid could have kissed Aimee right then and there. Actually, he could have kissed her anytime if he was willing to sport a bloody nose. Instead he pulled out his phone to call Doc Foyster. Doc was a semi-retired veterinarian who volunteered his time at the shelter when he wasn't providing low-cost spaying and neutering to the public. Having met at the shelter, David and Doc had become good friends through their mutual interest in old sci-fi movies and fantasy role-playing games.

The phone rang once, twice, three times. On the fourth ring, a pleasant female voice answered. "Foyster residence."

"Hi. May I speak to Doc Foyster, please? This is David Erickson."

"Oh, sorry, love, but Doc's still at the clinic wrapping up some paperwork, I imagine. Would you like to leave a message?"

"No, thank you. I'm close to the clinic, so I'll pop over." David smiled at Aimee and gave her a thumbs up. Doc's clinic was only a few blocks away.

"Guess we lucked out," Aimee commented. "You need help, or you think you got him?"

"I can manage," David said. He adjusted Goliath on his lap, making a semi-hammock with the poncho and tying the ends to each arm of his chair. He spun his chair around and headed up the alley toward Central Avenue.

Aimee walked her bike alongside David as he wheeled down the street toward Doc's clinic. Glancing at her, David was acutely aware of the movement of her long, slender legs as she walked next to him. *Aimee's got nice legs,* David thought, *not atrophied like mine.* David grimaced and shook his head, physically clearing his mind of any self-pity and focused back to a happy thought. *She could have been a model, kind of like Gabrielle Reese...only Asian and deaf.* David smiled.

"So, smelly cat, how did you get into the dumpster in the first place?" Aimee asked, staring down at David.

"Don't ask! It's a long story." David shrugged. He signed quickly and awkwardly over Goliath's body before giving another push on his wheel rims, sending his chair forward.

"Does it end with someone named Butthead Brian?"

"Yeah, pretty much." David nodded.

"How are we going to get back at him this time?" she asked, with an impish grin.

"Meh. Brian can wait. Goliath comes first."

David was starting to get tired pushing his wheelchair with Goliath on board. The extra weight was more than he was used to. By the time they got to Doc's clinic, David was breathing heavily and practically drowning in a river of sweat that ran down his back, soaking his shirt.

Aimee would have offered to push him, but she could tell David was still smarting from being found in the dumpster and was in one of his I-can-take-on-the-world-from-this-chair moods. Like he had been there for her when she had lost her hearing and had learned sign language with her, she had been there for him when he had lost the use of his legs and helped him adapt to living with wheels. She didn't let him ever throw himself a pity party, and she wasn't about to let him start now. But she also knew his moods enough to know when to give him some time to himself to work out internal issues.

When they did finally reach the clinic, Aimee left her bike leaning against the railing and tried to get her rusty old bike lock to click in place. After a few minutes struggling, it finally locked. "Stupid thing. So annoying!"

"You need to get a new one of those. Something bigger and made of titanium," David chided.

"Whatever," Aimee shot back then got behind David to push him up the ramp. He looked as frazzled and exhausted as a wildebeest escaping from a pack of lions after swimming through a crocodile-infested river.

With one hand gripping the wheelchair handle, Aimee plugged her nose with her index finger and thumb. "I have two words for you—personal hygiene. I hope Doc already had his supper or has a head cold. A stuffy nose sure would come in handy right about now."

"Ditto," David snickered as Aimee pushed them up the ramp and into the clinic.

Doc's clinic had a small waiting area decorated with animal posters and other bric-a-brac. Doc apparently had no sense of matching decorum. There was a hundred-year-old set of veterinary tools hanging on one wall while the wall next to it had a picture of what looked like a dog in jail with the caption *Don't breed or buy while the homeless die*. In one corner was an antique wooden writing desk with various handouts for everything from types of worms in dogs to the pros and cons of spaying your cat.

Opening the door had triggered the door bell, which loudly pealed *Who Let the Dogs Out*. Shortly afterward, Doc appeared from the back treatment area.

"What an unexpected surprise," Doc said pleasantly and walked around the reception desk. "Well, now! What do we have here?" Doc stooped down to look at Goliath. The dog eyed him warily and tentatively licked at the hand Doc placed in front of his nose to smell. "Someone's been in quite a fight, eh?"

"It's a long story, Doc. Can you help him? Please!" David pleaded. "I can pay you back, I swear!"

Aimee clasped her hands under her chin and added her voice to the cause. "Please! Oh, please, please, please!"

"Well, now! Who can resist that? Follow me then," Doc said, leading them into a treatment room. "And where did you come by this poor beast, my boy?"

He gently lifted Goliath from David's lap and placed him on the stainless steel exam table. Goliath had not moved since he was taken out of the dumpster, which was disturbing David. Seeing Goliath in Doc's capable hands lifted a heavy burden from David's shoulders.

Doc was a proper old English gentleman. He had the accent, he wore the cashmere sweaters instead of a lab coat, and he actually still wore bow ties! His black-framed eyeglasses continually slid down his long nose, so he spent more time looking over them than through them. He was currently looking over his glasses while inspecting Goliath's wounds.

"Um ... I kinda found him in a dumpster," David answered truthfully, hoping Doc wouldn't pry.

"You don't say. I never would have known from the smell." Doc smiled, gently prodding at Goliath's shoulder wound.

Aimee was bent over, looking into Goliath's face when he suddenly lifted his head and let loose with a deep, throaty "woof!" Aimee jumped, tripping backward and falling into David's lap. David tried his best not to laugh, but in the end he couldn't resist.

"Oh, shush joo! He startled me," Aimee said sheepishly and climbed from David's lap. "I wasn't expecting him to lunge at me like that."

"Ah, so you are alive!" Doc patted Goliath soothingly on the head. Doc had a calm, firm voice to which most animals responded favorably.

Goliath stared intently at Doc's Maine Coon cat, Ernest, who up until now had been observing the proceedings from the top of a medicine cabinet. Without invitation, Ernest jumped down from his perch and climbed up onto the table right in Goliath's face.

"Look out!" David cried out in alarm, not sure how Goliath would respond to another animal. Didn't he read that pit bulls were supposed to be animal aggressive? Did they have a crazy prey drive?

"Hold on there, Ernest, not everyone likes cats," Doc chided his overly large feline friend who pointedly ignored him. Before anyone could stop him, Ernest rubbed up against Goliath's face as if daring him to complain while purring loudly. Goliath cocked his head sideways and sniffed at Ernest in bewilderment.

"I guess he passed the good-with-cats test with flying colors," Doc said. Aimee picked up the huge feline and placed him outside the room. "Unless, of course, he's still in shock. As far as I can see, though, most of these wounds are superficial, although there are a few puncture wounds that will need staples or drains placed, especially this shoulder, but everything else looks to be in good order. He'll need antibiotics as punctures can be a nasty business on their own, but to top that off with being in the garbage... well, now that certainly didn't help.

"I'll give him an injection of Baytril tonight along with some pain killers and anti-inflammatories, and we'll start the oral antibiotics tomorrow along with a topical ointment to put into the punctures. They'll also need to be flushed twice daily. We'll want to make sure no infection has set in the punctures before they close. A good bath, some tender loving care, a few good meals, and this lad should be peachy keen in no time."

Doc looked pointedly at the large clock on the wall that displayed dogs of various breeds where the numbers should be. He took Goliath off the table and placed him on the floor. Goliath sprawled out where he was placed. Obviously, he wasn't planning on going anywhere. "You two should probably be getting home. I'll keep this old boy for the night. I'll call my assistant to come in and help clean him up and get him fed. He looks like he could use a decent meal on top of everything else the poor chap's gone through. You can come by tomorrow to pick him up."

David and Aimee looked at each other, both of them visibly averse to leaving Goliath.

"Don't worry. It's for the best that he stay here tonight. He'll be fine." Doc ushered them toward the reception area door.

"Thanks so much, Doc...for everything!"

"Don't mention it, my boy. That's why I got in this business after all...to save animals. Now go home and get cleaned up. I'll see you both tomorrow at eight a.m. sharp."

Reluctantly, David pushed his wheelchair out the front door and turned to wave goodbye to Doc who locked the clinic doors behind them.

After opening the lock, Aimee mounted her bike and stopped to look at David. "Thanks for calling me. It totally made my day. I feel so good that I could help. That I could make a difference You don't understand how bummed I was when I got the text. And now I'm so full of warm fuzzies, I could puke!" She smiled, but her eyes sparkled with what looked like unshed tears.

David shrugged and smiled back. He always seemed to get tongue-tied around girls when conversations started turning serious and talking about...feelings—and what was that but a crappy song? Sure, he could be a laugh a minute but having to deal with sincere emotions made him nervous. Even with Aimee, who he had known since they were in kindergarten together, made him feel uneasy recently. Especially Aimee! If she started crying, he wouldn't be able to run away fast enough— literally! Avoiding eye contact, he gave her a hurried thumbs-up before giving his chair a push and headed for home.

"Oh, and, David, make sure you get your legs checked out?" Aimee ordered.

"Yeah, sure," David muttered. "Thanks for your help, Aimee."

Aimee moved her bike in front of David. "What did you say?" she asked.

David signed, *Thanks for your help tonight. See you tomorrow morning.*

Aimee smiled and patted him on the back. "Anytime, brah! What are friends for?"

11

Goo Gone

I t was almost nine o'clock by the time he wheeled up the sidewalk to his house. Rolling up the front ramp, he put his key in the lock and quietly opened the solid wooden door. Wheeling inside, David quickly typed in the security code and deactivated the door alarm before shutting the door behind him. *So far, so good.* Breathing deeply to calm his racing heart, he gagged. *Ok, bad idea. Boy, do I smell rancid! Hopefully, no one's around.*

The front entrance of the one-story ranch-style house was tastefully decorated with an antique-looking wooden bench and coat rack. His parents favored earth colors and had painted everything in the house in shades of autumn or, as David liked to say, "pukey pastels". From the entrance, the house split into three different areas. Left led past his sister's room to the room shared by his two baby brothers while right went into the kitchen with an open dining room. Straight ahead led to the backyard and covered pool area. David's bedroom was at the back of the house but he would have to travel past his parent's offices.

David quietly wheeled down the hallway littered with his brothers' numerous toys and carefully maneuvered around each obstacle. He heard *Here is Gone* by the Goo Goo Dolls. *Ah. Gutterflower. Good CD.* And a bonus that it blared from his mom's office, so she wouldn't hear him. Passing her door, he peeked inside at his mother grooving in her chair while typing away at her computer keyboard. *So embarrassing.*

That woman has no sense of rhythm! Good thing no one's here to witness this atrocity. Well, it could be worse, David thought. *She could be singing!*

It appeared that Lady Luck was with him as his younger siblings were in bed and not wandering the house with "I need to pee!" or "I want water!" excuses. His luck ran out though when he neared his dad's office and ran over a doll that practically screamed, "Will you sing a song with me?" Fortunately, his dad was involved with a computer game and merely asked, "Hey, buddy, have a good night?" as David jetted past the office door.

"Yeah, it was different," David replied without stopping to elaborate. "Night, Dad!"

He made it to his room and locked the door behind him. Getting undressed was always a bit of an ordeal for David. Getting his shirt off was easy enough. His arms worked fine. His pants represented another problem altogether. Walkies take for granted being able to stand up and drop their drawers. David was now adept at getting dressed and undressed, but it had been a challenge for him at first. He pulled off his Converse and socks easily enough by bending forward and reaching down. He had long arms.

To get his pants off, he turned a cheek, literally, and slid his pants and boxers down that cheek then turned the other cheek and repeated his earlier performance. Having cleared his buttocks, he then dropped his pants and boxers down both legs at the same time. Making sure his weight was centered in the back of the chair, he reached down and slipped his pants off over his feet, tossed them into the laundry hamper, and wheeled over to the bathroom.

His shower had been modified slightly with handles along the walls and rims of the tub to allow him to transfer independently in and out of it. Independence was important to David, and he had no intention of asking for help from anyone unless he absolutely had to, which was one of the reasons he insisted on not having a motorized wheelchair. Although his legs didn't work all that well, David had a strong upper body from working out. He had suffered an incomplete thoracic spinal cord injury, which meant he had good upper body function.

Pulling a wooden sliding board from behind the toilet, David got a towel down from the closet and placed it on top of the sliding board. Putting one end of the board under his butt and the other end on the bath bench that was placed partially in and partially out of the bathtub, David was able to slide over to the bench. Then he lifted his legs one at a time into the tub. Reaching up in front of him, he pulled down the shower nozzle which attached to a long hose. He hit the tap to warm water and waited several seconds for it to get warm. With a grateful sigh, he ran the water over his head, washing away the smell and grime.

With the water streaming over his head and face, his thoughts drifted back to the events of the day, and he couldn't help but smile. *I can't believe it! Finally! I've got my own dog! Of course, Brian's got some serious payback headed his way. On second thought, maybe I should thank the creep. Nah, I'm not that altruistic. I've gotta think up something extra sweet this time around. I can't believe he threw me in a freaking dumpster! But Brian can wait until I figure out what to do about Goliath. Good 'ole Goliath... I like the ring of that! But what am I gonna tell Mom and Dad? Well, at least tomorrow's Saturday, which will buy me a little more time.*

With his thoughts still racing, David finished his shower. He dried himself off with a towel before transferring back into his wheelchair. Thirty minutes later, he was fully dressed and sitting comfortably at his computer, munching on a peanut butter and banana sandwich.

David's room was a tribute to old sci-fi movies and fantasy role-playing games. Posters and stickers from every game worth playing and even a few he hadn't finished plastered his walls. His cabinets contained some of his inventions, as well as an assortment of spy wanna-be equipment; such as walkie-talkies, pen cameras, infrared cameras, listening devices, tracking devices, and other surveillance equipment. David also had an assortment of computers he had pieced together, and he was currently using one of the more powerful ones to go online. He wanted to look up anything he could find on pit bulls and what to expect.

To David's surprise, there were millions of hits on pit bulls. There were tons of pages advocating the breed, touting how kind and gentle they could be. He read numerous news stories on pit bull heroes saving people from burning buildings or even from other people. One of the top US drug-sniffing dogs was a pit bull rescued from a drug bust.

There were several rescue organizations rehabilitating pitties and speaking out against breed specific legislation. It appeared there were several counties where pit bulls were no longer allowed, even if they belonged to responsible pet owners. People's pets were being taken from homes and killed, even without any history of aggression. Little puppies were killed based on someone thinking they looked like they could have pit bull in them. Fortunately, David didn't live in the Miami/Dade area where the breed had been banned. There were many online petitions opposed to breed specific legislation (BSL).

There were also a number of pages on dog fighting and the exploitation of the American Pit Bull Terrier breed. Although it was illegal in all fifty states, there were still many people raising and fighting dogs. David thought about the wounds on Goliath's body and skimmed past the dog fighting pages. He wasn't yet ready to face the nightmare that had been Goliath's life.

There were several media stories on pit bull attacks on people. In almost every case, the owners seemed to be at fault. Unfortunately, reading the comments on the articles, it appeared many people blamed the dog breed instead of the irresponsible owners. In typical human fashion, people didn't take responsibility for mistreating or not training or socializing their dogs properly. In the majority of cases the dog owners were either not present during the attack or had no control over their dogs. David vowed not to be one of those owners.

12

Dog Eat Dog

Sunlight weaseled its way through the blinds on David's bedroom window, and the first warm rays caressed his face as they crawled across his pillow—right before alarm sirens blared. A small helicopter flew up from the base of the shrieking alarm clock. Groaning, David rolled onto his stomach, bunched up his pillow, and stuffed his head underneath it. The screaming sirens finally tore through the curtain of sleep, and he remembered there was something important he had to do today. *Goliath!* Sitting bolt upright, pillow flying off the bed, he looked at the clock on his bureau—7:15 a.m.

Throwing off the covers, David reached down beside the bed to pick up the fallen helicopter. He slammed it back on its base to turn off the obnoxious alarm. He then lifted himself into his wheelchair and wheeled into the bathroom to urinate before getting dressed. Grabbing the urinal, he positioned it before draining his bladder so it wouldn't spill. When he was done, he checked to make sure his urine didn't show any signs of blood or pus in it before dumping it into the toilet.

After the accident two years ago, David had undergone extensive therapy, and one of the things he had been taught was that blood or pus in his urine meant he had a kidney or urinary tract infection. As he flushed the toilet, he thanked his lucky stars that he didn't have to use a catheter with a leg bag like so many other people he knew with spinal cord injuries.

By 7:30 a.m., he was dressed and in the kitchen making his breakfast. His parents had the counters in their house specially designed to allow a wheelchair to fit underneath. Most of the drawers had special cabinets that slid out so David didn't have to reach inside. Thankfully, this morning he had the kitchen all to himself. Since it was Saturday morning, he didn't have to maneuver his way around his siblings and parents during their normally hectic morning routine as everyone bustled to get ready for school and work.

At exactly 7:45 a.m. sharp via satellite by the atomic watch strapped to David's right wrist, he headed out the front door. He left a note for his parents to let them know he would be spending the day at Doc's clinic helping with the animals, which he did many Saturday mornings.

Ten minutes later, he rolled up the walkway to Doc's clinic, slightly winded but too excited to even notice. Aimee's mountain bike was already parked outside with her broken lock ineffectively hanging around the back wheel. As he entered the clinic, Hoku came bounding over to greet him. The Basenji slammed on the brakes at the last second and sat directly in front of David's chair, her curly tail trying to thump the floor but missing by a few inches. She threw her head back and yodeled, either in greeting or complaint at being left alone in the waiting room.

"Hi, Hoku! Good girl," David said and scratched her behind the ears. "Where's Aimee, girl?"

Hoku whined softly, looking over her shoulder. Sometimes she had an uncanny ability to understand people. Bouncing to her feet, she looked pitifully at David then ran toward the treatment room and scratched at the door. The door stubbornly remained shut despite her attempt, and she huffed in agitation. Not getting an answer from Aimee, Hoku trotted back to David.

"Okay, okay, I get the message. You weren't invited in, and you're not happy about it." David patted Hoku's head in commiseration. Hoku barooed softly and laid her chin on top of David's knee, milking the sympathy gig as much as possible. David smiled down at her. *You're laying it on thick this morning!*

"You're such a ham, Hoku!" David laughed, sweeping a hand over her wrinkled brow.

Hoku blinked up at him and patted his leg with her paw. She whipped around and made a mad dash for the door when she heard movement from the other side. David was obviously forgotten and put back on the shelf.

Quietly, Aimee opened the treatment room door a crack and stuck her head out and said, "About time you got here".

"Sit, Hoku. Good girl. Yes, you are! You're such a good girl." Aimee patted Hoku's head affectionately and bent down to kiss her nose before opening the door further for David to enter. "Stay, Hoku." Hoku whined softly but held her position.

David was through the door and wheeling around the corner when he abruptly stopped. On the floor in front of him lay Goliath licking the last morsels from a bowl between his forelegs. Doc looked up from where he knelt by the dog and smiled at David.

"Morning, Davey boy," Doc said with his usual good humor.

Goliath looked up from his bowl and ran his pink tongue across his nose, cleaning up any stray bits of food. He tentatively got to his feet and whimpered slightly at the movement. David inwardly winced at the sight of the battered body full of staples and criss-crossed with inflamed, red wounds. He frowned in consternation as Goliath limped over to the wheelchair.

David couldn't help but feel pity for the obvious pain Goliath was still in. *He probably wouldn't want my pity. I know I've never wanted anyone's pity.* Finally, the pit bull sat directly in front of the wheelchair. Turning his head first one way then the other, he regarded David for a few moments before placing his blocky head on the boy's lap, turning to gently lick David's hand.

David sat quietly, smiling like he had won the latest and greatest Xbox—complete with a year's worth of games! He'd never owned a dog, even though he'd wanted one for as long as he could remember. He had always been jealous of Aimee for having her little star Hoku. And now, finally, he had one of his very own. He felt a little in awe at the simple gesture of his own dog sliming up his hand. This was all like a dream come true. He was sure that any minute he would wake up and it would all go away. He pinched himself quickly and grinned even wider at the slight pain.

"Well, I guess that settles that." Doc winked at Aimee. "We were wondering if he would remember you, Davey."

Aimee beamed a smile at David. That was the moment he knew this was no dream. This was for real. He now had a dog! David saved Goliath and now Goliath was his. Suddenly, the world seemed to be a better place. For a few seconds at least David felt at peace with the world. It was a beautiful day. The sun was shining. The birds were singing happily.

"Sooooo...what did your parents say when you told them?" Of course, Aimee, ever so helpful, brought his happy day to a screeching halt.

"Um, yeah...my parents..." David squirmed in his chair. "Well, um, you see—I, um—haven't exactly told them yet."

"You're so kidding, right?" Aimee asked incredulously, her voice rising. "David!"

"What?" David replied, sounding slightly indignant in the face of her agitation.

Doc opened his mouth to make a comment, a suggestion, or pose a question, but was thwarted by Aimee's shriek of outrage.

"What? What! Goliath isn't some toy you can sneak in the back door and hide in your closet! He is a living, breathing creature who, by the way, needs some serious TLC at the moment. Have you given any thought to this at all?" Aimee finished with an exasperated sigh. Throwing her hands in the air, she asked with withering sarcasm, "So what's your master plan now, genius? Should we throw him back in the dumpster?"

David looked to Doc for support. He heard Hoku's undulating banshee howls from the waiting room as the frustrated Basenji reacted to the anger in Aimee's voice. Doc placed a calming hand on Aimee's shoulder to stop another possible scathing tirade.

"Davey boy, she does have a valid point. This is a sick dog, possibly in mind, as well as body. You have to be one hundred percent sure this is a responsibility you want to undertake."

Thanks, Doc, David thought darkly. *So, maybe I don't have a plan. How many great inventors started out with an idea and then developed a plan? Probably most of them.* That thought made David feel a little better. Looking at Aimee, however, made him feel infinitely worse, like he would feel if she had sucker punched him in the gut after accidentally wheeling over Hoku's foot.

Suddenly overwhelmed by the realization that Goliath's life might hang in the balance on the decisions that were made here today, David regarded the badly battered pit bull who had landed in his lap, figuratively speaking, and began to formulate a plan. Goliath needed him, and David realized he needed Goliath, too. He would make this work. He had to. Now that he'd found Goliath, no one was going to take his dog from him.

"What if I boarded him with your agility trainer and got help training him before I took him home?" David smiled tentatively in the face of Aimee's glower. When she didn't smile back right away but continued to stare at him steadily, his smile slowly faded. Maybe she hadn't been able to read his lips that time.

Aimee looked at Doc and then back to David. "You know, that is the first sensible thing you've said in two days." Aimee finally beamed a smile in David's direction, and he felt the tension leave his body. "What do you think, Doc? That way Manny's dad will be able to teach Goliath some things to help David out, too. You know, besides the normal obedience things. More service animal oriented. Of course, we'd have to get him to pass his Canine Good Citizen test. And then get his service certification. That way you'd be able to take Goliath everywhere you go. Like me and Hoku. Not everyone can go into a restaurant with their dogs—only the special people!"

"Before you look at kenneling him somewhere, we better give him all his shots starting from scratch since we don't know his history. We might want to test him for dog aggression as well." Doc looked meaningfully toward the waiting room door.

"Should we do that right now?" Aimee frowned. "He's so big and my baby's so small!"

A vision of No. 9 attacking his cage to get at Smiley popped into her mind again. She didn't want that type of dog anywhere near her baby. She glanced nervously at Goliath. "Like, right this minute? Are you sure that's a good idea?"

"There's no time like the present." Doc took a nylon collar and leash down from the shelf and fastened it around Goliath's neck. Goliath swung his head from David's lap to look questioningly at Doc as the man slid a basket muzzle over his mouth. "It's okay, old boy, just a little insurance." Doc patted Goliath on the head and called him.

Goliath looked up at David.

"It's okay, boy. Go on," David said soothingly, pushing Goliath toward Doc. "Good boy."

At those words, Goliath's ears perked up. He couldn't remember being called "good boy" in a long time. Reluctantly, he stepped away from David and sat in front of Doc, waiting, his stubby tail thumping hesitantly against the tile.

"Okay, Aimee, let Hoku in." Doc gripped the leash firmly in both hands.

Aimee wasn't so sure this was the best idea, but she made her way to the door and grabbed the doorknob. Turning around, she looked at Doc and then down at Goliath. She chewed briefly at her bottom lip before asking again, "Are you sure, Doc?"

"No one is going to get hurt. Now call in your pooch." Doc smiled reassuringly.

Aimee read his lips but still hesitated at the door. She looked from David's excited face to Doc's calm reassuring one. David signed for her to open the door like she hadn't understood what Doc had said. Sending him a warning glare, she slowly opened the door.

Aimee called Hoku who still sat outside the door waiting to be released from her earlier "stay" command. Hoku bounced into the room, happy to finally be included in the excitement. She bounded through the door and jumped up on Aimee, nudging the girl's hand with her nose. Goliath came up on all fours, body rigid, alert and ready to fight. The hairs on the back of his neck were raised, and he bared his teeth menacingly. David held his breath, worried about Goliath's immediate reaction.

After getting affection from her guardian, Hoku quickly turned her attention to Goliath. Prancing around the pit bull, Hoku seemed not to notice that Goliath was not inviting her to play. In her mind, she was adored by everyone. Without further ado, she stopped directly in front of Goliath and dropped her front end down and whined expectantly. Goliath had braced himself for an attack but had never encountered this particular tactic before. He cocked his head to the side and stood there, staring in confusion at Hoku's antics.

Hoku who was not always patient—as in hardly ever!—yodeled at Goliath in that strange Basenji voice that was part wolf howl, part dingo yap. Wagging her tail to show she only wanted to play, she rose up on her hind legs and lightly batted Goliath on the head with her paw. David smiled at her boxer-like moves. Goliath moved forward with Doc in tow. The two dogs sniffed each other front to back and back to front.

David assumed Hoku was checking out okay since Goliath's back hair had flattened back down, and he no longer looked so aggressive. Hoku grew tired of all the sniffing, whipped around, barooed at Goliath, and took off running around the examining table. Mystified by this strange behavior, Goliath looked up at Doc and sat down, whining softly.

"Basenji zoomies are a thing to get used to, my furry friend," Doc laughed.

"Okay, Hoku, that's enough for now. Come. Sit." At the command, Hoku made one more hind-legged feint at Goliath before streaking to her human. Aimee picked up the Basenji and held her on her hip as if the dog were a human baby. The girl affectionately cuddled her dog, scratching Hoku behind her ears. "Silly girl. Goliath thinks you're crazy." Hoku chirped in response and leaned her head to rest against Aimee's.

"So, did he pass?" David asked excitedly. He wheeled over to where Goliath sat and rested a hand on Goliath's head.

"It's a good start," Doc replied and took off the muzzle. "He still needs to learn basic obedience and behavioral training, how to interact with other dogs, as he doesn't appear to know how to play. He also needs to get neutered."

"I'll tell you what, Davey boy. Since you rescued this poor beast, you did him a good turn. It's only fair I reciprocate and do you a good turn. We'll get your boy up to date on his shots. Let's keep him here for a few days so that I can keep a good eye on those puncture wounds, and if they're looking good with no sign of infection, we'll bring him over to Sanchez in about a week or so. We'll try to add a few more pounds to his frame while we're at it."

"Neuter! Hasn't the poor guy been through enough? Now you want to put him through surgery for no reason? Do we have to?"

Aimee kicked the wheel of David's chair and glared at him. "Did you ask the stupidest question ever? Did I read that right? You volunteer at a shelter! You, of all people, should know how many pit bulls come through the door every year. Every day over two thousand pitties are killed in shelters in the US alone. And you ask why Goliath needs to be neutered? I think I need to smack you."

"Well, I meant that he's hurt now, you know? Covered in stitches. I didn't mean never neuter him!"

"Ah, well, then we should have him recover from everything all at once!" Doc Foyster smiled. "Don't worry. He'll be fine. He's a tough young lad! Neutering males is a simple procedure, and one he will recover from quickly. He'll be tip-top in no time."

"Awesome! Totally awesome! Thank you! Thank you so much, Doc!" David was grinning so widely that he wondered briefly if his smile was as huge as the Joker's—only hopefully not so maniacal, although with the giddy, ecstatic way he felt, he thought it could very well be. He leaned over to envelope Goliath's head in a bear hug. Goliath flinched as David reached for him.

"Easy, boy, it's okay" David soothed, returning to an upright position. He slowly extended his hand toward Goliath, palm up, for the dog to sniff. Goliath noticeably relaxed and licked David's fingers.

"Congrats, David. Looks like you got yourself a keeper." Aimee patted David on the back before giving Doc a one-armed hug. "And, Doc, you are the bomb!"

Doc chuckled and stood there awkwardly, not sure how to react to this outburst of affection. He gently detached himself from Aimee's grasp and patted her arm. "All in a day's work, my dear, all in a day's work. Speaking of work, I have lots to do. The two of you can visit for as long as you like. I'm sure I won't be getting any work from you lot today. Come get me when you're ready to leave. I'll be in back taking care of my other patients."

After Doc left the room, Aimee turned to David and asked, "So, do you know what you've gotten yourself into? Are ready for this responsibility?"

"What? You think I can't take care of him because I'm in a wheelchair?" David replied in sign language.

"You're gonna go there? For real?" Aimee smirked. "No, it's not because you're in a wheelchair. It's because you were planning on keeping a dog in a dollhouse in your backyard. I'm not questioning your physical ability—I'm questioning your intellectual ability."

"Ouch," David winced. "I think I'd like it better if you were questioning my physical ability. Of course, I know how to take care of a dog. I volunteer at the shelter, don't I?"

"Oh, really?" Aimee placed a hand on her hip. "So when do you feed him? How much do you feed him? What do you feed him? Do you feed him once a day or leave a bowl of food out? How much do you think he should weigh? How often do you give him heartworm meds? Flea meds? Crate or no crate? How often should you walk him? Do you know what to brush his teeth with? Or how to clip his nails?"

Aimee's barrage of questions continued until David threw up his hands in surrender. "Okay, I get your point. Goliath comes with more instructions than a flipping Mogwai! Geez, woman, I don't know as much as you do about dogs. Does anybody?"

Aimee said smugly, "Well, now that you mention it, probably not. But that's beside the point."

"So, are you going to beat me over the head with more questions, or are you planning on helping me out here, Sensei?"

"Well, before the dog can be trained, you have to be trained!" Aimee laughed.

David spent the majority of his first day as Goliath's owner-to-be wishing that he had brought a notebook and a pen. Or even better a recorder. He felt like he needed to take notes as his brain was inundated with information. He had read a lot about pit bulls and training them—among other things—the night before. But reading was one thing and hands-on experience was another.

Aimee taught David how to flush Goliath's wounds before putting in the topical antibiotic cream and the trick of hiding pills in a blob of peanut butter, while Hoku taught Goliath how to find the squeaker in a plush toy and how to get the treats out of a Kong. By day's end, they were all exhausted and extremely happy.

13

Training Brah

After his first week of dog ownership, David had to admit the fantasy of having a dog was not the same as the reality. You have to walk them (or wheel them) several times a day, feed them, water them, clean up their crap, train them in basic obedience, and the list goes on and on and on... like the Energizer Bunny. Who knew? Imagine all those unsuspecting kids who get their first puppy for Christmas. Boy! Were they in for a surprise! But then again, no wonder so many Christmas puppies become pound puppies instead. Dogs were a lot of work!

Now that he had rescued a dog and knew firsthand the time and commitment required, David would advise anyone even remotely thinking about getting a pet to volunteer at a shelter or with a rescue group first. Being a shelter volunteer, he knew what happened to all those poor rejects dropped off at the shelter after Christmas because people didn't have time for them or they were no longer cute little puppies.

Well, that wasn't going to happen to Goliath. Not if David had anything to say about it. For one thing Goliath wasn't a cute puppy rescued on a whim. And for another thing David and Aimee had spent every evening at Doc's helping out and getting to know the amiable pit bull they had rescued. There was nothing spontaneous or whimsical about David's desire to be Goliath's forever guardian.

The week had gone by quickly and Goliath was healing remarkably well. It was a rainy Saturday morning when Doc's front door bell began to sing. David nervously wheeled up to the door and paused for a second to take a deep breath before he reached out to grab the door knob and pulled.

"Hi, I'm David. Come on in. We've been waiting for you," David said nervously.

He invited Mr. Sanchez into the clinic. The week had gone by so fast he had almost forgotten that Goliath's life could depend on this man who he barely knew. If Aimee's trainer thought Goliath had a chance of being rehabilitated, then there was a slim chance David might actually be allowed to keep the dog he'd rescued. David shook Mr. Sanchez' hand.

A wiry teen about his own age slipped by David and into the waiting area.

"Hey, dude, I'm Manny." Manny held out his hand. When David reached out to shake it, the boy quickly pulled it away and slicked back a mop of dark hair from out of his eyes. "Gotcha!"

"Manny!" Mr. Sanchez said, frowning slightly at his son. 'Behave. It's a pleasure to meet you, David."

"Hey, brah," Aimee said, punching Manny on the arm and saluting Mr. Sanchez.

"Aimee!" Manny grumbled, rubbing his arm. "Not so rough on the merchandise. I bruise easily."

"I take it you know each other?" David asked and signed for Aimee's benefit.

"We train together," Manny said matter-of-factly. "I'm Dad's right-hand man. We're like the dynamic duo. The local dog whispers. The amazing Sanchez family trainers. I'm surprised you haven't heard of me."

"Sorry. I'm new to dog training," David replied, eying the fidgeting teen skeptically.

"Where's the dog I'm here to evaluate?" Mr. Sanchez asked, rolling his eyes at Manny.

"Juan, welcome," Doc said, walking out from the back room. He smiled broadly at the trainer and led Goliath to them on a short leash.

Goliath's back hairs bristled when he saw Mr. Sanchez and Manny. His lip wrinkled back to show his canines, but before he could growl, Hoku squeezed through the door. She slithered under his legs and barooed loudly, dancing around the two newcomers.

"Easy there, old boy." Doc reached down and placed a hand on Goliath's head reassuringly. Goliath still eyed the two strangers warily.

"Hoku, you bad girl! Come here and sit," Aimee commanded and her reluctant self-appointed-greeting-committee Basenji obeyed.

"What do you know of his history?" Mr. Sanchez asked, nodding to Aimee approvingly.

"Not much," Doc admitted. "David here found him in a dumpster about a week ago."

"The police raided a dog fight last week," Mr. Sanchez said. He looked thoughtful, as he put the dots together. "I heard some handlers escaped with their dogs."

"We don't know for certain Goliath was part of that," David said, not happy with where the conversation was heading.

"That may be, but you need to be fully aware of what you're getting into, David." Mr. Sanchez made eye contact with David. Aimee intently watched their interaction, reading David's tension, carefully reading their lips. "Have you contacted the shelter to ask if anyone reported a lost dog?"

"I am in close contact with Greta at the shelter, and there have been no reports of missing dogs fitting Goliath's description," Aimee cut in, a hard edge creeping into her voice. "And even if there were, there is no way we're giving him back to someone who would do this to him!"

"Alright now, Aimee," Mr. Sanchez said, holding up his hands in a placating gesture. "No one said anything about giving Goliath back to anyone."

"I have already applied for and gotten him a license in David's name. He's now newly neutered," Doc added. "His shots are all up to date, and he's been vaccinated for kennel cough. As far as I'm concerned he's ready to go."

"I see." Mr. Sanchez walked around Goliath, observing the dog while keeping his distance. Goliath had remained guarded and continued to watch Mr. Sanchez carefully. Then Mr. Sanchez did the unexpected and sat cross-legged on the floor directly in front of Goliath with his body sideways to the dog. "Let out his leash, please."

Curious, Goliath moved closer and sniffed the sitting man. He was rewarded with a small piece of dog biscuit tossed on the floor by his feet. Snatching up the biscuit, he moved closer and sniffed the seated man from head to toe. All the while Mr. Sanchez ignored him completely. Every few seconds the trainer dropped another treat on the ground.

Still ignoring Goliath, Mr. Sanchez explained what he was doing. "He appears to be more confused than aggressive. I am getting down to his level to allow him to approach me without being afraid I will do anything to him."

Gobbling down another treat, Goliath walked around in front of Mr. Sanchez and sniffed his hands for more food. Mr. Sanchez opened his hand and allowed Goliath to take the treat hidden there. "It's good that he's curious. I don't think dogs should always be rewarded with treats, but this poor guy has probably never been given anything except punishment and pain. I want to gain his trust before I ask him to join my pack."

"He's been good with us," David replied. "He likes food."

Mr. Sanchez reached out his open hand for Goliath to sniff and then gently scratched under the pit bull's chin. Goliath stiffened slightly but did not pull away.as the man gave him another treat with his free hand. "He may be fine with you, David, but it's going to be important he learn to greet new people he meets with calm confidence if you expect to use him as a service dog."

Goliath stretched out a paw and batted Mr. Sanchez's treat pouch. He whined softly, then without being asked, he sat on his haunches and tilted his head to the side. Mr. Sanchez pulled a treat from the pouch and held it out in his open hand. When Goliath went for the treat, Mr. Sanchez closed his hand and waited. Goliath sniffed the hand then began licking it softly.

"Can you train Goliath as a service dog?" David asked.

"No," Mr. Sanchez said with a shrug, opening his hand and letting Goliath take the offered treat.

"But I thought ..." David trailed off, not able to hide his disappointment.

"No, I will not be training Goliath as a service dog," Mr. Sanchez said with a wry smile. "But that isn't the question. The question is—can you train Goliath as a service dog?"

"But I was hoping you would work with him..."David started to whine before Aimee slapped him on the back of the head.

"And people think I'm deaf! Mr. Sanchez told you that he's going to help! He doesn't train dogs—he trains people!" Aimee beamed her winning smile at Mr. Sanchez who chuckled and nodded his head.

Getting slowly to his feet, Mr. Sanchez took the leash from Doc's hand and led Goliath around the room. He offered treats when Goliath followed him without struggling. Within a few laps of the room, Goliath was trotting beside Mr. Sanchez and looking up expectantly for the next treat to come his way.

"He can come home with us today. He needs to learn to be around other dogs and people in a positive environment. Every dog has an innate desire to be part of a pack."

"Awesome!" Manny, who had been waiting patiently in the background, exclaimed. "Amigo, have I got an offer for you."

14

Training Wheels

Goliath spent the first week at the Sanchez residence learning to be a dog again. At first he bristled and stiffened any time another dog ventured near him, and several times he tried to attack other dogs if they approached too quickly. Since he missed out on key socialization with other dogs as a puppy, Goliath had a hard time initially differentiating overly friendly behavior from aggression. The more exuberant the greeting, the quicker Goliath responded with a growl and lunge. Each time he reacted inappropriately, Mr. Sanchez patiently corrected him. After a week of this treatment, Goliath no longer stiffened at another dog's approach and would even allow the smaller dogs and younger ones to bounce on him without growling.

After two weeks Goliath was allowed to run free in the large fenced backyard with Hoku and some of the less dominant dogs in Mr. Sanchez's training pack. David was finally allowed to start participating in the training process. Goliath's training for this week was to learn the game of fetch. David was given a ball thrower and a dozen tennis balls. His job was to toss balls across the yard for Goliath and any of the other dogs who wanted to play. All of Mr. Sanchez's pack was trained to fetch and retrieve on command.

"Why am I playing games when he doesn't even know how to sit?" David asked, trying not to sound as frustrated as he felt.

"Exercise, obedience and affection—in that order," Mr. Sanchez replied. "You need an easy method of exercising Goliath while you train him to sit and heel and stay. It may be a while before you can walk him safely."

"Oh, I see," David said, not convinced at all.

David was given his own treat bag and instructed to give Goliath a treat each time he brought the ball back. After ten minutes of play, it became apparent Goliath didn't need the food incentive. In fact he ignored the food and eyed the ball thrower with an intensity that bordered on fanatic. After watching the first few ball tosses, he decided to join in the chase. After the third or fourth throw, he was racing across the lawn with his eyes locked on the ball.

After twenty minutes, most of the dogs wandered away to find other entertainment—but not Goliath. Panting and beaming a huge pit bull smile from ear to ear, he eagerly raced across the yard each time David lobbed a ball into the air. And each time Goliath came racing back almost as fast to deposit the ball directly into David's lap without ever having to be told to do so.

"Pit bulls can be single-minded when they want something," Mr. Sanchez explained to David. "That's one reason they're used as fighting dogs."

"He sure loves to play. How could that be used to make a dog want to fight?" David asked, stopping his game to look at Mr. Sanchez.

"Good fighting dogs don't back down and they don't give up," the trainer replied. "And they stay focused on what they're doing long after other dogs would give up or wander off. Pit bulls will fight to the death upon occasion."

"Why would anyone want a dog to do that?"

"Some people are cruel and sadistic, David. They think it's a sport. They usually bet money on the dogs." Mr. Sanchez shook his head. "At least for Goliath, that part of his life is behind him."

"It makes me so angry to think someone made him fight other dogs for fun and then threw him away like garbage when he got hurt," David growled. "I hope there's a special place in hell for people like that."

"Karma," Mr. Sanchez replied. "There are lots of good people out there trying to put an end to dog fighting. Even famous people are being caught and punished."

"Not punished enough if you ask me," David said. "They should be banned from ever owning another animal."

"I agree."

"So, what does being good at fetch have to do with training Goliath to be a service dog?" David asked, letting some of his anger go for now.

"Good service dogs have to be good around people and animals but also need to be focused on their jobs," Mr. Sanchez said. He pointed at Goliath who continued to sit at attention in front of David's wheelchair, eyeing the now dormant ball thrower expectantly.

"I don't understand," David admitted.

"Try waiting him out," Mr. Sanchez replied with a wry smile.

"You're on!" David said.

He laid the plastic ball thrower across his legs and crossed his arms. He absently watched Manny run around the yard with his little blue Chihuahua Chiquita chasing after him. After thirty minutes, Goliath still hadn't moved from the spot, his eyes fixed on the ball, his mouth open, tongue lolling as he panted in eager anticipation.

Heaving a deep sigh, David called to Mr. Sanchez who now sat on the patio drinking iced tea. "Okay, you win. I see your point. He's got some serious focus skills."

"Yes, he does. And we are going to use that focus to train Goliath to be an excellent service dog," Mr. Sanchez called back.

By week four, Goliath had learned to come, sit, lay down, and stay with verbal and visual commands from David. He followed David everywhere the boy went and would not play with the other dogs unless David was stationary and in line of sight, even after receiving the "go free" command. If David moved or attempted to leave the yard, Goliath was by the teen's side in an instant, his strong bond to the boy clearly evident.

As the weeks passed, David became friends with Manny and some of the other teens who brought their dogs to the Sanchez's training center on a regular basis. Of course, it didn't hurt that Aimee was one those teens. During his second month of training, David had been invited to join a small group of kids Mr. Sanchez had recruited to promote responsible dog ownership. They travelled throughout the area with their pets, educating and entertaining crowds of people and fundraising for the Sanchez Training and Animal Rescue.

Goliath was slowly learning to trust again, and he would even allow new people to pet him as long as they approached slowly and didn't try to reach for his neck. He still had a mistrust of males he didn't know but was becoming less guarded on a daily basis. Mr. Sanchez felt Goliath was no longer a high risk for attacking other dogs and allowed David to take him on walks off the property.

Part of Goliath's new job as a service dog was to pull David in his wheelchair. It was a job the sturdy pit bull took as seriously as playing fetch. At first David had been reluctant to be pulled because he didn't feel he needed the help, but when he realized how much Goliath loved to pull, he soon gave in and even began to enjoy the experience. After all, people go bike joring, ski joring, scooter joring with dogs of all kinds. Both humans and dogs seemed to enjoy that sport. There seemed to be no end to Goliath's energy and David often wore out before his dog did.

Goliath loved to run and David took him out every day, rain or shine, for several miles of exercise. He would let the determined pit bull pull him for a while then he would push himself. To his surprise, he and Goliath were both gaining muscle and endurance. *There is something to this exercise stuff,* David mused, easing into a semi-fast race with his new best friend. Goliath for his part never got more than a few feet ahead of David so it was difficult for David to tell if he was getting faster or if Goliath was letting him catch up.

Gaining confidence by the day, David decided to take Goliath to a pet store to look for a better pulling harness. The pit bull marched obediently beside David once inside the store and together they travelled up and down the aisles looking at pet products.

Coming to the end of an aisle of leashes, Goliath stopped dead in his tracks and David nearly ran over him with his wheelchair. The dog yelped, startled, as David's left wheel nicked his side before stopping.

"Sorry, buddy." David rubbed Goliath's side in apology. "A little warning you're about to stop would be nice."

Goliath looked at David and whined softly. He had stopped in front of the cat adoption room window. Turning his head to the side, he eyed a small calico kitten batting at the window, mere inches from his nose. Dropping his front end down into a bow, Goliath let out a loud woof, indicating he wanted to play.

At that exact moment an older couple led by a beagle walked from behind an adjoining aisle. Hearing Goliath bark, the beagle raised its hackles and growled menacingly. Ignoring the other dog, Goliath continued to play bow and bounce to the kitten. The elderly man let out the retractable line, allowing the agitated beagle to advance menacingly toward Goliath. Fearing the worst, David moved his wheels between Goliath and the oncoming beagle.

"What's the matter, kid?" the older man asked. "Your dog not friendly?"

"My dog is fine." David was about to explain that their dog was in an excited state and wanted to attack instead of play with his dog. "It's your dog who's..."

"Bill, that's one of those pit bulls from the news!" the woman with Bill hissed. "Quick! Grab Buster before that thing kills him!"

By this time Goliath had stopped playing and had turned to curiously regard the beagle.

Bill suddenly realized his prize beagle was about to be eaten by one of those vicious fighting dogs. Cursing, he grabbed his dog by the collar and lifted it into the air before tucking it under one arm. The couple quickly retreated back down the aisle.

"It's okay, buddy. You didn't do anything wrong." David fumed in his chair, too stunned to move. Goliath licked his hand as if sensing he was uneasy. They stayed there for several minutes while David tried to make sense out of what had happened. Were people that stupid?

"Excuse me." A store representative walked up to David and Goliath.

"Yes?" David turned his chair to face the employee and place himself between her and Goliath.

"We've had several complaints about your dog being aggressive," the woman said. She eyed Goliath with an inscrutable expression on her face. She was a tall thin black woman who looked to be in her early twenties. She had a treat bag attached to a belt at her hip. Reaching her hand into the bag, she pulled out a treat and approached Goliath. "May I give him a treat?"

"He wasn't being aggressive," David replied irritably, trying to remain calm. He had known some people would be prejudiced against pit bulls but hadn't been prepared for this. Goliath hadn't even acknowledged the other dog.

The woman stood waiting. When David didn't reply, she asked again. "May I?"

"He's working," David shrugged noncommittally. "I usually don't let people pet him or feed him when he's working."

"So, he's a service dog?" the woman asked in a conversational tone.

"Well, technically, he's still in training." David liked educating people about his best friend.

The woman held a treat in her hand by her hip but didn't offer it to Goliath. He sniffed the air, nose high, before looking at David. His ears moved to droop along the sides of his head as he gave David his best mournful hang-dog expression. David wanted to laugh. Obviously, the treat must have smelled pretty tasty. David shook his head. Goliath snorted his disappointment but didn't move from David's side.

"He's seems well behaved to me," she said. "I'm Tisha, one of the store's trainers, and I told the couple who complained that I would talk to you to determine if your dog was too aggressive to be in our store."

"What! Goliath didn't do anything," David sputtered. "It was their dog who tried to attack him."

"I know," she said calmly. "That little guy has tried to bite more than one dog in here before today."

"Then why are you harassing us?" David asked. "Kick them out of the store!"

"Actually, I recommended they take their dog to obedience classes and they left without buying anything." Tisha smiled sweetly.

"Oh," David said, losing some of the anger. Goliath pushed his nose under his guardian's hand to get petted and David obliged without even realizing it. "Why do people have to be so stupid? Why are so many people prejudiced against pit bulls?"

"You're asking me why people have to be prejudiced?" Tisha quirked an eyebrow and looked down at David.

"Sorry, I didn't mean anything," David looked at Goliath, his face starting to feel hot.

"People fear what they don't understand. Not to mention the coverage pits get in the news. Why! You would think every dog bite in this country was done by a pit bull. And if isn't a pit bull, it doesn't even make the news. No one talks about labs mauling anyone, even though it happens all the time!" The woman sighed. "Mind you, I'm not saying that pit bulls don't bite people or attack other dogs."

"Yeah, I know," David replied sadly. "But blame the deed and not the breed. Any dog can bite."

"Exactly," she agreed. "And sadly, more pit bulls suffer at the hands of people than the other way around. But the pit bull hate mongers aren't screaming for those statistics."

Goliath had moved closer to the woman and sat down with a loud thump. Looking from David to the woman, he seemed to be saying this person is okay. David almost laughed out loud. Goliath sighed deeply as if he understood and agreed with the conversation. "You can pet him if you want to."

Tisha offered her treat-free hand for the dog to sniff. Goliath smelled the appendage thoroughly before gently pushing his head underneath it to get pet. He liked being touched by people now that he understood that most people were not going to hurt him. Tisha opened her other palm, holding out the treat, and Goliath looked back at David who nodded. Grinning, tongue lolling, Goliath sniffed excitedly at the treat before gently taking it from Tisha's hand. She scratched under his chin as he happily chomped away, holding his head higher to expose more scratching areas.

For the next ten minutes Tisha talked to David about training a service dog and how to deal with people like the ones who had reported Goliath. By the time they left the store with Goliath's new harness, David and Goliath had made a new friend and David had learned a few new strategies for dealing with people who were ignorant or afraid of his dog.

***

Two months of daily training had made a huge difference in both David's ability to handle Goliath and Goliath's ability to understand David's direction. Goliath turned out to not only be extremely loyal to David, if lovey dovey eyes were anything to go by, but also eager to please his guardian. The amiable pit bull was quickly becoming the talk of Mr. Sanchez's students.

"Hey, Wheels, watch what I taught Hoku to do," Aimee shouted.

David looked toward Aimee and Hoku. He had been watching Goliath play with Chiquita. The little Chi-warrior bounced on Goliath's head and chewed on his ears while the pit bull lay quietly on the ground with a soulful look on his earnest face. He wasn't sure how to play with this rambunctious tiny terror who darted underneath his paw every time he would slowly raise it to bat at her gently.

"Hoku, backflip!" Aimee commanded.

The feisty Basenji leaped into the air and did a little summersault before yodeling loudly at her owner. It was difficult to tell if Hoku understood Aimee couldn't hear the multitude of sounds she was able to make. David found it ironic that the girl who was hearing impaired had the most uniquely vocal dog of all his new friends.

David alternately clapped his hands and shook them in the air while shouting, "Bravo, bravo!"

"Why, thank you, kind sir," Amiee said, taking a bow alongside Hoku who also did a little bow. "How is Goliath's training coming along?"

"Why, I would say excellent, as you can see from how well he maintains the long down-stay position even in the face of such adversity," David replied, looking away from Aimee before he finished talking. Chiquita had a hold of Goliath's collar and was pulling at the pit in an attempt to drag him out of position.

"What did you say to me?" Aimee asked, irritably.

"Oh, sorry," David said, turning back to face Aimee, signing the words as he said them. "My bad."

"I hate it when people use that expression." Aimee said. She walked over to stand in front of David. "My bad...what does that mean anyways?"

"Um, the opposite of my good?" David replied weakly. Changing topics, he released Goliath. "Goliath, go free!"

Giving his head a shake, Goliath dislodged Chiquita and stood up. He leaned forward, dropping his front end and stretching even as Chiquita darted in to nip at his ear. Looking toward David, Goliath cocked his head to the side and sat down almost on top of the little Chihuahua who now nipped at his hind legs in an attempt to get the bigger dog to play with her.

"It's okay, buddy," David said reassuringly. "Go play with Chiquita before she rips a piece out of you."

Heaving a deep pittie sigh, Goliath whipped his head around and lunged at the little dog, causing her to yelp and jump back in surprise. Nudging her gently with his wet nose, Goliath sniffed Chiquita then took off around the yard in crazy, circling zoomies that left her standing bewildered for all of five seconds. Realizing she'd been tricked, Chiquita let out a series of excited barks and gave chase to Goliath's quickly receding backside. Hoku batted Aimee's leg with her paw and barooed loudly.

"Silly girl," Aimee chided the Basenji. "Go play if you want."

"Do you think it's okay for them to play rough like that?" David asked, watching Hoku streak after the other two dogs.

"Dunno," Aimee replied, looking at David with a mischievous twinkle in her eyes. "Chiquita can be a little rough on him and Hoku can kick butt with the best of them. Are you worried she'll hurt your baby boy?"

"Funny," David rolled his eyes and signed. "You know what I mean. Goliath was trained to fight other dogs."

Chiquita had finally caught up to the pit bull and Hoku ran circles around Goliath, yodeling noisily and attacking him with her front paws like a boxer. Goliath lowered his head and woofed at her before doing a quick circle and using his rump to push the Chihuahua back.

"Honestly, David, I don't know," Aimee said with a serious tone. "Who knows how long he was abused by those jerks. You hear stories in the news all the time about dogs who never got into any trouble suddenly attacking other dogs or people totally out of the blue."

"Do you believe that?" David asked.

"Nope," Aimee shook her head. "I think those dogs gave lots of signs and the people who owned them didn't notice or maybe didn't understand. Goliath likes playing with Chiquita and Hoku. Besides he hasn't even growled at another dog in several weeks. I think he'll be fine. But you always have to be sure to supervise him and do slow introductions. I mean, our dogs are easy peasy, but who knows what he'll do with a freaky deaky one?"

"Yeah, I guess you're right." David sighed. "I don't want anything bad to happen to him."

"You worry too much, Wheels," Aimee punched David on the arm before he could move out of the way.

"Ouch," David tried unsuccessfully to run over her toes, but she was too quick on her feet and nimbly danced out of harm's way. "Remember! I don't get angry...I get even!"

"Lookit me! I'm so scared," Aimee taunted him. "Not!"

Goliath raced by the two kids with Hoku and Chiquita hot on his heels, interrupting David's witty reply. Truth be told, David never knew exactly what to say to Aimee who seemed to always one-up him despite being deaf and not always hearing the entire conversation. He was always amazed at how well she had adapted to her disability. It would take a trained ear to notice the slightly monotone quality to Aimee's otherwise normal speech patterns.

David wished he had adapted as well to his own disability. Life in a wheelchair was not something he would wish on anyone else. Sure, he got around okay and did have a cool set of wheels thanks to his parents, but what he wouldn't give to be able to run around the yard with Goliath. David stared at the playing canines and sighed.

"Can I join your pity party?" Aimee asked with saccharine sweetness, smiling at David condescendingly.

"No!" David shot back. "Members only."

15

Break a Leg

Four months had passed by quickly. David had still not broken the news to his parents, and Mr. Sanchez was pressing him to take Goliath home since he was now healthy and fit. With two weeks left until summer break David was running out of time. He had tried several times to approach his parents but couldn't work up the nerve. How do you say to your mother, *"Mom, I rescued one of those fighting dogs you see attacking people on TV all the time. Can I keep him?"* Probably not! Remember this is the mother who tried some serious covert, spy-type actions when David wheeled himself to school the first time after the accident. Oh, yeah, she'd totally let him have a killer dog and let it sleep in his bed.

Of course, he couldn't go back to his original idea of keeping Goliath in his sister's castle. There was the small but not inconsequential fact that Goliath had a mammothly loud bark. No, not loud. Try earsplitting or deafening (unless you were Aimee, of course). Let's say that anyone who came within a few hundred feet of the place would drop a load in their pants when Goliath let out his warning war whoop.

The only real option left was to run away from home. Unfortunately, it's hard to run when you've got wheels. So, David did the next best thing—he invited both his overly busy parents to a dog agility fundraiser that Mr. Sanchez's rescue was putting on at the local shopping mall.

David and his new friends all had two things in common. One was a love of animals and the other was the fact that all but one had suffered from a childhood disability. Not to say they were handicapped by their individual disabilities. On the contrary, the group was all about their abilities. Thus the name they gave themselves was Ability Inc. Actually it was Manny who came up with the idea and the name.

Their animal companions currently consisted of five dogs and one ferret. Most of the dogs were CGC-certified, meaning they all had passed the Canine Good Citizen testing. This certification allowed the non-service dogs to enter nursing homes and hospitals. Goliath, however, was the only dog in the group who was not yet CGC-certified. He was still in training, so it was a good thing that the first demonstration David was to participate in was at the local mall.

For David, today was D-day or hopefully THE-day he got to take Goliath home. His new friends had helped him come up with a simple plan. He and Goliath would perform tricks they had learned over the last few weeks, and his parents would be so impressed they would immediately fall in love with Goliath and want to adopt him from the rescue. Okay, the plan had a few holes in it, but David was an optimist after all was said and done. His parents knew David was working with dogs at the Sanchez shelter but he had neglected to tell them that one of the dogs was his.

The first pair to go onstage was Siobhan O'Rourke, a legally blind teen and her huge Irish wolfhound Oenghus. Oenghus obviously was not a typical seeing-eye dog. Size alone would deter most people from wanting him as a companion. Siobhan wasn't like most people. David immediately liked the diminutive, feisty redhead whose deep green eyes saw more than most normally sighted people. She could see some shadows a few inches in front of her face but couldn't make out details. She could read brail, memorize verbal instructions (word for word after the first reading), and was a black belt in Jui Jitsu, which was way cool in David's mind.

Siobhan and Oenghus sauntered onstage with Siobhan tapping her way to the center, using her walking stick. Normally with Oenghus, she never used her stick, but this was to show the audience she was blind. Once they were center stage, Siobhan dropped her walking stick before she and Oenghus negotiated a difficult obstacle course at a run without so much as a misstep.

It was obvious Siobhan trusted her canine companion completely and Oenghus took his job seriously. They finished their run with a warning for people not to try this at home. Oenghus then scooped up her walking stick in his mouth and placed it under her hand to grab. The audience applauded loudly. Taking her stick, Siobhan cued Oenghus who sat on his haunches and gave her a high five before leading her offstage.

Following Siobhan was her identical twin Niamh who didn't have an obvious disability, although Niamh, tongue-in-cheek, counted having Siobhan as a sister a disability. Ironically, though they were identical twins, Niamh and Siobhan were opposite in many ways. Siobhan had a huge dog while Niamh had a wee ferret. Niamh had her silver-mitt ferret Maeve curled up in the hood of her shirt. Reaching behind her head, she snapped her fingers, and Maeve slinked her way out of the hood and onto Niamh's shoulder.

Not as exciting as Oenghus but definitely cuter, Maeve hopped and crawled through a miniature obstacle course before fetching a variety of objects for Niamh. Niamh made Maeve seem smarter to the crowd. By knowing what objects Maeve liked, such as jingling keys, a stuffed ferret, and a squeaky toy, Niamh could make it seem that Maeve was retrieving an item that Niamh specifically asked for. In reality, the ferret had no clue what her human master was saying besides "fetch".

Putting one of Maeve's objects in a line with other things Niamh knew wouldn't interest the ferret, she would ask Maeve to get the keys or toy. Knowing she would get a raisin reward, Maeve was a good fetcher. This was always a crowd pleaser. They were always impressed with Niamh's little trick. Niamh and Maeve exited with the ferret leaping and bouncing after Niamh off stage. Only Maeve knew that Niamh had a fistful of raisins.

Kameron Lloyd and his red Doberman Pinscher Watson were the next to perform. Kameron was from South Africa. His family had immigrated to America when he was only five years old. At sixteen, he was already a lanky six feet tall and still growing. Unfortunately, Kameron's dad had not only given him his gene for height, but he also passed on the gene for diabetes.

David watched closely as the pair started their round.

Kameron expertly took Watson through a series of agility obstacles as the crowd ooh'd and aah'd. With seemingly effortless movement and little communication with Kameron, Watson ran up and over teeter-totters, jumped through hoops, crawled through tunnels, and zig-zagged around weave poles. For their climax, Watson jumped/climbed over a seven-foot-high wall, landing smoothly on the other side. As an encore, Kameron knelt on one knee and Watson jumped back and forth over his back several times.

David peeked out from backstage looking for his parents. Goliath sat quietly, his blocky head on David's lap, shaking slightly. There was one more act to go, and then he and Goliath were on. He suddenly had the urge to puke. What was he doing here? There was no way he could go out on stage in front of all these people! He was a gimp in a wheelchair. His hand automatically went to Goliath's neck and began scratching.

A delicate female hand gently touched his shoulder—not likely! Aimee punched him on the arm and then slapped him on the back of his head, almost knocking him out of his chair. David sometimes wondered if she could read his mind.

"Ready to go, brah?" Aimee smiled sweetly down at David.

"Yeah, you bet," David said and patted down his hair.

"I know you're probably getting stage fright. Everybody does their first few times. You may even think that being in a wheelchair puts you at a disadvantage to some people here. Or maybe you think some peeps in the audience will look at you strangely or feel sorry for you. But you know what? You can do things with Goliath that no one out there can do. By the time you're done, they'll be eating out of your hand."

Aimee brushed the hair out of David's eyes. "I remember the first time I went onstage with Hoku. I ran out first, and I was giving commands and gesturing like a mad woman. When I turned around, there was no Hoku behind me. Instead she was peeking out from behind the curtain." Aimee knelt down and cupped Hoku's face in her hands. Speaking more to Hoku than to David, she continued, "All you could see was this cute Basenji face. Do you think that little Basenji would come when I called her? No way, hosehead. She totally sat there and became as deaf as me!"

Aimee laughed until she saw David wasn't laughing with her.

"Oh, I feel so much better. Thank you!" David replied sarcastically once he caught her eye. He was seriously going to hurl any moment now. "Why don't I go home now and save myself the humiliation?"

Aimee shrugged and stood up. "Okay, so maybe that wasn't the best inspirational story. But here we are! We're still doing it, and we're totally awesome. Of course, maybe not all the time. Hoku is a Basenji after all, and you know how temperamental Basenjis can be! At least you have an easily trained dog. Not like Goliath is a Lab or anything, but compared to Hoku, he might as well be." Aimee laughed and patted Goliath's head.

Hoku jumped up and placed her paws on David's knees in front of Goliath. She yodeled at Goliath several times before raising a paw and bopping Goliath on the noggin. David and Goliath exchanged glances.

Apparently it was true that owners and dogs shared the same personality traits. The longer they were together, the more similar Hoku and Aimee became. It dawned on David that Goliath was probably thinking the same thing.

Hoku barooed a few more times for good measure. Goliath let out a grumbling sigh. David chuckled when he realized that once again Aimee and Hoku had made him feel better. Hoku gave Goliath a few parting licks before returning to Aimee's side.

"Don't sweat it, David. You and Goliath will be fine. Just follow the program and break a leg." Aimee gave David another affectionate pat on the back that had him nearly swallowing his tongue and wandered over to congratulate Kameron and Watson, who were coming off stage.

Manny, dressed in prison garb, ran past David with Chiquita. As Manny bounded onstage, Chiquita was close on his heels, barking savagely (well, as savagely as a Chihuahua can) and grabbing at his pant leg. Falling to the floor, Manny rolled over as Chiquita jumped on his chest and growled menacingly in his face. Pulling a tiny treat out of his pocket, Manny rewarded his pooch and stood up, lifting her high in the air so everyone could see her little police dog shirt.

After the applause died down, Manny threw Chiquita up onto a high platform where she expertly walked across a narrow board and climbed into a box. Next she pulled on a string that caused the box to drop down to the ground. Leaping out of the box, Chiquita ran over to a small trampoline and jumped, bouncing up onto Manny's shoulder.

Asking for help from the audience, Manny blindfolded Chiquita and handed her to the volunteer with instructions to release the dog after Manny had hidden. Manny went back onstage and sprayed a wooden chest with several types of perfume before climbing inside. The volunteer took the blindfold from Chiquita and set her down on the ground with the command, "Find Manny."

Chiquita ran across the stage, sniffing every obstacle she passed. As she passed the chest, she stopped briefly and sneezed several times as she got a good whiff of the perfume. Whining softly, she circled the trunk several times before jumping on top of it and barking excitedly. Manny tried to open the chest, but Chiquita would not move. When the lid opened a little bit, she would jump up and down, shutting it again on Manny's head, to the laughter and applause of the crowd. Finally after several minutes, she jumped down from the chest and sat quietly in front of it. Manny sheepishly climbed out and passed her a treat. The pair left the stage with Chiquita running zigzag patterns in and out of Manny's legs as he walked.

Taking a deep breath, David commanded Goliath to "heel". Goliath had been fitted with a special harness that had a sturdy handle on it that David could use to have Goliath pull him. Goliath ignored other distractions when he had a job to do, which was exactly what Mr. Sanchez felt the powerful pit bull needed. Today David was going to demonstrate some of the jobs Goliath had been trained to do as a helper dog. Of course, Goliath still had lots to learn, but he had mastered the basics in a short time with Juan's expert guidance.

16

Exit, Stage Right

Goliath quickly assumed his position beside the chair and touched David's leg with his paw once to signal he was ready to work. Goliath loved to pull things, especially David in his wheelchair.

"Pull, Goliath," David commanded.

Pull, pull, Goliath thought, his stocky body waddling slightly from side to side.

"Faster," David commanded.

Goliath sped up to a light trot. Pulling David onto the stage, Goliath hardly noticed all the people watching them. They didn't matter to him now. The only thing that mattered was David. There was a plethora of different smells assaulting his sensitive nostrils in the mall—cheap perfume and tangy lotions, the wafting aroma from the food court, sun-kissed people coming from the beach, little kids with sticky faces and hands. He ignored them all and looked expectantly up at David as they neared center stage.

"Whoa!" David commanded quietly. Goliath slowed to a walk and stopped, waiting for the next command. "Good boy." David patted him on the head and handed him a small treat. Goliath gently took the offered treat and swallowed it whole. He wanted to lick David's hand but held back the urge. Instead he wagged his stumpy tail.

"Goliath, go get my towel. Towel, Goliath!" David commanded letting go of the harness' handle.

Goliath walked around the stage for a several seconds before seeing the dresser he was familiar with. Jogging over to it, he used his teeth to pull open the top drawer and sniffed a big towel that smelled like Mrs. Sanchez and that soapy stuff that tasted bad and Chiquita who had slept on it recently.

Then the command "towel" echoed in his mind. *Stop sniffing and get towel.* He gingerly grabbed the towel with his teeth and pulled it from the drawer. He turned to go back to David before remembering something. Turning back to the drawer, he gave it a push with his paw, closing it tightly. Returning to the wheelchair, he dropped the towel on David's lap and touched his leg with one paw. David patted his head and told him he was a good boy.

Goliath had learned early on that the praise "good boy" was a type of reward. Good boy meant good things happened—like treats, ear rubs, belly scratches, and the wonderful game of catch. "Good boy" had been a dim memory of a life before fighting. He was glad he could be good again. Goliath wanted to please David. David spent a lot of time with Goliath and never once beat him or teased him with food or kicked him or tried to make him fight. He didn't fight anymore.

He lived in a pack with a whole bunch of other dogs and no one fought. No one wanted to fight. Sometimes he had to do things the people told him to, but they weren't bad things. And instead of punches and kicks, he got treats and time to play and run and roll around in a big field. And he was never hungry or hurt. So, he did what David told him to—contentedly.

Goliath performed a series of other basic tasks at David's command. David dropped his backpack. Goliath grabbed the backpack, but as he put it on David's lap, a book fell out. Goliath scooped up the book gently in his mouth and held it out to David. He did a series of retrievals and small tricks like balancing a biscuit on his nose.

Soon Goliath had the audience clapping every time he did something. The noise was distracting. Goliath looked out at the audience, at all the people. The smell was different, but the noise was similar to a dog fight. The clapping, the shouting, the whistling. Goliath didn't like the noise. He liked it quiet. He trotted to the backstage curtain and looked over his shoulder. He wanted to leave now. David called for him to heel. Goliath hesitated. He wanted to leave. David called again. Obediently, he trotted over to David's side and sat down with a whine.

"It's okay, buddy. We'll leave in a minute. We're almost done," David spoke softly and patted Goliath reassuringly. Goliath had no idea what David had said, but he was reassured by the tone of David's voice and his gentle touch.

Suddenly, Goliath was on his feet and alert with his muzzle high in the air. His sensitive nose picked out a familiar scent. A scent he hated. A scent he feared. A man-scent he would never forget drifted across the stage. Goliath growled and scanned the audience for the man who had kept him caged and forced him to fight.

"Goliath, sit!" David commanded.

Goliath ignored David and started toward the crowd, his head high, moving slowly from side to side as he continued to sniff out the direction of the hated man. Hackles raised and teeth bared, Goliath barked loudly to warn the man to stay away from David. He would protect David, no matter what. Finally at the back of the crowd, he spotted the threat.

Before Goliath could leap off the stage to go after the hated man, Mr. Sanchez was onstage and had grabbed his collar, commanding him to sit. The trainer tapped him lightly on the neck, getting his attention, and then commanded him to sit again. Goliath responded automatically to his pack leader and sat where he was. He continued to growl deep within his throat as he stared at the hated man across the room.

"It's only a case of stage jitters, folks! This is Goliath's debut performance." Mr. Sanchez spoke to the audience before leading Goliath backstage with a red-faced David wheeling right on his heels. The audience quickly forgot the incident as Aimee and Hoku hurriedly trotted onstage to perform their fly ball and agility act.

***

"Boss! Boss! Doesn't that look like Goliath?" Carlos stopped walking abruptly, pointing at the pit bull barking on stage. "I guess we know why he wasn't in the dumpster when we went back. Boss, that's him!"

"That's Goliath all right," Hank sneered. "What's that cripple kid done to my fighting dog?"

"He doesn't look like much of a fighting dog now, Boss."

"Shut up, you idiot!" Hank hissed angrily at Carlos. Firmly gripping the other man's arm, Hank tugged Carlos behind him and hastily moved away from the agility show toward the mall exit.

"But that was Goliath! Didn't you see him?" Carlos was practically yelling as he tripped behind Hank. "He sure saw you! Ay yi yi! If looks could kill, you'd be one dead gringo."

"For the last time, shut up!" Hank slapped Carlos across the back of the head. "Do you want the whole place to hear you?"

Carlos, looking somewhat irate, finally closed his mouth and yanked his arm from Hank's grasp. Speaking in a hushed voice, he went on, "But that kid has Goliath."

"I know that, you imbecile," Hank replied, twirling his lucky silver dollar between his thumb and index finger. "We're gonna wait in the parking lot until they leave and follow them home. Don't worry. We're gonna get that useless dog back, and good ol' Goliath is gonna have a final comeback fight. His last fight ever."

Hank and Carlos chuckled as they exited the mall.

17

Adopt-a-bull

David was beside himself with worry. Everything had gone as planned right up until the end. Now what was he going to do? He couldn't very well say to Mom and Dad, "Can I have Goliath? He's a perfect helper dog. Oh, sure, he brings me my clothes and picks up my books and on occasion may attack someone unexpectedly. But as a bonus he'll make a good guard dog!" David looked down at Goliath whose head rested contentedly on his knee.

Frustrated, David kneaded Goliath's ear to help calm himself down. Things weren't going as well as previously planned. He didn't want to think about what would happen if his parents didn't let him keep Goliath. Maybe he could stall the meeting? Was it too late for him to run away and join the circus?

"What was that all about?" David asked Mr. Sanchez.

"I'm not sure, David. He was behaving in a protective manner. My guess would be that he thought he needed to protect you from someone." Mr. Sanchez scratched his head. "I guess he smelled someone he didn't like in the audience. Someone definitely spooked him."

"Great! Is he going to do that every time he smells someone he doesn't like? I'll have to make sure there are no stinky people in my entourage then. Smelly people need not apply. I'll have to arm myself with a stink-o-meter to keep Goliath from eating up the smelly people," David grumbled and started working Goliath's other ear.

"Remember all this is completely new for him. Since entering training, he hasn't been around many people other than you and the rest of our group. And he hasn't shown any aggression toward people whatsoever. Stinky or otherwise. He's a good dog who had a bad beginning, David." Mr. Sanchez smiled at David, hoping his words helped to alleviate some of the boy's worry. "Some scars take longer to heal than others."

"David! David, over here!" David's dad called from the end of the stage.

David gentled pushed Goliath's head from his lap and tried to hand the leash over to Mr. Sanchez. The trainer held up both hands, refusing the offered leash. "David, eventually you will need to tell them about Goliath," he said, patting David on the shoulder.

"You knew all along?" It was more of an accusation than a question.

"Yep. Doc told me the day Aimee asked if I would work with Goliath," Mr Sanchez replied.

"But you never said anything." David felt his body temperature rise as he got angry. Was the whole world against him?

"I figured you would talk about it in your own time." Mr. Sanchez wasn't apologetic.

David's anger wilted away as he realized Manny's dad was not his enemy. "Thanks, Mr. Sanchez," David said. "I really mean that. Thanks for everything you've done."

David guessed that maybe it would be good to have the truth finally out in the open. About as good as having bamboo shoots stuck underneath your nails or walking on burning coals with your bare feet or laughing so hard milk flew out of your nose and sprayed the shirt of the cutest, most popular girl in school. At least Aimee eventually forgave him for that one.

His fear of losing Goliath was real, but at least he might get some help from his new friends. Maybe they could kidnap his baby brothers, Darryl and Dylan, and hold them until his parents gave in to his demands. After all, Dylan was still in diapers and Darryl still had plenty of accidents, so they both fell under the category of stinky. Maybe it wouldn't be a good idea for them to be around Goliath until Goliath got over his stinky people aversion.

Mr. Sanchez patted David reassuringly on the shoulder. "Don't worry. You found yourself a good dog. It'll work out okay."

Yeah, yeah, and maybe flying pigs would shoot out of his nose and wing Goliath and him to Old MacDonald's farm. Reluctantly, David wheeled over to where his parents and siblings waited. Goliath trotted obediently by his side in the "heel" position until they reached David's family. At David's command, Goliath sat down, thumping his stumpy tail against the ground in greeting.

His little sister, Darcy, had a huge grin on her face and couldn't contain her bouncing. Darcy was a spazzy eight-year-old. She constantly had springs on her feet. She never walked. She never sat. She bounced. Even her pigtails bounced.

"David, that was so cool!" Darcy gushed before bouncing on top of Goliath, enveloping him in a girly-version of a bear hug. Goliath looked inquiringly at David. David smiled and shrugged at Goliath.

David's mother looked him straight in the eye and asked nonchalantly, "Anything you'd care to discuss, David?"

"Um, Mom, Dad... can I have a dog?" David smiled weakly and averted his eyes from his mother's penetrating stare. She was a lawyer and knew how to stare someone down when she wanted to. It was intimidating. Even when she had a rugrat on each hip.

"Puppy!" Darryl shrieked, shaking himself free and slithering down his mother's leg before launching himself at Goliath. Resigned to his fate, Goliath sat there quietly, enduring the torment of an over-exuberant two-year-old. While the two children hugged all over Goliath, he sniffed them from head to toe.

"Darryl, no! Darcy, stop that! That's not how you approach a strange dog!" their mother said, kneeling down beside Goliath who acted like he had known the children his entire life.

Goliath could smell bubble gum, fruity shampoo, and vanilla lotion on the little girl. His nose followed a trail of cookie crumbs that started on the little boy's pants and ended at the boy's face. For the first time since he had been stolen, Goliath licked the crumbs from a child's face and sighed contentedly. David's dad reached down and scratched Goliath's ears.

"Well?" David prodded his parents for a reply. "How about it? Can we adopt a dog?"

David's dad looked up, winked at David, and replied before his mother could, "What's wrong with the one we already have?"

18

Ungrateful Mutt

Cursing under his breath and slamming his fist against the steering wheel, Hank followed the disgustingly happy family as they drove away in their Suburban—with his prize fighting dog! It was bad enough they had stolen Goliath from the dumpster where he had thrown him. And now they were driving down the road with that ungrateful pit bull hanging his ugly mug out the window, taunting Hank with his fat tongue lolling in the wind.

"We're gonna follow them home and take back my dog," Hank growled at Carlos who looked like he was about to jump out the window at any minute. "What's wrong with you?"

"I got a bad feeling about this, Boss," Carlos whined.

"What don't you got a bad feeling about, idiot?" Hank snarled back at his lackey.

"You don't understand, amigo. Juan Sanchez knows a lot of people, and you don't want to cross him when it comes to dogs..." Carlos tried to explain but was cut off.

"Shut your pie hole!" Hank slapped the cowering man across the chest with the back of his hand. "I'm sick and tired of your whining. I don't give a rat's patootie who's training him—I'm taking him back. He's mine! Do you understand me? Mine!"

"Okay, Boss." Carlos rubbed his chest and looked away. "Whatever you say."

"That's right and don't you forget it." Hank drove by the house where the Suburban had pulled into the driveway. He kept driving for another block before pulling the van into an alleyway and stopping.

"Now we wait."

At dusk the Suburban left the driveway with the man and crippled boy inside but no Goliath. Hank couldn't believe his luck. There would be no one left inside but the woman and kids and, of course, his dog. Slapping the snoring man sleeping beside him, he opened the van door and stepped out.

"Time to earn your keep," Hank sneered. He opened the van's back door and grabbed a steel choke collar and length of rope. Then he picked up a tire iron and handed it to his henchman. "Let's go get my fightin' dog back."

19

Hos-pit-ality

Goliath explored his new home with curious enthusiasm. Traces of David lingered everywhere. He followed David to a room filled with the boy's presence. He happily jumped up on the bed and rolled onto his back, wiggling his body back and forth, covering himself in his boy's scent.

"Wait a minute, big guy!" David laughed at Goliath's antics. He wheeled over to the window side of the bed and pointed at a thick-padded dog bed lying on the floor. "Your bed is right here."

Goliath stopped rolling wildly on top of the bed and jumped off to sniff at the thing David pointed at. Unlike the bed it barely smelled like David. He pushed his nose under the dog bed and flipped it over to see what was hidden underneath. Not finding anything of interest, he began digging at the bed with his paws.

"Goliath, stop that!" David commanded. Then as Goliath continued to dig, he remembered that wasn't a command. "Goliath, leave it."

Sitting on his haunches, Goliath looked at David with his head tilted to one side. Did David want him to get it since he was pointing or leave it alone like David commanded? Sometimes his boy could be so hard to understand. It was as if he didn't know what he wanted himself. Goliath let out a loud woof and jumped back onto David's bed. He spun in a circle three times before lying down with a contented moan.

A soft bed filled with the scent of his boy. He closed his eyes and pointedly ignored the boy still sitting in the wheelchair glaring at him.

Cracking one eye open, he watched David roll himself into the bathroom. When David's wheelchair moved out of sight, Goliath was on his feet and charging through the door before it could be closed.

"Oh, I see...now you want to be with me." David chuckled as Goliath squeezed past him. "There goes my privacy."

David felt extremely exposed as he undressed with the big-eyed pit bull watching his every move like the fate of the world depended on it. Not to mention the fact that the pit retrieved his pants whenever he tossed them in his laundry hamper. After the third time, Goliath finally got the idea that he was to leave the pants in the hamper.

Turning on the shower, David slid across his transfer board and settled onto the shower bench. The warm water ran over his head and down his body. He leaned back against the wall and closed his eyes only to be interrupted by a loud thump that nearly caused him to fall off the bench. Goliath had decided to climb over the edge of the bathtub to join him.

"Really? Really! Can I have no privacy at all?" he asked, splashing water at Goliath, who sat down and began licking David's outstretched hands. "Oh, all right. But if you're gonna be in the bathtub, you're gonna get a bath."

A half hour and four towels later, Goliath was scrubbed from head to toe, dried off and resting peacefully on his new bed. David got dressed and wheeled out the door before his stalker could squeeze out with him. Dad had agreed to take him to the store to get more supplies and food for Goliath. Although Goliath would eventually be allowed to go everywhere David went, he wasn't a certified service dog yet and David didn't want to get into any trouble so soon after bringing him home.

Goliath was on his feet once the door closed and he scrambled across the room, sniffing at the crack under the door. He could hear his boy and the friendly man leaving the house, and he whined softly. He didn't want to be left behind. His whine soon became a howl as he heard the Suburban drive away. Becoming frantic, he began clawing at the door when it suddenly popped open.

"We'll have none of that!" David's mother said in a no-nonsense tone that Goliath understood was meant for him. He tried to shoulder past the woman, but she agilely blocked his path and grabbed his collar before he succeeded. "You and I need to come to an understanding if you're going to live in my house."

Goliath looked up at the woman and whined then turned his head toward the garage door David had left through. His intent was so obvious David's mother relaxed her grip and knelt down to scratch his neck and chin. "I know how you feel. But David can handle himself, and sometimes when you love someone, you have to let them go out on their own. Now sit."

Whining softly, Goliath licked her hand and sat down obediently. No sooner did his butt hit the ground then one of the twins careened out of his bedroom, screaming, arms flailing with a soft dog toy clutched in one hand as he flew down the hallway.

"Goliath...get me!" Dylan screamed, trailing the hand with the toy behind him. Goliath looked up at the woman, his stumpy tail threatening to wiggle right off his butt.

"Can I trust you?" she asked. Goliath whined excitedly but held his seated position.

"Dylan, stop that and come here!" she commanded. The toddler stopped running away and came back to his mother with his eyes downcast.

"Play with doggy," he stated, assuming his mother hadn't understood his intention.

"I know, honey, but you've just met Goliath. And we don't know how much he likes spastic little boys." She tousled his hair affectionately.

A second later Darryl emerged from their bedroom with a plastic sword and took a swing at his brother. Goliath growled and instinctively crouched down, expecting to get hit.

"Darryl, put that down!" David's mother ordered and patted Goliath's head. "It's okay, Goliath. No one here is going to hit you.

"Now, you two! Front and center!" she ordered the twins who both contemplated making a run for it until they made eye contact. They knew when their mother used that voice, they had to obey—or else! Goliath visibly relaxed when the sword hit the ground.

"Goliath is a new addition to our family, and I need both of you munchkins to be extra nice to him." She knelt down to be eye level with her twins. "Do you understand?"

Darryl looked everywhere but at his mother's face while Dylan nodded his head. She released her hold on Goliath and got slowly to her feet. "Okay, it's almost bedtime. Anyone want a snack before we brush our teeth?"

The two boys dashed around her and down the hallway toward the kitchen, screaming, "Cookies! Cookies!"

Telling Goliath to heel, she marched after her two brats and into the kitchen where Darcy was finishing her nighttime snack. She directed her two siblings to their place at the table. "Sit down if you want something."

The boys climbed eagerly into their booster seats and started banging the table with their greedy little hands. "Cookies! Cookies!"

"No cookies tonight. I'll make you fruit and veggie smoothies for snack time," David's mother said, gesturing for Goliath to lay down on the mat by the kitchen door. Goliath obediently sprawled on his belly and sniffed at the mat and under the door where the scent of his boy still lingered.

"Good boy," she said and tossed him a dog biscuit.

Goliath decided he liked the lady as he caught the treat in midair. He began chewing it while listening to the three small humans arguing with each other. Although he still missed David, he was not locked in a room and had his new pack to keep him company.

An hour later David's mother tucked Darcy into bed as Goliath hovered nearby and watched the proceedings. Darcy, being eight years old and almost grown up, at least in her mind, was the last to go to bed. She crawled under the blanket then suddenly remembered something. She quickly threw off the covers and jumped back out of bed.

"Honey, it's bedtime," David's mother said with a deep sigh.

"Kiss. I want a kiss!" Darcy pleaded.

"Oh, alright." David's mother smiled and bent down for a kiss.

Darcy giggled and slipped past her mother and dropped to her knees, wrapping her arms around Goliath's neck. Goliath groaned but didn't move—not even when the little girl planted a kiss on his forehead. Then his stumpy tail wagged slowly back and forth, and he returned the kiss with a slobbery tongue against Darcy's cheek.

"Goodnight, Goliath," Darcy said sweetly then got to her feet and gave her mother a quick hug before diving back into her bed.

"Goliath, heel," David's mother commanded.

Goliath obediently trotted out of the room on her heels. David's mother pulled the door partially shut behind her. She then made her way down the hall and into the living room where she sat down on the couch and searched for the TV remote. "Where is that darn remote control?"

She flipped over a pillow and moved the blanket covering the couch but didn't see the remote anywhere in sight. Dropping onto the floor, she checked under the couch and beside the end table. Nothing there. After several minutes of fruitless searching, she turned to look at Goliath and asked, "Do you know where the remote control is?"

Goliath looked at her for a moment as if he were contemplating the question. Then he got up from where he sat and sniffed along the right side of the couch. Not finding anything of interest, he moved along the front of the couch and then to the left side. David's mother watched him for a minute then got to her feet and walked over to the TV and pressed the button on the side of the unit. "It was worth a try. I guess you're no Einstein, huh?"

When she turned to go back to the couch, she stopped dead in her tracks and eyed the pit bull who sat smugly beside the couch with a wet-looking remote control wedged between his pearly white canines. "I stand corrected. May I have that please?"

Goliath cocked his head to the side and regarded the woman. She moved toward him and reached for the remote control but did not give him the command to release it. At first he wasn't sure what she was going to do as her hand reached toward his neck, and he bristled slightly, curling his upper lip in warning.

David's mother had grown up on a farm with several large breed mutts for company and knew how to handle big dogs. Instead of grabbing for the remote, she knelt down beside Goliath and pulled a small dog biscuit out of her pocket. She held out her hand. "Trade you?"

Goliath sniffed the treat then dropped the remote on the floor and reached out to accept the offering. Ignoring the remote control, David's mother gave him the biscuit and scratched behind his ears, all the while telling him what a good boy he was. Goliath gobbled down the treat then licked her hand, hoping there was more to come. Picking up the remote control, David's mother sat down on the couch and pulled a blanket up around her.

Goliath laid his big head on her lap and sighed, eyeing the empty space on the couch longingly. Clicking the remote, David's mother turned on the evening news and pointedly looked away from the forlorn pit bull. Goliath heaved a deep sigh and looked up at her and whined softly.

"Cut it out," she chided and switched the channel.

Goliath's eyes moved from David's mother to the empty spot on the couch and back again.

"You're worse than the twins!" She tried to push his head away, but he leaned into her with all his weight and groaned some more. "Oh, all right then. Come on. Get up! But only this one time."

Not needing a second invitation, Goliath leaped over her legs and landed dead center on the empty spot. He did a few quick circles then dropped down, resting his head contentedly on her lap. She laughed, despite trying not to, and gently patted his big head. He closed his eyes and drifted off to sleep, snoring loudly.

20

Bite Me!

Hank pulled the balaclava over his head and pushed the other one into Carlos' waiting hand. "Put this on."

"Why do we need these, Boss?" Carlos asked, taking the mask and sliding it over his head. He had left his cowboy hat in the van so no one would recognize him. He didn't see why they needed woolen ski masks—they weren't robbing a bank. In his mind people were more likely going to notice two guys walking down the street at night in the middle of summer with ski masks on, but he kept that opinion to himself.

"Shut up!" Hank growled then snickered. "When I want your opinion on something, I'll ask for it—then shoot myself."

"Stupid gringo," Carlos muttered under his breath then quickened his pace to match strides with his grumpy employer.

Skulking down the sidewalk, the two would-be dog thieves checked both directions before turning into David's driveway and scrambling over the solid wooden fence surrounding the backyard. Hank went first then turned to regard his henchman. Carlos hovered on the brink of the fence, rocking back and forth on his fat stomach, unable to get over.

"Boss, help! I'm stuck!" Carlos hissed.

"Get down here, you idiot!" Hank snarled at the hapless man who teetered on the fence, arms and legs flailing. Grabbing his lackey by the shoulders, Hank gave a mighty heave that unbalanced Carlos and caused him to tumble off the fence. Carlos emitted a loud squeal of pain when he struck the ground on his side.

"Stop your whining!" Hank hissed, pulling Carlos roughly to his feet. "Let's try the back door first."

"But, Boss," Carlos whined plaintively. "The crippled kid's mother is still home."

"And?" Hank sneered, hefting his crowbar. He moved to stand with his back against the house and began sliding along the wall. Carlos hung his head and trudged along behind Hank, not even pretending to be stealthy. When he reached the big picture window, Hank stopped and held up a fist for Carlos to stop walking. Carlos, who'd been looking over his shoulder into the neighbor's backyard when Hank stopped abruptly, walked directly into the raised fist and let out a startled yelp.

"Shhh!" Hank hissed and grabbed Carlos, pulling him down below the level of the window as the woman inside stepped into view and peered outside. With a flick of her wrist, she closed the blinds and blocked Hank's view of the interior. Hank snarled at no one in particular, "Damn it."

Still grumbling under his breath, Hank continued to creep along the wall, making his way around the side of the house into the back yard. Carlos followed closely at his heels.

Without any warning, the back door swung open and the woman from the window walked out, leading Goliath on a short leash. Hank whipped his head back and threw out his arm, slamming Carlos against the wall behind him. "It's Goliath. Get back!"

Goliath growled loud enough for the two men to hear him as they scrambled toward the front of the house. Hank pushed Carlos to get him to move faster. He clearly heard the woman ask Goliath why he was growling. *Stupid woman, he's growling because he's a fighting dog and not a house pet!*

"Goliath! Come back here!" the woman shouted.

"Oh, crap!" Hank hissed, passing Carlos and making a beeline for the front fence. "Run!"

Goliath charged around the side of the house like the fabled hellhound Garn from Norse mythology. Fangs flashing, huge paws digging up clumps of earth, saliva dripping from his open maw, he looked possessed and ready to kill something. Realization hit Hank like a fist in the face. The something that Goliath wanted to kill was him.

Snarling, Goliath passed Carlos and came at Hank with a ferocity he had never shown in the fighting ring. All thoughts of stealing Goliath gone, Hank was at the fence and already climbing over when he felt sharp canines tear through his left pant leg, removing his jeans at the knee. Thankfully, it was only his jeans and not his leg. Landing on his knees, Hank was vaguely aware of Carlos scrambling over the fence beside him, screaming at the top of his lungs. He had never seen his partner move so fast. Sprinting down the driveway, he could hear Goliath slam repeatedly against the fence, claws raking the wooden planks in an attempt to get at him.

"That's right! You two better keep running and don't come back! Next time I may not be here to stop him!" the woman yelled. By the time she got to the fence and looked over the top, the two men were racing down the street for all they were worth.

Reassured the men were indeed gone, David's mother turned her attention to the determined pit bull still frantically digging under the fence, a piece of denim firmly gripped between his teeth.

"Goliath, that's enough! Settle down," David's mother commanded, grabbing his collar and tugging it to get his attention.

Goliath resisted the pull on his neck and slowed down his digging. In a stern voice, David's mother commanded Goliath to heel. She pulled Goliath forcefully away from the fence, and reluctantly, Goliath stopped digging and obeyed the command he was given. Looking over his shoulder one last time, Goliath let out a muffled warning bark before entering the house.

"Good boy, Goliath," David's mother cooed.

She shut the door and slid the deadbolt into place. Squatting down to eye level, she pulled a treat out of her pocket and offered it to Goliath in exchange for the shredded denim. Goliath refused to release his trophy and growled softly.

"Leave it," she said firmly remembering the command she had heard David use. Holding out the treat, she repeated the command. Understanding that she wanted to trade, Goliath loosened his grip on the piece of cloth and accepted the treat.

David's mother picked up the denim between her thumb and index finger, smiling despite herself. "Well, I guess we've added a little more bite to our security system."

Goliath looked up at her and wagged. The lady wasn't like the hated man. She didn't hit him, even though he hadn't come when called. And she had offered him a treat and called him a "good boy." Goliath wanted to please the lady, but he would attack the hated man again if he got the chance.

With a sigh, he dropped to the floor and rolled over to get a belly rub. He stuck out his paw and tapped David's mother's leg, and she reached down and scratched all his itchy spots. Goliath moaned with pleasure. Life was good.

21

I Spy ...

The next day, the kids of Ability Inc. and their animals met at Manny's place. Having successfully participated in their first event, David and Goliath were now official members. This was like icing on the cake for David. He was already on cloud nine after learning he could keep Goliath; he even had his mom's unexpected full endorsement. Sitting in the backyard by the pool, the kids discussed the fundraiser and congratulated each other on a job well done. The dogs didn't join the discussion but instead decided to swim and retrieve tennis balls in the pool. Maeve opted to take a power nap in Niamh's hood.

"So, David, which shelter did you say you adopted Goliath from again?" Kameron asked between bites of pizza.

"I didn't say. Because I didn't adopt him. I actually found him in a dumpster," David replied with a smirk.

"No way!" Niamh giggled, assuming David was joking.

"Way," David laughed.

"It's true. I actually pulled both of them out of a dumpster with these guns." Aimee flexed her biceps to the sarcastic oohs and aahs, and giggles of her friends.

"Get out!" Siobhan exclaimed.

"I remember the day well. It was a Friday evening, the last day of February. There was a chill in the air. And then out of the blue I get this weird text from David asking—no—pleading for me to rescue him. I was at work and having a total craptastic day because a group of dogs had been brought in from a dogfighting raid the night before, and Greta said a lot of them would be euthanized because they were too aggressive and unsuitable for adoption. So, I get this text and it's all, like, I've fallen and I can't get up! I mean, how would you take that coming from him?" Aimee tossed her head in David's direction.

David laughed. "Come on. I didn't write that!"

Aimee rolled her eyes. "Oh, yes, you did! Hello! Am I not a female? Do I not have uber memory? Remember it's a male shortcoming of not remembering dates and details, not a female one."

"Or birthdays!" chimed in Niamh. "So sad. Missing out on all those presents. Tragic, really."

"And you can kiss those anniversaries good bye 'cos they'll never remember those dates either," Siobhan added.

"We're not like that at all," Kameron protested.

"Au contraire, mon fairy! You have the mind of a sieve. Anyho! You should have seen him at the bottom of that dumpster. Too funny and way super smelly cat!" Aimee and David told the rest of the story of Goliath's rescue.

"You know, the night before that, Siobhan and I were on a stakeout of that lab that still uses live animals in its product testing," Manny stated. "They say they don't use live animals anymore, but that crazy animal activist group says they still do. So, we were casing the joint, trying to get some evidence. Unfortunately, we didn't get anything and decided to call it a night. When we left the place, we were crossing the street and almost got run down by this idiot driving a white van."

"Yeah, they took out my stick! And they call me blind." Siobhan shook her head.

"White van?" Aimee asked. "What kind of van was it?"

"I'm not sure. I didn't get a good look at it," Siobhan answered with a chuckle.

"It was a Ford cargo van with no windows in the back or on the sides," Manny replied. "And I got the first three digits of the license plate number."

"You're not a typical male," Niamh giggled with a smirk. Manny winked at her and looked smug.

"David, wasn't there a white cargo van parked beside the dumpster I pulled you and Goliath out of?" Aimee asked.

"Um, there was a white van?" David looked confused.

"I rest my case!" Aimee exploded with laughter. Niamh raised her hand, and the girls shared a giggling high-five.

"Hey! I was recovering from a concussion!" David complained, causing the girls to erupt into further laughter.

Kameron groaned with impatience. "We can stop with the male bashing at any time now."

"Never mind, you cranky pants! Ohmigod, it's gotta be more than a coinky-dink!" Aimee was excited now as the pieces of the puzzle fell into place. "Do you think that Ford van you saw could have been the same one by the dumpster?" She looked closely at Manny. "Do you think the cops caught them?"

"I doubt it. The cruiser was pretty far behind, and he stopped to ask if we were okay." Manny looked somewhat confused.

David finally understood where Aimee was going with this. Obviously, he was the only one and would have to spell it out for the others. He felt somewhat redeemed for not having remembered the white van. "Don't you get it? Dogfight—white van—Goliath in a dumpster? It's all connected. The people who dumped Goliath were being chased by the police, so they ditched the van and tossed poor Goliath in the trash to get rid of evidence."

"Ohmigod!" Niamh exclaimed when the light bulb in her head turned on. "Poor Goliath."

"I hate dogfighting! It's all kinds of wrong," Siobhan added. "I wish we could do something to help the police catch those losers."

"Maybe we can!" David had an idea. "Aimee, wasn't your grandfather a cop?"

Aimee had been kneeling over, giving the irresistible beggar bum that was Hoku a bite of pizza. She had been facing away from David as he spoke. When she turned back toward him, all eyes were on her. "What? Do I have pizza sauce on my face?" She self-consciously wiped at her mouth.

"Sorry. Sometimes I forget you're deaf. I mean, hearing-impaired," David shrugged apologetically.

"Funny. I never forget you're a dork ...der! Paraplegic," Aimee shot back.

"Touché. But I'm not a paraplegic. I'm a person who suffers from paraplegia," David stated smugly.

"Would you like another piece of pizza to ease your suffering?" Aimee stuck out her tongue.

"Gah! You win," David said in resignation. "Now, was your grandfather a cop or not?"

"Don't I always win?" Aimee asked sweetly. When David didn't reply, she continued, "Pops has been retired from the New York police force for about thirty years now."

"Do you think he has any police friends here in Florida?" David asked.

"You know there's tons of New Yorkers that like to winter in our sunny state." Niamh smiled at David.

"Dunno." Aimee shrugged. "I can find out easy enough. Why do you want to know?"

"Manny saw the license plate of the van. He's got those digits. Maybe your grandfather can run a plate check to find the address of the guy who owned it. We can case the joint. Then we can bust him and stop him from hurting any other animals. I might even let Goliath rough him up. You know, let Goliath have some ring time with the ring leader. Goliath could give him a few matching scars. Now wouldn't that be sweet?" David finished his tirade and, somewhat winded, stuffed another piece of pizza into his mouth.

"Maybe Greta's boyfriend, Officer Slim Jim, can help us," Aimee mused out loud.

"Greta has a boyfriend?" Niamh exclaimed.

"Not!" Aimee and Siobhan snickered simultaneously. Niamh rolled her eyes at them, which, of course, was lost on Siobhan.

"I don't want them to know what we're up to until we have proof. I don't want this guy getting off with a slap on the wrist and a fine," Manny said angrily.

"No kidding. He needs to go to prison and get the electric chair or something equally nasty," Siobhan added. "Speaking of prison, maybe you guys can help Manny and me with another animal rights problem we have. Remember Manny said we were staking out a lab that tests on animals the night we saw the van?"

"Yeah, so what were you doing anyways?" Aimee asked.

"That's just it. We didn't find anything at the lab. But I know they're using animals for their product testing, but we need proof for anyone to take us seriously. We need, like, photos or video or something, and you all know how well I handle a camera. For some reason, all my photos come out too dark." Siobhan smiled.

Aimee laughed and gave her a friendly shove.

"Hey! I have some surveillance equipment at home. We could set up a twenty-four-hour camera linked to a laptop and tape the place." David was excited to finally be able to use some of his spy equipment.

"For real?" Kameron asked.

"Yeah, for real," David smiled. "I have infrared, night-vision goggles; video camera pens; pin-sized microphones; sound-amplified speakers; GPS tracking devices, etc. You name it and I probably have it."

"Cool! I want to go over to your house and play!" Kameron chuckled.

"It's settled then. We'll help you nail the lab jerks and you help us shut down the dogfighting idiots." Aimee made a fist and held out her arm. David was the first to put his fist on Aimee's before everyone else followed, Niamh leading her sister's hand on top of David's.

"Ability Inc. is on the job. Watch out, animal abusers! Move over, X-men! There's a new sheriff in town," Manny said, adding his fist to the pile. Everyone cheered and threw their arms in the air.

22

Dog-gone It

C arlos began snoring loudly, and his head bobbed up and down as he tried to sleep in a sitting position. A line of drool slid unchecked down the right side of his cheek. Hank whacked him sharply against the side of the head.

"Wha? What is it?" Carlos jerked awake, looking around for someone to hit back. Wiping the drool on his sleeve, he looked guiltily at Hank. "Oh, it's you. I wasn't sleeping. I was resting my eyes."

"Whatever, you idiot... now stay awake! The little cripple is coming out with Goliath." Hank pointed at David wheeling his chair down the street, Goliath running obediently beside him.

"Hey! I ain't going anywhere near that crazy mutt again," Carlos whined. That statement earned him another whack on the side of the head. "I don't think we should mess with one of Juan Sanchez's kids anyways, man." Carlos sounded scared. But then Carlos always sounded scared to Hank.

"Shut up, you idiot!" Hank made a threatening fist but didn't strike this time. "I don't give a rat's tail who's untraining my dog. Good old Goliath is going to have one more fight—his last. No dog bites Hank and lives to gloat about it."

Carlos turned the key and started the engine. Shifting into drive, he slowly pulled the van out into the street. Hank pulled a case from under the front seat and opened it. Pulling out a long-barreled tranquilizer gun, he loaded a dart.

"The little creep in the chair is gonna learn that he should've left well enough alone. Let's get my dog back. Pull right up beside them," Hank ordered Carlos.

"Whoa, whoa, whoa, wait a minute! No one said anything about shooting anyone," Carlos stammered and maneuvered the van around a parked car.

Eyeing the gun in Hank's hand, Carlos wasn't about to remind Hank that he pretty much threw Goliath away. Carlos wondered if Goliath was worth all this trouble. Wouldn't it be easier to get another dog? Goliath was no good as a fighting dog now. Not after becoming a family pet. The dog deserved a break after being Hank's dog.

"It's not a real gun, stupid! I swear! Some of the things that come out of your mouth and pea brain amaze me! It's a tranquilizer gun. I stole it from the lab guys the last time we were there. I thought it would come in handy when we're out hunting for stray animals to sell to the lab." Hank scowled at Carlos and pulled his lucky dollar out of his shirt pocket. "Tell ya'll what, I'll flip you for the privilege of darting Goliath."

"Yo, David, wait up!" A tall black-haired teen came barreling out of the driveway on a mountain bike with her mutt running alongside.

"What the heck! If we didn't have bad luck, we'd have no luck at all." Hank closed his fist around the coin and looked like he was about to explode. "We don't want to attract too much attention. Back off, Carlos. We'll have to follow them and wait for a better chance."

As they passed the Sanchez residence, Carlos said a quiet prayer that Juan Sanchez didn't see them. When he was finished, Carlos crossed himself and said "amen" out loud. Juan Sanchez was a legend to the local people. He had helped many influential people train their dogs and was not someone you crossed lightly. Carlos had a sudden epiphany. It might be time he started looking for a new job before it was too late.

"What? What did you say?" Hank asked crossly.

"Maybe that lucky coin of yours ain't so lucky," Carlos muttered.

23

Operation Spy Kam

The following day David got up early and organized his spy gear. He quickly gathered everything he thought he might need and began stuffing it into a duffel bag. First he added a battery-operated camera with a built-in recorder that had a motion sensor and could record night or day. He decided to put it in a metal case that looked like an outdoor electrical box that could be attached to a telephone pole or to the side of a building. Then he added a laptop computer to the bag, so they could watch the video feed remotely. Since he hadn't actually been to the building yet, he added all the tools that he might need into Goliath's backpack then rolled toward the front door. Goliath followed closely at his side, the backpack swaying from side to side as he walked.

"What are you two doing today?" Dad inquired when David sped past the kitchen. Dylan sat in his booster chair, slamming away at the tray. Darryl and Darcy must have still been sleeping, most likely in his parents' bed with his mother.

"Just chillin'," David responded.

"Great! Then you can help me with a project I'm working on once your mother wakes up from her beauty sleep and can take over the baby duties," Dad said cheerfully, cutting up a banana and sliding it onto Dylan's plate. Dylan made a face and smashed a piece with his spoon.

"Um, well, actually I was going to hang with Aimee and the rest of the gang for a while." David figured staying close to the truth was the best approach. "We want to practice for our next fundraiser."

Goliath had taken the opportunity to walk up to Dylan's chair. He licked up some tasty smears on the floor before attempting to clean the plate. However, after receiving a stern look and hand signal from David, he snorted and reluctantly returned to his guardian's side.

"Oh, shoot, I thought we could spend some father-son-dog time together." Dad sounded disappointed.

"Can we do it this afternoon instead? I should be back by two or so." David felt guilty about dissing his father but setting up the stakeout was important. His peeps were depending on him.

"Sure. No prob, buddy. Catch ya later, dude," Dad said, sounding like a real dork, especially while dodging toddler-thrown banana pieces.

Why, oh, why do adults try to be cool with their kids? Inquiring minds want to know. David shook his head and wheeled out the door and down the front driveway toward the street. Flipping open his cell, he called Kameron, who informed him that his ETA was less than five minutes. Sure enough, within minutes, the familiar SUV came down the road and stopped at the curb directly in front of David and Goliath.

Niamh opened the back door and jumped out. After giving Goliath a big hug, she then punched David on the arm.

"Suppies, dork meister?" She smiled playfully.

"Ah, you, too," David sighed in mock indignation. "I get no respect, no respect at all."

"Aimee asked me to do that. Sorry if it makes you uncomfortable. I won't do it again. Did I hurt your arm?" Niamh sounded genuinely concerned and touched his arm gently with her hand. Her attention and touch wasn't that unpleasant.

"Nah, Aimee has a much stronger punch than you do. I think she's done permanent nerve damage to that arm, so I don't feel much there anymore." David chuckled. Girls were a mystery to him. Who could ever figure them out? One minute they were bruising your arm. The next minute they were apologizing for it.

Niamh wore a leg-revealing summer dress and a mesh, front-pouch carrier that wiggled when she moved. As the breeze picked up, her long straight red hair danced wildly around her neck like red ribbons swirling around a May pole. David hadn't realized how elfin-like Niamh and Siobhan were until that moment. Now that he thought about it, Niamh was pretty with slender features and a natural grace missing in many girls her age.

A fuzzy head poked out of the opening in Niamh's front pouch and dook-dooked in greeting. Rising on his hind legs, Goliath sniffed the tiny animal. As his nose almost touched Maeve, the little ferret snapped forward, trying to bite him. She hissed, and the hair on her body and tail poofed up. She looked like someone had gone crazy rubbing a balloon all over her. Either that or a weasely-type of dandelion. Goliath jumped back, bumping into David's chair, and almost fell over in his hurry to get away. Niamh and David both laughed at their antics.

"Geez! You'd think they'd be used to each other by now." Shaking her head, Niamh carefully moved Maeve back inside the carrier and zipped the top shut. Maeve hissed and vigorously scratched at the zipper to show her displeasure.

The passenger window rolled down, and Watson popped his head out as David grabbed the door handle. Turning his head to one side, he gave David a look that said *"and what exactly are you trying to do?"*

"Don't tell me. Let me guess. You've got shotgun?" David looked at Watson as if expecting an answer. Watson tilted his head to one side and regarded David quizzically.

"Sorry, mate, but he insists on riding in the front. He gets car sick if he rides in the back." Kameron looked slightly apologetic, while leaning over Watson to talk to David. "I doubt you'd want dog puke on the back of your head."

"No problem. I can get in the backseat easier anyway. Niamh, can you put my wheels in the back, please?"

After opening the rear-passenger door, David slipped his hands beneath his knees. Lifting his feet off of the foot pedals, he moved his legs out of the wheelchair and onto the ground. He then put one hand on the back of the front seat and one hand on the door. He lifted himself out of his chair and pivoted onto the back seat. Once seated, he pulled his legs into the SUV as he turned to face the front. David was able to fold his own wheelchair and place it behind him in a car but had difficulty in a vehicle as high as an SUV. And it didn't hurt to have a lovely assistant at his beck and call.

Speaking of lovely assistants, he shot Niamh a grin and scooted over to make room for her to sit down after she made his chair disappear in the back of the SUV. Goliath sat patiently on the sidewalk until David gave him the command to "come". Without waiting for a second offer, Goliath leaped into the back of the vehicle and snuggled between David and Niamh. He laid his big, blocky head on David's lap, staying as far away from Maeve as he could.

"Shouldn't the dogs be contained in a crate or a seatbelt harness or something?" Niamh frowned.

"They'll be fine," Kameron shrugged. "We always travel this way."

"Well, I don't think it's safe or responsible."

"I'll keep that in mind. All aboard!" Kameron did a passable imitation of a train conductor, rolling up Watson's window and locking the doors and ignoring Niamh's disapproving glare. Shifting the SUV into gear, he started down the road. "Aimee, Siobhan, and Manny went over to Aimee's grandfather's place to see if he could do the license plate trace. We'll all meet up after at Manny's place and compare notes."

Kameron checked his rearview mirror and did a double take. "No way! No frigging way!"

"What? What's up?" David asked. Goliath sat up abruptly and placed his paw on David's shoulder. "What? Oh! I didn't mean get up! I meant what's up." Goliath tilted his head questioningly. David sighed. "Bah. Nevermind."

Niamh giggled when Goliath licked David's face. As she stroked Maeve's head, she said, "There's the dog whisperer—and then there's David, the dog befuddler."

"Don't be obvious, you two, but look behind you and tell me what you see." Kameron intently watched the rearview mirror.

Following Kameron's instructions to a T, David, Goliath, and Niamh whipped their heads around and looked back at the same time. Goliath put his paws on the back seat and leaned forward to get an even closer look at the vehicle following them. He whined worriedly.

David almost fell out of his seat. It was the white van, or at least a white van. What were the chances of having a white van following them down the street at 8:00 a.m.? Okay, given the number of white vans in Florida, the chances were probably good. But still the coincidence was creepy.

"Subtle, guys, real subtle. Webster's defines obvious as easily seen through because of a lack of subtlety. Me, I'd define it as you three at the moment. Why can't you all be more like Watson?" Kameron asked with an exasperated sigh.

"Well, excuse me for living, Kam, but you don't think that's the-with-a-capital-T white van, do you?" Niamh's voice quavered.

Standing on his seat, Watson stepped on the button, rolling down his window, and stuck his head out to get a better look at the vehicle. Ears flopping in the wind, jowls pulled back into a grin, Watson barked several times at the van following them.

"Et tu, Watson, et tu?" Kameron asked the Doberman before reaching across the console and grabbing Watson's collar to pull him back into the SUV. Hitting the button on his side, Kameron rolled up Watson's window and hit the window lock. Watson reached a paw up to his face and rubbed drool off his muzzle, splattering Kameron's leg with dog spit. Yawning, he circled three times before lying down on the seat. He looked anything but contrite.

"Maybe it is the van, maybe it isn't. Who can tell? Come on, guys, it's a white van. They're a dime a dozen. I mean, seriously, let's not freak out." David wasn't sure if he was trying to convince himself or his friends. He patted Goliath reassuringly and looked from Kameron to Niamh. Goliath growled deep in his throat.

"Well, I most certainly think it's the white van. Amazed that these imbeciles would be that stupid, but then again...they are dog fighters so obviously not that high on the IQ scale to begin with. Let's take some side roads and see if they follow us." Kameron didn't seem the least bit put-out at the prospect of being followed. In fact, it made Niamh nervous that Kameron was smiling for a change.

24

Pop Rocks!

With a squeal and a hiss, the bus shuddered to a stop. The driver grabbed the door lever and gave it a yank, snapping the doors open. Manny and Chiquita weaved past several elderly passengers who puttered along, taking their own sweet time down the aisle. Of course, to Manny and Chiquita, anyone not moving at warp speed was puttering along. Both of them had only two speeds: warp five and stop.

Next came Aimee with Hoku prancing obediently at her heels. Extending her arm, Aimee assisted one of the ladies off the bus while shooting Manny a withering glare. Manny stopped bouncing a ball for Chiquita long enough to give Aimee a what's-your-problem shrug.

"Thank you, dearie," the elderly lady said to Aimee and bent over slightly to pet Hoku on the head. "What a good little puppy you are." Hoku yodeled her agreement.

Chiquita dashed away from Manny. The Chihuahua yipped and bounced spastically in front of the lady, begging for attention, touching her leg one moment and bouncing in circles the next. Her little tail whipped in circles like a helicopter blade.

"Oh my! You're a frisky one, aren't you?" The lady gave Chiquita a small pat before moving away as Oenghus stepped off the bus. Oenghus led Siobhan carefully down the stairs. Holding onto Oenghus' harness, Siobhan used her stick to tap the edge of the step and the ground before she stepped down to the sidewalk. Oenghus led her to where Aimee and Manny waited. Together they marched up to the independent-living apartment complex where Aimee's grandfather resided.

Entering the building, they approached the front desk attended by a bored, matronly looking receptionist. Beady, little eyes peered over the top of thick, black-rimmed bifocals that sat at the tip of her witchishly crooked long nose. Aimee's first thought was that the lady looked like someone with a good sense of humor or poor eyesight had helped her put her wig and makeup on. Oops, maybe that wasn't a wig after all.

Like a skeptical child sitting on Santa's knee and contemplating tugging on his snowy beard, Aimee wondered if the receptionist's hair was real or fake. Thanks to the nattering of the cricket on her shoulder, she stifled the urge to reach over the counter and grab a fistful of hair to see if it would come off. Aimee always followed Jiminy's advice and did the right thing—not! *Is my nose growing any longer*, she wondered, self-consciously rubbing her nose to check its size.

"I'm here to visit Peter Whelan in Room 606," Aimee said.

"No pets allowed!" the tie-dyed wig-wearing receptionist exclaimed, making stabbing gestures toward the sign above her work station.

"Manny, you'll have to wait outside," Siobhan snickered.

"Bow wow." Manny barked and growled at Siobhan. All three canines looked at him with their heads cocked to the side, most likely wondering if Manny had finally gone off the deep end.

Missing the joke entirely, the receptionist continued with her tirade. "You can march right back out the door you came in. And whoever you're here to visit should have told you about our pet policy. Who do you think you are anyway?"

"Aimee Whelan, Peter Whelan's granddaughter," Aimee responded, only understanding about half of what the lady said. Trying hard to focus, she carefully watched the bright red lips opening and closing. *Wow! Way too much makeup, Granny. Nice smudge on those dentures, by the way! Get out, demons of stupidity! Must focus here.*

Aimee leaned over the counter. "I come here once a week to visit and I always bring Hoku with me. She's a service dog I'll have you know. Not a pet! Are you new? Maybe you need to get out your policy and procedures manual and look at page thirty-one, paragraph three, subsection two. It clearly states under the *no pets allowed rule* that there will be an exception made to service dogs for disabled individuals. In case you don't understand what that means, let me break it down for you. She's blind, I'm deaf, and he's dumb!"

"Hey!" Manny protested. "I represent that remark."

Siobhan tapped her cane sharply on the ground. "You realize this is all covered under the ADA, which is the Americans with Disabilities Act. 'Any guide dog, signal dog, or other animal individually trained to do work or perform tasks for the benefit of an individual with a disability, including but not limited to guiding individuals with impaired vision, alerting individuals with impaired hearing to intruders or sounds, providing minimal protection or rescue work, pulling a wheelchair, or fetching dropped items.' So, basically, where we go, our dogs are allowed to go...without question...and especially without harassment. We'd hate to alert the authorities and, of course, your boss!"

"Humph." The receptionist looked over her glasses, examining Manny and Siobhan with a critical eye. "And what's his disability?"

"I am so ready to put this on FaceBook!" Manny threatened, whipping out his cell phone and snapping a picture.

"Look, I don't have the time or the patience for this today." Aimee grabbed Manny's phone and began dialing her grandfather's phone number. "I'll call Sergeant Whelan, and you can explain to him why you're giving his hearing-impaired granddaughter and her friends such a hard time."

"How do I know you're deaf? You don't speak like someone who's deaf," the woman said, suspicion evident in her voice.

"Oh, no, she didn't!" Manny exclaimed, feigning shock. He looked at Aimee apprehensively wondering if a Hawaiian volcano would explode and rain the terror of Pele on this ignorant woman's head.

Aimee's face flushed with anger. "So, you have a lot of deaf friends, do you? You're an expert on the speech patterns of deaf people?"

"Well, I never..." the receptionist started to say before Aimee cut her off in mid-sentence.

"You either let us go or I'm calling Sergeant Whelan right now. And he gets seriously cranky when people make fun of the way I speak!"

Aimee's voice had gone up a few octaves and was garnering attention from other people in the waiting area. The receptionist could see a few people shaking their heads and looking at her in disapproval. Realizing that she was losing control of the situation, she switched gears before it could escalate any further.

"That will not be necessary, young lady. Aimee, is it?" The receptionist pushed her glasses back up her nose. "Sign the guestbook and be on your way. I am busy and don't have time for any more of this nonsense." With that remark, she turned away from the trio and began shuffling some papers on the desk in front of her.

Aimee felt several choice words slide toward the tip of her tongue, and to her credit, not one of them escaped. She angrily signed her name, making big sweeping strokes with the pen, nearly cutting the paper in two. Manny signed after her and then helped Siobhan by placing her hand with the pen on the paper so she could sign her name. Without another word, they left the front desk and headed for the elevators.

"Um, Aimee, how do you talk on the phone to your grandfather?" Manny faced Aimee, smiling mischievously and spoke while signing.

"Shut up, Manny! I was seeing red and couldn't think of anything else to say. Do you believe the nerve of that bi...."Aimee swallowed hard and took a deep breath. *Get control of yourself, girlfriend*, she told herself. *Now was not the time to go postal on some annoying old spinster. Maybe her wig was on too tight.* Giggling, she pushed the elevator button and leaned against the wall. Then she began laughing hysterically.

"What's so funny? Do I have something on my face again?" Siobhan asked, reaching up self-consciously to touch her cheek. Manny did the same thing at almost the same time.

"No, it's not your face. It's the wig!" Aimee said and laughed even harder. She should've pulled the old biddy's wig off to see what she would have to say about that. Damn that Jiminy! Whoever heard of having a cricket for a conscious anyway?

"But I'm not wearing a wig!" Siobhan protested.

Aimee looked from one to the other and continued laughing so hard she thought she was going to pee. Soon Manny and Siobhan began laughing with her.

After a few seconds, they all stopped, and Manny asked in a serious tone, "What were we laughing at anyway? Which one of you is wearing a wig?" That brought on another round of laughter that continued until the door opened, and they all walked out of the elevator, holding their sides and wiping their eyes.

Aimee's grandfather was ninety years old and still going strong. He exercised every day and was into natural medicines and health foods. Aimee loved him dearly, but lately, she had noticed that his mind wasn't as sharp as it used to be.

"Pops!" Aimee hugged her grandfather after he opened the door to let them in.

"Amelia, it's about time you got home." Pops had confused Aimee with her mother again.

"Pops, it's me, Aimee. Mom died four years ago." Aimee kissed his cheek affectionately.

"Right, I remember now. You look so much like your mother," Pops said with a sad glint in his eye. He seemed to accept Aimee's explanation easily today. "I should have known it was you since you're never without little Hoku!"

Pops patted his thigh, encouraging Hoku to come get attention. She warbled in greeting before standing up against his leg as she'd been taught. With her paws on his thigh, the Basenji threw her head back and yodeled loudly. Aimee's grandfather laughed at her exuberance as he lavished her with affection.

"And who do we have here?" he asked, reaching out to shake hands with Manny. Before he made contact with Manny's hand, he touched the top of Chiquita's head. She bounced quickly up and down in front of the boy seeking attention.

"Sit, Chiquita, sit. Show some manners," Manny scolded her gently. Obediently, she stopped her spastic bouncing, and with barely contained energy, she sat at Manny's feet, her body quivering, tail quickly whisking the floor.

"Pops, these are two friends of mine, Emmanuel Sanchez and Siobhan O'Rourke." Aimee introduced her friends one at a time. Pops shook Manny's hand and then reached for Siobhan, who stood there smiling. Unlike Chiquita, Oenghus sat obediently by her side. He yawned widely, looking bored.

"What's wrong with you? Didn't your parents teach you any manners, girly?" Pops asked somewhat crossly.

"Huh? Who? Me?" Siobhan asked, somewhat taken aback by the sudden change in Aimee's grandfather's tone.

"Pops, Siobhan is visually impaired," Aimee intervened quickly.

"Blind, you say? Is that why you have that stick and the big dog with you? I thought the stick was to beat the big dog when he didn't listen."

"Pops! I can't believe you said that!" Aimee responded before Siobhan could say anything. Siobhan stood in shock, not sure of how to address the cantankerous old man.

"Don't get your knickers in a twist! I was joking. Where's your sense of humor, you young whippersnapper?" Pops pinched Aimee's cheek affectionately. She grimaced and wondered what perverse thrill old people got by doing that.

Pops reached out and gave Siobhan a hug. "It's okay, honey, I guess I was the rude one then."

Siobhan stood awkwardly for a few seconds before deciding to go with it. She reached out and hugged him back and said, "It's okay. People make that mistake all the time."

Aimee's grandfather ushered the trio into the living room area and asked Aimee to go into the kitchen to get them some lemon water to drink. Manny picked up Chiquita and sat with her on a chair. Oenghus nudged Siobhan and guided her to the couch before lying down at her feet. Having been here numerous times before, Hoku sprawled out on the most comfortable chair in the room.

Aimee obediently went to the kitchen and got the drinks and checked out her grandfather's grocery supplies while she was there. Some seniors didn't eat well when they lived alone. Pops was not one, and his fridge and cupboards were well stocked. Aimee and her dad saw to that. They not only bought his groceries for him, they also pre-made some of his meals every Sunday so he didn't have to cook too much. He used the microwave oven like a champ.

Aimee returned from the kitchen with a tray of drinks and granola cookies for the humans and a bowl of water and dog biscuits for the canines. After everyone had taken what they wanted, Aimee cleared her throat and looked at her grandfather.

"Pops, do you still have any friends at the police station?"

"A few...at least I think I do," her grandfather replied. "Why do you ask?"

Aimee watched his lips carefully, making sure she heard/saw him correctly then proceeded to tell him the whole story about David and Goliath, and how she thought the white van was somehow involved. She finished by saying that they were hoping some of his police friends could do a license plate search. Her grandfather listened closely to the story, asking questions here and there to better understand what was going on. When Aimee finished, he picked up the phone and made a few phone calls.

"Hello, this is Sergeant Whelan. Can I speak with Lieutenant Dan Maters, please?" Pops was making his last phone call. "What? He retired ten years ago? Thank you for your time, young lady. Have a nice day." He hung up the phone and shook his head, a look of disgust on his face. "They're all gone, retired, ten years ago. Ten years. Has it been that long?" Pops looked at Aimee regretfully. "Sorry, honey, guess I'm a little out-dated."

He got up and walked into his bedroom, returning with a shoe box. Opening the box, he pulled out an old-style 38-special and laid it on the table and pushed it toward Manny. "Well, if you're going after those scumbags, you're going to need some protection," Aimee's grandfather said.

"Now that's what I'm talking about!" Manny said and reached for the 38-special.

"Pops!" Aimee smacked Manny's hand, pushing the gun back. "We can't take a gun! It would be totally illegal, not to mention dangerous! Manny doesn't even know how to use a gun."

"Hey, how do you know what I know how to do?" Manny protested indignantly. "I could be a government sniper for all you know."

"Puh-leez! You couldn't hurt a flea," Siobhan said. "Let alone sit still long enough to be a sniper."

"Young people today! Do you even know how to wipe yourselves after you go?" Pops sounded totally disgusted. He put the gun back in the box and pulled out a stun gun and some small pepper spray canisters. "Can you use these?"

"No, Pops. We'll call the police when we get some evidence on the dog fighters." Aimee was relieved when her grandfather put everything back into the shoebox. "We've gotta go now, Pops."

"Well, that's just as well. I have a shuffleboard competition in half an hour," Aimee's grandfather said, turning away from Aimee before heading to the door to see them out. Aimee and Hoku both got up and followed him. Aimee hugged Pops tightly at the door before exiting to the hallway. Oenghus stood up at Siobhan's command. Holding onto the harness handle, Siobhan said good-bye as the wolfhound led her out. Manny got up last and reached into the shoebox. He grabbed something he thought might come in handy and stuffed it quickly into his pocket. It's not like he was stealing since Aimee's grandfather had offered it to him.

Chiquita peered at Manny and whined. Manny shook his head at her. "Shush, Chiquita. It's our little secret."

25

Banshee's Wail

Kameron continued driving casually down US-19 where the traffic was heavy. He tried not to drive suspiciously. No weaving in and out of traffic, sticking to the middle lane, and keeping to the speed limit. So far the white van was still on their tail, staying about four cars back.

"I think we should call the police if we're being followed," Niamh repeated for the hundredth time. She reached into the pouch and stroked Maeve's head, more for her own comfort than the ferret's.

"Yeah, right! We'll say, 'Hi! We're being followed by a white van—send out the troops!'" David couldn't hide his sarcasm. "I think they'd hang up on us, Niamh. Chill. They haven't actually tried to do anything yet."

"I think David's right, Niamh. The police would laugh at us. Besides, I can lose them any time I need to. Hang on! I'm gonna try something." Kameron's hazel eyes gleamed mischievously.

Maneuvering the SUV into the right lane, Kameron slammed on the brakes. He whipped into a gas station parking lot, and the SUV listed to its side like a pirate ship in heavy seas. After the white van sped past them, he peeled the vehicle back out into traffic. Like any good sea captain, Kameron spun the wheel, causing the SUV to right itself with a stomach-dropping bounce.

Feeling seasick, David reached up and latched onto the J-bar above the window. Thankfully, Niamh didn't notice his cowardice as she clutched onto her own bar for dear life, her eyes squeezed shut. David soon realized the screeching was no longer coming from the SUV's tires but from Niamh.

Poor Goliath, not having a J-bar to grab, flipped sideways onto Niamh's knees with his head thumping against Maeve's pouch. Before he could right himself, an indignant ferret poked her head out and gave him a glare that seemed to say, "Get your fat head off me!" Hissing, she bit the end of his tender nose before diving back into the safety of her pouch. With a yelp, Goliath jumped back from Niamh and onto David's lap.

Captain Kameron and his first mate Watson fared better in the front seat. Legs braced wide apart, Watson calmly rode the storm like an old seadog. *Obviously, this isn't his maiden voyage with the Dread Pirate Kameron,* David thought.

"Now! Let's see who's in that van, shall we?" Kameron hit the accelerator, pulling up behind the vehicle. "David, get a picture of the license plate."

"Aye, aye, Captain! But go easy on the wheel, I'm about to heave, me hardee."

"What are you talking about now?" Kameron asked, totally perplexed by David's randomness.

"Never mind." Releasing his J-bar and flexing his fingers to get the circulation back, David took out his phone and quickly pulled up his camera app. He snapped off a few quick shots before Kameron whipped the SUV into the left passing lane.

"I can't see anything on this side. The windows are tinted," David complained.

"I've got an idea," Kameron said, changing lanes. "Niamh, if you could open your eyes for a second and stop screaming like a banshee, you could get out your cell phone and get a picture of these creeps. When I pull up close beside them, try to snap off a few shots without being obvious... you know... subtle like."

Slowly opening her eyes, Niamh stopped screaming and smiled sheepishly. "If you didn't drive like a maniac, I wouldn't be screaming like a banshee. Banshees are harbingers of death. So keep that in mind the next time you decide to pull a Ricky Bobby!"

"Thank you, mighty Morrigan. Queen of the Banshees!" David looked up from reviewing his camera photos and grinned at Niamh. "Can we get on with the car chase now, people? Oh! I got the license plate."

David was thinking James Bond-style now. Maybe when Kameron pulled alongside the van, he could pull himself out the window and climb on top of the van. Humming the theme song to *Mission Impossible*, Niamh held her pink Hello Kitty blinged phone out in front of her as Kameron pulled the SUV alongside the van. David looked down at the roadway passing by at fifty-five miles an hour and lost some of his gusto. *Okay, maybe a few pictures and let the police handle the rest*, he thought, leaning back into his seat. After all, unlike James Bond, he didn't have a stunt double. Maybe when they made the movie of his life . . . his thoughts were rudely interrupted.

"David, can you see into the van? The windows are tinted on this side, too." Niamh shook David's arm.

"Huh?" David had always been verbally gifted around girls. It was part of his charm. "What? Oh, yeah, the van. Nope, not a thing. I can't see a thing."

The van made a lane change to the right, then did a quick turn at the next intersection, leaving the SUV behind. Realizing he missed the turn, Kameron got into the right lane and gunned the engine as he headed down the street. Stopping at the red light, everyone peered down the street to the right, almost expecting the van to be sitting there waiting for them.

"Sorry, guys. Looks like I lost them." Kameron sounded miffed.

Watson growled menacingly and turned to face Kameron. Suddenly, a head poked through the window. Yelping, Kameron raised his hands defensively and fell back from the intruder. David barely managed to latch onto Goliath's collar before the pit bull could lunge into the front seat.

26

Hang Dog

Aimee, Manny, and Siobhan were seriously bummed out after leaving Pop's place. Aimee had been so sure Pops could help them. She hadn't considered the possibility he wouldn't be able to solve her problem. So, what to do now?

"Well, that sucks." Manny had a knack for stating the obvious. "So, what's the plan, Stan?"

"Let's get on the bus, Gus," Siobhan chimed in.

Aimee rolled her eyes. "Let's get back on track, Jack!"

"Maybe we can go to the police and let them follow up on it," Manny said, ending their rhyming session.

"Aimee, what about Greta and her policeman? Maybe Officer So-and-So can help us?" Siobhan tapped her cane against the bus stop bench. "If only we could think of some other reason why we needed the license plate number."

"Siobhan, you're a genius! We can tell them the story about your cane getting whacked by an erratic driver and how you want to send him a bill or something like that." Aimee grabbed Siobhan's arms and swung her around in a circle.

Manny stood back and eyed the two girls, not sure whether to join in or head for safety. Oenghus sat with a perplexed look on his face and woofed loudly, while Chiquita joined the girls, yipping and jumping at their heels. Not to be left out, Hoku madly dashed around their ankles.

Releasing Siobhan, Aimee continued excitedly, "Officer Slim Jim can do it! I bet you Greta can convince him to help."

Two buses and thirty minutes later, Aimee opened the door to the Animal Rescue Co.

"This is where you work, Aimee?" Manny asked. She walked past without responding. "Oops, keep forgetting she can't hear," he said, shrugging his shoulders apologetically at Siobhan before remembering she couldn't see him. "Gah, you two are gonna drive me nuts!"

Siobhan giggled and slapped Manny accurately on the arm. Aimee turned around in time to see Manny jump back and stick his tongue out at Siobhan. Shaking her head, Aimee smacked him on the other arm and handed him Hoku's leash. She gave him a push towards the waiting area as she proceeded to the back rooms where the animals were kept.

Greta was in the holding area working with the young pit bull Smiley. Smiley bounced over to Aimee and tapped her playfully on the leg with his paw then dropped on his belly to get patted. Greta called him to her, and he responded immediately, coming back and sitting at her feet, his tail sweeping the floor clean of dirt behind him.

"Good boy, good boy, Smiley." Greta's eyes were puffy like she had been crying, which would be weird since Greta was a pretty tough nut.

"Is everything okay, Greta?" Aimee was genuinely concerned for her friend.

"Hi, pumpkin. No! Everything is not okay." Greta wiped her sleeve across her face, drying her eyes somewhat.

"What's up?" Aimee was uncomfortable being around adults when they cried—it felt weird and disconcerting.

"The director decided today that No. 9 is not going to be a suitable candidate for adoption because of his extreme dog aggression. He has such a strong prey drive...and he wouldn't be safe in the general public. Oh, he's a total love bug with people...but not a fan of dogs. Who can we trust him with so he doesn't potentially hurt or kill another dog or dogs?" Greta blew her nose into a tissue she had grabbed from the table.

"I'm so sorry, Greta. This totally sucks!" Aimee started crying. Not being adoptable was a death sentence for No. 9. She walked over and gave Greta a hug, then dropped down on the floor and buried her face in Smiley's fur. For his part, Smiley gently licked Aimee's hand and snuggled as close to her as he could.

After crying for a while, Aimee remembered why she was here and her friends sitting outside waiting for her. Getting back to her feet, she wiped her face and nose with a tissue, then stood directly in front of Greta.

"I need a favor, Greta." Aimee was more determined now than ever to get these guys and shut down their operation for good. Instead of telling Greta the lie they had concocted, she decided to go for the truth.

Greta looked at her and smiled sadly. "What do you need?"

"Well, it's a long story. You have to promise it'll be our secret or I won't tell you."

"Before I promise, I have to know if it's illegal."

"It's not illegal. It's a story about David and his special dog."

Greta looked surprised. "Our David? He has a dog? Where did he get a dog? Why didn't he adopt one from here!"

"Well, Greta, that's part of the secret. Seriously, you have to promise not to rat us out, and you have to help me help David."

Greta and Aimee had been friends for a while and Greta trusted Aimee. She thought of Aimee like a little sister and would do anything to help her if she truly needed it. She knew Aimee well enough to know the teen wouldn't involve her in anything illegal. "Okay, pumpkin, okay. I promise. Now spill the sauerkraut and don't leave anything out!"

Aimee started from the beginning and told Greta the whole story about David and Goliath and the white van. When she finished, Greta had an inscrutable look on her face. At that moment Aimee's cell phone began to vibrate with an incoming text message.

27

Papyrophobia

P aper? You wanna buy a paper?" the pimply faced kid asked after Kameron stopped screaming.

"Nope. We don't need a paper today. Don't mind the girly man in the front seat. He has papyrophobia." Niamh waved at the boy from the backseat. "Thanks anyway!"

The paperboy looked through the window and gave Niamh a broken-toothed smile before shrugging and moving on to the next vehicle. Kameron could hear him mutter as he walked away, "Freakin' weirdoes."

Niamh pushed the back of Kameron's seat and asked, "Who's the banshee now?"

"I think I dropped a load in my pants." David laughed weakly and released his grip on Goliath's collar. "I guess things were getting a little tense there." Goliath lost interest as soon as he realized the paperboy wasn't a threat. With a half-hearted bark, Goliath circled three times before lying back down next to David.

"Papyrophobia?" Kameron asked, glaring at Niamh before slowly pulling out into the intersection.

"Hello! Fear of paper!"

David laughed before stating to no one in particular, "I better text Aimee and give her the license plate number so the police will be able to find the address easier."

"We have the license plate number. Let's go put the surveillance equipment up and then meet the others." Niamh shuddered. "This whole thing's given me the willies!"

"Good idea." Kameron for once was not going to argue. It was getting late and the lab would be open soon. If they didn't put the equipment in before lunch, they would have to wait another whole day. Who knows what torture those poor animals were being subjected to in the name of cosmetics?

It didn't take long to get to the lab from where they were. David opened his bag and took out the equipment, handing the surveillance camera to Niamh. Flipping open his laptop, he tested everything one last time before showing Kameron and Niamh what they needed to do.

"Stay, Watson," Kameron commanded his sidekick before getting out of the SUV. Watson heaved a deep sigh, curled up on the seat, and went to sleep.

Niamh pulled Maeve's pouch over her head and laid it on her seat as she got out of the vehicle. Giving David and Goliath a stern look, she warned them, "Do not, under any circumstances, let Goliath step on my baby!"

David snapped Goliath's leash on and pulled him closer. "Ten-four on that, Mama Bear. Not to worry. The situation's under control."

"You better see that it is." Niamh left the threat hanging. David nodded and tightened his grip on Goliath's leash. Niamh glared at David one last time before shutting the door and moving to the back of the vehicle.

Kameron walked around to the back of the SUV and got out two bright orange vests. He handed one to Niamh and put on the other. Then he picked up two orange work helmets, the kind construction or electrical workers wore. He put one helmet on and got out a tool belt, then turned and handed the other helmet to Niamh.

"Um, I don't think so," Niamh said, putting a hand on one hip while shaking her index finger in the air in front of Kameron's face. "Not on this head. I don't do construction worker, sorry."

Kameron plopped the helmet on her head and walked around to David's side of the SUV.

To her credit, Niamh stood speechless for at least a couple of seconds before she exploded. "How dare you, jerk! I said no way and no means NO!"

Niamh followed Kameron and grabbed his arm, turning him around to face her wrath. Both Kameron and David looked at Niamh with puzzled expressions.

Niamh realized she was overreacting. Sometimes she hated her Irish temper. Refusing to let her temper get the best of her, she simply handed the helmet back to Kameron instead of throwing it at him and turned away from him, childishly crossing her arms in front of her chest and pouting.

"Um, yeah, anyways, as I was saying, put this Bluetooth earpiece on, and I will guide you through the installation process. Niamh, are you in or out?" David didn't have the time or patience to be subtle or understanding. Guess he wasn't going to be one of those sensitive guys girls always said they wanted. Funny that... even though most girls said they wanted a sensitive guy, none of them actually ever dated sensitive guys—go figure.

"Fine. I'll wear the stupid helmet this time, but next time, get someone else to be your lookout." Niamh grabbed the helmet back and walked across the street without looking for traffic. Luckily, there were no cars coming either way.

"Whatever," Kameron muttered. He followed closely behind her and headed for the telephone pole they had picked out for the installation. Strapping on his spikes, Kameron wrapped his utility belt around the pole and started to climb. When he reached the top, he spoke into the Bluetooth, and David began giving him instructions for the camera placement.

Niamh stood on the sidewalk below Kameron's position and practiced waving her sign back and forth, pretending there was someone there. She explained to the imaginary person that there was a power outage and that they would have to walk carefully to the other side of the street.

This continued for several seconds until Kameron, exasperated, shouted down at her, "Will you shut up! You're the lookout. You're not trying out for a major motion picture."

"Well, excuse me for living!" Niamh said, looking up at Kameron who seemed oblivious to her usual charms.

The whole process of setting up the surveillance equipment took less than fifteen minutes. When everything was finished, David remotely activated the camera and focused the lens on the back door of the lab.

"Okay, that's a wrap. Get down from there and let's get outta here." David spoke into his Bluetooth and was answered with a ten-four by Kameron. He could hear Niamh loudly humming the *Mission Impossible* song in the background. Watson, hearing his guardian's voice, sat up and looked out the window whining softly. He impatiently waited for Kameron to return. His whole body wiggled and wagged, as Kameron and Niamh finally approached the SUV.

Kameron and Niamh took off their gear and stowed it in the back before climbing into the vehicle. Niamh picked up Maeve's pouch and slipped it back over her shoulders. As the pouch nestled against Niamh's chest, Maeve popped her head out and gave Niamh a few welcoming kisses. Reassured that Maeve was okay, Niamh glanced over to see what David was up to.

Oblivious to the fact that he was being scrutinized, David adjusted the zoom and focus on the camera they had installed. Niamh leaned over Goliath for a peek, placing her hand on David's lap for support. David looked at her and smiled uncomfortably. He sighed. Girls made him nervous for some reason.

Kameron drove the SUV out into the street and stopped at the intersection. While he waited for the light to turn green, he switched on the radio and quickly flipped through the stations, looking for some music. No one in the SUV noticed the white van pulling up beside them in the left lane. The passenger window rolled down, and a pistol barrel slowly moved out, pointing directly at Kameron.

28

Rainbow Bridge

Brutus liked the lady who entered his kennel. She spoke softly, always gave him treats, and scratched all his itchy spots. Today she had a sad smell on her and her face was wet. He gently licked her tears when she bent down to attach his leash. Usually a leash meant fighting but not here. Here fighting was not allowed. Brutus had never been near so many other dogs and not commanded to fight. He was confused by this place. Reaching into her pocket, the woman took out his favorite squeaky toy. He carefully took it from her hand.

The nice lady led him down a long hallway and into a room that smelled strongly of medicine and sweat and other dogs and cats. Brutus knew the smell of medicine. His old master had used many different smelling things on him when he had been injured in numerous fights. Some things hurt while others felt good. Brutus shivered and cowered down as the lady tugged on his leash. Brutus trusted the lady, but this place smelled of death. Brutus had known death. He had lived with dead things all around him most of his life, and he hated the smell. He feared the smell.

The lady talked softly to him, encouraging him to follow her. He wanted to please her, so he followed even though he was scared. The lady was not like his old master. She didn't punch him or kick him or twist wire collars around his neck until he couldn't breathe. She always talked softly and played with him. He had never played before and didn't know what to do at first, but eventually, he understood what she wanted. She laughed. He liked hearing her laugh. He wanted to please the lady. He liked her. He especially liked when the lady threw his favorite squeaky toy and he would bring it back to her. It never ceased to amaze him that no matter how often he brought it to her, she would throw it away again...and again...and again. She was a lot of fun. But today she didn't throw anything for him but instead stroked his face and hugged him.

Soon other people came into the room wearing white coats. Brutus didn't like the white-coats; they poked sharp things in him and hurt him. Brutus growled warningly at the white-coats. The nice lady patted his head reassuringly and he quieted down. He trusted the lady but he was afraid. She led him to a comfortable blanket and sat down in front of him. Holding his collar firmly in both hands, the nice lady kept talking to him in a calm husky voice that soothed him. He began to relax when he felt a sharp prick in his back leg. One of the white-coats had hurt him again. Growling, he tried to turn to face the white-coat, but the lady held him tightly.

Then without warning, his legs buckled, and he slid down onto the nice lady's lap. He looked up at the only person who had ever been kind to him and tried to lick her hand, but his tongue wouldn't move. Brutus didn't understand why he couldn't move. He was afraid and began to whine. The lady was still there. She sang to him. He could feel her stroking his neck and back. Her hands sliding sweetly over his jowls and massaging his ears. Her comforting scent lingered in the air around him, but he couldn't see her anymore as his vision faded. Her soft crying and soothing voice were the last sounds he heard. With a deep sigh, he closed his eyes and drifted off into eternal sleep.

"Bye, bye, No. 9, my sweet," Greta whispered, her voice hitching. The vet gave Greta's shoulder a sympathetic squeeze. "Finally, you are in a safe place and will be at peace. You will never have to fight or be hungry or feel pain. And most importantly, no human will ever be able to abuse you ever again. I'll see you at the Rainbow Bridge, my sweet, sweet boy."

After seeing to the cremation of No. 9's body, Greta went to her desk, picked up the phone, and stabbed the keypad buttons purposefully. She was on a mission and would not rest until the men responsible for abusing dogs like No. 9 were all locked up and rotting in jail.

"Hello, Slimka here. How can I help you?" Officer Slimka's deep baritone voice asked.

The sound of Mike's voice always turned Greta's legs to mush. Good thing she was sitting down. Greta knew she couldn't ask Mike to run a license plate check on someone. And she sure wasn't going to tell him Aimee's story as she had promised. This left her with a real moral dilemma. She couldn't lie to Mike since he was a good friend. What she finally concocted was a story she thought was close enough to the truth and believable enough that Mike would help. David had sent the rest of the license plate number by text message, so it shouldn't be too hard to track.

"Hallo, mein schätzchen," Greta said teasingly into the phone. "It's Greta over here at the Animal Rescue Co. How are you today?"

"Hanging in there," Mike replied noncommittally. "Greta, how can I help you?"

Greta went through her story about a dog owner who was seen abandoning a dog on the side of the road and how a group of kids had gotten his license plate number and given it to Greta. Greta hoped Officer Slimka could run a plate check for her, so she could pay the owner a visit to see if they should press charges.

"I can do that for you, Greta. Do you want a squad car to go by with you?" Mike was always the practical one.

"I want to check out the story first, Mike, in case the kids got the wrong number or something." Greta wanted these guys bad but not only on abandonment charges. She wanted to catch them red-handed at a dog fight, and this time they wouldn't be getting away with any dogs. These scum bags needed to do some serious jail time. No. 9's last minutes where vividly etched in her mind as she hung up the phone and got out her cell phone to let Aimee know everything had gone as planned.

29

Get Lost!

Niamh, giving her eyes a break from the computer screen, looked out the driver's side window and let out another ear-piercing banshee scream. For a little person, she had a big, big voice. Maeve disappeared inside the safety of her pouch carrier. Both David and Kameron covered their ears and looked at her. Watson snarled and moved toward Kameron, his head over the boy's shoulder. Goliath, growling threateningly, climbed over David and tried to claw his way out the back window.

Kameron looked to his left and saw the gun barrel pointing at his head at the same time the traffic light turned green. Not considering the danger, he gunned the accelerator, sending the SUV barreling into the intersection, cutting off a white Bronco attempting to run the red light. The Bronco screeched to a halt and Kameron banged on the horn. He skillfully maneuvered the SUV around the other vehicle before heading down the street, leaving the white van temporarily stuck at the intersection.

David tried to calm Goliath down as Kameron pushed Watson back into the passenger seat. "That's it, Buddy. You're definitely getting a harness."

"I told you it was dangerous to have dogs loose in the car! But did you listen to me? No..." Niamh, of course, couldn't resist taunting.

"So, you think loose dogs are more dangerous than a gun pointed at us?" Kameron asked, surprisingly calm and level-headed.

"A gun?" David squeaked. Goliath gave a warning woof from the back, still looking out the window.

After a few blocks, Kameron eased up on the accelerator and checked his rearview mirror. "I think we lost them."

"Oh my God! They were going to shoot us!" Niamh was beside herself. "That's it. I don't care what you guys say! I'm calling the police." She whipped out her cell phone and started dialing 911.

"No, don't do that, Niamh," Kameron said, casually for someone who had almost been shot a few minutes ago. "That wasn't a real gun. It was a dart gun. They were trying to scare us."

"You're just saying that!" Niamh was not ready to be pacified yet. Her thumb remained poised over the one button.

"How do you know it was a dart gun, Kam?" David asked.

"Duh, remember? My dad is retired military?" Kameron said. "I could tell you more, but then I'd have to kill you."

"Yeah, okay, Mr. Bond. Seriously, how do you know it was a dart gun?" David asked a second time.

"Dad has one like it at home," Kameron stated. "He does some large animal extraction work from time to time that requires a precision instrument that can efficiently neutralize the threat without endangering the target."

"Oh, cool!" David nodded.

"Could you say that again in English instead of in geek speak, please?" Niamh blinked repeatedly as if that would help her better understand Kameron.

"Whatever. Dad uses a dart gun to tranquilize animals that stray into human territory. He helped relocate two Florida panthers on Alligator Alley last week." Kameron turned down a side street and checked his rearview mirror again.

David looked over his shoulder as a white van suddenly rounded the corner behind them. He didn't want Kameron to get a speeding ticket or smash up his dad's SUV, but he was beginning to get worried about the people tailing them. Maybe they were psychopaths after all. For a moment he was tempted to let Niamh call 911. Fortunately, the moment passed. He came up with a brilliant plan instead. Okay, maybe not totally brilliant but workable...he hoped.

"Kam, our company's back," David said, tapping Kameron on the back. "This time I have a plan."

David quickly filled them in on his plan. Kameron kept driving as if he hadn't noticed the van was back. Heading nowhere in particular, he kept to the speed limit and took every right turn he came to as David had instructed. Before long the van pulled farther and farther behind as their pursuers tried to be inconspicuous.

"It's working." David checked and didn't see the white van. "Okay. After the next turn, follow the plan."

"Roger that," Kameron saluted David in the rearview mirror.

"Your plan better work, David. 'Cos if you guys get me killed, my mum and dad are going to kill you both! We have IRA connections, you know!" Niamh threatened, half-jokingly.

"Well, good thing you're a twin. And if one of you disappears, your parents will still have one left." David winked at Niamh.

Niamh heaved a deep sigh, which of course they also ignored. *Boys were such stupid Neanderthals most of time, even smart ones like these two. David was cute though—in that needs-someone-to-take-care-of-him way. Bet he wouldn't like that thought.* Niamh giggled. David looked at her with raised eyebrows. She looked away and stifled more giggles. Goliath reached over and licked her face as if sharing the joke. Niamh only laughed harder and hugged his head. "You know what I'm talking about. Don't you, Goliath?"

After taking the next right, Kameron gunned the accelerator and sped down the street. Hitting the brakes hard, he whipped the SUV into a service lane and then pulled into someone's driveway, hiding behind a pickup truck.

Looking out the side window, David watched the white van pass the service lane and head down the street toward the next right-hand turn without realizing they had lost their prey.

"Alright!" David and Kameron did a high-five. Niamh tried to give David a high-five but missed and ended up smacking him on the forehead instead. She shrugged at him and smiled sheepishly. David smiled back and rubbed his aching forehead. Who could understand girls?

Goliath snuggled closer to David and whined. David patted him reassuringly on the head and spoke softly to his best friend. "Don't worry, buddy. No one's ever going to hurt you again as long as I'm alive."

David meant every word. He realized at that moment how strongly he felt about what had been done to his best friend. He was more determined than ever to get those scumbags put behind bars for a long, long time.

Kameron drove the SUV out of the service lane and took David home. He parked next to the curb outside of David's house and got out to take the wheelchair from the back. David opened the door, swung his legs out of the SUV, and waited for his wheels. Kameron unfolded the wheelchair and pushed it close to David. First putting his legs on the ground and then grabbing the inside door handle and back of the front seat, David gave a strong heave and transferred himself back into his chair. It never ceased to amaze him how lost he felt without his wheels underneath him.

Niamh gave Goliath a hug and then waved goodbye to David. At David's command, Goliath jumped down beside him and waited, his stumpy tail vibrating with anticipation.

"See you tomorrow morning at Manny's?" Kameron asked David, climbing back into the vehicle.

"Yup, yup." David pulled the laptop out of his backpack and handed it to Niamh. "Give this to Aimee when you get to Manny's?"

"Say please?" Niamh teased.

"Please with sugar and mustard on top." David stuck out his tongue.

"Ewww, gross." Niamh scrunched up her face and picked up the laptop.

"Get a room, you two," Kameron interjected.

David looked at Kameron then back at Niamh and felt his face redden. Had he looked closer, he would have noticed that hers was a few shades darker than his. It was time to go. Saying a final goodbye, he wheeled his chair over the curb and headed toward the house with Goliath following. As the SUV drove off, David opened the front door and wheeled into the house looking for his dad.

As it turned out, Dad's big surprise was a pair of kayaks. David had mentioned a few weeks ago that he'd like to learn how to kayak. So, his dad had gone to a local supplier, rented two kayaks, and had paid for lessons for the two of them. David didn't mention that his main reason for wanting to kayak was that Aimee was somewhat of an expert kayaker. Aimee's dad was a marine biologist who worked for Stoerm Enterprises, a privately funded marine science center. Aimee spent a lot of her free time (not that she had a lot between the shelter and her sports) helping her dad and going out sailing with his nemesis for her attention, Skyler Stoerm.

The supplier had a pool where they taught lessons and would also take people out on the open water when they were ready. David and his dad spent the rest of the day in the pool learning the basics of paddling, steering, and even rolling and righting a kayak. David couldn't remember the last time he and his dad had so much fun together.

30

Do It!

By ten a.m. everyone but David had arrived at Manny's house. Niamh gave Aimee David's laptop then went over to sit with Siobhan who played fetch with Oenghus. No one knew exactly how Siobhan was able to know where things were when she couldn't see them. It was like she had some weird spooky sixth sense, especially at night when her extremely limited vision was even more limited. Niamh reached inside her front pouch and idly scratched Maeve's little head.

Manny played tug of war with Watson. The Doberman gave the rope toy a good shake when out of nowhere little Chiquita attacked. Snarling viciously, she ran under Watson, playfully chewing on his legs. Distracted, Watson turned to woof at the quick Chihuahua, losing his grip on the rope toy. Taking advantage of Chiquita's surprise attack, Manny grabbed the rope out of the Doberman's mouth, holding it up triumphantly. Chiquita ran for cover behind her guardian, peeking out between his legs at the confused Watson.

"Hey! No fair! You guys cheated," Niamh shouted at Manny. "Two against one isn't fair, is it, boy?"

Watson looked at Kameron and let out a whine as if he agreed. Everyone laughed at the confused Dobie as he eyed the rope toy, no doubt wondering how his royal highness had lost against the puny human and his tiny mutt.

Manny tossed the rope toy for Watson and Chiquita to run after and came over to sit beside the twins. He sat for less than a minute before he started tapping his foot and running his fingers through his hair.

"Don't you ever sit still?" Niamh asked Manny.

"Not if I can help it," Manny shot back, crossing his arms across his chest to keep them from moving. Siobhan snickered and reached down to give Oenghus' belly a good rub.

"He has ADHD, Niamh. What do you expect?" Siobhan explained.

"Yeah, well, where is the Ritalin when you need it?" Niamh asked cleverly.

"Ouch, don't even say that jokingly." Manny had bad memories of going to doctors' offices and listening to them explain to his mother that Ritalin would be the best thing for him. He crossed and uncrossed his legs several times, constantly adjusting his position. Thankfully, his parents had decided to try diet and exercise before drugs.

"Sorry. I was joking."

Niamh sighed and stood up. She walked to where Aimee and Kameron huddled around the laptop. Niamh looked over Aimee's shoulder at the streaming video coming in from the spy camera she'd helped set up the other day.

Chiquita bounced over to Niamh and jumped up onto her lap without being invited. Being small and cute had its perks. You could get away with little transgressions as long as you sucked up a lot—and the little Chihuahua was a master at sucking up. Chiquita barked at the pouch until Maeve popped her fuzzy little head out.

"You wanna play, huh?" Niamh laughed at Chiquita. Opening the pouch, she let Maeve out. With a loud dook and two spastic, wiggling, sideways bounces, Maeve did the weasel war dance around the yapping Chihuahua. Before long, the two were playing on the ground under Niamh's watchful eye.

The morning passed by uneventfully. By lunchtime everyone was wondering where David was, so Aimee sent him a text message. **Where R U?**

Right behind U, David texted back. He let go of Goliath's harness and wheeled up behind Aimee who jumped after he touched her shoulder.

"Dork!" She aimed a punch at his arm but missed because Goliath intercepted, inserting his big blocky head between the two. Goliath happily licked Aimee's closed fist in an enthusiastic greeting. "Oh, silly butt! I wasn't gonna hurt your boy... much!"

"You couldn't hurt me if you tried...not with these guns!" David scoffed, flexing his biceps.

"Oooh! Has someone been working out?" Aimee mocked.

"Do you two need some alone time? There's a half dozen empty kennels over there," Siobhan snickered, pointing in the opposite direction of the empty boarding kennels.

Niamh threw her twin a withering glare, which of course was completely wasted.

"Shut up," Aimee laughed.

David's face turned several shades of red.

Quickly changing the topic, Niamh touched Aimee on the shoulder to get her to look then asked. "Can you see anything on the spy camera yet, Aimee?"

"Yeah, is anything going down yet?" David was eager to change the topic as well.

"Yes and no," was Aimee's cryptic reply.

"Um, which is it? Yes or no?" Kameron asked and peered over Aimee's shoulder when she didn't reply. Out of sight and out of hearing, he sighed.

Aimee was looking at David and so she didn't hear Kameron's question. Before he could move in front of her or sign his question, she saw something onscreen.

"Everyone come over here and look at this!" Aimee squealed excitedly, startling Hoku who had been napping at her feet. Goliath woofed at her excited tone and jumped up, placing his front paws on the picnic table to peer at the laptop.

"Sure, I'll be right there." Siobhan stood up, cane in hand, and walked over to stand behind Aimee, with Oenghus trailing closely behind her. "Now would you mind telling me what I'm looking at since I left my reading glasses at home?"

"It's the white van again. I don't believe it! If those are the same guys, they so need to go to jail!" David said.

Goliath growled. He leaned forward and barked at the two men on screen.

"Jerks! I bet they have cats in those carriers." Aimee was getting angrier by the minute. "We need to do something!"

"What sleazy looking guys," Niamh stated unnecessarily, picking up Maeve who was trying to bite her big toe.

"Come on, you guys, blind girl over here can't see them. Can someone describe them to me already?" Siobhan demanded, as Watson returned with the rope toy and tried to entice Oenghus to play. Hearing Oenghus' playful whine, she patted his neck and said, "Go free."

David tapped Aimee's shoulder to get her attention and signed to her that she needed to describe what she saw online to Siobhan. Aimee grinned sheepishly at him and mouthed, "My bad!" before saying out loud, "Well, one of them is a white guy with a scruffy looking face, at least six feet tall. Believe it or not, this guy is all business in the front and a party in the back! And if you didn't get that reference, he's sporting a serious mullet. Can you say redneck? He looks mean. Not only is he a sadistic animal abuser, he's fashion disabled!"

Aimee made the camera zoom in. "The other one is a short, stocky guy and looks like the hired hand from a dude ranch. In fact he's so bow-legged, he looks like one of those cowboy action figures that you slip on and off a plastic horse. He looks like a reject from those old spaghetti Westerns. He even has a big old mustache and a cowboy hat on. All he needs now to complete his outfit is a poncho and he's all set to star with Clint Eastwood."

David laughed at Aimee's commentary. Goliath whined as he watched Oenghus chase Watson around the yard. "You wanna go play, too? Okay, Goliath. Go free!"

Goliath streaked away, Chiquita following closely at his heels since Maeve had abandoned her.

"That dude in no way is a representation of my people," Manny added, somewhat defensively.

"And that loser with the mullet is in no way a representation of my people either! And I love country music!" Niamh chimed in.

"Those guys are in no way a representation of human beings period," Siobhan corrected them both. "So, how are we going to take these jerks down?"

"I think we need to call Greta, and she can get the Animal Rescue Co. and the cops involved," Kameron suggested.

"The cops can't do anything, Kam. There's no law against using poor, defenseless pets for experimentation," Siobhan said angrily.

"This sucks. We need to go kick some butt!" Manny paced back and forth.

"We need to plan and not go off half-cocked." David had already given it some thought and had the beginnings of a brilliant snatch-and-grab plan. At least he thought it was brilliant. Okay, on reflection, maybe it was a good blueprint for a plan. Okay, okay, he had an idea that might work, maybe... hopefully.

"What if we take the video tapes to the police and show them the guys taking the cages into the lab?" Niamh asked.

This started a debate on the merits of going to the police versus rescuing the animals themselves. As far as Manny was concerned, this was talking way too much and taking way too long. Frustrated, he tapped Siobhan on the shoulder, and the two of them quietly walked away from the discussion.

"Come on. I'm tired of discussing this. Let's go free some animals," Manny whispered in Siobhan's ear."

"How are we going to get there?" Siobhan whispered back.

"We'll take my wheels."

"But what about Oenghus? Chiquita might fit on your bike, but he sure won't."

"Don't worry about it. We'll leave them with the others. Come on. It's not like it's the first time we've gone out without them. And technically it's not like we're leaving them alone. The gang's here. It's all talk and no action. They're talking the rescue to death. Besides with all the yammering they're doing, we'll be back before they even know we're gone."

Manny and Siobhan covertly slipped through the gate and around to the front of the house where he had parked his moped. Oenghus and Chiquita continued to play, oblivious to the fact their guardians had fled the scene.

Meanwhile everyone else still argued over how best to go after the bad guys. They had never discussed what they would do if or when they caught the bad guys in the act. The plan had been to get video of lab animals entering the building. No one had thought about what to do after that. Now that the problem stared them right in the face, they were not at all sure which direction to take.

"Anyone see Siobhan?" Niamh asked.

Everyone looked around the backyard, but Siobhan was nowhere to be found.

"And Manny..." Aimee said.

"You don't think they went to the lab without us, do you?" David asked, not expecting an answer. David, who had been signing as much of the conversation as he could to Aimee, cracked his knuckles. "That'd be a long walk, doncha think?"

Kameron smirked. "Yeah, it might be. If Manny didn't have a moped."

"Oh my gawd!" Niamh screeched. "You don't think they'd be stupid enough to go alone!"

"Maybe they went for a ride," David said doubtfully.

31

Candid Camera

Siobhan wrapped her arms around Manny's waist and closed her eyes and mouth tightly. One of the drawbacks of being blind was that you couldn't see the bugs coming, not that you could see the bugs coming at thirty to forty miles an hour anyway. Manny's moped zoomed down First Street South toward the lab. A bug smacked into Siobhan's helmet and she ducked her head behind Manny's back. She didn't like motorcycles or mopeds or any other vehicle where you sat unprotected on the outside. Maybe it was the fact that she was blind and couldn't sense things coming like she could when walking or maybe it was not being able to take Oenghus with her. She prayed silently that they would make it to the lab in one piece to free the cats.

These guys most likely didn't raise the cats from kittens, which meant they went around stealing people's pets or trapping strays. Either way she wanted to get them and make them pay for their cruelty. The lab guys were also at fault since they bought the animals after going public to say they didn't test their cosmetics on live animals.

After what seemed like an eternity to Siobhan, the moped slowed down and then came to a halt. Manny held her arm as she climbed off and handed her the white cane she used to feel the ground when Oenghus wasn't with her.

Manny led Siobhan past the white van still parked by the back door of the lab. The lock and chain on the back door proved it was their bad guys. As he reached for the door, Manny remembered they were under surveillance. Turning to face the telephone pole where he thought the camera had been mounted, Manny made funny faces and waved in that direction.

"What's the hold up? Why did we stop?" Siobhan asked.

"Smile! You've been Punk'd." Manny laughed at his own joke.

Unfortunately, it was lost on Siobhan. "What?"

"Remember? They're spying on us."

"Right!" Siobhan grinned and started waving enthusiastically for the camera.

"Um, Siobhan... you're waving at the door," Manny muttered.

"Oh!" Siobhan turned and waved at the wall. "You think they can see us now?"

"I hope not," he smirked.

"What?"

"Nevermind. Let's go!" Manny said, testing the door. To his surprise, the door swung open. "Hmmm, I thought it'd be locked. So, you sure we should do this?" he asked, not so sure of himself now that he was actually looking through the door and into the lab. He felt exposed under the bright fluorescent lights illuminating the long hallway. Once they entered the dragon's lair, there would be no turning back. And worse, there would be no place to hide.

"Yes, I'm sure," Siobhan said. She walked past him and through the doorway into the unknown. "Go home if you're scared."

"I'm not scared. I was making sure you wanted to do this." Manny hurried to catch up to Siobhan who was already tapping her way along the polished ceramic tile. The noise echoed loudly down the hallway.

"Geez! Could you be any louder with that stick?" Manny asked nervously. As the door ominously slammed shut behind them, Manny had a sinking feeling he would regret his hasty decision.

32

Mutiny

"Oh my gawd!" Niamh wildly fanned her hands in front of her face and looked like she was either going to faint or win a Miss Teen America contest. "It's them!"

"Who?" David asked, before approaching the computer.

Aimee saw Niamh's frantic movements while playing with the dogs. She threw a Frisbee one more time and watched for a second as Hoku passed Oenghus and Watson and leapt high in the air to grab the Frisbee.

"That's my girl!" Aimee said proudly before rushing over to the group to stand behind David and peer at the laptop.

"Siobhan and Manny. They're at the lab!" Niamh sounded slightly hysterical as she continued to watch the live video feed.

"Not good. Now what are we gonna do?" Kameron watched the computer screen intently. "And who's Manny waving at?"

David panned and zoomed the camera to the area Manny faced. "There's nothing there," he stated and changed the camera angle back to focus on his two friends. "And now we have Siobhan waving at the wall."

"Ohmigosh! Maybe they're trying to tell us something." Niamh grabbed and shook David's arm. "Do you think it's a code or something? You're good with puzzles! What do you think they're trying to say?"

David freed himself from Niamh's grasp. "Wait! I think I know what they're trying to say." Niamh held her breath, waiting for David's interpretation. "We're two complete morons who are going to be on house arrest for the next decade."

"By jove, I think you've got it!" Kameron quipped. "Who's got the bail money?"

"Whatever, you guys! We have to go help them." Aimee grabbed up the laptop and headed for the front yard, turning to stare at David. "Well, are you coming or not?"

Hoku rushed up to Aimee and dropped the Frisbee, Oenghus and Goliath hot on her heels, Watson and Chiquita bringing up the rear. All the dogs sat obediently in front of Aimee, waiting patiently for the next throw.

David wheeled his chair around and moved in behind the dogs. "Count me in."

"Okay, okay, count me in, too," Kameron added. "Since I'm the only ride you have."

"You're not leaving without me! That's my not-too-bright sister going in there," Niamh said matter-of-factly. "Where she goes, I go. And she is going to get an earful when I get my hands on her. I can't believe she left without us."

"What about Goliath?" David asked, "And the rest of the pack?"

Hearing his name, Goliath swiveled his head to look back at David, anticipating a command. Chiquita whined impatiently for the next throw and glanced around, looking for her boy. Not seeing Manny, she started dashing around the yard, searching. Picking up his scent, she followed it to the front gate.

"We better leave them here, so when we do get arrested, they won't be sent to the pound," Kameron said dryly, patting Watson on the head.

Aimee stared at Kameron and made a face. "Shush joo! Why so negative? David and I will meet you in the SUV after you two kennel everyone."

Aimee and David made their way to the vehicle while Niamh and Kameron rounded up the pack and got them settled into empty boarding kennels. The Sanchez's had plenty of room since they did boarding as well as training. Niamh made sure everyone had water. Kameron made a quick trip to the freezer and grabbed some frozen Kongs. He tossed a treat-filled Kong into every kennel. Before leaving, he double checked the latches on each door.

Goliath paced in his kennel and woofed mournfully several times in a failed attempt to get Kameron's attention. Watson, Oenghus, and Chiquita contentedly chewed on their Kongs. Ignoring her treat, Hoku rattled the door and barooed her displeasure.

"Sucks to be you!" Kameron teased the Basenji before walking away.

"That wasn't very nice, you know. Basenjis aren't as forgiving as Dobies. It may literally come back to bite you in the butt." Niamh glared at Kameron, who shrugged and walked away before she could fully unleash her Irish temper on him. "Whatever, you're so rude."

Niamh flounced sulkily behind Kameron who ignored her completely. When they got to the SUV, David was already seated in the back. Aimee had folded up his chair and was putting it into the storage area. Niamh slid into the seat next to David and gave him a shy smile. At least David was easygoing and not difficult like Kameron.

"Did you get everyone settled in okay?" David returned Naimh's smile.

"Yeah. Goliath and Hoku weren't too happy about it, but I'm sure they'll settle down soon. Kameron gave everyone Kongs to keep them busy while we're away."

Hoku was anything but settled. Instead, using the wire mesh to her advantage, she climbed over the kennel gate. She pranced over to Goliath's kennel and stretched up to reach the latch. Barooing excitedly, Hoku pawed persistently at the latch until it popped opened. Then she jumped back as Goliath barged past her and headed for the exit.

Seeing Goliath dash past his kennel, Watson scrambled over his kennel door, landing with a thud on the other side. Hoku raced after Goliath, passing Chiquita who had managed to squeeze her little frame under the kennel gate. She yipped excitedly, as she joined the other two at the exit. Watson bounded over to Oenghus' kennel. Oenghus whined as Watson pawed frantically at the latch.

Goliath stopped at the door and barked loudly at Hoku. She pawed ineffectively at the round doorknob. The pit bull nudged Hoku aside and reared up, scratching at the doorknob with both front paws. Within seconds, the knob turned. Goliath crashed through the open door with Hoku leaping over him and Chiquita charging under his legs. Unable to unlatch Oenghus' kennel, Watson barked in frustration before turning and racing after the fleeing trio.

A crashing sound erupted from the rear of the house. David and Niamh whipped around in the direction of the commotion. Aimee finished storing David's wheelchair in the back, totally unaware that behind her, Goliath, Watson, Hoku, and Chiquita were all making a beeline for the SUV.

Watson climbed over Niamh before she could protest and jumped into the front seat, taking up his co-pilot position. He looked sheepishly at Kameron, gave a deep woof, and then looked away, clearly not going anywhere. Little Chiquita was all over the place, first in the front seat then the back, then over the seat and into the back storage area. Good thing she was only hand-sized or her tail would have knocked everyone unconscious.

Goliath crawled under Niamh's legs and planted himself beside David, turning his head to the side, panting and smiling widely as only a pittie can. He looked pleased with himself. Hoku leaped into the back storage area where Aimee had finished stowing David's wheels. In typical Basenji fashion, she yawned and waved her paw at Aimee before lying down and turning away as if to say, "I'm going, case closed, get over it."

"It appears we have an animal mutiny on our hands," Aimee said, scowling at Hoku who was cleaning herself vigorously and pointedly ignoring her guardian. Aimee shut the back door before slipping in next to Niamh.

David patted Goliath on the head. "Did anybody think to lock the kennel door?"

"I don't mind them coming if you guys don't," Aimee stated.

Kameron looked put out since he didn't feel that the dogs should be with them. He didn't mind getting in trouble, but he hated the thought of something happening to Watson. But knowing that it would be more trouble to keep the dogs at Manny's, he acquiesced. "Fine, but someone will have to stay in the SUV with them if we go inside the lab because it's too hot for them without the AC running."

David was more than happy to have Goliath along for the ride. He'd deal with the problem of who would stay with the dogs when they got to the lab. For now he needed to come up with a plan to help Manny and Siobhan. Oenghus' mournful howls could be heard as they drove away from the house. David and Niamh shared guilty looks as the dog's cries faded.

"Maybe we should go back for Oenghus," Niamh said.

"No time. Manny's parents will be home any minute now, and we don't want to have to explain why Manny isn't with us," David said.

"I wonder if you'd say that if Goliath had been the one left behind!" Niamh snapped, turning to glare out the window in an obvious snit.

Looking from Niamh to David, Aimee asked, "What did you say to her? What did I miss?"

"Never mind," David said, turning to stare out the other window and ending that conversation.

A short time later, Kameron parked the SUV around the corner from the lab. Aimee had decided on the way that she and Niamh would stay in the van with the computer and animals while Kameron and Watson did some reconnaissance around the building. David's job would be the riskiest since he was the decoy, or dummy as it were. Yeah, David the crash test dummy.

Okay, so maybe the brilliant plan wasn't so brilliant but, hey! It was tough being a genius. There was a lot of pressure. Everyone looked to David now for leadership. How that had happened he had no idea. One day he was the school nerd, the next day he was the leader of his own gang. Thanks in part to Goliath.

"Hey, dork!" Aimee punched David's arm, effectively interrupting his fantasy. "Be careful out there. If anything happens, yell like the girl I know you are, and I'll come rescue you." She snickered at her own joke.

David had the wildest impulse to lean over and give Aimee a quick kiss, but he stifled it and instead crossed his eyes at her. He scooted to the edge of his seat and grabbed the J-bar above his head.

Seating adjustments were made as Kameron and Watson left the vehicle and retrieved the wheelchair and set it by the door. Goliath leaped into the driver's seat to get a better view, and when space was made, Hoku moved up to nestle next to Aimee.

With one hand on her pup's head, unconsciously kneading the Basenji's worry lines, Aimee opened her laptop and booted it up with the other hand. She looked over at David lowering himself into the wheelchair. With a mock evil glare, she said menacingly, "Remember Big Brother is watching you."

"Yeah, whatever." David rolled his eyes at her and wheeled away from the SUV.

"Be careful, David," Niamh called out, her anger momentarily forgotten. David rounded the building and headed for the front entrance to see what trouble he could cause. Niamh groaned and grabbed a strand of hair to nervously chew on the tip. "Oh, this is so not good! I'm worried about him already. And I'm going to kill my sister!"

Of course, Aimee didn't acknowledge Niamh's comment because she was looking away, already engrossed in setting up the computer for their covert operation.

33

Cat's Meow

Hank and Carlos unloaded the last of the cat crates from the van and went to the back office to get paid.

A tall, thin man dressed immaculately in a dark business suit sat at a desk, punching numbers on a computer keyboard. Hank stepped inside the room and waited for the suit to acknowledge him. He impatiently tapped his foot loudly against the linoleum. Carlos stood nervously behind Hank with a cat crate in one hand and a soda in the other. He swiped the back of his hand against his sweaty brow. The suit stopped typing only to grab the pencil behind his ear and start scratching numbers on a sheet of paper in front of him, blatantly ignoring the two who stood before him.

After a few minutes, Hank got tired of waiting.

"Hey, buddy! We don't have all day. Pay up!" Hank stepped up to the desk and placed both hands down on top of the suit's papers.

"Always the impatient one, Mr. Kruger. Please take your filthy hands off my research and be patient." The man glared over the top of his black-rimmed glasses and down his long, pointy nose.

"Look, buddy, I got places to go and people to see." Hank glared right back at the suit behind the desk and didn't move his hands. He wasn't about to be intimidated by a pencil neck in a lab coat.

"Fine. How many did you bring me tonight?" the suit sighed, leaning over to pull open a desk drawer.

"Twelve healthy kittens." Hank smiled. "At a hundred dollars apiece, that's one thousand and two hundred dollars."

"Your math skills never cease to amaze me," the suit remarked somewhat sarcastically.

"Yeah, well, I didn't go to no college like you, but without me, your little research projects wouldn't get very far," Hank replied. "So, put that in your eye liner and wear it."

Carlos snickered. The suit was not amused. He reached into the drawer and pulled out a lockbox. Opening the box, he pulled out twelve, crisp, one-hundred-dollar bills and slid them across the table to Hank.

"Do you still need the fish bait you asked for last week?" Hank asked, counting the bills. You never knew if one of these suits would try to short change you.

"Why, yes, I do. As much as you can get. I need it delivered to the docks by this time tomorrow. Look for the Russian ship *The Dangerous Lady*," the suit answered.

"That's original," Hank sneered. Carlos, who had taken a gulp of soda, snorted and started coughing while soda spewed from his nostrils.

"Charming," the suit remarked, his tone indicating it was anything but. "You need to house train your dog better, Mr. Kruger."

"Yeah, well, he ain't the sharpest tack in the pack, but he gets the job done and don't ask questions," Hank answered, stuffing the bills into his pocket.

"Admirable qualities to be sure," the suit sneered. "Make sure you are at the docks no later than ten tomorrow night or the ship will not be there. I will pay you upon receipt of suitable product delivery."

Carlos had finally gotten his coughing under control and proceeded to wipe his nose with the back of his shirt sleeve.

"Our business is done for today. Now take your unkempt self and unwashed sidekick and get out of my office. Don't come back until you have more animals." The suit turned back to his computer, dismissing Hank and Carlos.

Grumbling under his breath about "stuck-up richie types think they're better'n everyone else", Hank stalked out the door and down the hallway.

"How long we gonna keep bringing that dude animals?" Carlos asked.

"Until we get a better gig, man. Now hurry up! There must be a few more stray animals kicking around town, and if there ain't, I'm sure someone's let their cat out for the night. Let's go check our traps and see if we got any," Hank answered.

"Where are we gonna get that fish bait, man?" Carlos asked.

"Where do you think? Stoerm Enterprises. They owe us bigtime for all the work we did for them," Hank answered, flipping his lucky dollar into the air. "Our luck is about to change, Carlos."

"Hank, we got fired for stealing. I don't think they were planning on paying us after that," Carlos said innocently.

Hank grabbed Carlos' cowboy hat and whacked him across the back of the head with it.

"Idiot! I didn't say we were gonna ask Mr. Big Shot Ash Stoerm for anything. I said they owed us something and I intend to collect it."

Hank handed Carlos his hat back and the two of them proceeded down the hallway. Carlos grumbled his displeasure and placed his hat back onto his head. Walking around the corner, they came face to face with two of the cripple kid's friends.

"Siobhan, run!" the boy shouted and pushed the girl behind him.

"Not so fast, kid." Hank smiled at the opportunity presented to him and motioned for Carlos to move forward. Moving faster than his demeanor suggested he should have been able to, Carlos passed the two teens and trapped them between himself and Hank.

"Back off or you'll regret it. I know karate and I'm not afraid to use it." The boy sounded serious.

"Now hold on, kid," Hank said. He spread his hands wide and tried to look non-threatening. "Let's talk this through like two adults. You and me, kid."

"Manny, move aside and let me deal with this," the girl said, unfolding her white cane into three sections, each attached with a thin wire cord.

"Siobhan, it's okay I got this," the boy turned his head as he replied.

Seizing the opportunity, Carlos swung a wild punch at the boy's head, connecting solidly with his jaw. With a loud thud, Manny collapsed in a heap on the floor, leaving the girl standing there, looking confused.

"Well, well, what do we have here?" Hank leered at the young girl who stared blankly ahead.

"Manny? Manny, are you okay?" The girl tapped her foot on the ground, trying to find the boy. "What did you do to, Manny?" she demanded angrily.

"I'd worry more about myself if I were you, sweet cheeks." Hank grinned evilly.

34

Underdog

David wheeled his chair right up to the stairs. These stairs were definitely inaccessible to wheelchairs. Bonus! He wouldn't have to fake the anger part. David hated when he was denied access to a building. Oh, sure, the government made all new businesses put in wheelchair-accessible ramps or elevators for potential clients. That didn't do much for all those businesses that weren't new or ignored the new building codes. Granted, he wasn't really denied since he could go up and down stairs easily on his own, but it was inconvenient if he was in a hurry or the stairs were wet or dirty.

It figured that the lab would be inaccessible by wheelchair. Anyone who used live animals to test cosmetics didn't care for the rights of others on this planet, like say, disabled people. Now that David had worked himself up to angry, he talked to Niamh via his Bluetooth earpiece.

"The eagle has landed."

"Dork," Niamh's voice sounded in his ear. "Sorry. Aimee made me say that."

"Uh huh," David replied. "Tell her she needs new material. It's getting old." David took a deep breath and cracked his knuckles. "Ready, girls? It's show time!"

David began shouting at the building's front door. Before long a couple of security guards came out of the building and approached David.

"Move along, kid. Go home. We're closed," the tall, older security guard said, his tone weary.

"I'm not going anywhere until I talk to the manager of this place!" David practically screamed at the guards. "Disabled people have the right to wheelchair-accessible ramps! How are people like me supposed to get into your building?"

"People like you have no need to get into our building. Now get out of here, kid, before I call the cops and get you booked for trespassing." The stocky younger guard was obviously less intelligent and more belligerent than the older guard.

David targeted his next attack at the younger man. "Make me, cop wannabe."

"Look here, son. You need to move along now." The older guard put a restraining hand on the young guard's arm as the man approached David.

"This building discriminates against disabled people. You only have one wheelchair parking spot in your whole parking lot and no way to get inside the building." David was working himself to rant now. Can someone say Oscar performance? David wondered if he could make himself spit when he yelled at the guard without looking too obvious. "Do you even have handicap accessible bathrooms available? Or are we supposed to piddle in our pants? I'm going to sue your boss and their bosses and you, too, if you don't get a manager out here right now!"

"Okay, don't go too overboard," Niamh cautioned into his earpiece. "Kameron almost has the door open."

Kameron knelt on one knee in front of the back door to the lab with a lock pick kit he had bought online. It was amazing the things one can find online. Carefully, he inserted the thin metal pick into the lock and wiggled it from side to side as the book described. Nothing happened. Niamh's babbling into his earpiece every few minutes wasn't exactly helping his concentration either. It was amazing how different the twins were while looking exactly the same. Siobhan was the quiet, take-charge type while her sister Niamh was the nervous, social butterfly who incidentally never shut up.

"Did you get it yet?" Niamh's voice sounded off in his earpiece for the umpteenth time. "David's gone totally over the top. You better hurry before he gets himself into trouble."

"Shhh! Be quiet! I can't concentrate with all the chatter." Kameron's voice came across a little harsher than he had intended it to be.

"Excuse me for caring. I'll be quiet if that's what you want." Niamh's voice clearly conveyed her annoyance through the earpiece. "Not to worry. If you don't want to talk to me, you don't have to. It's not like I need you to talk to me or anything! I mean, I have lots of friends, I don't . . ."

Kameron nearly blew a gasket. "Be quiet!" he hissed into the Bluetooth and immediately regretted it. At least he was rewarded with silence. Complete and utter silence from the other end. Did Niamh hang up on him?

Watson looked at him and whined softly. Sitting he offered his guardian a paw and tilted his head to the side, inquiringly. If he could talk, he probably would have said, *"Lighten up, man—life's too short to be so grouchy,"* or *"Hey, man—why are you growling at the door?"*

Kameron looked at his best friend and laughed and patted him on the head. "Okay, okay, I'll lighten up. Sorry I growled."

"Apology accepted. I knew you'd come around. I mean, everyone says, 'Kameron is way too serious.' And I'm, like, maybe you just need to get to know him better. There is a kind heart under all that bluster ..."

Guess she didn't hang up after all. Groaning, Kameron switched off his earpiece. The silence that followed was sweet. It wasn't that he didn't like Niamh... he did. But when she got nervous, she couldn't shut up, and since Aimee was hearing-impaired, she couldn't tell Niamh to shut up because she probably didn't even realize Niamh was talking his ear off. Besides if Aimee could hear, Niamh would probably be talking her ear off instead of his.

Kameron pulled his lock pick out of the door and sighed deeply. He couldn't understand why it wasn't working. He was getting frustrated now. Watson eyed his guardian carefully than jumped up on the door with his front feet and pushed. The door swung open. Apparently, even though the door was still locked, the lock hadn't been engaged all the way.

Watson stepped inside the door and stopped, looking back at Kameron with a self-satisfied look on his face. *"You through playing?"* he seemed to say. Kameron chuckled and stepped inside the building's long empty hallway. Switching his earpiece back on, he was immediately inundated with questions.

"Did you lose the connection? Hello, are you there? Kameron, are you okay? Ohmigod, Aimee! He isn't answering me! We have to go help him. Kameron? Kameron! Are you there? Are you okay?" Niamh's voice rose an octave higher with each passing second he didn't answer.

"Shhh! I'm inside the building," Kameron whispered. "I need you to be quiet since this earpiece carries sound almost too well."

"Oh, thank God, you're okay," Niamh replied in a loud whisper. Still whispering she went on, "I mean, I was so worried that maybe something had happened to you and Watson."

"Everything is A-OK. Now please, pretty please with sugar on top—be quiet!" Kameron whispered.

"Okay, okay! You don't have to tell me more than once. I'm not deaf. Oops, sorry, Aimee!" Niamh giggled then whispered into her

Bluetooth device, "I forgot she can't hear me because she's looking the other way. So does that count? I mean, if the person doesn't hear you, is it still considered offensive?"

Kameron took a deep breath and turned his Bluetooth device down as low as it would go. "Maybe you should check in on David."

"Good idea! I mean, ten-four on that," Niamh said.

David had both guards standing at the bottom of the stairs and trying to get him to go home. He played the upset wheelchair user to the max. He even bumped his chair against the bottom step several times to show the men there was no way he could get up those stairs. The older guard was still talking quietly to him, trying not to make a scene. However, the younger man was at the end of his patience and grabbed the back of David's chair and tried to push him down the sidewalk.

"Help! Help! I'm being attacked. I'm being manhandled by a huge baboon! Someone help me!" David screamed at the top of his lungs. He hoped Aimee didn't come running around the corner to kick some butt as that would be a bad thing. He was only trying to get the guards' attention long enough to let Kameron get inside the building.

"Okay, sonny, you've had your fun. Now it's time to move along or we'll have you charged with trespassing." The older guard had taken out his cell phone and started dialing a number.

David's own phone began to vibrate against his side, so he reached up and hit the switch on his earpiece. Niamh's voice whispered in his Bluetooth device, "The Doberman has landed!"

"What are you..." David started to ask before remembering where he was and who he was surrounded by. He grabbed his wheel rims and gave a strong push, pulling his wheelchair out of the younger guard's hands. "I'm out of here now, but I'll be back with my lawyer. This isn't over! You can count on that!"

"Whatever, kid!" the younger guard muttered, before turning his back and heading back to the building.

David rolled to the corner and did a quick check over his shoulder to make sure the guards weren't following him. Apparently, they were satisfied he was leaving and had gone back inside. As David rolled up to the SUV's window, he was greeted by Goliath's deep woof and the thumping sound of Goliath's enthusiastic wiggling body and Chiquita's yip-yip. Hoku, on the other hand, sat wagging her curly little tail, not making a sound.

"Any news?" David asked Niamh.

"Not yet, but Kameron and Watson are on the inside," Niamh said.

Aimee plugged away at the keyboard. "Finally, I got it!" she whooped looking up to see David outside her window.

"Got what?" Niamh and David asked simultaneously.

"The blueprints to the lab building," Reading David's lips, Aimee stated smugly. "Now I can give Kameron better directions."

David raised both hand and signed, "Awesome."

"Sweet beans," Niamh piped in and dialed Kameron's cell phone number.

Kameron's voice answered the phone in a whisper. "What now?"

"We have the blueprints for the building, Mr. Cranky Pants," Niamh said teasingly.

"Cool," Kameron replied, ignoring Niamh's little jibe. "I'm at the first intersection about to see if Watson can track Siobhan."

Kameron reached into the right leg pocket of his camouflage pants and pulled out Siobhan's hair band, the one she had left at Manny's house. Holding it to Watson's nose, he gave the command to "find Siobhan". Watson sniffed the hair band carefully then began sniffing the ground. He immediately moved off toward the left corridor.

"Okay, he's got her scent and we're heading down the left corridor. Who knew that those hide-and-seek games would actually pay off?" Kameron followed closely behind Watson, on the lookout for more guards. He only hoped Siobhan and Manny were okay since neither of them had called in or answered their phones.

35

Ice Ice Baby

Shivering, Siobhan tried to push the heavy metal door open for the hundredth time. Manny had finally woken up but had a bad headache. He sat in the corner with his back propped against the wall and his head held in his hands, moaning. They were locked in a freezer and both of them were getting closer to hypothermia.

"Manny, get up. I need your help." Siobhan felt her way over toward the moaning. Reaching down, she grabbed Manny's arm and pulled. He resisted at first, but she pulled harder, practically dragging him to his feet.

"My head is killing me and I'm f-f-freezing. It's so c-c-cold in here," Manny complained between chattering teeth. "We're going to freeze to death."

"No, we're not! Now stay on your feet and think." Siobhan wanted to throttle him for giving up but resisted the urge. "Describe the room to me."

"It's a freezer, Siobhan. Need I say more?" Manny whined.

"Manny, just do it!" Siobhan was losing her patience and someone was looking for a hiney whoopin'!

"Okay, okay, already! D-don't get your knickers in a knot." Manny stuck out his tongue, knowing full well Siobhan couldn't see him.

"Stop that," she chastised. "Help me get out of here and we can hold you a pity party later."

Raising an eyebrow, Manny wondered how she managed to do that. "There is a locked d-d-door. There are no windows and lots of boxes and a barrel that smells terrible."

"Oh, I thought that was you," Siobhan said.

"Har de har har. Hold on, I'm opening the barrel." Manny heaved on the cover, and it let go with a quiet popping sound. "Holy crap on toast! It's filled with dead cats."

"We need to get out of here and stop these monsters from testing on any more animals!" Siobhan was getting fired up despite their current predicament.

"It's hopeless, Siobhan." Manny stated flatly putting the cover back on the barrel. "We're trapped and there's no way out."

"I can feel air blowing from somewhere. What about on the upper walls or ceiling? Are there any vents or wiring?" Siobhan asked, ignoring Manny's last comment. She was not going to think about the ones they were too late to save.

"Yeah, there is a small vent of some kind, but it's way too small for a person to fit into." Manny didn't see the point in describing the room. There wasn't a way out. "There are no exposed w-w-wires that I can see."

"Try your cell phone again." Manny thought Siobhan sounded a little less sure of herself or maybe the cold was starting to affect her.

Manny flipped up his phone and checked the signal bar. He couldn't get a signal anywhere he walked in the room. He tried the phone anyway. All he got was a message telling him what he already knew... there was no signal. "Nothing, nada, no signal!" He was almost crying now. His head hurt so much.

"Wait a minute, Manny. Let's stack some of these boxes up in the corner." Siobhan grabbed a frozen box and handed it to Manny. "Manny, come on and help me," Siobhan pleaded.

"Okay, okay, but I don't see what good this will do." Manny grabbed the box and carried it over to the corner. When he dropped the box, he blew on his fingers. They were starting to go numb. He had never been anywhere colder than Florida and wondered if this was what frostbite felt like.

After a few minutes, the boxes were piled almost eight feet high. Manny had to stack boxes in a stairway-type pattern to be able to place the boxes on top. When he put the final box up, he stepped back and realized he wasn't as cold anymore. All the work had warmed him up at least for the moment.

"There. That's as high as we can put them. Now what?" He looked at Siobhan who also didn't look so cold anymore.

"What do you think? Climb up there and try your cell phone again." Siobhan gave him a shove toward the boxes.

Manny climbed to the top and pulled out his cell phone. When he flipped up the cover and moved the phone around, he was rewarded with one signal bar. "I got it! I got it! You're a genius, Siobhan!"

"Yeah, I know." Siobhan smiled and shrugged her shoulders. "It's a burden I bear."

Manny quickly dialed Niamh's number and waited. There was a long pause after he dialed. Crossing his fingers, he looked anxiously at the phone. The number he dialed still showed on the screen, but there was no dial tone yet. He moved the phone up and down and from side to side, trying to get a better signal.

"Well?" Siobhan asked impatiently.

"Nothing yet," Manny replied, trying to hide his disappointment. Turning up the volume, he held the phone up to his ear listening intently for someone to answer.

Without warning, a barrage of hysterical chatter exploded from the phone. Grasping his head in pain, Manny dropped the phone. "Manny? Ohmigod, Manny! Is that you? Ohmigod, Aimee! Manny's on the phone!" Niamh sounded like she was talking with marbles in her mouth, but there was no mistaking who had answered his call. Manny quickly scooped up the phone and lowered the volume before holding it back up to his ear. "Manny, are you there? Talk to me. Where's my sister? Is she all right? Where are you!"

"Niamh, slow down! I'm here. Siobhan's here, but we are in some seriously deep doo-doo and need help," Manny replied.

"Well, duh! And who's fault is that? If you hadn't taken off like that, you'd be here with us outside the lab instead of in it! Where are you now?"

"We got jumped, so I'm not exactly sure where we are. It looks like we're in a freezer. There's a small air vent in the ceiling, but that's about it. We can't get out."

"Kam and Watson are in the lab now. Watson's trying to sniff out Siobhan. I wonder how that would work through the freezer. I can't believe the mess you've gotten us into! I hope you've learned your lesson. And I can't believe my sister would totally follow you into this disaster!"

Manny sighed. "Look, Niamh. It's freezing in here. We're sorry, but c-c-could you stop lecturing long enough to help us out?"

"Hello? Hello! Manny! Manny, are you there?" Niamh asked. "Oh! Wait! Hold on! I'll jump outside the van and try to get better reception. Manny, can you hear me now? Hello! Can you hear me now? What about now? Can you hear me now?"

Without warning, Manny's cell phone went dead. "Bah! The battery died."

"Come and take mine," Siobhan said, reaching up as high as she could in his general direction.

He climbed down from the box and grabbed Siobhan's cell phone and checked it. Unfortunately, it was dead as well. With a disappointed sigh, he climbed down from the boxes and gave Siobhan back her useless phone.

"Dead, too," he said, unnecessarily. "Well, at least the gang is all here. Everything will b-b-be alright now."

Slowly, he sat down on a box and wrapped his arms around himself and began shivering uncontrollably. Siobhan came over and sat beside him and snuggled as close as she could get. Manny placed his arm protectively around her. Combining their body heat seemed to help.

"Don't get any ideas," Siobhan warned but didn't move away from him. "I heard it from an audio survival book. It's better to sit close together to keep warm. I hope they come soon. I'm freezing."

36

Heads or Tails

Hank still limped after being hit in the shins by the blind Samurai girl's cane of pain. Holding his crotch, Carlos hobbled along beside him. After nearly getting the snot kicked out of them, they had finally managed to get the three-sectional cane away from the little spitfire and had been able to hit her with the Taser. While she was down, they dragged her and the boy into the cold storage room. The door locked from the outside and didn't have a safety handle on the inside. It was about time these young punks learned a valuable life lesson—no one messes with Hank Kruger and gets away with it.

"Oh, man, that stings," Carlos moaned for the umpteenth time. "What are we gonna do with them kids, Hank? We can't let 'em freeze to death. That's Juan Sanchez' kid in there! I can't believe I punched out the Sanchez kid!"

"What is with you and that Sanchez guy?" Hank sneered at Carlos. "And yes, I can let them freeze to death. They're outta my hair now. I'm going home to get some rest. We need to get Goliath back by tomorrow night for the big fight. If some of their friends disappear, it might knock some of the cockiness out of those little pukes."

"Come on, Hank. They're kids. You're not serious?" Carlos watched Hank's back as he walked away.

"Wanna bet?" Hank pulled his silver dollar out of his shirt pocket and turned back to face Carlos. "Heads we let them go. Tails we leave 'em."

"I dunno, Boss," Carlos said reluctantly.

Ignoring Carlos, Hank flipped the coin into the air and caught it. Flipping it onto the back of his hand he looked to see who had won. "Tails it is. Now get back to work."

Carlos sighed and shook his head. He had come to the U.S. seeking his fortune but had somehow gotten involved with Hank. And now he was being asked to commit murder. It was all too much. After their next payday he was going to find another way to make a living. With that thought in mind he ambled down the hallway after Hank before the other man decided he needed another knock on the head.

37

Mission Chihuahua

Aimee sat in the SUV, looking at David expectantly. Niamh stood next to him with the cell phone against her ear, looking at him like she expected him to have all the answers. Unfortunately, he had no idea what to do. Things had spiraled out of control too quickly. At first they were on an adventure and now they were stuck in a nightmare. Manny and Siobhan could be freezing to death while they sat out here doing nothing. Did freezers run out of oxygen? What would James Bond do if he were in this predicament? He knew what Bond would do—most likely call in the stunt double to take his place before the action started.

"David, wake up, dork! We don't have time for the daydreaming. You need to figure out what we're going to do." Aimee eyed him as if expecting a brilliant plan to come tumbling out of his already overtaxed brain. "Well, any ideas, genius?"

"Hold on! Kameron's on the line." Niamh held up her hand for them to be quiet. "He says Watson lost the trail. Apparently, the janitor had recently washed the floor with some strong smelling chemical cleaner or something. It's like super smelly in there, but in a clean way, and Watson can't follow the trail anymore. He's coming back out!" Niamh's shoulders slumped. She pulled Maeve out of the pouch and hugged her to her chest.

"Now what, David?" Aimee asked for the second time. "Do we go door to door?"

David looked at Goliath and then at Chiquita, trying to come up with a plan. Goliath jumped out the open back window and sat in front of David as he too was expecting a brilliant plan. David reached down and scratched under Goliath's collar. Absently, he ran his fingers along the GPS device he had attached to Goliath's collar last week. He wasn't going to take any chances on losing his best friend. Chiquita's little head popped in and out of sight at the window as she jumped up and down, whining excitedly.

David was suddenly struck with a brilliant flash of lightening that nearly knocked him out of his wheelchair. Okay, in reality it was more like he had a sudden inspiration. Grabbing Goliath's collar, he removed the GPS device and rolled over next to the back window.

"Chiquita, come!" he spoke firmly to the little Chihuahua.

Chiquita obediently jumped out of the SUV and landed on David's lap. She happily jumped up and licked his face and rolled her eyes at him as if saying, *"It's about time you came to your senses."*

"You finally have a plan, don't you, David?" Niamh smiled knowingly and kissed the top of Maeve's head. "I know that look."

"Maybe." David smirked then signed for Aimee. "Can you determine distances on the blueprint?"

"You're such a funny guy," Aimee replied. "Can a crow fly? Can the sun shine? Can I, like, do that in my sleep?"

"I'll take that as a yes." David laughed, pointing at the vent exhaust on the side of the building. "Manny said there was an air vent in the freezer."

"Yeah, so?" Niamh wasn't getting it.

"Dude, have you lost your marbles?" Aimee looked at David and then down at Chiquita. "David, we can't do that. What if she gets lost or worse, like, stuck? I don't think we can risk that."

"What's our alternative? Do nothing?" David held up Goliath's GPS then snapped it onto Chiquita's collar. It was a little big but it fit well enough to work. Holding her up in front of his face, he said to the little dog, "You can find Manny anywhere. Can't you, girl?"

At the sound of her guardian's name, Chiquita started whining and wiggling so much that David nearly dropped her. Bringing her back down to his lap, David turned his chair around as Kameron and Watson came running around the building.

"Okay, so do we have a plan B?" Kameron asked, panting only slightly after running.

Watson and Goliath sniffed each other before both lying down beside David's wheelchair.

"As a matter of fact, we do," David said, holding up Chiquita. "Meet plan B."

"You're joking, right?" Kameron looked at Aimee and Niamh for confirmation. Aimee shrugged at him, her face impassive. Niamh shook her head. "What possible good could one little cheese dog do? Quit with the bogusness and tell me what the real plan is."

David outlined his plan. His friends listened. Niamh smiled and called him brilliant. Kameron nodded and said he thought it would be doable. Aimee merely shrugged. It was hard to tell if they thought he was a genius or an idiot. Maybe they thought he was both. What did you call that? Idiot-savant. No, that was someone who had genius in one area but was not very good in any other areas. Like someone with a low IQ who could do advanced mathematics. David was good in more than one area. At least he thought he was good in more than one area, sort of. Maybe ...

"David, focus, man." Kameron looked down at him and snapped his fingers in the air. Even Goliath had gotten up and was touching his leg with a paw, his head tilted to the side. "Let's get this show on the road and that Chihuahua in the vent."

"Ok, Aimee, test the GPS to make sure it's working," David said, forgetting to sign. He never lost his amazement that Aimee understood most of what people said to her by reading their lips. He still had a habit of signing to her when there was a lot of discussion since it was more arduous for her to look from person to person and follow some of their heated debates. She could do it if she wanted, but he wanted to protect that lovely neck from whiplash.

"Done already, dorkus maximus, while you were daydreaming." Aimee smiled patronizingly. "And I linked the GPS tracker to the blueprint map using a basic algorithm program I pulled from the net."

"Huh?" Niamh faced Aimee who sniggered at her confused stare.

"Never mind, dear. Don't worry your pretty little head over it. It's kinda complicated." Aimee smiled and nodded. Boy, was she on a roll—a condescending roll with cheese on top.

"No, it isn't that complicated. I know how you did the algorithm. Duh! I used to do those in, like, the fifth grade. I was wondering where you got the program on the net." Niamh smirked and looked at her nails. *Take that and stuff it in your little red wagon*, she thought smugly.

Aimee's mouth dropped and for a fraction of a second she actually looked stunned. However, she recovered her composure quickly. "We need to talk more about algorithms, Niamh." Aimee eyed her friend with new respect. Who knew that she had a brain under all that inane chatter? "But not right now. I'll email you the web page later."

"If you two are done talking mathematical gibberish, would it be too much to ask that we get going?" Kameron held Chiquita under his arm like a little, blue, hairy, wiggly football. "David, can you cover us with another distraction? When you left the front, the guards did a sweep of the building, and Watson and I almost got caught on our way out."

"Sure. No problemo." David opened the back door and ordered Goliath to get back into the SUV.

For a moment Goliath sat there and whined softly, a worried look on his face. But at David's stern unrelenting stare and pointing finger, Goliath reluctantly jumped up into the backseat beside Hoku who had been sleeping peacefully. Waking with a yawn, Hoku waited for Goliath to sit down before putting a paw on his head to hold him still while she licked his ears clean. You've got to love Basenjis and their everyone-must-be-clean fetish. If cleanliness was next to godliness, then Basenjis were as close to God as dogs could get.

Kameron took out his multipurpose tool and unscrewed the cover on the outside vent and looked inside. It appeared to go into the building as far as he could see. Looking at Chiquita one last time, he lifted her up to the vent and gave her the command, "Find Manny."

Chiquita didn't have to be told twice to find her boy who had been gone for several hours. She hit the vent at a dead run like a black-footed ferret after a prairie dog. Kameron watched until she disappeared into the darkness. Loosely closing the vent cover, Kameron walked to the back door and slipped inside with Watson close on his heels. As he carefully moved down the hallway, he whispered into his Bluetooth device, "Okay, Chiquita is off and running."

"Ten-four, roger that... good buddy," Niamh answered back immediately with a mix of military-trucker lingo.

Kameron sighed deeply. That girl was going to drive him nuts. Coming to an intersection, he said, "I'm at the first intersection. Which way do I go?"

There was a short pause as Niamh relayed the information to Aimee. Before long she was back whispering in his headset, "Go left and then right at the next intersection. That little Chihuahua is booking it."

Kameron hurried down the left hallway, listening for footsteps that would signal approaching guards. He made it to the next intersection without any trouble. Looking down, Kameron noticed Watson's back hairs stand up before he began growling.

"Easy, boy." He grabbed Watson's collar and ran back down the hallway, trying to find an open door. Finally, he found an unlocked janitor closet. He led Watson inside and shut the door. Kneeling down, he covered the dog's mouth with his hand and softly commanded him to be quiet.

Two sets of footsteps could be heard moving down the hallway toward where Kameron and Watson hid. One person walked with an audible limp, almost dragging one foot. As the footsteps reached the janitor's closet, they stopped. Kameron grabbed the doorknob with his free hand. He felt the doorknob begin to turn and squeezed as tightly as he could. Watson jerked his head, trying to free his mouth from Kameron's other hand, and began to growl deep in his throat.

38

Best Supporting Actor

David wheeled himself yet again to the front of the building. Shouting loudly, he waved his arms. He could barely see the older security guard sitting behind the front desk. Getting up from his chair, the guard moved toward the front door, talking into his walkie-talkie as he came out to see David for the second time.

"Look, kid, you have about a minute to get out of here before I call the cops." The guard was obviously done tolerating David's antics.

David tried to explain to the guard that he was on public property, being still on the sidewalk. He didn't scream this time. He tried to keep his tone calm and low. He needed to buy time for Kameron and Watson. However, the guard was not interested in conversation and appeared to be annoyed. This time around wasn't going well at all.

Within seconds two other guards stormed out of the building. One of them was the young hothead David had met earlier. All three men surrounded David and things were not looking too promising. Things were going from bad to worst. David had a temporary sense of déjà vu— only adult cop wannabes surrounded his chair instead of testosterone-filled teenage jock wannabes.

"You back again, you little gimp?"

Apparently, Brian had an older brother who worked as a security guard. What were the odds of finding two unrelated people who looked alike and thought alike, or more accurately didn't think at all. David swallowed his witty reply and tried to wheel his chair around to leave.

The Brian look-a-like grabbed the arm of his wheelchair and held it in place. "What's your hurry, kiddo? Where do you think you're going?"

"Ah ... I am an American citizen with a disability and I know my rights," David blurted out, trying to wheel away with the guard dragging behind. Unfortunately the guy was as strong as he looked and smelled.

"You shouldn't have come back," the guard leaned down and growled in his ear.

39

Camera Shy

Carlos, carrying a mop and bucket, followed Hank down the hallway. This place was the most sterile place he'd ever been in and he didn't think the scientist guy would like the blood they had left on the floor after their scuffle with the two kids. Hank sent him to the janitor's closet to get a mop and bucket to clean up the mess. Carlos was still having second thoughts about those kids locked up in the freezer. He had decided he'd make an anonymous phone call to the lab security once they left the building. Hank would never know it was him and the kids would not be able to identify them because the girl was blind and the Sanchez kid went down so fast he couldn't have seen much.

"Hurry up, Carlos. We don't got all night," Hank growled from up ahead.

"I'm coming, Boss. This bucket is heavy." Carlos huffed and puffed as he limped down the hallway.

"Come on, you lazy bum. It's about time you did some honest work." Hank snickered at his clever putdown.

Carlos wondered what Hank would do without someone to pick on and bully. Most likely take it out on the dogs. What a sick gringo he had gotten himself messed up with. Thinking back to when he first came to this country he wondered where he had gone wrong. He had originally intended to make some quick money doing farm work or even orange grove or nursery type of work to help his family back home. After a cock fight, he and some friends had gone to a dog fight where he met Hank, and things had gone downhill from there.

Everything had sounded good at first. Raise some fighting dogs and get rich quick. So far that had not panned out and now he was locking kids in freezers. Maybe it was time to go back home where things made more sense. He missed his family and wondered what they did with the money he sent them. At least his work for Hank had paid off well, even if he wasn't rich yet. There was no way he would have made this kind of money at home, no way at all.

"Carlos, today, man. Get the lead out!" Hank stood in front of the closet door. "Did you lock the door when you got the mop and broom out?"

"No. I left it open like you told me to," Carlos replied and set the bucket and mop down. "Let me try it."

Grabbing the door knob, he twisted it one way and then the other way. It felt weird. The knob moved and didn't feel locked, but the door wouldn't open. It was probably jammed. Carlos shrugged his shoulders and looked to Hank for suggestions.

"Stay here and I'll go get the key again." Hank shook his head, stomping down the hallway. "You idiot! I told you not to lock the door. Can't you do anything right? I don't know why I don't fire your sorry carcass. You hear me, Carlos? Your days are numbered, amigo."

Carlos leaned against the door and took out a cigarette and lit it up. He knew smoking was bad for him but figured he would be dead long before he got cancer or some other smoke-related disease. There was a low rumbling growl sound coming from somewhere behind him. It sounded like a dog but not quite. It was like a dog growling underwater or something. No... more like a dog with a muzzle on. Yeah, that was it—a muzzled dog.

Carlos turned around and eyed the door curiously. What would a dog be doing in the janitor's closet? Maybe the sound came from the room behind the closet. That made more sense since the lab did use animals for research. To think some people thought dog fighting was sick. What about these lab guys who tortured animals day in and day out to test makeup? *Like chicks don't already have enough lipstick and eyeliner*, he thought.

At least with dog fighting, the dogs get tons of exercise and get out of their cages daily. These poor buggers never get to leave their cage and usually get killed after they're of no more use. Not like he cared about these animals. As long as the lab needed animals, he and Hank would make good money stealing pets that were left unattended outside by their owners or getting them free off the internet.

The noise had stopped and Carlos put his ear to the door to listen closely. The dog must have been in the other room. Carlos finished his cigarette and dropped it into the mop bucket. Heaving a deep sigh, he sat down beside the door and pulled his hat down over his eyes. It was siesta time. Who knew when Hank would come back? The guards were never in the same place twice in this building. It might take him half an hour or more to find the key.

Within a few minutes, Carlos nodded off, snoring loud enough to be heard halfway down the hall. Hank and the locked door were quickly forgotten and he entered a dream about being the handler of a champion dog.

***

Hank cursed angrily under his breath after walking up to the security office only to find it empty. Opening the door he walked inside and went over to the key holder to get the janitor's keys himself. A dozen monitors scanned every hallway and alleyway around the building.

Twirling his lucky coin between his index and middle finger Hank decided to have a look around.

He made some modifications to the camera and tape that would have shown him, Carlos, or the kids in the storage room. Before deciding it was easy money to nab other people's pets or strays, he had previously been on the security payroll himself. His previous position gave him the knowledge of the ins and outs of the building and the equipment.

While erasing the tape that showed Carlos and him dragging the kids into the room, Hank stopped and looked at one camera that currently showed a view of a familiar looking SUV parked outside the building. It couldn't be those kids again...or could it? Peering closely he saw the blind girl stick her head out the window and look around.

How was that possible? He had locked her in the freezer less than thirty minutes ago. There was no way they could have gotten out so fast. Adjusting the knob on the camera, Hank was able to zoom in on the SUV. Hank continued to watch the girl when a familiar head poked out of the back window. Goliath! Hank zoomed in to get a better look. Sure enough. There was Goliath sitting all comfortable in the back of the SUV.

"Well, well! Don't that beat all?" Hank flipped his lucky coin into the air, caught it and slapped it down on the back of his hand. Looking down he smiled at Lady Liberty's face. He turned back to the key rack and lifted off one of the master keys to the building. "Guess today's my lucky day. Should go get me a lottery ticket before the day's over."

40

Stinky Business

Kameron loosened his grip on the door and put both hands on Watson, trying to calm him down. Watson was having none of it. The men outside the door didn't smell right and he wanted at them. His guardian was in danger and he was going to protect him.

Lowering his voice to a slight whisper, Kameron tried to comfort Watson while holding his mouth shut. The guys at the door had stopped trying to turn the door knob and everything was quiet. Kameron put his ear against the door and listened carefully. Watson still growled but not as loudly as before.

"Are you okay Kameron?" Niamh's voice erupted from his headset.

Kameron's heart nearly leapt out through his mouth. He swallowed hard before answering in a hushed voice, "Shhh! I'd be better if you hadn't given me a heart attack! There were a couple of guys outside the closet we're hiding in and for a minute there I thought we were busted."

"Well, stop playing around and get going," Niamh verbally reprimanded him. "Chiquita is way ahead of you."

"Okay, okay, already. I think there's still one guy out there," Kameron whispered into his Bluetooth device. "Be quiet while I check it out."

Moving as slow as a sloth through quicksand, Kameron turned the doorknob and pulled the door open a crack. Looking out he saw a middle-aged Hispanic man sitting propped up against the wall with a big cowboy hat covering his eyes. If the volume of someone snoring was an indication of the level of sleep, then this guy was out cold. He wasn't merely snoring—he was sawing those proverbial logs like there was no tomorrow.

Taking a firm hold of Watson's collar, Kameron eased out of the closet and quietly shut the door. Watson pulled half-heartedly toward the man on the floor but didn't seem as upset now that he could see his adversary. He still growled but not loudly enough to be heard over the guy's snoring. Walking as if he was treading on egg shells, Kameron led Watson past the sleeping man.

Without warning, the man snorted and turned to one side. Heart racing, Kameron froze in place, no more than a few feet from the man. At this point he would make a run for it if the guy woke up. Hopefully, the guy was as slow moving as he looked. Letting out another snort, the man passed wind and settled back down, sighing peacefully before ripping out another snore.

Kameron blinked back tears as the gas cloud pummeled his nose. Watson sniffed deeply and then recoiled as his sensitive nostrils got a good whiff. Gagging as he plugged his nose and held his breath, Kameron quickly dragged a sneezing Watson past the guy and around the corner. After going to the end of the hallway, he bent over double and took in a deep breath of clean air, looking at his sidekick.

"Wow! That was bad. I mean B-A-D, bad!" Kameron laughed out loud, despite trying his best to contain it. Watson had finally stopped sneezing and rubbed his nose on the ground, scratching it with one paw.

"Kameron! Kameron, are you okay?" Niamh asked urgently. "You sound like you're in pain."

Kameron laughed all the harder, releasing the tension that had been building up. Taking several minutes to catch his breath, he finally replied. "Yes, we're fine. We barely survived a gas attack. So, which way do we go now?"

"What? Like the kind the riot police use?"

"What riot police?" Kameron asked, still laughing. "No, no...it's some old guy farting."

"Eww gross. TMI." Niamh tapped Aimee arm to get her attention. "He says it stinks in there."

Aimee shook her head. "Whatever. Focus, people! Tell him to go to the end of the hallway, and then take a left, and then a right. Pick up the pace! Chiquita is three or four hallways ahead of you."

Niamh repeated Aimee's directions.

Kameron commanded Watson to heel and the two of them raced down the hallway. There were no guards in sight, so David must have been successful in getting their attention at the front door. He only hoped David didn't get into too much trouble.

David was a gutsy kid for someone in a chair. Kameron thought about that then corrected himself. David was a gutsy kid period. His wheelchair was only an obstacle because other people saw it as one. David sure didn't. Kameron didn't have a lot of friends, but he considered David one of them. He used to feel sorry for himself because of the diabetes and dealing with the insulin pump and sticking himself all the time for blood draws and having to always keep in mind what he was eating and when. It was such a pain. But that was until he met David. It was the aphorism "I cried because I had no shoes until I saw a man who had no feet." And it helped that Aimee didn't allow anyone to have a pity party.

Rounding the next corner, Kameron asked Niamh for more directions. He was now entering into more of the actual lab area. As he passed a room with a large pane glass window, he stopped and looked inside. He had never actually been in a lab room before where they did experiments on animals. Through the glass barrier, he could see a dozen or so cats crammed into small steel cages. The room was meticulously clean and sterile. No blankets or toys lay in the cages, only the poor miserable-looking kitties lounging on steel mesh grating.

Watson stood on his hind legs and looked through the window. He whined softly and looked up at Kameron. "I know, buddy. I was thinking the same thing. Don't worry. Once we get Manny and Siobhan out, we'll come back and get them out, too."

Watson, apparently satisfied with Kameron's answer, dropped back down on all fours and waited to move on. Kameron spoke into his Bluetooth device, "Hey, guys, I found the animal holding area. Can you mark my position on the map so we can come back this way to get them on the way out?"

"Oh, those poor little kitties! Aimee, Kameron's found the kittens and, like, you need to mark it so they can go back. I hope those kitties are okay. It's horrible. The thought's too terrible to bear. I can't believe they still test on animals. It's heartless!" Niamh ranted then took a break. "Oh, Aimee says consider it done."

Kameron walked to the end of the hallway and then through the fire doors. This area was like most of the rest of the building. Sterile, cold, and uncaring, probably like the people who worked there. Kameron wondered how someone could go to work every day and torture animals then go home to their kids and pets and pretend that they didn't inflict needless pain on an innocent creature.

He vowed to pay more attention to the products he used since that was the best way to stop the cruelty. Hit the companies where it hurt—in the wallet. If enough people boycotted a product, the producers would be forced to change their testing practices. Many companies were already changing due to public pressure.

"Chiquita has stopped moving! Oh, I hope she found them and that she's not stuck. Geez! What if she's stuck? What are we going to do then? How are we going to get her out!" Niamh's voice rose with excitement. There was a brief pause. "Aimee says she thinks Chiquita's found them! Her location is a small room which could be the freezer. The blueprints don't list the room's uses so we can't be sure."

"Score! I'm on my way." Kameron broke into a run with Watson following closely at his heels.

41

Chilidog

Manny's thoughts were adrift with dreams of being on a warm sunny beach with his friends. He was lying down on a beach towel, letting the sun warm his face. Siobhan was lying beside him wearing a black bikini with a sarong over the top of it. Smiling warmly she offered him a drink of her Gatorade. He grinned back at her and took the drink. She leaned closer as if she had something important to tell him.

"Manny," she breathed in his ear.

They were so close he could smell the sunscreen she had rubbed on her milky-white skin only minutes ago. When she opened her mouth, her breath smelled of strawberry gum.

Their lips nearly touching, Manny closed his eyes in preparation and puckered up. As they kissed, Manny was surprised and slightly repulsed by the warm wetness of her lips. Wetness? *Were kisses supposed to be this wet*, he wondered. *Gag!* The wetness increased and soon she was licking his face and whining. Whining? Why was Siobhan whining?

This was getting gross to the extreme.

Manny slowly opened his eyes only to find Chiquita and not Siobhan licking his face. Chiquita barked excitedly as her guardian finally woke up. Bouncing from Manny's lap to Siobhan's, she wiggled and waggled her whole body, trying to be on both of them at once.

Siobhan sat beside him with a bemused look on her face. Sometimes he wondered how much she could see. Several things ran through the fog that was his mind at the moment. First of all, how did Chiquita get in here? Second, where was the rescue party? Third and most importantly, why was Siobhan smiling at him like that?

"Don't you think it's funny how some people talk in their sleep?" Siobhan taunted Manny.

Manny held his head and groaned. There was no way he talked in his sleep! Was there? Before he had time to get any more embarrassed, someone knocked on the door from outside. Siobhan was the first to the door and pounded back on it with short, angry jabs.

"Manny? Siobhan? Are you guys okay?" Kameron's voice could be heard faintly through the heavy door.

"Kameron, we're in here. Get us out of here. Hurry up! We're freezing," Manny yelled back through the door, hoping Kameron could hear him. Chiquita danced on the floor, jumped up on Manny's legs, and then ran around in circles, barking all the while.

Looking up, something caught Manny's eye. The air vent at the top of the boxes they had piled up was hanging open. Chiquita must have come in through the opening. Wow! His little Chiquita had probably saved their lives. Guess he'd have a certain something to say the next time Kameron called Chiquita a little cheese dog.

Siobhan reached down and Chiquita sprang into her arms. Siobhan picked up Chiquita, telling her what a good girl she was. Chiquita wiggled and squirmed for a few seconds before settling comfortably in Siobhan's arms. Normally, she would have refused to be held for very long, but Chihuahuas were not built for this low temperature. She snuggled into Siobhan's body as close as she could, giving Siobhan a thank-you lick every few seconds.

Within a few minutes Kameron had the door open and stood there with a peculiar look on his face. Watson barked excitedly. Kameron closed his hand around Watson's muzzle quickly before the dog could bark even more. Chiquita jumped down from Siobhan's arms and ran outside the freezer to do a little hopping dance of joy around Kameron and Watson.

"Took you long enough," Siobhan said, walking from the freezer with her hand held out in front of her, a shivering Manny close on her heels. Both of them looked about half frozen.

Manny teeth chattered slightly as he spoke. "Who had the idea to send Chiquita in through the air vent? That was b-b-brilliant."

"Who do you think?" Kameron said. He quieted Watson down and reached out to hold Siobhan's hand. It wouldn't be a good idea to draw too much attention to themselves now that they were free. There was still the business of getting the animals out.

"Niamh, I found them. We're on the way back!" Kameron whispered into his Bluetooth device.

There was no response. That was weird as only a few minutes ago Niamh wouldn't shut up. Dead silence was somehow eerie, like horror flick eerie, after all the noise she had been making over the last hour. A sudden feeling of dread gripped Kameron and wouldn't let go. Did he miss the insistent chatter that much?

At the next intersection, he couldn't remember which way he had turned, and Niamh wasn't answering. Well, at least, this time they had a Plan B. Patting Watson's head, he commanded "Home, Watson, go home."

Watson sniffed the floor momentarily then took off down the left hallway. Siobhan gripped Kameron's hand tightly and didn't stumble. Manny followed close behind. They were both still cold but starting to warm up. Manny rubbed his arms vigorously to stimulate his circulation. Chiquita danced between his legs as he walked and occasionally ran back and forth between Watson and her boy.

Leading the way, Watson hurried along the corridors, occasionally sniffing the ground before moving on. Their scent was so fresh he had no trouble following it. Kameron had taught him the "home" command while they were out rollerblading. Watson loved to pull Kameron behind him but would sometimes try to go up on the sidewalk so Kameron had come up with the run home game. It worked so well that Watson would now lead him back to their starting point from almost anywhere without yielding to distractions. Who knew a simple game would turn into a life saver some day? That's twice now in one day that two simple dog games had gotten them out of some serious jams.

After the next turn, they came to the place with the large glass windows. Kameron called Watson back and the group looked for the doorway. Fortunately, it was located around the corner but unfortunately securely locked with a high-tech sensor device that Kameron was unfamiliar with. After looking at the keypad for several minutes, he tried punching in different numbers to find the code. The indicator light stayed red.

"Any ideas?" Kameron turned to his two human companions who had been quiet since being rescued.

"Someone's coming."

Siobhan had almost superhero-like hearing. If she said someone was coming, no one argued the point. They quickly looked for a place to hide. They tried every doorway on one side of the hallway without any luck. Everything was locked tight. Kameron dropped to one knee in front of a plain, wooden door opposite the glassed-in area and got out his lock pick kit. Someone rattled a doorknob in the hallway.

"Hurry up, Kam!" Manny wasn't interested in being locked up for a second time—he was finally starting to get feeling back into his legs. He bent down and picked up Chiquita and held her little mouth shut so she wouldn't give away their position.

Now they could all hear footsteps as one of the security guards walked down the adjacent hallway toward them. Watson's back hair rose as he moved toward the hallway, emitting a low rumbling growl. Siobhan blocked him with her leg then groped along his body until she was able to grab his collar. Covering his mouth and petting him reassuringly, she whispered in his ear to be quiet. Reluctantly, he stopped growling but his back hair still stood up, an indication he was upset.

Another door rattled. This time the sound was just around the corner from where they had turned. Kameron whispered, "I almost have it...I only need a few seconds."

"Hurry! He's almost on top of us," Siobhan whispered back.

Whistling an old Russian tune, the guard rounded the corner and stopped. He thought for a moment he had heard a dog growl. These sterile buildings could be a little spooky at night, with their odd noises, flickering lights, and cold spots. Shaking his head, he walked up to the key pad and entered his security code. Opening the door, he walked into the lab and did a once around to make sure everything was okay. Satisfied that things were kosher, he walked back into the hallway and closed the door behind him.

Standing behind the door, Kameron held the knob tightly, waiting for the guard to try to open it. He didn't have to wait long. The familiar tug came, only this time the guard wasn't trying to get in, only testing the lock. He gave it one quick twist then moved on down the hallway. Kameron slowly opened the door and peeked out. The coast was clear. Unfortunately, he hadn't been able to see the guard put in his security code, so they were right back where they started.

Siobhan put her hand on Kameron's arm and whispered into his ear. "Take me to the key pad, Kam. I think I can open it now."

"What?"

Kameron looked at Siobhan like she was crazy. Of course, she didn't see him lift his eyebrows and cock his head to the side. Shrugging and looking at Manny, he led her to the key pad and placed her hand on it. Who could say no to a pretty blind girl? Especially a pretty blind girl with a painful right hook who could always seem to hit dead-on.

Manny leaned back against the wall and smiled. If Siobhan thought she could open it, then let her try. She punched every key, one at a time and listened carefully to the different sounds each one made. After doing this several times, she then punched a set of numbers and waited. Nothing happened.

"Well, it was worth a try," Manny fidgeted impatiently. His tolerance for standing in one place was about ten seconds. "Let's break open the glass."

"Shhh! No more suggestions from you!" Siobhan hissed at him.

Manny quieted immediately, rolling his eyes at Kameron. Kameron shrugged his shoulders and looked at his wristwatch. They were running out of time.

Siobhan tried another series of numbers and then another. On her fourth attempt, the lock clicked and the green light came on. Feeling along the door for the knob, she turned it and pushed the door open.

"Awesome!" Manny exclaimed.

"Yes, I know I am, but thank you for saying it anyway," Siobhan replied.

"How did you do that?" Kameron asked.

"Don't you worry your pretty little head over it, Kam." Siobhan slapped his butt as he passed.

"Stop that!" Kameron scooted forward quicker than he had intended.

Siobhan giggled and followed the boys into the room and shut the door behind her.

Once inside, the trio found discarded crates and started loading the scared kittens into them. Manny was surprised at how many cages were empty, but then he remembered the barrels in the freezer. *At least, we can save these guys*, he thought sadly.

There were twelve kittens in total and they were small enough to fit them into three carriers. That was one carrier for each of them. As they moved back toward the door, two men appeared outside the glass window. It was the guys from the white van.

Siobhan let out a startled yelped as Manny grabbed her by the shoulders and pulled her down with him. Kameron looked back at Manny, wondering what his friend was doing. Manny scrambled forward and grabbed his arm and yanked him off his feet and onto the floor beside him and Siobhan.

"It's those van guys!" he hissed, scuttling across the floor toward Chiquita.

Watson was at the door growling under his breath as Chiquita bounced up and stopped short, sniffing the door. Before Manny could reach her, she let out a series of sharp barks that echoed throughout the room. Thankfully, the bottom half of the door was steel and Chiquita was too short to be seen.

Manny finally grabbed her and held her close to his chest, covering her mouth and telling her to stay quiet. Chiquita obeyed her guardian but the damage had already been done. They hunkered down against the wall, under the window. Kameron held onto Watson and Manny had Chiquita. Everyone held their breath, waiting for the door to open.

After several tense minutes, Manny finally couldn't take it any longer and slowly lifted his head up and looked out through the window. The men were gone. Tapping on the glass, Manny realized that it was double thickness and most likely soundproof or close to it. Breathing a sigh of relief, he stood up and helped Siobhan to her feet.

"Close one!" Kameron whispered, letting out a deep breath. "Let's wait five minutes to make sure they're gone and then get the heck out of here."

"Yeah, way too close." Siobhan reached out and grabbed the arm closest to her, which happened to be Manny's. "I've had all the fun I can handle for one day. You two sure know how to show a girl a good time."

Exactly five minutes later, Kameron opened the door and checked the hallway. The coast was clear so he led the way out the door. Manny let go of Chiquita and placed a carrier in Siobhan's hand before picking up his crate of kittens. Once everyone was in the hallway, Kameron gave Watson the command to "go home"

"Cross your fingers we make it out without coming across those two rejects!" Kameron said, following Watson.

"Did anyone else hear that?" Siobhan asked and pulled back on Manny's arm, slowing him down.

"Hear what?" Manny asked, coming to a stop. Chiquita, who had been walking on his heels looking behind her, collided with him and let out a little yelp.

Not stopping to wait for their friends, Kameron and Watson rounded the next corner coming face to face (or crotch to snout in Watson's case) with a guard who had been walking down the hallway from the other direction. Everyone stopped moving. Kameron eyed the guard. The guard eyed Watson. Kameron opened his mouth to say something but closed it again since there was nothing to say.

Thankfully, Watson wasn't as spellbound as everyone else seemed to be. Growling low and menacingly, he pulled back his lips, exposing his fangs—sharp fangs that could shred a good-sized leg in a few bites if he wanted to. Apparently, the guard had come to the same conclusion. His hand moved slowly toward his stun gun.

"I wouldn't do that if I were you. He's trained to take down an armed thug. Think you can get us all before we bring you down?" Kameron asked the guard who immediately froze in place.

"Who is it?" Siobhan whispered to Manny.

"A guard," Manny whispered back. He picked up Chiquita who was trying to get a piece of the action.

"Put your hands on your head and turn around," Kameron ordered and placed a restraining hand on Watson's collar.

Moving slowly, the guard did as instructed. Kameron waved his arm behind his back, signaling Manny to lead Siobhan down the hallway.

"Don't move until I tell you to," Kameron said, following Siobhan and Manny down the hallway. "Or I let the Doberman go."

"Look, kid, you are in enough trouble as it is. Give up now and I'll see that things go easy for you." The guard started to turn around as he spoke.

"Run!" Kameron yelled as he passed the others, Watson close on his heels.

42

Snatch and Grab

Hank stopped by one of the labs and grabbed a couple of bottles of chloroform and some rags. He also confiscated some rope and two plastic animal crates. Hurrying back to Carlos, he dropped the equipment he carried and gave his sleeping compadre a good kick in the rear. Carlos jumped halfway to his feet, fumbling with his hat before falling back to the floor.

"Get up, stupid!" Hank hauled Carlos to his feet. "We got work to do."

Carlos finally managed to get his hat straightened out and clambered to his feet. "What's up, Hank?"

"Those kids came out here in full force and they brought Goliath with them. So we don't have to worry about how we're going to get him or when. The when is now and the how is with this." Hank held up the chloroform and rags. "Now let's go to the van, get my dart gun, and go get us a fightin' dog."

Once at the van, Hank pulled the dart gun out from its case. He inserted a tranquilizer dart into the chamber and cocked it. Together he and Carlos moved closer to the SUV, being careful not to be seen. The girl on the driver's side chattered away on a cell phone while the other one typed furiously on a laptop. No one even suspected they were there. Then Goliath's ugly head popped out the window.

Doesn't get any easier than this! Hank thought. *They were practically jumping into his lap.*

Signaling Carlos to move up on the SUV's passenger side, Hank took aim at Goliath and fired. Goliath let out a small yelp then disappeared inside the vehicle. Seconds later a smaller dog stuck its head out the window, looking around suspiciously. Hank couldn't believe his luck. Loading another dart into the gun, he took aim and fired. The dart traveled true, striking the other dog in the neck behind its ear.

Moving fast now, Hank approached the vehicle on the driver's side where the redhead sat. Soaking his cloth with the chloroform, he sidled along the SUV, keeping an eye on the rearview mirror, watching the redhead. She had whipped around in her seat, to peer behind her at the prostrate dogs.

"Ohmigod, Aimee!" she exclaimed. The redhead's hand shot out to shake the other girl's shoulder while she pointed frantically at the backseat. Frowning, the dark-haired girl leaned around to the backseat, reaching toward one of the dogs. At the window Hank looked inside. Both girls were now regarding the mutts in the backseat, their bodies twisted with their backs facing the windows; they didn't even notice him or Carlos.

Hank reached inside and grabbed the redhead by the hair, pulling her head toward him and covering her mouth with the cloth. Her eyes widened with fright and she let out what would have been a loud, piercing shriek if it hadn't been effectively smothered by Hank's hand and the chloroform-soaked cloth. She struggled for a few seconds, her hands protectively clutching her bag to her chest, before she passed out.

Attempting to mimic Hank, Carlos reached inside the window and tried to grab the other girl's hair. Having witnessed Hank take out her friend, this girl was a little feistier. She batted his arm away, and before he knew what was going on, she kicked the door open with him still hanging through the window. Carlos fell in a heap on the ground, his head bouncing off the ground, with the cloth hitting him in the face before he dropped it.

Jumping from the SUV, the dark-haired girl stopped to give Carlos a kick in the groin before darting off toward the building. His second groin shot of the day.

"Take that, you pig!" she hissed, before bolting toward the building. "Kameron!" she yelled at the top of her lungs.

Unfortunately for her, the kick was a costly mistake since it gave Hank time to run around the front of the vehicle. Aiming his dart gun at her fleeing back, Hank fired, hitting her below the shoulder.

She almost made it to where the van was parked before she dropped to her knees. Turning around, still on her knees, she faced Hank who was closing in on her. She looked more angry than scared. "I'll kill you if you touch a hair on Hoku's head!" she threatened. But it was an empty threat as her eyes glazed over and she passed out, falling face-first into the dirt.

"Yeah, I'm running scared, little girl," Hank muttered, quickly grabbing the sleeping girl and dragging her to the back of the SUV. Giving the stunned Carlos a kick in the side, he cussed several times. *Why do I always have to do everything myself*, he wondered. Carlos had almost let the girl get away. Good thing none of the guards came running. And to top it off, the idiot had chloroformed himself with the soaked cloth. Hank was tempted to leave the moron behind but thought better of it. He still needed someone to clean out the dog cages and do his grunt work, and Carlos, as lazy as he was, worked cheap and didn't talk back much. Hank reached down and shook Carlos until the man opened his eyes.

"Get up, moron!" Hank growled between clenched teeth.

Kicking Carlos a second time, Hank dropped the girl and pulled Carlos forcefully to his feet. *At least the moron hadn't gotten a full dose*, Hank thought, as his partner in crime started to wake up.

"Go get the van. We have some cargo to load up."

Hank pushed Carlos to get him started. He wondered for the hundredth time why he was so good to his stupid companion. Guess it was his good nature to take care of things weaker and more stupid than he was.

Hank checked the SUV to make sure the dogs were out cold. Both dogs lay on the back seat sleeping soundly. Hank hauled them both outside and gave them a good once over. The little dog wouldn't last long in the ring but would provide some entertainment. Goliath had put on some weight and looked good. The kid must have overfed him to get him so bulky. Hank shrugged as he pulled the red-headed girl out of the SUV and laid her on the ground beside the other girl and the dogs. Walking to the end of the alleyway, he looked both ways to make sure there were no walkers out. The coast was clear.

Carlos pulled the van up beside the sleeping bodies and stopped. Getting out of the van, he massaged his temples and yawned. Rubbing his eyes, he tried to focus. Hank walked to the back of the van and opened the cargo doors. Together they lifted the two girls into the vehicle and quickly tied them up, back to back. Then they shoved the dogs into the waiting cages. Hank wasn't taking any chances that Goliath might wake up while in transit and cause trouble.

Climbing into the driver's seat, Hank put the van in gear and drove it out of the alleyway. As he drove, he began to develop a devious plan for the girls. He already knew what he was going to do with Goliath. But the girls were an added bonus. He knew a Russian guy who would pay handsomely for two young girls. The teenage slave market was doing pretty good from what he understood.

Goliath and the other dog were another matter. Hank came up with an even better idea for tomorrow night's fight. He would do a last-dog-standing competition like they did in the WWF with wrestlers. Only Goliath and his little girlfriend would take on all comers, two at a time, until they were finally killed. It should be a good night. Hank was still amazed at how good his luck had been tonight. Already counting the money he was going to make, he drove off into the night with his captives securely bundled up in the back.

43

From Russia With Love

David sat quietly in his wheelchair, looking at the older guard across the desk. The security guards had actually carried him, chair and all, inside the building. He suddenly wished he had taken a more time to come up with a better plan. Beads of sweat trickled down his forehead and he wiped it away with his sleeve. His mom was going to kill him when she had to come and get him out—if that was what they intended. The younger guard had implied David was going to get what he deserved. That could mean almost anything in this crazy world of animal abusers.

None of the guards had spoken since they had brought David into the office. They were all still here and Brian's cousin was still glaring at him. This would be a crappy way to end his life. To survive a near-fatal car crash only to be killed by a group of bored security guards was almost too much for David. Maybe they were the Russian Mafia in disguise. He wondered if they would do cement wheels on his chair instead of shoes before they tossed him off a pier.

On the other hand, a quick death might be more agreeable than trying to explain to his mother what he was doing sitting outside a lab building creating a disturbance. He wondered if she would try to get him off on a plea bargain or try to teach him a lesson by letting him go to jail, like that rich girl in the news who got busted for a DUI and had to go to jail.

David was close to losing it. His friends should be free by now, but Niamh hadn't given him the okay to leave so he was still twiddling his thumbs, trapped in the security room. The younger guard kept taunting him with threats of punishment. He threatened everything from dismemberment to electrocution. The other guards rolled their eyes, making David realize the threats at least were hollow. That still didn't get him out of trouble as a call to the police wouldn't go over too well either. Normally, he would throw some one-liners back at the younger guard, but why push his luck? He could imagine explaining this one to his mom. She would never let him out of the house again.

Opening the door, a middle-aged man over six feet tall and dressed in a dark business suit entered the room. The guards immediately all stood up, looking as uncomfortable as David felt. Obviously, someone in charge had arrived. Maybe it would have been better dealing with a mere peon. Not waiting for an invitation, the balding man pulled up a chair and sat within a few inches of David's wheelchair.

"Good evening, young man." The man had a soothing, European accent. Maybe he was from Russia. He sounded like someone who was used to giving orders that would be immediately obeyed. "What brings you out to my lab today?"

Although his voice sounded pleasant, his eyes bore right through David, making him squirm in his seat. He felt like a trapped bug under some sadistic kid's magnifying glass; all that was missing was the bright shine of an interrogation light. David couldn't maintain eye contact.

There was something eerily dark and Ernst Stavro Blofield sinister about this man. He was definitely giving off bad vibes while maintaining cool politeness. David's stomach troll did back flips and somersaults and flying cannonballs. David thought he was about to vomit. This time he realized he was in way over his head.

"He was out front again creating a ruckus," the young guard said, trying to impress the older man. It didn't work.

"That will be all, gentlemen. I will handle our guest from here." He didn't take his eyes from David.

None of the guards said anything. As a group, they left the room without a backward glance, leaving David to his fate.

A number of awful scenarios flashed through David's overactive imagination. This was it! He was right. The boss was a Russian mobster and he was going to kill him without any witnesses. He had always wondered how they mixed the cement. *Guess I'm about to find out*, he thought morbidly.

"Well? I'm waiting for an answer, young man." The man looked at David expectantly.

"Huh?" David said intelligibly. He was doing that a lot lately.

"I said, what are you doing at my facility?" the man asked. His voice had dropped even lower and had a dangerous, no-nonsense-will-be-tolerated quality to it.

"Oh, that." David laughed nervously. "Well, you see, your lab is not accessible to disabled people in wheelchairs and you don't have many parking spaces set aside. That's discrimination, you know." His voice broke as he spoke. He could feel his heart pounding in his chest like it would explode at any second. Maybe he was like that guy on the show *Heroes* and was going to explode and blow up the whole city and everyone in it. A strong hand clamped down hard on his shoulder and brought him abruptly back to reality.

"For starters my facility has no need to be accessible for wheelchairs as I have no wheelchair-bound employees, and we do not deal directly with the public. That not withstanding, if you had gone around to the other side of the building, you could have entered through the wheelchair accessible door and gone up to any floor using the elevator. It is conveniently placed right by the door. As to the wheelchair parking outside, the city only requires one space be placed there. So maybe you should go and stake out City Hall and see if you can put some pressure on the politicians and city council members there to change the rules."

"Oh." David grimaced. Forget about being physically challenged, he was on a verbally challenged roll.

David wanted to ask about the animals in the lab but had lost his nerve seconds after the man entered the room. Suave, yet slimy at the same time. So maybe David did watch too many mobster-type movies, but this guy gave off some seriously bad mojo like someone who would definitely put other people in cement shoes. He wasn't someone David felt up to the challenge to, well, challenge. David was sure the man was about to crush his shoulder as the grip tightened, squeezing painfully.

"Now if you have no further questions, young man, I will see you to the door."

The pressure on David's shoulder eased up slightly. David gulped hard and wheeled quietly behind the man as he walked toward the front entrance. Opening the double doors, the man waved David through before walking out onto the top landing himself.

"There will be no more of this nonsense. Is that understood?" There was no room for argument in that question. It was more of an order than an actual question. This guy was used to being obeyed.

At the moment David was feeling obedient, not to mention he was scared shipless. "Yes, yes, sir."

David hadn't recovered his nerve yet and overcame an insane urge to salute the man. Usually he had some witty comment to make. His intuition warned him strongly to wheel out of there as fast as he could before this guy changed his mind. Without waiting for an invitation, David wheeled to the stairs and plunged over the edge. He had done this so many times at school it was almost second nature. He hardly needed to focus as he tipped his chair back slightly and bounced down the steps. Damned if he was going to let this guy help him down the stairs.

"Bravo, young man, well done."

The man actually clapped as David hit the sidewalk and quickly rolled away toward the side of the building without looking back. With the hair standing up on the back of his neck and his skin resembling that of a freshly plucked goose, David was sure he'd be shot in the back at any moment. He was practically holding his breath as he sped to the side of the building. Rounding the corner on two wheels like Speed Racer, he let out a sigh of relief and slowed down.

Wheeling toward the back door of the building, David realized something was different. Looking around he tried to figure out what had changed. Then he realized the white van was gone. He spun around in a circle to see if it had parked somewhere else close by. Crossing his fingers the tables hadn't turned and those losers weren't watching and waiting to jump on him and his friends, David wheeled himself over to Kameron's SUV.

"Hey, guys! There is one seriously scary Dr. Evil working in that place!" David called out when he neared the vehicle. "Umm, guys?"

There was no answer, no grinning dog face popped up in a window, and no non-stop chattering Irish girl to barrage him with twenty questions either. David's goose bumps came back. The silence didn't bode well. Beside the vehicle lay a bunched-up, white cloth that shined like a beacon of doom from the ground. He picked it up and immediately dropped the oily cloth after getting a good whiff. His eyes watered and he coughed several times. If he remembered his spy chemistry correctly, the cloth had been soaked with chloroform.

"Goliath, come!" David yelled and then whistled several times. Looking around frantically, he turned his wheelchair in circles and was about ready to go back inside the lab to look for them.

"Did James Bond ever have such a crappy night?" David muttered morosely, wheeling himself towards the back door.

Feeling as edgy as a mouse loitering in front of a trapdoor spider's lair, David wheeled himself underneath the building lights and dialed up Kameron's cell. While he sat there confused and trying to understand what the missing van and chloroform-soaked cloth might mean, the backdoor of the lab burst open.

44

Great Escape

Kameron, Watson, Siobhan, Chiquita, and Manny spilled out of the lab and toppled over and around David who sat directly in their path. If David wasn't so caught up in his own thoughts, he probably would have screamed at the sudden bang of the door slamming against the wall. But since he was preoccupied, he only yelped then jumped in his seat and fumbled with his phone to keep from dropping it. Watson dodged nimbly to one side as Chiquita ducked under David's chair, coming out unscathed on the other side. Siobhan let out a yelp of her own as she crashed into David and tumbled onto his lap, almost dropping her crate of kittens.

Manny and Kameron managed to go to either side of David's chair with Kameron, at the last minute, swinging his crate up and over David's head to avoid knocking him out. Kameron quickly set his cage on the ground and went back to shut the door. Grabbing a discarded piece of lumber sitting by the garbage can, he jammed it against the doorknob. Turning around he leaned heavily on the closed door. Within seconds someone started banging on the other side. Kameron jumped away with a start and picked up his crate. Going to stand protectively by his guardian, Watson began to bark loudly at the closed door.

"What happened inside?" David had so many questions, his hand on his wheel, already swiveling the wheelchair in the SUV's direction. "Where are Aimee and Niamh? Aren't they with you? Where's Goliath!"

"What do you mean? Where's my sister!" Siobhan screeched, climbing off his lap, being careful not to drop the cage she carried. "She's not with us! Aren't they still in the SUV?"

"We need to get out of here. In case you didn't hear all the banging on the door, the guards are right behind us." Manny hopped from foot to foot, full of anxious energy. "We can't stand out here trying to figure this out. Now's not a good time. Geez! Shut that dog up before he brings more guards out here!"

Kameron shot Manny a stern look. "We need to get out of here. Like now!" He pointed at the lab door that was being pushed open even as they stood/sat there.

"I'm not leaving Goliath and Aimee here with those guys," David snarled at Kameron.

"And what about my sister!" Siobhan interjected.

"Everyone getting caught isn't going to help anyone," Kameron said calmly. "We need to regroup and come up with a plan. Let's go, people!"

"Fine. Let's go," David grumbled, begrudgingly seeing the sense in Kameron's words.

"Good call," Kameron said. "Come on let's get out of here!

David took the cage from Siobhan and placed it on his lap. He then placed her hand on the back rest of the chair. Giving his chair a strong push, he called back to Siobhan. "Hang on."

Kameron and Manny ran toward the SUV parked on the other side of the parking lot. Watson and Chiquita kept pace easily, seeming to love this new game of chase. David and Siobhan were only a few strides behind and coming fast. David wheeled to a stop and handed the cage to Kameron who had already loaded the other two crates into the back cargo area. Chiquita bounced her way into the vehicle and over the seats. Siobhan felt her way along the side of the SUV to the door Manny had opened for her and climbed in.

"Those jerks took my stick," Siobhan complained.

Manny climbed in beside her. "I know, Siobhan, but at least we got out of that freezer." Manny sighed. Chiquita wiggled under his hand. "And we did rescue the kittens."

"Only to lose everyone else!" David quickly climbed into the back seat and angrily folded his wheelchair and swung it over the seat into the back cargo area with the crates. Kameron closed the cargo doors and raced to the front, jumping into the driver's seat.

"Where do you think they went?" Manny asked, looking at Watson who tried to make room on the seat beside the laptop sitting there still open and powered on.

"Do you think they went to look for us when we lost the connection?" Siobhan asked.

"Maybe, but wouldn't we have passed them inside?" Kameron asked, picking up the laptop and handing it back to David.

"I think someone grabbed them." David said quietly. "Aimee wouldn't leave her computer sitting on the front seat with the doors unlocked."

"Do you think the guards got them?" Manny looked out the back window. "Ah, guys, speaking of guards...let's get out of here!"

Kameron fumbled in his pocket, looking for the keys. He tried all his pockets but no keys. Frantically, he looked through the console tray, throwing papers and paraphernalia everywhere. Still no keys. Chiquita jumped up on the console, wagging her whole body.

Manny gave a play-by-play of the guard's progress. "Here they come. There's two of them. Big, beefy ones! Definitely not donut-eating types. They're pulling out their stun guns. Oh, that's not good. Not good at all. Here comes another one out of the door. There are three of them now. We need to get out of here. Like pronto! Kameron, do something— do something yesterday!"

Chiquita dropped what she carried, which jingled as it fell. She bounced up and touched Kameron's shoulder with both paws and barked excitedly to get his attention. Finally, Kameron looked over at her and saw that she stood on his keys. In fact, she was standing on two sets of keys.

"Sweet!" David blurted out. "Good girl. Wow. Now that's a good trick. You think she can find the others?"

"Maybe she can pull Niamh out of a hat," Siobhan said drily.

"Oh, no! My wheels! I can't leave it here for them to find!" Manny exclaimed, quickly grabbing his keys before leaping out of the SUV and running in the opposite directions from the guards.

David reached out and caught Chiquita in mid-jump as she tried to follow her guardian. He quickly slammed the door shut and locked it for safe measure.

Kameron rammed the keys into the ignition, turned the engine over, and pulled the gearshift out of park. The guard that was the Brian-look-alike reached through the driver's side window with his stun gun and aimed it at Kameron's neck.

Giving the guard his best cheesy smile, Kameron gunned the accelerator. The SUV lurched forward, dumping the unlucky guard onto the ground as he hit the button on his stun gun. As he fell, David saw him land on his own gun. His body was still jerking up and down as the SUV rounded the corner and sped down the street to freedom. The other guards stood by and watched the SUV disappear down the street. The last David saw of them, they were rolling their buddy over and appeared to be laughing. No doubt about it—they were a sadistic bunch. Good thing he got away from them when he did.

After several quick turns, Kameron slowed the SUV to normal speed and turned to David. "Well, what do you think happened to Aimee, Niamh, and the dogs?"

"Dunno, but did either of you notice the white van was gone?" David asked ominously. "I'm thinking that the dog fighting guys wanted Goliath back."

"But that wouldn't explain why they would take Aimee and Niamh," Kameron said.

"We need to call the police!" Siobhan was nearly hysterical. "If anything happens to my sister, I'll kill those jerks."

"Oh, and I found a cloth soaked in chloroform lying on the ground by the SUV before you guys ran me down." David, still in shock, explained what that meant. "Most likely they used the chloroform to knock everyone out."

"Oh, great. Just freaking great!" Siobhan started crying quietly.

"David, you're not helping." Kameron threw a withering glare David's way.

"Before we call the police, let's go back to Manny's place and meet up with him and make sure the girls aren't there," David suggested. "Maybe they got away and went home to get some help."

Although his optimistic words suggested otherwise, David had a sinking feeling in the pit of his stomach. What would he do without Goliath? And what about poor Aimee and Hoku? If those jerks did anything to hurt Aimee, he would make them pay. Tears welled up in his eyes as he tried to hold back the wave of nausea that threatened to overcome him.

As they drove up the driveway David noticed he had his feet on Niamh's *My Chemical Romance* purse, which had fallen on the floor in the backseat during the scuffle. Bending over he reached down and picked up the purse, placing it on Siobhan's lap. She held it close to her chest without saying anything.

45

Fit to be Tied

A imee woke up with her head pounding in her ears. Her arms and wrists were tied behind her back, and they felt numb and lifeless. She tried moving her legs but they wouldn't budge. Slowly opening her eyes, she tried to check out her surroundings. As far as she could tell, she was lying on the floor in the back of van. With a sinking heart, she knew it was the white van. Someone was tied behind her and she had a sinking feeling it was Niamh. She also realized the goons who nabbed them had to have been the owners of the white van that had been tailing David.

Using her head, Aimee bumped Niamh several times until the other girl gradually woke up. Aimee could tell when Niamh finally woke up by the way she attempted to move her arms and legs in vain as Aimee had done when she first came to.

"You okay, Niamh?" Aimee asked. Well, at least her voice was working, although her mouth and throat were as dry as the Mojave desert.

"Okay? What do you mean by okay? Like, do you mean am I okay with being tied up in the back of some van!"

Of course, Aimee couldn't hear Niamh's response but could feel Niamh's back tighten up. Niamh's body shook slightly as she started crying. Aimee could tell Niamh was losing it. With her forehead pressed against the scratchy carpet covering the floor of the van, Aimee made herself count to ten in order not to say anything snarky.

"Hey, easy there, girlfriend. Hysterics won't get us out of here." Aimee was not the panicky type. Address the problem and find a solution. She had dealt with her disability this way all of her life. Plus being captain of the volleyball team, you can't lose it on everyone no matter how lame it was of them to miss a spike or block or serve into the net. Assess the situation then come up with a plan. "We need to get untied first so we can talk since I can't see a thing. And even if you knew sign language, I'm no Helen Keller who can understand if you do it against my palm."

Aimee hoped Niamh was calming down since she had never been any good at dealing with girly girls and was definitely not into coddling and holding anyone's hand. Niamh had to buck up and get her act together for them to get out of this situation. Aimee hoped the other girl would get a grip on her own and she wouldn't need to resort to butting Niamh in the back of the head. "Can you see anything on your side that will help cut these ropes?"

Aimee felt Niamh's head swiveling in different directions as Niamh looked around at their surroundings.

"No, there is nothing in here at all but you and me."

Niamh knew Aimee couldn't hear her but felt the need to talk anyway. She always talked more when she was nervous. Something wiggled against her belly. Maeve! She could have crushed her! Niamh almost starting crying again at the awful thought of what could have been. Tears swimming in her eyes, Niamh looked down with great difficulty and talked soothingly to her little fuzzy friend. "It's okay, a chailín mo chroí. Mommy's tied up at the moment, but I'll get you out soon. I promise."

Maeve wiggled again and scratched against the carrier she was in. Her nose butted against the zipper, trying to get out. For a second

Niamh envisioned her little trooper clawing her way out of the carrier and chewing through the ropes that held her. Or maybe she could develop superhero powers and bust out herself. She took a deep breath and strained against the ropes with the tiniest glimmer of hope, imagining that she would be able to break free. The ropes could be rotten for all she knew.

With a sigh she crashed back to reality. What was she thinking! She couldn't believe that she actually tried to bust out of the ropes with her own lack of strength. This wasn't some fairy tale or made-for-TV movie where everything worked out with perfect happy endings. This was the real world. There would be no clever writer getting her out of this scene. She needed a plan and quickly. Who knew when those jerks would come back to finish what they had started? Forget those bozos! Who knew how hot it would get in the van? Her baby wouldn't be able to survive the heat! Niamh tried to tap down another burst of hysteria as Maeve vigorously scratched at the zipper.

Aimee began to get some feeling back into her legs and arms. She wished she was a Chinese contortionist or one of those Cirque du Soleil people, but it didn't look likely in this lifetime! She didn't even think she could touch her toes with her fingers, much less her head! Maybe she could wiggle her wrists out of the ropes that held her and Niamh tied together. She tried for several seconds but only succeeded in tightening the ropes more. Okay, scratch that idea. Maybe Niamh had a plan?

"Niamh, I can't think of anything. I'm totally brain dead. Have you got any ideas?" Aimee tried to think but her head was still in a fog.

"I've got nothing over here unless you think you can untie me from your end because my fingers kinda feel like sausages at the moment and there's, like, no way I would be able to untie you," Niamh replied. "Wait a minute. Hey! Maybe if we both move together we can sit up." Of course, there was no response from Aimee. "Then again, maybe not."

Aimee felt around, trying to get at her back pocket where she kept her cell phone. She could touch it but couldn't seem to reach inside. "Niamh, let's see if we can sit up. We go on three, okay? Tap my leg once if you agree."

Niamh tapped Aimee's leg. "Now didn't I just say that? I guess great minds think alike."

Together they both tried to roll over and sit up. Unfortunately, neither one of them had ever tried to work together tied up before. As Aimee tried to sit to the left, Niamh would go to the other side, pulling her back down. After several unsuccessful attempts, Aimee called a halt.

"Okay, we need to coordinate this a little better. Since I can't hear you, you'll have to follow my lead," Aimee said. "I'm rolling up to the right, which will be your left. Ready?" Aimee waited for the tap on her leg. Niamh tapped her leg that she understood.

Again they tried to sit up. This time they made it with some minor head banging against the side of the van. "Kewlies, we did it. Go, girl power!" Aimee said excitedly.

"Woot! Woot!" Niamh got caught up in the excitement.

From where she sat, Niamh could see through the bars into the front seat. Aimee faced the back cargo doors. Looking out the front window, Niamh could see a dilapidated building several hundred feet away. There were several other vehicles parked in front of the van they were in. The sun sat high in the sky, making it about noontime. Niamh noticed for the first time how hot it was in the back of the van. Thankfully, the windows were heavily tinted and they were parked under one of the many oak trees that dotted the field. If not for that, they would be fried by now. Some thoughtful person—yeah, right!—had left the front windows open.

"Niamh, can you reach my phone? It's in my back pocket."

Aimee tried to lift her butt cheek to make it easier for Niamh to get into her pocket. Niamh wiggled her fingers around, sliding them into

Aimee's back pocket, and grabbed the tip of the small device. Carefully, she pulled on the phone but it didn't budge.

"Drat! Remind me to tell you that you need to wear looser fitting jeans from now on."

Niamh wished Aimee could hear her. She could use some reassurance right about now. She was scared out of her mind. The thought of those two scruffy old guys coming back made her nauseous. She tried again and managed to get a good grip on the cell phone charm string. This time she got it all the way out. Now what? She couldn't bring it to where she could see to dial.

"Awesome, Niamh, you're amazing! I'll never make fun of you for being so prissy ever again. I swear!" Aimee knew her friend was terrified. She wanted to reassure her but also needed her to be strong. If they were going to get out of this in one piece, they needed to keep their wits about them.

"Now hold the phone up so Siri can hear you." Aimee only hoped that the rest of the guys had fared better than they had.

"Hey Siri, call David," Niamh said.

"Calling David. David is not available at this time and his voicemail box is full." Siri stated.

"David, I'm going to kill you! How can your mailbox be full? You only have six friends!" Niamh growled then tried again. "Siri, text message to David."

As Niamh finished dictating a text message to David, the front door banged open.

46

Plan B, C and D

O enghus was beside himself with worry until Siobhan entered his kennel. She barely stepped through the gate before he accosted her with his big tongue, soaking her upraised hands and face.

"Easy, a thaisce. Mummy's back," Siobhan said soothingly. She tried to calm her worried canine companion with gentle sweeping face strokes. "Sorry, I left without you. It won't happen again. I promise."

Oenghus woofed several times at David and Kameron as if to say, *"How dare you let her leave without me?"* He circled around his guardian protectively, brushing up so close to her legs that he nearly knocked her over several times.

"Okay, a thaisce, I said sorry. Now behave yourself." Siobhan gave him a reassuring pat on the head. "Sit, Oenghus."

Obediently, the wolfhound sat at Siobhan's side. Even sitting, his head reached Siobhan's chest level. As she waited patiently with Oenghus, David and Kameron checked the house, kennels, and backyard for signs of the others while Manny went to set up one of the kennels for the kittens they rescued.

"Okay, we've checked the house and the kennel. They are most definitely not here," David said, wheeling up to where Siobhan waited.

"We need to call the police, like, now." Siobhan used both hands to stroke Oenghus on the head as she spoke.

"And say what exactly?" David asked. "Hello, officer, we broke into a lab downtown and stole some kittens that were going to be used for experimentation and some of our friends were kidnapped while we were committing grand theft larceny?"

"That wouldn't go over very well," Manny added unnecessarily, joining David and Siobhan with an armful of Big Red sodas. "I can't go to prison. I'm far too pretty."

"Too pretty to die!" Siobhan snorted, trying not to laugh. "You're not all that."

"Awesome!" David laughed and reached over to help himself to the sweet, red soda. Manny put a can in Siobhan's hand. "I totally needed the sugar rush."

"We can't sit here and do nothing!" Siobhan shouted in David's face. David was always amazed at how well she could find people when she wanted to. Maybe it was like a fae force. But at the moment he was getting more of a taste of her Irish temper. "Now that you're getting refueled with sugar and caffeine, you need to do something. Come up with a plan, genius!"

David's phone began to ring before he could reply. Thankful for the respite, he got out his cell and flipped open the cover. He didn't recognize the number. "Hello?"

"David, this is Greta from the Animal Rescue Co." Greta's voice spoke into David's earpiece.

David turned on the cell's external speaker so everyone could hear.

"Hi, Greta. Is Aimee with you by any chance?" It was worth a shot.

"Nein, not today, sweetie," Greta said. "I do have some good news though. I have the address from the license plate number Aimee gave me."

"That's great!" David began to formulate a new plan in his head. "Let me get something to write with."

Kameron, who had returned after searching the backyard, took out a pen and small notepad to write down the number. David sent Manny to get the laptop computer so they could locate the address. Maybe there was still hope of finding the girls and Goliath and Hoku before anything terrible happened.

"Now you promise me that if I give you this address you won't do anything silly? You have to promise this to me. I'm already taking a huge risk helping you out. I don't want to lose my job over this."

"No worries," Kameron reassured, holding the pen at ready and crossing his fingers with the other hand. "I'll keep an eye on the kids for you... make sure they don't do anything rash."

Greta chuckled and read off the address. "I'll wait for your phone call and I'll be ready to mobilize the troops if you find anything. Remember... do not go on the property! Call me right away if there are any signs of dogs or other animals being abused. Then I will go out and investigate. We need proof before I can get a search order and police back up."

"What? They won't come out on your hunch, Greta? I thought you had more clout than that. Didn't Aimee say you had a certain police officer eating out of the palm of your hand?" David teased.

"Such a silly boy!" Greta giggled. They could almost hear her blush over the phone. "Oh, I have another call. Now you must promise me to be careful. Do not take any risks! Look around only and call me." Greta hung up the phone.

Manny rolled his eyes and handed the laptop to David. "Hmmmm, I guess it's a good thing we didn't tell her about the kittens. You think she'd give us the address if we had?"

Siobhan snickered. "She probably would have had kittens!"

"Ohmigod... kittens! Why didn't I think about that before?" At everyone's blank stare, David continued as he booted up the laptop. "What have we been staking out?"

Manny's face broke into a huge grin, and he jumped up and down excitedly. "The cameras!"

Kameron smiled. "Good thinking. We'll see what definitely happened to them."

David rewound the surveillance tape and they watched their friends' kidnapping in fast forward. Siobhan nibbled on a thumbnail while her other hand fiddled with Oenghus' ear. "Did you find it yet? Do you see them? You have to tell me what you see!"

Kameron winced. "Oh, that's gonna leave a mark."

Manny smiled. "You go, Aimee! Too bad that guy shot her."

"What!" Siobhan's hand involuntarily tightened on Oenghus' ear and he yelped, shaking free.

"With a dart," Kameron calmly explained. "They darted the dogs then chloroformed Niamh. But they didn't surprise Aimee." Kameron chuckled. "She got in a good kick before she got darted."

David frowned and snapped the laptop shut. "It's them. The guys from the white van. Those losers took our friends and we're going to get them back!"

Manny bounced on the balls of his feet. "We've got the address so let's go already!"

"Geez, that sounds familiar. This time don't get me locked up in a freezer again," Siobhan muttered.

"Ha, ha, you're funny, Siobhan. You're a riot, I tell ya. A total riot." Manny rolled his eyes and grabbed her hand.

David's phone burst into song. He flipped up the phone and saw who he received a text message from. "It's from Aimee!" He smiled and oddly enough almost felt like crying. "They haven't been hurt but they don't know where they are. And here's the clincher—they're in a van somewhere!"

Siobhan started crying softly. "She's okay! Niamh's okay." She grabbed Manny and hugged him tightly.

"Well, as Sherlock Holmes would say, 'the game is on'!" Kameron got up from his chair and headed to the SUV. "Come, my dear Watson, let's go rescue our friends and get these scumbags thrown in jail."

47

Slim Jim

G reta chewed her lower lip whenever she was nervous. It was a bad habit she had developed as a child growing up in a strict German family. Her dad believed to spare the rod was to spoil the child and he didn't spoil his children. After leaving home at a young age, she discovered she had a love for animals. She attended a veterinary technician program as a teenager and realized what she wanted to do was help abused animals.

There was a spiritual component to Greta's love of animals. She strongly believed God had placed humans on earth to take care of the planet and not abuse it. This belief transferred to all of God's creatures but especially to companion animals since Man did domesticate them after all. Greta felt God wanted her to protect the animals that could not protect themselves and she was tireless in her efforts to do so. She was their voice. She was their God-appointed protector.

After saying goodbye to David and hanging up the phone, she wondered if she had gone too far this time. If her boss found out what she had done, she would most likely get fired. An image of No. 9's lifeless body, lying limply in her arms after being euthanized, flashed through her mind's eye. No. She had done the right thing. They were good kids. They were smart enough not to take any risks. What she needed to do now was get ready to move out on a moment's notice if the kids called back with any information.

Picking up the phone, Greta called Officer Slimka to give him a heads up on the possibility of a dog fight going on in the area this week. She only hoped she would be able to rescue more dogs this time and put their owners behind bars for a long, long time.

48

Deja Vu

Goliath woke up to familiar surroundings—a cage that he had almost forgotten. Hoku lie beside him. He opened and closed his eyes several times to try to clear his vision. Getting shakily to his feet, he closely surveyed the room outside the cage. Sniffing the air, he caught the scent of more animals. Some of them were in pain. There was the smell of feces and urine and the smell of death. Too well he remembered that smell.

Something moved to his left. It was the hated man. He no longer thought of the man as his master. A metal rod poked through the crate, hitting Goliath painfully in the ribs. Turning to face the man, Goliath snarled and leapt at the cage, trying unsuccessfully to reach the man on the other side.

"So, you do remember your old buddy, Hank, doncha, mutt?" the man asked before spitting out some chewing tobacco in front of the cage. "Good thing. Hopefully, you remember how to fight cause you're gonna get your chance again tonight. You and your little girlfriend. Since she's such a little thing, I don't think she'll last all that long."

Goliath didn't understand what the man said, but he did understand that the man meant Hoku and him harm. Growling threateningly, he moved to stand protectively over Hoku who was still out cold.

Hank stuck the rod through the cage again, intending to poke the Basenji to see if she was even still alive. Before the rod got anywhere close to her, Goliath grabbed it in his powerful jaws and wrenched it out of Hank's hands. Cursing loudly, Hank kicked the cage several times before stomping out of the room.

Goliath released his grip on the rod and sniffed Hoku, who lie quietly on the floor of the cage. She whined in her sleep when his cold nose brushed her skin. Being careful not to hurt her, Goliath nudged his pack mate toward the back of the cage where he could better protect her. Satisfied Hoku was as far away from the front of the cage as he could get her, Goliath began gently licking her face, trying to wake her up.

After a few minutes, Hoku began to move her head and, before long, opened her eyes. She gazed at Goliath inquiringly, not sure what had happened or where they were. She was reassured to find the pit bull standing protectively over her but wondered where her girl was. Aimee never left her alone for long and never in a cage. Something wasn't right. Hoku whined softly before slowly getting to her feet and looking around.

There was a myriad of smells in the room they were in, smells that were foreign to her sensitive little nose. There were at least a dozen animals in other cages in the room—many of them hurt. However, the strongest scent she could detect was that of fear. Hoku sensed many of the animals were terrified of something or, more correctly, someone. She sniffed the steel rod still lying on the floor of the cage and caught the scent of a man. Goliath sniffed the rod and growled warningly. Hoku understood Goliath was warning her that the man was bad.

Still shaky on her feet, Hoku moved around their cage, sniffing here and there, looking for a way out. She tried digging at the floor, which was plastic and unyielding to her claws. Then she clawed the bars and finally tried pushing on the door with her shoulder. Nothing worked and she began to get frustrated. She wailed her displeasure at the world. The undulating, eerie howl did not bring anyone to get her out of the cage. So she finally gave up and laid down beside Goliath. Whining morosely, she waited for Aimee to come get her.

The door opened and two men walked in, carrying long sticks with ropes on one end. Hoku got up to greet them, eagerly wagging her curled tail. Finally, someone was coming to get her out of this place! Goliath growled warningly and moved protectively in front of her.

Proceeding cautiously toward the cage, the two men talked nervously to each other. The short one smelled of smoke and sausages while the tall one reeked of alcohol and tobacco. Goliath bared his teeth at their approach and growled deep in his throat, his ruff standing on end.

Hoku was confused. No one had ever tried to hurt her before, and she had been raised to trust people. People always gave out treats and belly rubs and hugs. But Goliath and all of her own senses screamed at her that these men were bad and that she should be afraid of them. The short man approached the cage and slowly opened it.

With his powerful jaws snapping, Goliath rushed the door before it was fully open. Taken by surprise, the man fell back as Goliath slammed his full weight against the door. Goliath's head craned around the door and latched onto the man's pant leg. The man yelped and with his feet slammed the door tight against Goliath's shoulder to keep him wedged in the cage. Hoku watched as the second man stuck the rope end of the pole over Goliath's head and pulled it tight. Goliath fought valiantly against the rope but couldn't reach the tall man because of the long stick he held between them.

Hoku decided it was time to come to the rescue. Charging forward, she darted out of the cage and through the legs of the short man who was getting back on his feet. Sounding like a Tasmanian Devil on Red Bull, she attacked the tall man, ripping his jeans and some flesh off his calf. Her jaw may not be as powerful as Goliath's, but she still had a mouth full of sharp teeth. She had never tasted blood before and didn't like it, but she knew they were in danger and chose to fight rather than run.

The man let out a high-pitched scream and guttural curse when Hoku grabbed his leg, but he still retained a firm grip on the pole holding Goliath captive. The Basenji held on tightly and shook her head from side to side, trying to make him let go of Goliath, while Goliath swung his head wildly and whipped his body back and forth.

"Get this stupid mutt offa me!" Hank screamed in pain, louder than the two snarling dogs. For all of his tough-talking ways, Hank was a coward when he didn't have a weapon in his hand. With his hands full trying to hold onto Goliath, Hank could only ineffectively kick out at Hoku.

"Sorry, Hank! Almost got her!" Carlos wanted to laugh but was too shocked by the viciousness of what he thought had been a placid little dog.

Growling savagely, Hoku released the man and turned around as a rope wrapped around her neck. The short man pulled tightly, choking her. She realized, too late, the mistake she had made in turning her back on the bad-smelling, short man.

Snarling and clawing at the rope, their bodies thrashing wildly, Goliath and Hoku tried unsuccessfully to break free of their captors. It was a useless effort. These men knew what they were doing and had no intention of letting go of either dog.

Hank aimed a kick at the struggling Hoku. "Count yourself lucky, you stupid dog!" Hank growled before limping across the room.

Hoku had no idea the tall man would have killed her then and there if he hadn't already booked the fight headlining Goliath and planning on using her as warm-up bait for the crowd.

After dragging the dogs across the room, the two men stopped pulling on the sticks and loosened their grips on the poles. The short man handed his stick to the tall one and moved out of sight. Hoku took a deep breath and sat down, thankful for the respite. She was more of a lover than a fighter. Goliath kept on his feet and never took his eyes off of the tall man. He continued to growl threateningly.

"Useless cur! I shoulda drowned you instead of dumping you in the garbage! Strung you up from a tree like the piece of crap you are!" Hank taunted Goliath.

Goliath bared his teeth and didn't drop his gaze from the man's stare.

Without warning a torrent of cold water doused Hoku and Goliath as the short man squirted them with a hose. Hoku tried unsuccessfully to squirm her way out of the restraining collar to no avail while Goliath closed his eyes and stoically endured the stinging spay. After completely drenching both dogs, the men proceeded to drag them toward the fight ring set up in the middle of the room. The short man handed his rod to another man standing by the ring entrance and walked away.

"Gonna go check on them girls in the van," Carlos whispered to Hank before ambling out of the room.

49

Breath Mint

Niamh froze in place and tried to signal Aimee not to move either. There was no way to tell Aimee not to move without knocking the phone out of her hand. She sat there rigidly and stared at the grizzly-looking man who popped his head in the door. Sensing the tension, Maeve stopped her futile digging at the zipper.

"'Bout time you was getting up," the man said.

"Why are you keeping us here? What did we ever do to you! And where's Goliath and Hoku? You better not have touched a hair on their heads or you'll be sorry!" Niamh said, shrilly and loudly. "I demand to be released!"

The man chuckled and moved closer to the bars separating the back of the van from the front seats. "Later, little one. I'll come back and see you later. No one is going to hurt you."

Niamh shivered involuntarily when the man's strong sausage and garlic breath wafted toward her, nearly making her vomit. She didn't believe a word he said. He didn't look overly scary, more hang dog actually. But still, he did kidnap them, so he obviously meant them no good...no good at all. Whatever he intended for them, it would not be pleasant. Niamh felt the tears well up in her eyes, threatening to spill over her cheeks any minute.

"Ugh! What is that stench?" Aimee turned her head around enough to see the man and her eyes opened wide before narrowing into an icy glare. "You scumbag!" She practically hissed at him, banging her feet on the floor of the van. "Come a little closer, why doncha?"

The man involuntarily backed away. Without another word, he reached into his back pocket and pulled out a bottle of water and stuck it between the bars where it hung suspended.

"Get back here, you jerk! I swear if you hurt Hoku I will kill you! You touch a hair on that perfect head of hers and I will skin you alive! Rip you apart limb from limb!" Aimee screamed in fury, twisting viciously to get out of her bonds. She pushed with her feet to try to swing around Niamh and face her captor. "When I get out of this, you'll never have children again!"

Eyeing Aimee nervously, Carlos quickly backed out of the van and slammed the door closed.

"He was scared of you. Wow! And I'm supposed to be the one with the Irish temper!" Niamh said, amazed at her friend's bravery. "I was scared to death when he opened the door and here you are ready to take him on."

"Lucky for him I'm tied up. That's all I can say." Aimee ranted for a moment more until the water bottle caught her eye. "Hey, Niamh, can you reach the water bottle?"

"I can try," Niamh replied.

Niamh caught herself again. It was weird because Aimee could speak fluently and didn't rely on sign language to communicate. Aimee was awesome at lip reading. David normally did all the signing for the group. Even though he didn't need to, he had learned it to make it easier for Aimee. Niamh had picked up some basic signs, but that was about it.

As she thought about it, it wasn't fair for Aimee to make all the effort of communicating with others.

"When we get out of here, Aimee, I promise to learn more sign language." As she leaned forward, her grip loosened on the phone and it clattered to the floor. "Shoot, I dropped the phone. Stupid, stupid Niamh. Sorry, Aimee, I dropped the phone."

"Did you drop the phone, Niamh?" Aimee asked, feeling the metal brush against her fingertips.

Niamh tapped her leg to signal yes. Aimee sighed.

Wriggling toward the bars and reaching as far forward as she was able, Niamh managed to grab the water bottle in her teeth and yank it through the bars. Then she realized the next problem. There was no way to hold the water and open it at the same time. Maeve scratched at her carrier, still trying to get out. The little ferret was getting more agitated and Niamh could hear more gasping hisses coming from the pouch.

Now that the girls were sitting, Niamh was in a better position to try and open the ferret pouch. Tapping Aimee's leg to get her attention, Niamh dropped the water bottle and leaned forward, making Aimee curve backward. With her chin pressed awkwardly against her chest and with Aimee's weight pressing on her back, Niamh crunched down and grabbed the carrier's zipper with her teeth and pulled.

Maeve's little black nose poked through the opening before she pushed her head out. Placing her two front paws on the zipper, she strained forward to give Niamh's chin a lick to say hello. Then she agilely climbed up onto Niamh's shoulder and surveyed her new surroundings.

Snuggling her head close to Maeve's face, Niamh made little chirping sounds as the tears rolled unchecked down her cheeks. "Ah, a chailin mo chroi," she whispered, all choked up.

Aimee tried to look around the van but couldn't see anything that might help them get out of this mess. She was unable to reach her phone since it had been so skillfully dropped or to get the water bottle that had fallen in front of Niamh.

"Can you see anything in the front that might help us get these ropes off, Niamh?" Aimee asked.

Aimee could feel her friend shaking and assumed she was crying but didn't want Niamh to know that she knew. Trying to sound braver than she felt, especially now that her rage had abated, she tried again. "Niamh, pull yourself together, girl, and look in the front for something to get us untied. We don't have much time. So snap to it!"

Niamh tapped Aimee's leg, signaling that she understood. Taking a deep breath, she looked through the bars into the front seat. She could see a set of keys, a stack of papers, a tobacco can, a small pocket knife, an open coke can, and a half-eaten sandwich. Right on! A pocket knife! Sudden inspiration flooded her and she enthusiastically tapped Aimee's leg.

Moving as close as she could get to the bars, somewhat hindered by Aimee's weight, Niamh nudged Maeve. It wouldn't take much to get Maeve to crawl between the bars into the front seat. Maeve was an adept explorer and a natural packrat (but she definitely wasn't a rodent!). She liked to collect things when given the opportunity, and climbing was a definite passion of hers, which made it that much easier to train Maeve to fetch.

"Fetch, Maeve! Fetch!" Niamh commanded.

Niamh worried at her bottom lip as the ferret did the weasel war dance on the front seat, happily dooking away. Unfortunately, this fetching wouldn't be staged with her favorite toys, so hopefully Maeve would bring back something useful before she realized that Niamh didn't have any raisins. Turning sideways, both girls sat against the bars and watched as little Maeve got distracted from her bouncing and sniffed her way toward the front of the van. She waddled over the console and disappeared under the driver's seat.

Niamh held her breath for the longest time. There was still no sign of Maeve. Hopefully, she wasn't stuck under the driver's seat. What had she done to her poor baby? Why didn't she leave her at home? Why was she always insisting on taking Maeve everywhere she could? It was hot out! She should have known better!

Niamh knew only too well how heat sensitive ferrets were. During the hot summer months, Niamh always wished that Maeve had sweat glands so she could travel with the gang instead of staying at home in the air-conditioning. And she was always paranoid in case the AC went out, especially when it was running overtime in the summer.

A few more hours in this heat and little Maeve would be in poor shape and could even die. Luckily, it was overcast and the temperature inside the van was only warm and not unbearably hot as it could well be this time of year. There was always a story on the news about little kids and dogs found dead from heatstroke inside parked cars. Niamh wished she could reach her fingernails; she needed something to chew on.

A fuzzy little head peered over the driver's seat. Niamh let out her breath and giggled. Maeve was still going strong and heading in the right direction. She rummaged around on the seat and picked up someone's baseball hat and headed back to Niamh with it.

Struggling to pull the hat through the bars, Maeve grunted and hissed until the hat finally slid through the bars. Bouncing and waddling over to Niamh's lap, the little thief deposited the hat and headed back through the bars for more loot.

Next she brought back the tobacco can but couldn't get it through the bars and finally gave up with that one. In order of retrieval, she brought back a gum wrapper, a sock, a bandana, keys, a cigarette butt, breath mints, and finally—after about what seemed like an hour—the pocket knife. Dropping the pocket knife on top of the small pile, Maeve weasel-wiggled her way back to continue her investigation of the front seat. There was still a lot of garbage for her to sift through.

Niamh got Aimee to lean over so they were both lying on their sides, and then she maneuvered herself over to the knife. She stretched her wrists through the ropes and felt along the floor with her numb fingers. She found the baseball hat first, then the keys, then part of the half-eaten sandwich, which squished messily between her fingers. A shudder coursed through her body; she gagged a little.

Grossed out to the extreme and almost in tears, she continued. Her beautiful hands were most likely ruined. No hand modeling jobs for her. Barely holding back the sobs, she finally closed her fingers around the pocket knife. Fumbling, she tried to open it but couldn't seem to make her fingers work properly. It was no use! She couldn't open the knife.

Aimee who had been quiet through all of this finally spoke up. "Come on, Niamh, don't give up now. Open the knife and cut the ropes. It's getting late and we need to get out of here—like yesterday!"

"I can't, Aimee, I tried and I can't do it." Niamh broke down crying. She knew Aimee couldn't hear her, but she needed to vent. "I'm not like you! I'm not pretty, I'm overweight, I can't kick butt, and I'm not heroic. I'm just a plain Jane!"

"Niamh, I'm sure you're babbling about something, but I have no clue what. I need you to focus here and open that knife and cut the ropes. I know you don't think you can do it but I know you can. I believe in you. You can have your girly cry fest later. Now open that knife and start cutting because it's getting dark outside. We don't want to be here after dark." Aimee tried not to sound as frightened as she was.

Niamh sniffed back the tears and tried again. This time her hands brushed against a small button and the knife popped open in her hand. She was so surprised she almost dropped it, but fortunately, she had a better grip on it than on the phone. Smiling to herself, she felt around for the ropes and began to cut.

"Yes! Yes! Yes! I knew you could do it!" Aimee blinked back tears. She wiggled her wrists, testing the partially cut ropes.

As the sun set over the roof of the old building, Niamh and Aimee rubbed their aching wrists. Although it was painful to feel the circulation flowing back into their tingling hands and fingers, it still felt good to be untied. While they took turns drinking from the water bottle, Maeve came waddling back, pulling the phone across the floor to the pile of her stash. Niamh scooped up Maeve and the phone. The water was warm but tasted sweet to the two girls who hadn't had a drink all day. They saved a quarter of the water for Maeve. Niamh let the ferret drink her fill from the water bottle cap before wetting the ferret down to hopefully keep her cool.

A lot of traffic passed the van as more vehicles arrived, some with dogs, and others with men and women who came to watch these poor wretched dogs fight for sport. Some sport! Two half-starved dogs trying to kill each other. Aimee scowled, wondering what had happened to Hoku and Goliath. If that scumbag laid a hand on her little Hoku, she vowed to impale him on a stake Dracula-style. Feeling the circulation returning to her arms and legs, Aimee moved back to the rear cargo door and tried unsuccessfully to push it open. Someone had locked it from the outside. It wouldn't budge.

Angrily, she turned to face Niamh. "We may need to fight our way out of here, Niamh. Are you going to be able to help?"

"Against those men?" Niamh spoke in a small, scared, little girl voice. "Have you gone completely nuts! There's only the two of us and all of them! How do you think we'll manage that? You're totally insane! Untying ourselves is one thing I can handle—but fight?"

Since it was getting darker, it was more difficult for Aimee to watch Niamh's words; however, she did manage to get the gist of what Niamh said. "Not men, Niamh! We'd fight those scumbags who think they're men. When I get through with them, they won't be hurting any more dogs. That's for sure! They'll be lucky if they can walk."

Niamh took strength from Aimee's anger and straightened her shoulders and nodded in agreement. Facing Aimee, she spoke slowly. "How are we going to get out of here?"

Aimee picked up her phone and handed it to Niamh. "Let's call in the cavalry."

50

Crocodile Tears

David peered out the window as Kameron slowed the SUV down. It was past noon. He checked the address on the mailbox. This was the place alright. A long graveled lane led to a fenced area overgrown with shrubs, palmettos, and other unkempt vegetation. Large trees surrounding the area made it impossible to see into the property or to the end of the road that disappeared behind a huge oak tree.

It reminded David of something out of a late night horror flick— of the cheesy, cliché, yet-still-scary horror flicks. *Here we go, into the woods to find Little Red Riding Hood. I hope the wolf isn't home,* he thought, envisioning a patrol of werewolves waiting to hunt his party down. Now that they were in front of the place this didn't seem like such a good idea.

"Are we there yet?" Manny asked, twitching in his seat like he was about to explode.

Siobhan sighed. "Ohmigod, Manny, sometimes you sound like a broken record. Do you have to pee or something?"

"This looks like the place," Kameron said, not sounding as sure of himself as he had when they left Manny's place. His hand crept over to rub Watson's chest, an unconscious move to bolster his courage. "The address matches."

"Creepy place," Manny added for Siobhan's benefit. "Looks like a place you would feel right at home in, Siobhan."

"Oh, yeah? Why is that?" Siobhan asked, raising one eyebrow inquiringly.

"You know the whole wicked witch thing you do," Manny said. He waved his arms in the air, trying to look like he was performing some magic ritual. Siobhan punched him solidly on the arm.

"Wiccans have a creed that says do what thou wilt, as long as it harm none. Good thing, too, or you would have been a toad by now." Siobhan stuck her tongue out and pulled her door open. "You guys coming? My sister is in there somewhere and I'm going to get her out."

"We can't drive down the driveway and politely ask to have our friends back," Kameron stated in his annoyingly calm voice of reason.

"We don't even know if they're here," Manny added.

"We need to stake out the place for a while and see who comes and goes," David suggested.

Kameron drove the SUV further down the road and parked. "Okay, now what?"

"Now we wait," David said, opening the laptop cover. "When we spot the white van then we act."

The afternoon dragged on without anything unusual happening. Since none of them had gotten any sleep last night, they slowly drifted, one by one.

"Wake up!" Manny shouted, shaking David.

"What?" David groggily opened his eyes and pushed Manny away from him. It was almost dark outside now and there were vehicles turning into the driveway they were staking out.

"Shhh..." Kameron hissed at Manny. "You don't need to wake up the whole neighborhood."

"What is it?" Siobhan asked sleepily.

"There are a bunch of cars going down the lane," David replied. "But no white van yet."

"Maybe they're already here," Kameron replied thoughtfully.

"I have an idea," David said. Wiping drool off his keyboard, he began typing. Within a few seconds, he cheered excitedly. "I got it!"

"Got what?" Siobhan grabbed David's arm. How did she do that?

"Satellite image of the building."

"Well duh, why didn't you think of that before?" Manny bounced up and down in his seat.

"Whatever." David grabbed for the door handle. "Time to go. There's a big white van sitting right beside an old farmhouse!"

Manny tightly gripped the cold metal object he had taken from Aimee's grandfather, which was now snug in his pocket. He had a score to settle—and this time there would be no sucker punching. "Count me in. Chiquita, come," he commanded. He exited the SUV and went around back to get David's chair.

Within minutes the troops had mobilized and were ready to start their trek into the unknown. As darkness descended, they made their way cautiously down the laneway. Siobhan and Oenghus led the way, followed by Kameron and Watson, Manny and Chiquita with David bringing up the rear. They had several flashlights but were walking (and wheeling) in the dark to remain undetected. Siobhan walked unerringly beside Oenghus while everyone else stumbled along behind.

"I can't see where I'm going," Manny complained.

"Ditto," Siobhan shot back at him. "Oh no! I think I've gone blind."

"Not funny," Manny replied.

"Shhh! We're getting close to something. I can see a faint light behind that big tree," Kameron whispered.

Everyone quieted down as they approached the ancient oak. Siobhan stopped and David took the lead. The gang stood quietly while

David donned a pair of night vision googles. He cautiously peeked around the tree, reporting back to the others.

"I see the front gate. It's open and there's a guy the size of a gorilla standing guard beside it." David didn't sound as optimistic as he had a few minutes ago.

"What else do you see? Describe more of the surrounding area," Siobhan asked, nonplussed.

"Well, the lane continues to a house with a dark outbuilding beside it. It looks like an old stable or storage barn. It's hard to tell in the dark. There are a lot of cars parked outside," David explained. "I can see the white van. At least I think it's the same one."

"Where?" Manny poked his head around the corner of the tree.

David pointed at the white van and Manny nodded his head. That was it alright, with the chain on the back doors. This was the place, and it looked like they were either having a party or there was a dog fight in progress. The muted hum of many talking voices, laughing, and clapping with sounds of growling and barking dogs could be heard coming from the building behind the house.

"We need a plan and quick," Siobhan said and turned unerringly to face David.

"Uh, um, yeah, right. Another plan," David stammered. All eyes focused on him. Why was he the plan man all the time? The pressure!

Oenghus began whining and started moving toward the gate, trying to pull Siobhan with him. She signaled him to sit and he obeyed, although it was obvious he didn't want to.

"Shh! It's okay, Oenghus. What's up?" Siobhan asked her usually calm canine partner.

Oenghus only whined louder then he licked Siobhan's hand. Lifting one massive paw, he gently clawed at her pocket. Pushing his paw down, Siobhan put her own hand in her pocket and pulled out a hairband belonging to her sister. She had borrowed it yesterday and had forgotten all about it. As she held the soft, cotton-covered elastic band, she realized what Oenghus was trying to tell her. Holding the band in front of Oenghus, she spoke so everyone could hear her.

"Is Niamh here?" she asked Oenghus while he obligingly sniffed the band in his guardian's hand. His whole body shook, and he thumped his massive tail against the ground, whining excitedly. Siobhan gave him a hug and turned to face her friends who had been watching her skeptically.

"Niamh is here! This is her hairpiece I borrowed yesterday, so it still has her scent on it." She held up the band.

"Look, guys, I think this is way over our heads. This is some serious bad news stuff going down here. I'm talking Fed time! I'm talking guns. I'm talking Swat team stuff!" Kameron eyed the guard standing a few hundred yards away. "Let's call the police."

"I agree with Kameron. We aren't the police," David said.

"Ok, look, you guys!" Siobhan was barely able to contain her anger. Her hands clenched into fists at her side. Concerned, Manny looked at Siobhan's whitening knuckles and moved quickly behind Kameron. "My sister is in there somewhere and she needs help. We are standing right here! And the police are nowhere in sight. You guys are my best friends and I really, really need your help."

Siobhan began to cry. She hid her head in Oenghus' fur and waited. There was an awkward silence as Manny, Kameron, and David wondered what they should do. Finally, David couldn't take Siobhan's heart-wrenching sobs any longer.

"Well, of course, we're going to help," David said, looking at each of his friends for confirmation. "I think we should call for backup."

"Yeah, let's call the cops before we get Niamh and Aimee out of there," Manny said excitedly.

"We'll call Greta and be in and out before the cops come." Kameron put his hand on Siobhan's shoulder in an attempt to comfort her.

Siobhan kept her head buried in Oenghus' fur, not because she was still crying, but because she didn't want her smile to give her deception away. Boys were so easy to manipulate. A few tears and they melted like butter. She stifled a giggle, took a deep breath, and straightened herself up, making a big production of wiping her eyes and face.

"I think I have it," David said, an idea beginning to blossom. He quickly outlined his plan for the others and made a quick call to Greta. Before long they were ready to go.

Everyone adjusted their Bluetooth earpieces. David spoke softly into his own device. They were now connected via a group connection he had set up, using their phones' walkie-talkie feature. David had a sudden scary thought.

"You don't think they're going to make Goliath fight, do you?"

No one looked optimistic that Goliath wouldn't be in a fight given his origins and the ruthlessness of his captors. David had only worried that he would never see his best friend again. Now he realized Goliath could be in real trouble if they were making him fight. He could get seriously hurt or worse, maybe even killed. He promised Goliath he would protect him. Then there was poor Hoku who wouldn't hurt anyone. What would those goons do with her? David straightened himself in his wheelchair and grabbed his wheel rims.

"Never mind what Greta said. Let's go kick some butt!" he said and moved determinedly forward, leading the way.

51

Double Trouble

G oliath was pushed through the gate into the large cage set up in the middle of the pit area. He had been in a pit similar to this many times and knew what was coming next. It was fight night. He shook himself free of the rope as soon as the tension eased up. Charging at the hated man, his teeth closed on empty air as the cage door slammed in his face. He paced back and forth in the twelve-by-twelve foot enclosure, growling menacingly. His hackles raised, the hair along his spine stood on end, and his head was low and hunched between his shoulders. He never took his eyes away from the man he loathed with all his being. Goliath growled deeply, baring his teeth.

Hoku sat quietly in the corner, licking her paws and whining softly. Where was Aimee? Why hadn't she come to get her already? She didn't like it here. The men here smelled of nasty things and were mean to her. No one had ever hit or kicked her before, and she was confused and scared.

Goliath stopped pacing and sat by Hoku, nudging her with his big, blocky head. Hoku stopped licking herself and instead decided Goliath's ears were dirty and needed immediate attention. Goliath sat quietly and allowed her to lick his ears clean. He looked over his shoulder periodically as more and more people and dogs arrived.

A few dog owners stopped beside the cage and encouraged their dogs to attack Goliath and Hoku from the outside. Goliath turned his back on them. He knew they couldn't reach him through the cage. Hoku licked harder and even nibbled on a particularly stubborn sticky spot on his ear. Goliath let out a little yelp of surprise, which sent a wave of laughter throughout the assembled crowd.

Two men approached the entrance with their dogs closely in tow. One man wore a tattered football jersey and jeans. He smelled of beer and sweat. His dog was a stocky black bruiser missing an ear with scars crisscrossing his muscular body. The other was an Asian man wearing a brown business suit that looked meticulously clean for someone attending a dog fight. He smelled of cologne and whiskey. A brindle pit bull mix with a huge head and sturdy chest walked beside him. Of the two dogs, the black one looked like the more dangerous one.

The man with the suit signaled the other man with a nod of his head. Football-jersey man opened the door and pushed his dog into the cage, followed closely by the second dog. Neither dog was used to fighting in a cage like this. Both dogs growled at each other and began circling. The fights tonight had been booked as death matches, so no referee was needed. There would be no outside interference. No breaks. The dogs would be on their own until only one dog remained standing.

"Let's see how fast those two useless mutts can go down." The jersey-wearing man snickered and ordered his dog to attack.

Goliath stood protectively in front of Hoku, who tried to move around him to greet the other dogs. Not taking his eyes from the two new arrivals, he blocked the smaller dog from passing him by using his rump.

Without further prodding, the two dogs, teeth bared and snarling viciously, lunged for each other. Hoku tried to pass Goliath for a second time, wanting a piece of the action, or more likely trying to break up the fight like she did at home or at Manny's place with the pack. Goliath blocked her with his side and pushed her back against the cage, trapping her in place for the moment. He knew this fight was out of her league.

Braced against the corner of the cage, Goliath watched the brindle and black dogs attack each other again and again, until finally, they broke apart one last time. Breathing heavily and bleeding profusely, both were losing some of their initial fire. Without warning or provocation, the black dog turned suddenly and rushed at Goliath. Goliath braced himself for the impact while keeping Hoku pinned against the back of the cage.

52

Can You Hear Me Now?

Even though she technically didn't work on the weekends, Greta couldn't stay away from the dogs. She had finished toweling Smiley dry after his bath when her phone rang. Slipping a lead around his head, she began walking him back to his kennel. She swiped the phone with her thumb to take the call and held it to her ear.

A distraught girl whispered frantically, "Ohmigod, Greta, you have to help us!"

Greta was instantly disturbed by the girls fearful tone. "This is Greta. What's going on?"

"It's Niamh, Aimee's friend. Ohmigod, I'm so glad you answered the phone. You have to help us! They have us trapped here in the van. And Goliath and Hoku are gone! We don't even know where they took them and Aimee's freaking out."

Greta's heart nearly stopped as the girl spoke. "Who has you? Where are you!" Greta's voice came out clipped and angry.

"I don't know!" Niamh's voice shook. "All I know is that these guys in a white van knocked us out when we were in a friend's SUV. When we woke up, we were tied up in the back of the van and the dogs were gone! And now the batteries are dying in Aimee's phone. Oh, please, Greta, come get us."

The white van? Greta felt a moment of relief. At least she had a lead on the van. "Have you called the police yet?"

"No. Aimee told me to call you. She said you would be able to take care of it because we don't have much juice left."

"You tell Aimee to stay put. I'm calling the police. I think I..." And then the phone went dead. Greta was beside herself with worry, but before she had time to call the police for help, another call came in on her phone.

"Hey there, Greta!" David sounded breathless and hushed. Greta closed her eyes and prayed he hadn't been kidnapped, too. "The address you gave us checked out. We know there's a dog fight going on 'cos there's a bunch of cars here. We thought we would let you know that. You know... so you can call in the cavalry."

"Do you see Aimee there?"

David paused. "How do you know..."

"Never mind that, David. Do you see the white van?"

"Yes." David was surprised at Greta's angry tone. "What about the white van?"

"Nevermind, don't worry about it, David. I'm calling the police. You need to let them handle it. Do not go anywhere near the building or the fighting. Those are dangerous people you are dealing with," Greta growled in David's ear.

"But they have our friends!" he whispered, angrily.

"And if you do something stupid, they'll have you, too! Do me a favor and leave now! I don't want anyone else to get hurt. Promise me you won't do anything foolish. Now please—go home!"

Greta hung up on David before he could argue further and dialed Officer Slimka's number. She hoped they would be sensible and go home, but since they were already at the property, who could say what the teens would do? Greta felt a tension headache coming on. If something should happen to those kids, she would never forgive herself. She rubbed her temples and tried not to cry as she called Officer Slimka.

Officer Slimka answered his cell phone on the first ring. Greta didn't waste any time with pleasantries. She gave him the address of the dog fight and a brief explanation of what had transpired earlier with the kids. Mike listened quietly. When she finished speaking there was a long pause on the other end. Greta hoped Officer Slimka wasn't too upset with her. She was beating herself up already for helping the kids get into trouble in the first place.

As it turned out, Mike was all business and only asked a few questions. Then he said goodbye to Greta after agreeing to meet her at the property. Greta picked up the phone again and began calling in other Animal Rescue Co. officers who would be needed to help with the animal capture after the police raided the place and hopefully located Aimee and Niamh.

Greta still remembered poor No. 9 as she packed dog crates into the company SUV and got ready to leave. It wasn't long before the others began arriving, and she soon became too busy organizing everyone to think about anything else but getting to the raid.

53

Dumb and Dumber

"Hey, Pete, is that one of the fighting dogs?" Garth asked. He leaned against the gate and looked at the Doberman Pinscher who stood a few yards away from the gate, barking at him.

"Nah, he's too clean looking. That's someone's pet. Most likely got out of his yard and is checking out the smell of the other dogs here. Good lookin' dog, though," Pete replied, spitting out some chewing tobacco.

"Annoying dog, more like it. Why don't we catch him and have some fun?" Garth asked. He pulled out a stun rod he used to keep the peace.

Both men moved outside the gate and walked casually toward the Doberman. The dog sat on his haunches and regarded the men curiously. Pete went to the right while Garth came at him from the left. As they got within a few feet, the dog looked over his shoulder then got up and ran a few yards away from them and sat down again then continued barking.

Neither man knew much about training dogs so they followed him until they were out of sight of the gate they had been paid to guard. If they had been dog trainers, they might have thought it suspicious the dog kept looking over his shoulder as if seeking guidance before sitting and barking. Since the men were so intent on capturing the dog, neither one of them gave it a second thought. Apparently, it doesn't take a big IQ to work as a security guard for a dog fighting gang, only muscle and a weapon.

Watson looked over his shoulder at Kameron and waited for his next command. He liked this game. He didn't like the two men walking toward him, though. They both smelled of alcohol and smoke. Kameron gave him a signal to run in a large circle around the men. This was like a herding move, only the purpose was to avoid capture and not herd the men. Watson obediently got to his feet and started running.

Both men stood where they were, confused for a moment by the dog's antics.

Meanwhile David, Siobhan and Oenghus, and Manny and Chiquita moved unhindered through the gate and down the laneway toward the dog fight. Kameron pulled out his silent dog whistle and blew several short notes before moving through the gate to wait for Watson's return.

The Dobie darted into the underbrush and away from the two stunned guards, leaving them standing several hundred yards away from the gate. Where they were standing, neither guard could see the gate or Watson.

"Damn dog was playing us for fools," Garth said, now in a foul mood.

"No. I think he got scared and ran off," Pete replied, shrugging his shoulders and turning back toward the gate. "You are scary looking at night, man."

"Shut up," Garth said and took a mock swing at Pete's head with his stun rod. "Come on back to work."

"I wonder how the dog fight is going," Pete asked. "I remember Goliath's last fight where he could have killed Brutus but wouldn't. Some fighting dog that is. Not much of a killer but a mighty fine fighter."

"Well, tonight he isn't going to get away that easy. They'll have him fighting until he gets killed or kills his opponents. It's a last dog-standing type of match and that means to the death usually," Garth said. He walked back to the gate and took up position on the left side while Pete took the right side. "It sucks we're missin' all the fun."

"Yeah. Wish we could break early and watch the fight, man," Pete whined. "Good night for a fight. There's not much that could go wrong on a night like tonight."

"No kidding, man," Garth answered. He tried to look out into the darkness beyond the lights of the gate. "Only fools and stray dogs would be out this time of night."

54

It's About Time

David was the first to reach the parked cars. He rolled up to a black sedan and tried to peer through the tinted windows. Everything was pitch black inside. Leaning sideways in his chair, he put his face right up to the glass to get a better look. Snarling fangs dripping saliva lunged at him from the driver's seat. David jumped back, nearly falling out of his chair, as the dog inside the sedan attacked the window a second time.

Siobhan placed a hand on David's back and whispered in his ear, "I don't think he likes you."

"Ya think?" David replied cynically. "Look! There's the white van. Aimee and Niamh are in there!"

"Where!" Siobhan asked, whirling around as if she could actually see.

"Straight ahead at twelve o'clock about two hundred yards," David replied.

"Find Niamh, Oenghus, find Niamh!" Siobhan instructed even as Manny set Chiquita on the ground.

With a little excited yelp, Chiquita was off and running, passing Oenghus who also headed straight for the white van. When she got to the vehicle, she bounced up and down on the tailgate and barked.

Siobhan and Oenghus arrived at the van right on Manny's heels, almost knocking him over, followed closely by David. Manny tried to pull the padlock off the door, but it wouldn't budge. Reaching down, he gave Chiquita a pat on the head and told her to be quiet. There was a lot of noise coming from the dogfight in the building, but he didn't want to take a chance on being discovered.

Kameron and Watson came running up to the van and stopped. Kameron bent over double, trying to catch his breath from the run. Watson stood by his master, panting heavily, and waited to play more games. He loved to run.

Straightening up, Kameron made a fist and pounded loudly on the door panel. "Hey! Aimee! Niamh! You in there?"

David groaned at how loud Kameron was. Everyone but Kameron held their breaths and looked around, tensely waiting for someone to run out of the building to investigate. Fortunately, no one appeared. There was, however, a series of bangs coming from inside the van.

"Get us out of here!" Niamh's shrieked, her voice carrying easily through the open front windows. "Hurry up! Goliath and Hoku are inside that building!"

Manny quickly ran around the vehicle and tried all the doors. They were all locked. He saw the partially open windows but was afraid to unlock the doors from the inside in case it triggered an alarm system.

David felt his heart sink. Goliath could already be dead. He was too late. There was nothing a kid in a wheelchair could do to stop something as big as this. He looked around the area for something that might help. Where was Greta? Where were the police? She said she was calling them. Shouldn't they be here by now?

"David, do something," Siobhan pleaded and tugged on David's arm, bringing him out of his reverie.

Kameron stood beside the padlock, trying to pick it open with his tools. It was a big lock and it wasn't budging. David glanced at Siobhan's worried face staring at him pointedly, then to Manny who also looked at him while bouncing with impatience from foot to foot.

Sitting there feeling helpless, he finally let go of two years of frustration at being disabled, and his fear changed to something different—anger. He felt his face flush then his ears turned red and hot. Goliath and Hoku needed him! Aimee and Niamh needed him! It was time to stop making excuses and to do something. He may not be able to use his legs, but his brain was working just fine.

Reaching behind his wheelchair, David pulled out a brand new, oversized titanium bike lock he had bought to replace Aimee's broken one. Pushing Kameron aside, he swung the lock over his head and brought it down with all his strength. Once, twice, a third time he lifted the bike lock and hammered the padlock with it. It felt good to hit something—maybe a little too good. He lifted the lock for the fourth time and paused.

Manny tugged on his arm. "Good one, dude! You whacked it right off."

"Why didn't I think of that?" Kameron muttered. He pulled the mangled lock off the chain on the door and slid it out of place. Grabbing the handle, he pulled the doors open and moved aside as Aimee and Niamh tumbled out.

"About time you guys got here!" Aimee punched David on the arm.

"Ah, I got this for you ..." David mumbled and held up the now mangled bike lock.

"You're awesome! I needed a new lock," Aimee said, tossing the lock over her shoulder. Someone yelped off in the distance in the direction the lock had flown. Aimee gave David a big hug. He wrapped his arms around her awkwardly, enjoying but not comfortable with the close contact.

Siobhan and Niamh hugged as well, both crying at the same time. Maeve's head popped out of the pouch; Oenghus let out a happy howl that brought everyone back to task. Siobhan quickly slapped a hand over his muzzle. "Shush!" she commanded, as Niamh hugged Oenghus' huge head.

"Come on! We have to get Hoku and Goliath out of there!" Aimee looked frantically toward the building where her baby Hoku was in danger. Turning on her heels, Aimee was ready to sprint for the building, but David quickly grabbed her wrist.

"We need a diversion," David said and pulled his backpack out from behind him. He called everyone into a huddle and began outlining his plan.

55

Law and Order

O fficer Slimka slammed on the brakes of his cruiser and skidded to a stop. He practically jumped out of the vehicle and rushed to the back. Rummaging through the trunk, he pulled out his Mossberg 590 sawed-off shotgun and donned his Kevlar vest. Adjusting his Glock 22 in its shoulder harness, he closed the trunk. Other vehicles began stopping nearby. If Greta was correct, they would finish what they had started a few months earlier. Too many of the dog owners had gotten away from their last raid, including the organizers.

"Ready here, Mike. Remember, everyone, this isn't just a dog fight but also a possible kidnapping," Officer Connelly reported over the two-way radio. This time they had set up a perimeter around the property to catch anyone who managed to escape the initial round-up.

"Okay. Let's do this!" Officer Slimka waved for the others to move out. A dozen officers spread across the field toward the outer perimeter of the fence. Officer Slimka and three others went straight up the laneway to the gate where they could see two guards.

Officer Slimka signaled his men to come at the gate from either side. Moving swiftly through the thin woods surrounding the property, he closed in on the unsuspecting guards. Within minutes he was a few yards away from the larger of the two thugs. Taking a deep breath, he raised one hand and made a fist. This was the sign for the others to wait for him to move first.

Gripping his Mossberg firmly in both hands, he stepped out into the light and spoke loudly. "This is the police! We have you surrounded. I want your hands behind your back and both of you down on your knees!"

Both guards looked stunned at first then the larger one came at Officer Slimka with a cattle prod. Instead of shooting the man, Mike knocked the rod aside and hit his assailant in the solar plexus with the butt end of his Mossberg. The man doubled over and an officer moved in to pin him to the ground and place the handcuffs.

The second guard dropped his rod on the ground and raised both hands in the air. Officer Slimka ordered him to drop to his knees and another officer handcuffed him. The whole incident took less than five minutes and netted two eager informants. Within seconds of being captured, the larger man began spilling the beans on the whole operation. Then they were taken back to the squad cars as Officer Slimka proceeded toward the main building where he now knew without a shadow of a doubt that a dog fight was in progress. What he didn't know was that a group of young people had beaten him to the dog fight and had plans of their own to disrupt things.

Officer Slimka called his partner. "Ed, you can send in the troops. We've secured the gate."

"Roger that, Mike. Everything okay?" Officer Connelly asked.

"Ten-four. We got two goons who were watching the gate and they are spilling the beans like a couple of Boy Scouts," Officer Slimka answered.

"Okay, buddy, be careful in there," Officer Connelly said.

"Ed, make sure you watch the road. No escapes this time, okay?"

"Ten-four, Mike," Officer Connelly replied.

56

No Rain, No Gain

Aimee, Siobhan, and Oenghus waited outside a boarded-up side door. From their location they could see where Niamh, Manny, and Chiquita crouched and faced the front of the building. David, positioned at the rear, whispered into his headset that he was ready. Siobhan touched Aimee's shoulder to indicate everyone was in place.

Scaling an old wooden ladder, Kameron and Watson had climbed up to the roof. Looking over the edge, Kameron whispered into his headset they were ready as well. The roof top was flat with several raised skylight-style windows that gave them the only view of the inside of the building.

Carefully lifting the window, Kameron held his breath and peered twenty feet down into the smoky room. He heard dogs viciously attacking each other but couldn't make out details from this angle. Watson whined and growled quietly. Kameron patted his neck and told him to be quiet.

Scanning the room, Kameron found what he was looking for only a few feet from the skylight. In a hushed voice, he let everyone know he was in place but couldn't see much below. He also reported he had found what they needed for their diversion.

"Plan Save Goliath and Hoku is a go," Kameron whispered. "David, get inside and do some reconnaissance. We need to know if they're even inside before we go in guns blazing."

"Okay, roger that." David whispered back. "Going into silent mode."

"We brought guns!" Niamh's grabbed Manny's arm and her voice blared in everyone's ears. "No one said anything about guns."

Manny looking guilty, fidgeted with something in his pocket and quickly looked away from Niamh's penetrating glare. "Why are you looking at me?"

"Be quiet!" Kameron said, exasperated. "It's a figure of speech."

"Oh, sorry," Niamh giggled nervously then released her death grip on Manny's arm. "My bad."

David set his wheelchair in motion, moving quickly over to the back entrance. He carefully tried the door and found it unlocked. Slowly, he opened it and peeked inside. Fortunately, no one was anywhere near this side of the barn. Everyone faced the other way, watching the fight in the center of the room.

The room reeked of smoke, alcohol, and other less pleasant smells. Trash littered the floor while liquids of dubious origin spilled randomly throughout the place. Everyone was yelling and laughing, encouraging the dogs to keep fighting. It made David sick to his stomach and something else—it made him furious.

David recognized the layout from the net search he had done on dog fighting. He could make out the top of a large cage placed in the center of the building's fight pit. His internet search hadn't mentioned caged fights so he guessed this was something different. Checking around the room one more time to make sure no one was watching him, he took a deep breath, steeled himself, and entered the building.

Spying a set of makeshift bleachers, he wheeled quickly behind them, keeping out of sight. Once hidden, he turned around to face the back of the crowd and waited for Kameron to do his part. While he waited, he reached behind him and pulled his poncho out of his backpack and slipped it over his head. One never knew when it might rain.

"All clear, Kam. There's a fight going on in a cage in the center of the room with at least two dogs," David whispered urgently, giving a thumbs up towards the skylight. "I can't see Goliath and Hoku yet. You need to hurry. Make it rain!"

Kameron crawled back over to the open window, signaling Watson to stay by the ladder. He pulled a pack of matches out of his pocket and lit one. Reaching inside the window, he held the match up to the water sprinkler and prayed it was still functioning in this dilapidated old building.

Nothing happened and eventually the match sputtered and went out.

Reaching for another match, Kameron looked down in time to see David duck behind the bleachers and give him the thumbs up. He watched a woman walk behind the bleachers from the other side. There was no way to signal David that he was about to be exposed. Watching with growing horror, he waved his arms in a wasted attempt to get David's attention. It was obviously no good.

He pressed the button on his Bluetooth device and spoke softly into the little headset. "David's in the building and about to get caught. Can anyone down there help?"

"David can handle himself, Kameron," Siobhan's calm voice spoke into his earpiece. "Now get the sprinklers going. He'll do his job. You do yours."

"Alrighty then." Kameron sighed then looked to Watson for support. Watson whined worriedly and pawed at Kameron's arm. "Et tu, Watson?"

Quickly lighting the match, he fumbled with it and dropped it to the floor below, hitting someone on the shoulder. Kameron ducked away from the window as the man looked up, obviously cursing. Risking being spotted, Kameron peeked back inside the window. The man had gone back to watching the dog fight.

"And the Almighty said, 'Let it rain!'" Kameron whispered.

Lighting another match he held it directly under the water sprinkler and waved it back and forth. Something clicked in the sprinkler and water suddenly erupted from the entire sprinkler system throughout the building.

"And it did." Kameron snickered. It was like a good old Florida downpour, only it was inside instead of outside. Taking one last look down into the building, he spotted David who was now turning to face the woman stumbling his way.

57

Let It Rain

Hank and Carlos watched as the money continued to add up. They were set to take in over fifty grand tonight if Hank's calculations were right. As he watched Goliath protect his little girlfriend, Hank almost had a moment of doubt about what he was doing. Then another mark came up to him to place a bet on Goliath, and the moment was lost. It was good to be back in business. He absently twirled his lucky silver dollar between his thumb and forefinger as he waited for more bets to be placed.

Goliath held his own against the two dogs in the ring. The little Basenji dodged under his legs to attack the other dogs, much to the amusement of the crowd. She would dart out, quickly bite one of the dogs, and disappear back behind Goliath. So far the other two pit bulls were getting the worst of it. If they kept fighting each other and Goliath, they would both probably go down soon.

Not that Hank cared which dog took Goliath down. He had come up with a new fight idea and it was going over well. If these two couldn't beat Goliath, the next two would or the two after that. Who cared? The longer Goliath lasted, the more money Hank made. It was a win-win situation for Hank.

Hank looked over at Carlos, who gazed up at the ceiling. *Idiot! What was he doing now?* Stalking over to Carlos, he grabbed the man's arm and turned him around.

"What are you gawking at? You're supposed to be collecting bets," Hank snarled. He slapped the back of Carlos' head, knocking his cowboy hat off.

"But, Boss, what's that guy doing on the roof?" Carlos asked, before bending over to pick up his hat.

As Hank looked up, the sprinkler system erupted, sending a torrent of slimy warm water down on him. Chaos broke out in the room as everyone covered their heads with anything they could find and ran for the nearest exit. Even the dogs in the ring stopped fighting and looked around—no doubt wondering what new torture their masters had devised for them.

***

David turned to face a middle-aged woman who had come up behind him and touched him on the shoulder. She looked like someone out of a badly scripted, low-budget movie. With too much smeared makeup on her face and a cigarette in one hand, she could pass for the extra in almost any B-movie for that matter—no, make that a D-movie, a destined flop. The woman wore a low-cut skirt and blouse that revealed more than he needed to see. She was obviously undernourished with sores on her face.

The woman's face was hard and heavily lined, obviously having seen better days and too much sun. It looked like she was going to say something but then leaned over and puked behind David's chair. Totally shocked and thoroughly disgusted, David moved away from her as the sprinklers went off, drenching everyone in the room with warm, rotten egg-smelling water. At first everyone froze and looked around confused by the sudden, unexpected indoor shower.

"Fire! Fire! Fire!" David yelled hysterically at the top of his lungs from behind the bleachers.

Someone screamed then pandemonium broke out. Everyone rushed the doors to escape the nonexistent flames. David pushed his chair into the chaos and headed for the cage in the middle of the ring. Before he got more a few feet he spotted the guy from the white van standing in the center of the room, holding a hand full of wet bills with a confused look on his drenched face. Changing course David made a beeline straight for the loser who had tortured his best friend. Building up speed, he plowed his way through the panicked crowd and bore down on the scumbag who had kidnapped Goliath.

Shouting incoherently, David rammed his chair into the man, hitting him behind the legs and sending him toppling forward. Stunned, the guy went down face-first and landed hard on the wooden floor. David growled like a feral animal as he launched himself out of the chair and landed on top of the man's back.

People roughly jostled each other to flee the building, and several of them tripped over or kicked David and Hank while trying to escape the nonexistent fire. Of course, none of them stopped to help David up or see what they were stepping on or stumbling over. For once David was glad he had less feeling in his legs because he was getting hit from all sides as people ran over him in their haste to get away.

"This is for Goliath!" David screamed in Hank's ear then punched him in the back.

"Get off me, kid!" Hank growled, trying to roll over.

David sprawled sideways across Hank and pommeled the older man for all he was worth.

"And this is for Hoku and Aimee!" David punched Hank over and over again. "And this is for all the other lives you've ruined, dirt bag!"

His head pounding, his ribs aching and his bruised fingers throbbing, David's anger finally ran out. In hindsight this hadn't been one of his better plans. He rolled off Hank and managed to crawl under a nearby table to get away from the crowd. With his anger abated and lying on the floor separated from his wheels, David felt more helpless than he had in a long time. He watched in morbid fascination as Goliath's abuser rolled over and looked around in confusion.

Hank got slowly to his knees and continued to look around the room. He spotted David under the table, an evil sneer on his already ugly face. Standing, he angrily grabbed a broken chair leg and came at David, swinging his makeshift club and cursing savagely. David rolled farther under the table and furtively scanned the room for an escape route. What would James Bond do in a spot like this? *If only I had a laser pen... or a bomb watch.*

"Now what, genius?" David muttered to himself. "At least we got here in time to stop the fight." He looked toward the cage in the middle of the room and finally saw Goliath. "They're here. Goliath and Hoku are in the ring with two other dogs. Get in here now!"

58

Out of My Way!

A imee grabbed a loose board and pulled it off. She took hold of another one and tugged hard, but it wouldn't budge. Aimee tried futilely to get the board off. She could feel the board waver under her grip, but it remained steadfast.

Frustrated, Aimee grabbed Siobhan's hands and guided them to the board. "Siobhan, pull!"

Their combined strength was enough to yank the board free. Within seconds they had the side door exposed. Aimee pushed on the door knob, and the rotten piece of plywood fell completely off its hinges into the building. Stepping over the door, she entered with Oenghus and Siobhan following closely on her heels.

Men and women ran toward the front door in one congested crowd. Some attempted to climb out the broken windows. Dogs ran around free from their owners. Only a few were fighting, while others scavenged at the fallen food on the floor, and many others dashed between legs for the front door and freedom.

Pushing and shoving, Aimee and Siobhan moved through the mob toward the center of the building. Aimee recognized the sleazy guy who had given them water in the back of the van. She was tempted to go after him but saw a flash of black and white out of the corner of her eye.

With her heart in her throat and anger giving her added strength, Aimee bulldozed her way to the fighting cage where she had spotted a little tri-colored Basenji darting out from behind a big, white pit bull with a liver patch over his eye. There were two other dogs in the cage, and they were closing in on Goliath who looked like he had taken the brunt of the attacks. Aimee savagely elbowed and shoved any person caught between her and the cage that held her baby. Nothing was going to slow her down now that she had Hoku in her sights.

Moving as quickly as she could, Aimee opened the cage door, screaming Hoku's name. Before she could enter, she was nearly knocked off her feet as Oenghus rushed past her into the cage. Grabbing the closest dog around the neck with his powerful jaws, Oenghus spun the black pit bull around. Off balance and not expecting the rush from the wolfhound, the pit bull flailed and fell to the ground heavily on his shoulder. Oenghus pushed forward and pinned the pit bull to the floor. The brindle pit bull, seeing the open cage door, fled past Goliath and the wolfhound, leaving droplets of blood in his wake.

With an excited yodel that her guardian would never hear, Hoku leapt from behind Goliath straight into Aimee's waiting arms. Falling to her knees, Aimee held her baby close and cried. That had been way too close. She made soft, choking noises and scratched Hoku's neck. She looked a little dirty but didn't appear to be injured. Hoku wiggled and squirmed and ecstatically licked her girl's tears.

Goliath moved over by Oenghus and nudged the black pit bull who growled weakly as he lay helpless on the ground. Oenghus released his grip on the other dog's throat and moved back. Injured, weakened and unwilling to face two dogs, the black pit bull got to his feet and limped from the cage, his master nowhere in sight.

"Oh, crap, David!" Aimee scrambled to her feet, Hoku held tightly in her arms.

At the sound of the boy's name, Goliath's head whipped toward Aimee. Growling, he raced through the open cage door and into the chaos. Oenghus stood in the center of the cage for several seconds, watching Goliath leave before he realized someone was missing. Scanning the crowd, he spotted his guardian.

Siobhan stood trapped in the center of a group of drunken gamblers, wielding a broom handle like it was a martial arts Bo staff. Twirling the stick, she lashed out and caught one drunken man in the shins. He dropped to the ground, holding his injured knee with both hands and cursing loudly.

Without pause Siobhan whirled around and jabbed another man reeking of alcohol in the solar plexus, sending him sprawling over the top of a beer cooler and then onto the floor. Siobhan listened carefully, trying to distinguish between the men surrounding her and the people rushing to escape. A wooden plank creaked to her left and she whirled around, ready to dish out a little punishment to the man for getting too close. But then she heard the unmistakable sound of a hundred-and-fifty-pound growling Wolfhound charging toward her and smiled despite the seriousness of her predicament. Someone was in for a surprise.

Oenghus came snarling into the midst of the group, looking like one of the Baskerville hounds on a bad day. Circling Siobhan, he bared his fangs and lunged at the nearest drunken man. Watching dogs fight was one thing; being on the receiving end of a set of large canines was another. Quickly losing interest in Siobhan, the drunken cowards took flight in every direction like a flock of birds flushed out by a hunting Vizsla. Oenghus nipped one man on the rear as he ran by, tearing off a piece of the man's pants. He would have done more, but Siobhan called him to her and he obeyed immediately—if somewhat reluctantly.

59

Karma Bites

Kameron jumped down to a smaller outbuilding with a slanted roof that nearly touched the ground. Turning around he commanded Watson to jump like they did in practice. Watson only hesitated a second before leaping from the roof into Kameron's waiting arms. Kameron let out a whoosh of air as he caught his best friend and nearly tumbled backwards over the edge.

"Remind me to cut back on your food," Kameron groaned.

Watson licked his guardian's face, and Kameron lowered him to the roof. Not waiting for the command this time, Watson scuttled to the edge and jumped from the six-foot-high building, landing softly on the ground below. Kameron dropped down beside Manny who bounced up and down by Niamh.

The front door burst open and people came surging out. Everyone leaving the building was soaked. Sirens sounded off in the distance as police and fire fighters finally arrived in force.

Manny moved into the path of a short man wearing a cowboy hat and reached into his pocket. "Hey, dude, remember me?"

Slowing down, the man smiled nervously, exposing his rotten teeth. "Hey, amigo, what's up?"

"You're a disgrace and total waste of space, man." Manny moved back a few paces, keeping his hand behind his back.

Thinking he had the element of surprise, the man lunged forward, trying to grab Manny by the throat. Manny agilely sidestepped and whipped his hand out from behind his back even as the Chihuahua attacked. Growling a ferocious little battle cry, Chiquita lunged forward and grabbed the man's pant leg and pulled. Seizing the opportunity, Manny pointed the nozzle of the pepper spray he had borrowed from Aimee's grandfather and flipped off the safety. Pushing down on the button, he aimed the spray at the man's eyes and looked away.

The pepper spray hit Carlos full in the face. Screaming, he grabbed at his eyes and fell to the ground. Unfortunately for Carlos, he partially fell in front of the frantic crowd streaming out of the building. Chiquita managed to keep a tight hold of his leg while he got trampled by the escaping mob.

Not taking a chance that Carlos would get away, Manny and Niamh grabbed him by the back of the shirt and dragged him away from the mass exodus of wet bodies spewing through the front door. Niamh looked down at the cowering man. He didn't look so threatening at the moment, being bruised and battered, eyes puffy and red with tears streaming down his cheeks.

Then Carlos unexpectedly reached out and tried to grab Niamh's leg. She nimbly sidestepped his fumbling hand and kicked him solidly in the stomach. She was rewarded by a loud, whooshing sound as the air left his lungs, and he collapsed in a whimpering heap, still clawing at his eyes.

"Not so tough when you're the one on the ground, are you?" Niamh sneered.

Kameron and Watson raced into the building, pushing past several people trying to get out. Quickly surveying the room, Kameron spotted David rolling from side to side under a table with a tall man looming over him, trying unsuccessfully to bash his brains in with a broken table leg. Kameron groaned and moved toward them, hoping he could tackle the guy before he connected with David's head.

"Watson to David! Protect David!" Kameron curled his fingers around the Doberman's collar, using Watson's size and fearsome appearance to help him fight the crowd.

Then out of nowhere Goliath came bulldozing through the crowd and barreled into Hank like a dog possessed. The man never knew what hit him. Goliath leaped through the air and his powerful jaws grabbed a mouthful of Hank's jacket from behind. Two years of pent-up frustration and anger were released in that first bite. Growling savagely, Goliath shook Hank like a rag doll, dropping him to the ground on his face. Hank screamed as he fell, terrified of what was to come.

David was stunned by the ferocity of Goliath's attack. He had read how aggressive pit bulls could be but had never seen this side of Goliath before. He was having a hard time reconciling the sight of Goliath straddling the man's back and shredding his jacket to the gentle pit bull he knew and loved. The same pit bull who patiently tolerated Darcy dressing him up in her princess outfits. The same pit bull who gave up his favorite ball to the twins every time they wanted to play fetch. The same pit bull who spent five minutes covertly sneaking into David's bed only to flop down on top of him and snore loudly all night.

Recovering from his initial shock, David realized he had to do something. This wasn't the Goliath he knew. This was a vengeful Goliath who had been abused by the man lying beneath him. Goliath was slipping out of control, and David couldn't let that happen. Remembering his months of training, David stretched out his hand towards Goliath. The pit bull curled his lips and snarled at the boy, the jacket still firmly held in his jaws.

"Easy, buddy. It's only me," David said, trying to project calm assertiveness as he'd been taught. He placed his hand on Goliath's collar and firmly tugged on it. "Shhhhh. It's okay, buddy. It's only me," he spoke, soothingly, brushing his fingers against the dog's bloodied forehead. "Let the man go, Goliath. Please. Let him go. Goliath, leave it!"

Goliath's angry snarl turned to a grumble of confusion, but he didn't let go of Hank's jacket. David remembered that, after Goliath's outburst the first time they were on stage, Mr. Sanchez told him there would be a defining moment when he knew that Goliath was truly his dog. That moment would come when Goliath would obey David's commands regardless of the circumstances.

Taking a deep breath, knowing some people might think him crazy, he rolled closer so his face was only a few inches from Goliath's. Speaking firmly, he stroked Goliath's massive head and tense back.

"I know this man hurt you, Goliath, but you have to let him go... for me. You are my dog. He can't hurt you anymore."

Confused, Goliath whined softly but did not release his grip.

Continuing to pat Goliath, David spoke soothingly. "C'mon, Goliath. You can let him go. You're a special dog. You're the best thing that's ever happened to me. You're my best friend and I love you so much. So, please, let the guy go. He can't hurt you again. I promise."

Gradually, Goliath relaxed his grip on the hated man and eventually released him. David pulled Goliath close to him and patted his head and neck, crushing the dog to his chest. "You're such a good boy, Goliath! Such a good boy. You're the best." Goliath wagged his stumpy tail and licked David's face. At that moment, David knew Goliath was most definitely his dog.

"Good boy, Goliath. Good boy." David's voice broke as he laid his head on Goliath and cried. That had been close. He didn't know what he would do if Goliath had to be destroyed for being too aggressive. Both he and Goliath turned their backs on Hank as they huddled together under the table. Goliath licked away David's tears while they rolled down his cheeks.

With the dog now preoccupied, Hank saw his chance for a little payback. He pulled out the stun gun he kept in a holster near the small of his back and turned it on. He reached out toward Goliath, intent on getting even. "No one messes with Hank ..."

"Take him down, Watson!"

Kameron released his canine friend who sprinted past some stragglers and across the room, heading straight for Hank. Hank screamed as Watson grabbed his arm and dragged him forcefully away from the table. The stun gun went sliding across the floor. Kameron pushed a running passerby out of the way to grab the weapon. Growling low and menacingly, Watson stood over Hank as the man huddled in a fetal position.

"Stay there, you coward, because I have no qualms about stunning you!" Kameron yelled at Hank quivering underneath the Doberman.

Kameron righted David's wheelchair and, with Goliath's assistance, helped his friend climb back into it. David wiped tears from his face and smiled sheepishly at the other boy as Kameron patted his back. Goliath stayed by David's side, pressing his big head against the boy's knee. By this time the sprinkler system had run out of water, and the room was empty except for David and company and a defeated Hank. Watson kept his position and guarded Hank, as the others gathered together.

Aimee came over to David. She kept a death grip on Hoku, her Basenji resting like a child on her left hip and held securely under her arm. She placed her other arm around David's neck and planted a solid kiss on his lips. David looked up at her but was too stunned to say anything. Giving him a quizzical look, Aimee reached her free hand behind David's head and pretended to pull something out of his ear.

"Oh, a silver dollar!" Aimee said, handing David the coin. He laughed at her and she shrugged. "I found it on the ground."

"Blood money—no thanks." David tossed the coin over his shoulder.

Led by Oenghus, Siobhan found her way over to them. Niamh raced through the door and grabbed onto her sister's arm. "Are you okay?"

"Oh, Niamh, you worry way too much, sis!" Siobhan laughed and gave her twin a big hug.

Officer Slimka was the next person through the door, followed closely by an excited Manny and an even more excited Chiquita. For that matter when were those two not excited?

Seeing something shiny on the floor, Manny reached down and picked it up. "Oh! Lucky silver dollar!" he crowed, pocketing the coin.

David smirked.

"I see you beat me to the bad guys," Officer Slimka said.

Keeping the stun gun pointed at Hank, Kameron commanded Watson to back off, and the Doberman stepped away from the man. Officer Slimka strode swiftly to the cowering criminal and cuffed him while reading him the Miranda rights. When he finished another officer took over and escorted Hank to a squad car.

Once Hank was out of view, Officer Slimka faced the teens. "Do any of you know how dangerous this stunt was that you pulled tonight?"

"Danger? You're kidding, right? We thought this was a slumber party," David said as he looked around. "Hey, where did my pillow and sleeping bag go?"

Greta rushed into the building, cursing at the top of her lungs in German. Apparently, she was furious with David for not heeding her advice and for going after Aimee. However, after a drawn-out tirade no one could understand, her anger subsided when she realized everyone was safe.

While giving all the kids a lecture, this time in English—the first of many they would get after their little adventure—she hugged each of them and made them all promise never to do anything that stupid again. Of course everyone said they would never do it again. None of the adults seemed to notice all the crossed fingers hidden behind their backs. Oh, well, there wouldn't be much of a story to tell if everyone always did what they were told, now would there?

60

After the Rain

After what seemed like hours—about fifteen minutes—of lectures from Officer Slimka and Greta, the gang was finally released to go to the hospital to get checked out. Their parents had all been called and were to meet them there. Officer Slimka made them promise that they would go to the station the next morning to give their statements. He was only doing his duty after all.

There were many tears and many more scoldings once they were at the hospital and had to face their parents. David had to endure his mother's disapproval while his father and siblings took Goliath and Hoku to the emergency vet. David had never been grounded before that night but he didn't care. Goliath was safe and he was responsible for that. Well, more correctly, Ability Inc. was responsible for rescuing Aimee, Niamh, Goliath, and Hoku from the scum bags who had kidnapped them.

David found out later it had taken the police and the Animal Rescue Co. officers most of the night to round up all the dogs and arrest the men and women attending the fight. All in all, there were over fifty arrests and twenty dogs rescued. Quite a good bust for Officer Slimka. Greta informed Aimee and David that many of the dogs were of good enough temperament to be rehabilitated.

As for Hank and Carlos, bail had been denied, and they were expected to enjoy a lengthy vacation in a Florida prison for running an illegal dog fight, gambling without a license, and kidnapping. Apparently,

Carlos decided it was time to distance himself from Hank, and he negotiated a reduced sentence for bringing to light all the nefarious dealings of his ex-boss. As it turned out, Hank's not-too-bright sidekick had an excellent memory and gave the police names and addresses of a dozen other dog fight organizers in the area. Hank would have a long time to reconsider his career choices since he wouldn't be eligible for parole for at least ten years.

***

After a month of sitting idly in his room doing homework when not training with Goliath, David was finally allowed to go to Manny's house for the twin's birthday party. The whole gang was there sitting around the picnic table piled high with brightly wrapped presents. David wheeled his chair into the backyard and pulled to a stop beside Aimee who, as usual, was glued to a computer screen. At David's release, Goliath took off to join Hoku and Watson.

"Hey, what's up?" David asked, laying his presents on the table.

"Huh?" Aimee looked up.

David quickly signed "hello" and "what are you doing?"

"I was going through some old videos and found some footage of the surveillance we took of the lab downtown." Aimee's eyes twinkled mischievously. "That got me thinking. What are the lab jerks up to now? Want to see what I found?"

"Sure." David leaned in closer to get a better look. He caught a whiff of coconut shampoo and stared dreamily at Aimee's small perfect nose. She looked cute when she was concentrating and wrinkled her nose that way.

"What?" Aimee said, glaring at David. "Is there something on my face?"

"Your nose," David said, smiling sheepishly.

319

"Dork." Aimee shook her head and gestured toward the laptop.

Embarrassed at getting caught staring, David looked at the computer screen and huffed. "No friggin way!"

"That's what I was thinking," Aimee agreed, watching David's reaction.

On center screen was the Russian guy from the lab supervising a group of sleazy looking men unloading small cages from the back of a cargo van. David counted at least a dozen cages being carried into the lab.

"I guess they found replacements for old Hank and Carlos," Kameron said, leaning over to look at the computer screen. "It didn't take them long to get a new supplier."

"This is all wrong," Aimee said angrily. "We need to do something to shut these guys down for good."

"Maybe Ability Inc. needs to become more proactive in stopping animal abuse," Manny chimed in.

"Yeah, let's all get arrested and grounded for the rest of the school year. We've already been kidnapped and nearly killed once... what's one more time?" Niamh added helpfully.

"I'm with Manny,' Siobhan said. "Less talk and more action."

Aimee, who had been staring at the computer screen, had missed the conversation going on around her. When she finally looked up, Niamh and Siobhan were arguing animatedly about something with Manny standing between them, trying unsuccessfully to separate them.

"There is no way you are going back into that lab!" Niamh practically screamed at her twin.

Manny tried to place a restraining hand on her and got nipped by Maeve who stuck her little head out of the pouch suspended on Niamh's chest.

"You're not the boss of me!" Siobhan yelled back. "If you're too scared to do anything, then go home and don't be a part of this conversation!"

"Ouch!" Manny complained, sucking on his bleeding finger.

Hearing her guardian's distress, Chiquita started barking at the ferret. That in turn got Oenghus' attention, and he came bouncing over to see what all the commotion was about. The big wolfhound made his way between the two arguing girls, pushing Manny to the side. Using his body weight Oenghus pushed Siobhan back a few feet, separating her from her twin.

"See? Even Oenghus thinks you're both nuts," Niamh said.

"Oenghus, stop that," Siobhan growled, trying to push the hundred-and-fifty-pound dog away.

With her Irish dander up, she was in no mood to be pushed around by Niamh or anyone else. She angrily pushed Oenghus out of her way, inadvertently kneeing him in the process. Oenghus yelped in surprise and Siobhan immediately regretted what she'd done. Her anger immediately dissipated. She reached out a questing hand until she found his neck and gently stroked his fur.

"Mummy's sorry, a thaisce," Siobhan murmured softly. She buried her face in his neck and gave him a big hug. Oenghus, already forgetting the knee in the ribs, took the opportunity to lick his guardian's face before she could protest.

"Seriously, what is going on!" Aimee asked, unable to follow the argument.

"Well, we're having a very happy birthday," Kameron summarized. "Manny and Siobhan think we should go after the lab guys again and Niamh disagrees. Apparently, Maeve and Oenghus agree with Niamh. Siobhan viciously kneed Oenghus in the ribs and is now suffering his slobbery wet kisses as they make up. Oh, and Manny's sucking the bloody finger that Maeve bit because he tried to get fresh with Niamh. And I'm wondering when we plan on cutting the cake."

"I did not get fresh," Manny complained.

"Did, too!" Niamh said, reproachfully.

Siobhan punched Manny on the arm and Oenghus woofed at him.

"Leave my sister alone," Siobhan growled.

"What? Guh ..." Manny grumbled and rubbed his arm where Siobhan had connected. "You two are both nuts."

"I think it's time we took Ability Inc. to a whole new level," David said with enthusiasm. "We can do more fundraisers and start an online campaign to stop animal abuse!"

"What about the lab jerks?" Aimee asked.

"I think it's time those guys were taught a lesson in economics." David grinned evilly. "What's the one thing that can shut down a big lab like that one?"

"A fire?" Manny asked.

"Manny, we're not terrorists!" Kameron laughed.

"Although we do have relatives back in Ireland who ..." Siobhan snickered.

David gave Manny a what-the-heck look then continued, "Um, no ... not a fire. Something even worse. Financial collapse."

"Oh," Manny said. "That was my next guess."

"Well, first, we have to prove they're doing something illegal more than merely unethical," Kameron said.

"I don't understand why people think it's okay to abuse animals to make money." Siobhan frowned.

Aimee watched the happy and well-loved dogs playing in the yard. "In a perfect world, animals wouldn't be abused period, whether it's dog fighting or animal testing or just being thrown away."

"But we don't live in a perfect world," David said. "Ability Inc. can be a voice for the voiceless. Together we can make a difference."

"Okay already. But right now it's cake time!" Manny said, cutting David off in mid-sentence. "First we eat. Then we change the world!"

Epilogue

David wheeled his chair down the alleyway toward home. It was his first day back at school and so far he liked his new classes and teachers. Things would be different this year. With pleasant thoughts of rescuing animals with his friends in Ability Inc., David continued down the alleyway and past the garbage can where he had found Goliath—where it all started.

Whack! Splat! Something soft and mushy hit him in the back of the head. Reaching up, he felt a gooey mess sticking to his baseball cap. Taking off his cap, he wheeled his chair in a quick one-eighty. Brian and his two thugs stood in the alleyway.

Déjà vu.

"Hey, gimp, miss me over the summer?" Brian asked as he snickered—or more correctly—snorted. Some things never changed, like say, Brian's piggish looking face.

"Miss you? Why I was lost without your witty repartee," David countered.

"What'd he say?" Leroy asked, looking at Brian.

323

"Shut up!" Brian said, spraying Leroy with drool.

"Have you ever considered running away with the circus, Brian?" David asked.

"What do you mean?"

"I mean, with your face and obvious lack of intellect, you could be a major player in the freak show," David responded.

Maybe aggravating Brian wasn't usually a good idea. Today, however, David didn't care.

"You're gonna be real sorry you said that, gimp. Real sorry," Brian threatened as he walked toward David. David ignored Brian and looked down the alleyway, crossing his arms casually over his chest.

Stopping directly in front of David's wheelchair, Brian reached down and grabbed the arm rests. "Ready to go back into the dumpster, loser?"

David looked over Brian's shoulder and smiled. "Not today, man, but feel free to help yourself."

"Come on, guys, give me a hand here!" Brian called over his shoulder.

No one came. After a few moments of staring into David's smug face, Brian finally turned around to yell at his cronies. The words died on his lips as he turned to face a snarling pit bull. Aimee and Hoku stood there as well, but Brian's little pig eyes were fixed entirely on the intimidating dog.

"Only because, oddly enough, I have you to thank for introducing me to my best friend, I'll give you a head start," David said mischievously. "I'll count to ten. One, two, three ..."

Brian started running when David said five. The closest escape was the garbage can and he made a beeline for it.

"Shoe, Goliath! Fetch the shoe!" David called out, pointing at the running boy.

As Brian heaved himself over the dumpster, he felt Goliath's sharp teeth tug the bottom of his jeans and rip the shoe from his foot. Scrambling as best he could, Brian crawled over the lip of the large dumpster and tumbled inside.

David laughed so hard he nearly knocked himself out of his wheelchair. Aimee, followed closely by Hoku, walked over to David and gave him a punch on the arm.

"Have you ever seen Brian move that fast on the football field?" Aimee asked loud enough for Brian, who still hid in the dumpster, to hear.

David whistled for Goliath who came running to his call without hesitation. He walked easily beside David's wheelchair, swaying slowly from side to side, a shoe still dangling from his mouth, as the four of them made their way to David's house.

Yeppers, it was definitely going to be a good year, David thought.

THE END

GLOSSARY

a chailin mo chroi . . . my darling girl

a thaisce . . . my treasure

Er ist ledig . . . He is single.
Gut zu wissen . . . Good to know.

Mein schätzchen … my sweet
Sie vorsichtig! . . . Be careful!

ABOUT THE AUTHORS

Garry MacDonald is a fiction and fantasy author who writes middle grade, young adult, and adult novels. He works as an Occupational Therapist by day and writes during the wee hours of the night before drifting off to a sleep filled with heroic people and mystical creatures demanding their stories be told. Garry enjoys reading, writing, and hiking nature trails with his family and a pit bull named Trinity. Garry lives in the Pacific Northwest with Patty and the kids and way too many animals to be practical.

Pate MacDonald is an author/illustrator who co-writes, edits, and creates artwork for middle grade, young adult, and adult novels. She graduated from Eckerd College in St. Petersburg, FL, with a major in Fine Arts. When not helping run a rock-and-roll inspired animal rescue or busy bottle-feeding puppies, she has a pencil or pen in hand to create the next character sketch or book cover. She resides in the Pacific Northwest with Garry, two crazy kids, a plethora of foster animals, and a menagerie of her own furry fiends.